D0201146

THE GIRL FROM HOME

Also Available from Adam Mitzner

THE GIRL FROM HOME

A Thriller

Adam Mitzner

GALLERY BOOKS

New York   London   Toronto   Sydney   New Delhi

G℡

Gallery Books
An Imprint of Simon & Schuster, Inc.
1230 Avenue of the Americas
New York, NY 10020

Copyright © 2016 by Adam Mitzner

All rights reserved, including the right to reproduce this book or portions thereof in any form whatsoever. For information, address Gallery Books Subsidiary Rights Department, 1230 Avenue of the Americas, New York, NY 10020.

First Gallery Books hardcover edition April 2016

GALLERY BOOKS and colophon are registered trademarks of Simon & Schuster, Inc.

For information about special discounts for bulk purchases, please contact Simon & Schuster Special Sales at 1-866-506-1949 or business@simonandschuster.com.

The Simon & Schuster Speakers Bureau can bring authors to your live event. For more information or to book an event, contact the Simon & Schuster Speakers Bureau at 1-866-248-3049 or visit our website at www.simonspeakers.com.

Manufactured in the United States of America

10   9   8   7   6   5   4   3   2   1

Library of Congress Cataloging-in-Publication Data

Names: Mitzner, Adam, author.
Title: The girl from home : a thriller / Adam Mitzner.
Description: First Gallery Books hardcover edition. | New York : Gallery Books, 2016.
Identifiers: LCCN 2016000319 (print) | LCCN 2016004508 (ebook) | ISBN 9781476764283 (hardcover) | ISBN 9781476764399 (ebook)
Subjects: LCSH: Life change events—Fiction. | Man-woman relationships—Fiction. | GSAFD: Romantic suspense fiction.
Classification: LCC PS3613.I88 G57 2016 (print) | LCC PS3613.I88 (ebook)
|
    DDC 813/.6—dc23
LC record available at http://lccn.loc.gov/2016000319

ISBN 978-1-4767-6428-3
ISBN 978-1-4767-6439-9 (ebook)

To my parents, Linda and Milton Mitzner,
who would have thoroughly enjoyed seeing their names in a book

Sitting in a prison in East Carlisle, Jonathan recalls that he often considered his hometown a prison unto itself, and it seems redundant for him to actually be incarcerated within it. Only a few months ago, a future of endless wealth and possibilities awaited him, but that was so far behind him now it felt as if he'd only imagined it. His more recent circumstances had required acceptance that his freedom might have an expiration date, but he had assumed that if he did go away, it would be a short stint, something to burnish his biography. Like the way some people talk about their time in the army. But this wasn't that. This was a murder charge. The rest of his life in a steel box.

The key was held by Jackie. The girl from home whom Jonathan had loved from afar all those years ago. Yesterday he thought of her as his savior, but today she might become his prosecutor.

The thought of being caged made people do things. Things that they might not have ever conceived of doing before.

Part **One**

March–December

1

March

Jonathan Caine's morning routine is to rise at five o'clock and run a seven-mile loop along the Hudson River. It is a point of pride that the circuit never takes him longer than forty-five minutes, and he's always back to his apartment in cooldown mode by six. Then he makes himself a health shake with the $2,500 commercial blender he purchased three months ago—it's at least the seventh he's had in the last two years, as he replaces them whenever he hears there is a better one on the market. He sips nutrients while checking the market positions from the club chair beside the window that captures a panoramic view of the harbor, the Statue of Liberty in the distance.

It is in these moments that Jonathan feels the full magnitude of all he's accomplished and imagines all that still awaits his capture. He finds it ridiculous whenever someone suggests that he has it all. If there's one thing Jonathan Caine knows with the utmost certainty, it's that there's so much more still to obtain.

This morning's quiet is interrupted by a phone call from Norman Solomon, a midlevel investor in the hedge fund Jonathan runs under the auspices of the international investment bank Harper Sawyer & Company. Jonathan's tempted to let Solomon's call go straight to voice mail, but even though he finds Solomon to be a first-class idiot, the man still controls a few hundred million dollars, and for all Jonathan knows, Solomon is calling to give him a little more of that money to invest.

"Norm, my man," Jonathan says jovially.

Jonathan is a firm believer that clients are vain enough to believe he's actually thrilled to hear from them before working hours. In Solomon's case, that went double.

"Did you see it?" Solomon says, panic in his voice. "Page three. Bottom left."

"Of course I saw it," Jonathan replies, even though he has no idea what Solomon is talking about.

Jonathan's determined to have Norm Solomon—and all investors, for that matter—believe that he knows everything that goes on in the world well before it happens. Investors are like children in that way. In order to sleep at night, they have to believe their fund manager is able to protect them from any danger.

Jonathan taps the track pad on his laptop and navigates to the *Wall Street Journal*'s home page. Once there, he scrolls through the top stories.

There's nothing on page three of the *Journal* that causes Jonathan any concern—or has anything to do with the investments made by his fund. The disconnect might be because a dinosaur like Solomon still reads the print version, which has a different pagination than the online edition. The other possibility is that Solomon wasn't referencing the *Journal* at all. It would be just like Solomon to think that the *Financial Times* was the source of go-to information.

Unable to find what the hell Solomon is talking about, Jonathan is about to go into full BS mode. He'll spout some garbage about interest-rate circularity, and then tell Solomon that the position is not only hedged but cuffed and collared, too. If that doesn't do the trick, he'll throw in some more nonspeak until Solomon relents.

But then Jonathan sees it. It's actually on page six of the online *Journal*, under the headline "Russian Hard-Liner's Growing Influence." He skims the text while Solomon continues to drone on, which makes it difficult for Jonathan to focus on what he's trying to read.

"I'd be the first to admit that I don't have a clue as to how you actually invest the millions I send you," Solomon is saying, "but I do know it has something to do with the Russian market, and so I figure that it requires that the Russians pay their goddamn debts."

Norman Solomon runs what is euphemistically called a "feeder fund." In reality, he's little more than a middleman, telling his clients that he performs the role of investment advisor. The one saving grace is that Solomon is self-aware enough to recognize he's a poseur, which is why he sends his clients' money to people like Jonathan, who actually know how to invest it.

The article is at least three screens long, and Jonathan hasn't skimmed more than a few paragraphs when Solomon's stopped talking. That means Jonathan now has to say something to calm him down. So Jonathan lies through his teeth.

"Norm, we've anticipated this long ago, and the fund is totally hedged. No matter what happens in the market, you're golden."

It's like Jonathan has discovered the chocolate chip cookie that actually makes you lose weight. His pitch to investors is that no matter what happens in the world—markets are up, markets are down, inflation, deflation, war, peace—his fund will still return a handsome profit each year because of his magic potion called "hedging."

"Okay, my brother," Solomon says. "That's all I got to know. Keep doing what you've been doing. Love seeing that thirty-plus ROI."

Return on investment, he means. The scorecard of investing.

Jonathan can't help but mutter "moron" the moment after he hangs up. Then he reads the *Journal* article more closely to see whether, despite that he just finished telling Solomon not to worry, there's actually cause for any concern.

* * *

An hour later, Jonathan's at his desk, seven o'clock on the nose. Like so much on Wall Street, the word *desk* is a term of art because it's not one in any conventional sense. It's actually two long tables that form an X, with thirteen traders sitting along each axis, and Jonathan at the vortex that floats in the center of a twenty-thousand-foot trading floor. The walls are covered with large screens, forever blinking numbers and ticker symbols with the market's changes. And it's loud. Very loud. The phones ring incessantly and the traders scream and curse nonstop, either into the phone or at one another.

Jonathan normally focuses on the Russian market first because it's still trading—Tokyo and the Indian markets having already closed for the day—but he has even greater interest in the price of the ruble today because of Norman Solomon's distress.

He's already checked the quotes three times this morning—the last time just fifteen minutes ago from the back of the cab on his way to work. The ruble has been consistently down, but not too much. A few ticks. The MICEX—the Moscow Interbank Currency Exchange—which is Russia's equivalent of the New York Stock Exchange, except it's only been around for twenty-five years, is up seventy points, nearly six percent. That's good news, but it doesn't make total sense for the ruble to be down against the dollar while the MICEX is trending up. So Jonathan does what he always does when things seem out of whack in the financial world—he reaches for the phone and dials Haresh Venagopul.

Jonathan deals with a lot of people for whom the accolade *genius* is bandied about. Some of them, like the Nobel laureates who created the fund's trading model, have the credentials to back it up. But for Jonathan's money, Haresh Venagopul has more raw candlepower than any other man on the planet.

Haresh isn't a trader, and therefore he doesn't sit on Jonathan's trading desk. His workspace is a cubicle a hundred feet away, in the bull pen with the other analysts. Despite the lack of immediate proximity, he's Jonathan's unofficial second-in-command, and holds that position because he's the only person on earth on whose judgment Jonathan relies besides his own.

"Yo, Haresh. Talk to me about the ruble."

Jonathan can hear the clicking of keyboard strokes. "Down four cents against the dollar. Two percent against the yen," Haresh says with an upper-crust British accent, even though he was born dirt-poor in Calcutta.

"I got a Bloomberg terminal, too. I mean, *why* is it down when the MICEX is up seventy?"

"Why?" Haresh laughs. "Because they're Russians. You know as well as I do that their system never makes any sense."

"Yeah, I know. But I just got a call from an investor this morning who was spooked by an article in the *Journal* that the Russians are going to default on their foreign debt."

"I read that too. Total nonsense. I'd sooner ask a six-year-old for investment advice before relying on anything reported in the press. I mean, last week the *Financial Times* ran this investigative report about the uptick in construction in Dubai, and the stats were at least two months out of date."

"Okay, if you say so."

"I say so, Jonathan. Nothing to worry about in Russia. But if you want something to lose sleep over, you should check out the Delhi Exchange. Hoo boy."

* * *

Two hours later, Jonathan's in the elevator on the way to the forty-seventh floor. A few minutes earlier, he had been summoned by Harper Sawyer's chief executive officer, Vincent Komaroff, via the head honcho's administrative assistant, who said that Komaroff wanted to have "a brief chat."

Virtually every other Harper Sawyer employee would feel panic about being called in by the big boss, but not Jonathan. He's acutely aware of his contribution to the firm's bottom line, so being sacked is the farthest thought from his mind. In fact, Jonathan firmly believes he could punch Komaroff in the teeth and still keep his job.

That doesn't mean he's happy to be going, of course. He hates being pulled away from the desk during trading hours. Especially if the reason is to kiss the rings of the suits on 47, which is usually why he's ordered up there—to have guys who don't know the first thing about investing harp on about reputational risk and overleverage, all the while reaping the rewards he brings to them by eschewing those very concerns.

If Jonathan had his way, Harper Sawyer's executive suite would be located in another building entirely. Maybe a different state even. He hates the idea that these men—and they're *all* men—work above him, fancying themselves as gods on Olympus, sitting in judgment over those below, all without contributing a goddamned nickel to the firm's bottom line.

Francis Lawrence, the firm's number two, greets Jonathan at the reception area. At six foot four and probably not more than 175 pounds, Lawrence is a gangly jumble of arms and legs encased in a vested bespoke suit.

"So glad we were able to pull you away from that desk of yours," Lawrence says with a smile as he shakes Jonathan's hand.

"Just as long as you realize that if there's a coup in Russia while I'm meeting with you, we could take a big hit," Jonathan says.

Lawrence grins. "Eh, we'll risk it. Come with me. The big man is in his office."

Jonathan wonders whether the "big man" reference is an attempt at irony, because Komaroff is practically a foot shorter than Lawrence. Together, they are the Frick and Frack of Wall Street. Komaroff, the son of immigrants, went to college on a wrestling scholarship and worked his way up from the mail room at Harper Sawyer to chief executive officer, whereas Lawrence epitomizes the expression of being born on third base and believing you'd hit a triple, as his father ran the firm back in the 1970s.

It's an open secret that Lawrence is not so patiently waiting for Komaroff to decide his CEO talents are ready for an even larger stage, so Lawrence could finally capture what he has always considered his birthright. Komaroff's immediate predecessor is now Treasury secretary, and the one before him had run, albeit unsuccessfully, for governor of Connecticut. Komaroff, however, did not strike Jonathan as the political type, and even a presidential appointment would mean he'd ultimately have a boss. Komaroff would likely find that to be beneath him, which meant Lawrence was going to be number two long into the future.

"Good to see you, Jonathan," Komaroff says. "Glad we could pry you away from the desk."

Jonathan smiles, but decides not to repeat the joke about a Russian coup.

Komaroff's office is large enough to accommodate all twenty-six of Jonathan's traders, which makes it something of a disgrace to Jonathan. Komaroff might just as well announce to anyone who enters here that he's got a small dick.

"Have a seat," Komaroff says, pointing to the sofa. Opposite it is a matching couch, but he and Lawrence settle into the chairs perpendicular to Jonathan. Surrounding their prey, as it were.

"First of all, I wanted to personally express my condolences about your mother," Komaroff says. "You got the flowers the firm sent, right?"

Vincent Komaroff doesn't give two shits about Jonathan's mother, and they both know it. Nevertheless, he's the boss, and so Jonathan plays nice.

"I did, yes. Thank you."

"It was the least we could do," Komaroff says, likely not realizing that he was speaking literally. Sending flowers was the very least Harper Sawyer could do.

Komaroff sits up straighter, signaling the meeting is now about to truly begin. "Jonathan, we asked you to come up here because we wanted to give you your number," he says.

Ah. The number. Jonathan's year-end bonus. Normally it just shows up in his March 15 paycheck. The fact that this year it justifies an in-person meeting can only mean good news. The question for Jonathan is—how good?

Komaroff and Lawrence are all smiles. They act as if they're Santa

Claus rewarding Jonathan for being a good boy this year, when in reality all they're doing is allowing him to keep a small percentage of the money he earns for the firm.

"Nothing is set in stone yet," Komaroff says, "but we wanted to tell you sooner rather than later that we are *very* appreciative of your efforts over the past year."

"I see," Jonathan says with a grin, not caring whether he's coming across as a little cocky. "How appreciative do you mean, Vincent? On a scale of one to a hundred million, let's say."

"Fifteen," Komaroff replies. The boss's own grin reveals that he actually thinks he's being generous.

Jonathan's mind is whirring like a calculator. At first blush, fifteen million does seem like a major haul, and it was a fifty percent bump over last year. But when you crunch the numbers, a lot of the zeroes fall away. Half of his bonus is paid in unvested stock, so Jonathan won't see a penny of that seven and a half million unless he's still employed by Harper Sawyer when the stock vests in five years . . . and on Wall Street, five years is an eternity.

That left the other seven and a half million, which he'll get in cash. Federal, state, and city taxes eat up more than half, so the check he'll wind up getting would be shy of four million. Not chump change, but a far cry from fifteen million.

* * *

The elevator opens up to the center of Jonathan's apartment. Straight ahead is a fifty-foot-long, twenty-foot-high wall of windows looking south and out over the black water of New York Harbor. The view is why he bought the place, and the primary reason it cost eight million, and that was before the gut renovation that turned it into a palace Natasha deemed worthy.

He calls out his wife's name, but nothing comes back. Jonathan is not surprised Natasha's out. He almost never comes home this early, and she almost always has something to do that involves rich and glamorous people.

Jonathan pours himself a glass of Johnnie Walker Blue and takes it over to the living room. He stares out his eight-million-dollar view and contemplates how this year's number will help him achieve what's next on his acquisition list: an oceanfront mansion in East Hampton. He's just finished his drink when he hears the elevator open, signaling his wife's arrival.

Natasha doesn't quite enter a room so much as dominate it. Part of that is her beauty, which is so undeniable that perfect strangers sometimes remark on how striking she looks, as if they were commenting on a museum painting. The other part is that she knows damn well the effect she has on others. If the Heisenberg uncertainty principle had a corollary, it would be the Natasha self-assurance construct, which posits that someone who knows she's being observed constantly changes the environment around her.

Jonathan has endured more than his fair share of disparaging comments about Natasha being nothing more than a Russian mail-order bride. She certainly fits the profile—fifteen years his junior, statuesque, platinum blonde, and a large chest. Sometimes, especially around those who were predisposed to believe it, Natasha even enjoyed playing the part. But the truth is that her family immigrated to Texas when Natasha was six, and she grew up in Austin, where her father taught economic theory at the University of Texas. Natasha sometimes jokes that she's the most overeducated trophy wife in New York City, holding a BA from Princeton in literature and a master's from Harvard in public policy.

They met four years earlier, at a benefit for the American Museum of Natural History. Natasha was there as the date of someone who made the mistake of leaving her unattended for too long, and she ended up going home with Jonathan. They married less than a year later.

Even while they exchanged their vows, promising to stay together for richer or poorer, until death did them part, Jonathan knew that their marriage would be based on something far less romantic. He would provide Natasha a life of luxury, and she would always look beautiful.

Right now, those vows are in full effect. Natasha is wearing a full-length black leather coat and red boots that lace up nearly to her knees. With her five-foot-ten frame, she looks today like a well-heeled dominatrix.

"You're home early," she says.

Jonathan detects an undercurrent of disappointment in his wife's observation. Normally he arrives home after midnight, and she never fails to complain about that, reminding him that the market closes at four thirty, which requires Jonathan to offer the rejoinder that he follows the markets in Russia and the subcontinent, and that investing is only a small part of the job. Getting the money to invest is what really matters, and that requires a lot of wining and dining, such that all the nights he spends in five-star restaurants drinking outrageously priced alcohol are still work related.

"Correct, and I have no obligations," he says. "So let's celebrate my being home early by going out for dinner tonight."

"That sounds lovely," Natasha says. Jonathan assumes Natasha had other plans, as sitting home alone was not her style. But whatever she had on tap for tonight can apparently be easily jettisoned, because she immediately says, "Should we go to Pavia's or that new Jean-Georges place on Madison?"

She's given him a choice between the two priciest options within a ten-block radius. But Jonathan has never thought twice about dropping four hundred dollars for dinner. He opts for Pavia's because he likes their rack of lamb.

When they arrive, the maître d' greets Jonathan by name, while the coat-check girl kisses him on both cheeks. After they're seated, and their drinks have arrived—chardonnay for her and another Johnnie Walker Blue for him—as nonchalantly as he can, Jonathan announces, "Well, today was Numbers Day."

This is enough to capture Natasha's full attention. Many of

their discussions over the past few months about their future expenditures—most significantly, about buying a summer home in the Hamptons, that section of God's country that juts into the Atlantic at the farthest end of Long Island, and where Manhattanites "summer"—have ended with Jonathan saying "Let's see what the number is."

"And? East Hampton or Southampton?" Natasha asks.

Meaning, is Jonathan's bonus enough to buy in East Hampton, or will they need to lower their sights and look in the slightly less ritzy Southampton?

"Maybe Bridgehampton," he replies.

Bridgehampton is geographically between East and Southampton. Jonathan assumes Natasha knows that he's being symbolic and that he'd never be caught dead buying a house in Bridgehampton.

Natasha has apparently had enough of their little game. "Jonathan, just tell me the damn number."

Jonathan takes a gulp of his scotch, as if he needs liquid courage to impart this news. "I'll spare you all the platitudes that they blow up my ass before getting to the bottom line, and of course it's all conditional on final approval, but they think the gross number will be around . . . ten million."

It takes Natasha the amount of time that passes for Jonathan to lift his drink back to his lips for her to compute the bottom line. "So, about two-point-five will be liquid, right?"

Given that Jonathan is lying about the actual number, he has to recalculate it in his own head before answering. "A little less," he finally says. "And don't forget that the first five hundred grand goes to pay down the firm credit line and we owe about a hundred thousand to Amex."

Jonathan's draw—his salary before bonus—is a half million dollars annually. That translates into, after taxes, take-home pay of twenty thousand a month, nearly all of which goes to the mortgage and maintenance on their co-op, the one hard asset they own. The rest of their living expenses—which includes Christmas in Aspen and Easter in Anguilla, the two hundred thousand for the summer house they currently rent in East Hampton from Memorial Day to Labor Day, the thousand a month that goes to the parking garage for Jonathan's Bentley (the car itself is on a three-year prepaid lease), and then whatever else catches their fancy throughout the year, and man, there's no end in sight on that front—comes from the five-hundred-thousand-dollar credit line Harper Sawyer provides him, which is always maxed out before Christmas. From that point on, they live off Amex until his bonus arrives in late March, and then the entire process starts all over.

"We have about four million in the brokerage account," she says. "If we put that down, plus what you clear from the number this year, and mortgage the rest, we'll be able to buy something nice."

"I'm not looking to buy something *nice*, Natasha. I'm only going to buy oceanfront, and only in East Hampton, and we don't have enough borrowing power for that. Not this year. I'd rather rent on the ocean and buy next year."

"This may come as a shock to you, Jonathan, but East Hampton has many homes that are *not* on the ocean. Some are on bays or, God forbid, landlocked, but I can assure you that in the ten-to-fifteen-million-dollar price range, they're still very habitable."

"Not for me," he says definitively.

Natasha sighs. "Jonathan . . . at least let me go see what's out there."

"Look, if you want to spend your time driving three hours each way to East Hampton, be my guest. But I want to be crystal-clear with you about something. I am not going to settle. If we can't buy something on the ocean this year, then screw it, we'll just rent on the ocean this summer and buy next year. I'm sorry, but I want what I want."

I want what I want. It was Jonathan's mantra, the credo on which he dedicated his life. He followed it with religious fervor, fully believing that he was destined to have whatever he desired.

2

Nine Months Later/December

Nine Crowne Road could be refitted as a museum exhibit depicting 1970s–1980s middle-class suburbia simply by placing a turnstile at the front door. In fact, Jonathan suspects a near replica of his childhood home is probably an attraction at Epcot.

By rote, he climbs the stairs and heads to his old bedroom. Nothing has changed since the moment he left for college. It still has the same baby-blue dyed wood paneling his parents bought because it was on sale at Two Guys, along with the old red-and-blue wall-to-wall carpet, which has always reminded him of the Union Jack flag. Even the lighting fixture hasn't changed—a basketball hoop with a red, white, and blue globe in the net—and it must be worth something now, given that the ABA hasn't existed since 1976.

Jonathan throws his suitcase on his twin bed and begins to unpack its contents. He carefully places his navy Brioni suit and white dress shirt on a hanger, and then hooks it over the doorknob, hoping the wrinkles fall away before he has to get dressed tonight. He realizes he forgot to bring dress shoes, so he'll have to wear his Gucci loafers, which he would otherwise never wear with a suit.

As he pulls out the rest of his clothing, it reminds him of one of those *GQ* articles about the eight pieces of clothing you need to take to a deserted island, or something like that. In addition to tonight's ensemble, he's packed running shoes and the related gear, even though he hasn't run now in months, a pair of jeans, two button-down casual shirts (one white, one blue), some T-shirts, his favorite Loro Piana cashmere sweater, a week's worth of underwear and socks, and a toiletry bag.

Seeing it all laid out, Jonathan reflects on his walk-in closet back in the city, stacked with thousand-dollar Berluti shoes and six-thousand-dollar suits. He shakes away the thought of what he's left behind and places his meager belongings into a single drawer of the dresser that still shows the outlines of the New York Mets stickers he had once plastered all over it.

When his clothes are put away, Jonathan explores the house as if it's uncharted terrain, and not the place he called home until he left for college. The living room with its L-shaped sectional—the one item of furniture not from his father's store, which, of course, made it his mother's favorite—the den with its dark-brown-and-rust-color theme; the downstairs playroom that his sister, Amy, claimed as her bedroom after Jonathan left for college, which at least had a decor that was more 1980s than the rest of the house, with a purple polka-dot color scheme inspired by the cover of Prince's *1999* album.

The kitchen is new, meaning that it dates from the Clinton administration. It was the big expenditure his parents made after Amy graduated and his parents were no longer burdened with tuition payments. It was still done on the cheap, but at least it's white, and not the avocado green Jonathan remembers from growing up.

Jonathan decides that if ever a moment called for some alcohol, by God this was it. His parents were never drinkers, but for as long as Jonathan could remember, his father kept the same bottle of scotch in the cabinet under the kitchen sink. It was purchased on the day Jonathan was born, with his father intending to open it on his son's eighteenth birthday.

Jonathan searches under the sink for the bottle. He finds it in the back, wedged against the pipe. Pulling it out, he examines the label. It's a blend, and a crappy one at that. A brand Jonathan had never seen in an advertisement or a liquor store or on a restaurant menu, and Jonathan can't help but shake his head in disappointment. Even when William Caine was trying to go all out, he was subpar. It only further fuels the mystery in Jonathan's mind of how it could possibly be that he had fifty percent of that man's DNA running through him.

For an occasion nearly two decades in the making, when the seal on the scotch was first broken, it occurred without any pomp. Jonathan was on his way to go out and celebrate with his friends when his father asked him to stay for just a minute longer and handed him a glass filled with a centimeter of amber liquid.

"I can't believe you're giving your just-turned-eighteen-years-old son alcohol right before he gets in a car," Jonathan's mother had said.

"It'll be just a sip, Linda. And, besides, I doubt he's going to like it much . . . To my son on his eighteenth birthday," William Caine had said, clinking his own glass with Jonathan's. "You're going to want to sip it very slowly. Just take a small swallow in your mouth, and then let it roll down your throat."

Jonathan followed his father's instructions. Even so, it tasted like smoke at first, and then morphed into fire as he swallowed.

The entire event lasted no more than ten minutes. His father mentioned making the scotch drink an annual birthday ritual, but the following years saw Jonathan spending his birthdays at college. He and his father never shared another glass.

The bottle appears just as full as it was twenty-five years ago. After pouring a generous amount, Jonathan takes a sip. As he had expected, it's barely drinkable. Jonathan hasn't had anything but top-shelf scotch since . . . maybe since the day he turned eighteen.

He takes the glass outside. Even in the bright sunlight, there's a sharp chill in the air. As cold as it is now, Jonathan knows it's going to get much worse before it gets better.

Much like his own life, come to think of it.

* * *

An hour later Jonathan pulls his Bentley into the Lakeview Wellness Facility parking lot. He hasn't yet seen any lake that might be viewed, although he leaves open the possibility that there's some body of water somewhere, so maybe every part of the name isn't a total lie.

Jonathan has no illusions that the *wellness* part couldn't be further from the truth. He's certain that no one ever gets well at Lakeview. Like the old Roach Motel commercials—people check in, but they don't check out.

An odd anxiety takes hold the moment Jonathan enters the facility. He fears that his father has just died, or will expire in the next few minutes—before he makes it to his old man's room. Less than a hundred yards away from his destination, Jonathan begins to jog through the halls, full of dread that he's too late.

When he reaches his father's room, his fear appears to be realized. William Caine lies there motionless.

Jonathan can feel his heart thumping as he approaches. His father does not stir, even as Jonathan reaches out to grasp the man's thick, hairy fingers.

They are warm to the touch. Then his father slightly moves his hand but still doesn't open his eyes. Nevertheless, it's enough proof for Jonathan that his father's alive.

Jonathan walks out of the room to the nurses' station. It's manned by three women, all wearing white nurse's uniforms. One is African American, and the other two appear to be Hispanic. Each is at least fifty pounds overweight.

"I'm Jonathan Caine," he says to none of them in particular. Then he points at the room he just exited. "That's my father, William Caine. How's he doing?"

"Oh, hi," says the African American nurse. "Yeah, you look like him."

Jonathan's heard for years that he resembles his father, and he always took it as a compliment. His mother had never made any secret that looks were the reason she had married William Caine. Sometimes she'd say it as the worst type of insult, as in, *Do you think I would have married him if I'd known what he was really like? But what did I know? I was twenty-two and he was the best-looking man I'd ever laid eyes on.* Those looks included chiseled cheekbones, a long, straight nose, a strong, dimpled chin, and piercing blue eyes, all of which Jonathan inherited.

"So how's he doing?" Jonathan asks again.

The nurse shrugs. "The same. He was awake earlier today. Talking a little bit."

"Do you think he's asleep for the night, or could he wake up?"

"No way of knowing."

Jonathan checks his watch. It's five o'clock, and the reunion starts at eight. He needs no more than an hour's lead time to get ready, which means he might as well spend the next two hours watching television beside his father, rather than doing so by himself in his father's house.

He goes back into his father's hospital room and settles into the red vinyl recliner under the window. Finding the remote on the night table, Jonathan clicks on the wall-mounted television and surfs the channels until arriving at the Michigan–Ohio State football game, and decides that's as good as anything else to pass the time.

* * *

Jonathan's mother died nine months ago. Cancer. Diagnosed in June and dead by March. She had been complaining about something being wrong with her husband's mind for at least two years before she got sick, although truth be told, she had been complaining about her husband's mental state for as long as Jonathan could remember.

The last time Jonathan saw his father was at his mother's funeral. During the drive home, he finally saw what his mother had been talking about.

"Johnny," his father said.

Jonathan let slide his father's use of his childhood nickname, which he hadn't answered to since high school. Like everyone else, his father had long referred to him as Jonathan, so the reversion to Johnny was just another sign of his old man's decline.

"I have something I need to ask you."

"Sure," Jonathan said.

"I don't know if you'll know the answer, but I know you're very smart, so I thought I'd ask."

"Okay."

"Did you hear that person who talked at the funeral and kept saying how your mother was an angel?"

That person was her brother, Alan. Jonathan's father had known him for more than fifty years.

"Yeah. Uncle Alan. Right."

"Well, is it true?"

"Is what true, Dad?"

"Is your mother an angel?"

Of all the descriptions of Linda Caine, *angelic* was not one that Jonathan would apply. Beautiful. Overbearing. Ill-tempered. Those fit. Angelic, less so.

"She loved you very much," Jonathan said.

His father violently shook his head. "No. I'm not asking about *me*. I'm asking about *her*. Is she an angel? Is she?!"

Jonathan found his father's anger even more disconcerting than the absurdity of the question. For all of William Caine's faults, losing his temper wasn't one of them. Jonathan could scarcely recall the man being forceful about anything in his life, yet now he was demanding to know whether his dead wife was an angel with the urgency that suggested innocent lives were hanging in the balance.

"Do you mean like in heaven?" Jonathan asked. "With wings and a halo?"

"Yes," his father said with utmost seriousness.

Jonathan sighed deeply. He truly didn't know what type of response was appropriate in such a situation, but figured that you responded to people with dementia the same way you did a child.

"The thing is, Dad, that angels exist only in heaven, so no one knows if Mom is an angel or not, because if she's an angel, it's in heaven."

His father nodded, seemingly satisfied with this answer. "That's what I thought," he said. "I knew that guy was lying, because he couldn't know if Linda was an angel. Nobody can."

Jonathan isn't certain whether any actual diagnosis has been made of his father's condition. His younger sister, Amy, has told him that the doctors have bandied about different medical-sounding things, which she often mentioned in connection with some celebrity who suffered from the malady. Parkinson's, like with Michael J. Fox, was ruled out, but Parkinson's syndrome, like with Muhammad Ali, was a leading candidate when the symptoms were physical only, most noticeably that his left leg dragged when he walked. When his father's mind began to falter, Alzheimer's became the new diagnosis, with Ronald Reagan getting top billing, but Amy's Internet research recently led her to conclude he might have Lewy body. Jonathan had never heard of that one, but Amy said Robin Williams had it, and she described the disease as like Alzheimer's, only with hallucinations, pointing out that their father was often talking about having different imaginary friends.

* * *

For the next hour, Jonathan watches football as William Caine snores beside him. Just as Jonathan's ready to call it a day, after Michigan stops Ohio State at the two, his father shows signs of coming to life. First there's a gargling noise, followed by a loud hack, and then his eyes slowly open.

"Hiya, Dad," Jonathan says. "How are you?"

His father blinks.

"It's Jonathan."

"I know," his father croaks.

"Here, have some water."

Jonathan takes the pitcher on the bedside table and fills the Styrofoam cup sitting beside it. For a moment he thinks he'll have to hold it to his father's lips, but then his father takes the cup out of Jonathan's hands.

His grasp is less than steady, but he nonetheless manages to take a sip without spilling it. The cup's return trip to the table has a rockier landing, but it touches down without falling over.

"Why are you here?" his father asks.

It's more than a fair question. When his mother was alive, Jonathan's parental contact—which even then amounted to little more than monthly phone calls—was confined to his mother, with his father listening on the other extension, but not saying much besides hello and good-bye.

Since his mother's funeral, Jonathan had been even more distant, such that the most accurate description of his paternal relationship would be that they were just shy of being estranged. He hadn't visited, and they'd spoken only a handful of times over the phone, and those conversations followed a nearly identical script:

Jonathan: How are you doing, Dad?

Dad: Still here. How's everything with you?

Jonathan: Good.

Dad: Any plans to come see your old man?

Jonathan: Sorry, but work's crazed now. Maybe next month.

Dad: Okay. 'Bye now.

The first response that pops into Jonathan's head to his father's query as to why he's visiting now, after all this time, is sarcastic—*Nice to see you, too, Dad.* The second one is a lie—*Because I missed you.* He goes with the bronze-medal answer.

"I'll be visiting a lot more from now on, Dad. I'm going to stay at the house for a little while."

"Your mother will be happy about that."

Jonathan searches his father's face for some tell that he meant the comment facetiously, but he looks serious as a heart attack.

"Mom's dead. Don't you remember?"

Jonathan's father offers only a shrug. If he had forgotten, the news of his wife's passing appears not to be all that distressing.

"Tonight is my twenty-fifth high-school reunion," Jonathan says to change the subject to something grounded in reality.

"That's nice."

"I hope so. Remember Brian Shuster? I'm not sure if he'll be there, but I'm hoping he will be."

Jonathan had read somewhere that people with dementia have an easier time recalling distant memories. Perhaps his father remembered Brian, who had been Jonathan's inseparable best friend throughout the 1980s, more clearly than the fact his own wife had died this past March.

Jonathan's reference to Brian Shuster, however, is met with a blank stare. He might as well be speaking Chinese.

"He lived on Clayton Road," Jonathan prods. "We played Little League together?"

"Who?"

"Doesn't matter. Just someone I knew once."

They fall into a silence. The Michigan–Ohio State game's first half ends and they watch the halftime analysis without a word passing between them. When the players take the field for the second half, Jonathan figures it's a good enough time as any to take his leave.

"Hey, I should be going now, Dad. I need to get ready for the reunion. But like I said, I'm going to be staying at the house, so I'll come by tomorrow again and tell you all about it. Okay?"

"You're staying at my house?"

"Yeah. I told you just before."

His father's deep brow furrows, as if he's trying to make sense of this state of affairs. Jonathan braces to once again have to explain to his father that his wife, Jonathan's mother, is still dead.

Instead, his father says, "Johnny, can you do me a favor?"

"Sure. What?"

"If you're going to come back tomorrow, can you bring Marty with you to visit?"

"Marty? Who's that?"

"Marty McMarty. My pet monkey."

* * *

Jackie Williams isn't sure whether the bruise over her left eye is still noticeable. It reminds her of a ghost that only she could see. And it terrifies her in the same way.

Jackie and Rick have been together for twenty-six years, if you

went by the first time he asked her out, which was the summer before their senior year at East Carlisle High School. It was twenty-one
years if the count began when they started dating the second go-
round, which was the summer after they each graduated from college.
Twenty years from their engagement, and nineteen from the day they
were married.

"You've been in there for like an hour, Jackie," Rick says from the
other side of the bathroom door. "Trust me, you're going to look better than the rest of your skank friends."

Jackie shakes her head in disgust. It was just like Rick to think she
was being vain.

"Hang on. I won't be much longer," she calls back.

Staring at her reflection, Jackie knows that she looks damned
good. At forty-three, with two kids, she could easily pass for ten years
younger. Same weight as back in high school, with most of it in the
same places as it was back then, too.

But the mirror undeniably betrays that something is off. Back in
the day, she had a killer smile. When she flashed it, everyone fell
under her spell—boys, girls, teachers, parents—it didn't matter. But
now, it looks as phony as a bad toupee.

It last happened a week ago. Rick was drunk, which was bad
enough because he'd driven home, but that infraction was nothing
compared to the fact that Jackie knew her husband hadn't been alone.
Rick's new assistant, nineteen-year-old Brittney, was his drinking
buddy.

Jackie had held her tongue all the other times her husband had
come home reeking of beer and drugstore perfume. She'd nod like
an idiot when he explained he was held up in a business dinner that
required a little extra lubrication to get the deal done.

This time, however, when he stumbled into the living room with
that self-satisfied grin on his face—as if cheating on the mother of his
children was only one thing he got out of his philandering, the other
being that he thoroughly enjoyed her inability to do anything about

it—for some reason she'd had enough. She wasn't going to let it go as she had a hundred times before. If she couldn't stop his infidelity, at least she could end her complicity in it.

"I hope you at least wore a condom," she'd said.

"What'd you say?" he responded, slurring his words.

"You heard me. Bad enough that you're with such trash, but I don't want whatever's on her going anywhere near me."

He moved closer. By the look in his eye, Jackie knew he was going to strike her. And it was almost like she wanted him to do it. Sometimes, when the bruises faded, she wondered if she'd imagined the assault, but if he hit her again, she'd have incontrovertible proof that her husband was a monster.

"You high or something?" he said.

"She must be fucking other people, too. I bet she has to after you. Got some twenty-year-old she calls up the moment you leave, so she can get herself off."

By now, he was so close she could smell the stink on his breath. At six-two, Rick towered above her. Although she had provoked this confrontation, Jackie was now afraid of what she'd wrought. She reached for the only shield she had: her children.

"The kids are home," she said.

She hated invoking Robert and Emma for protection. But through the years she'd tried every other tack: fighting back, hiding, threatening to call the police, and nothing else had ever worked.

The possibility that his children would bear witness to their father beating the crap out of their mother was not always a sufficient deterrent for Rick, however. It often depended on how drunk he was. Tonight he was very drunk, so nothing could save her.

He smacked her. Hard.

It was one shot, open-handed at that. But Rick had a big hand, thick too, and callused where the fingers met his palm, from the days when he worked construction. His imprint covered more than half her face, from right below her cheekbone all the way up to her scalp.

The contact made a crack loud enough that it sounded like a weapon had been used.

She crumpled to the floor, her hand instinctively rising to her cheek, to detect whether Rick had broken the skin. A trickle of blood at the corner of her eye latched onto her finger.

Jackie wanted to cry out, but feared that would only cause the children to leave their bedrooms to investigate the source of her anguish, so she stifled her scream by stuffing her hand into her mouth. For his part, Rick saw nothing but humor in the situation. He flashed a particularly sadistic smile at the sight of his wife curled up in the fetal position on the cold foyer floor. As if he couldn't be more proud of what he'd just done.

She braced for more. At his worst, Rick would shower her with punches and kicks. This time, however, he merely stepped hard on her back as he walked away.

She wasn't the only one Rick terrorized. When Robert was fifteen, Rick decided his hand no longer was sufficient and started to use his belt to mete out discipline, without regard to the severity of the infraction. After Robert fumbled on his way to the end zone in some meaningless JV game, Rick unleashed a particularly furious beating on his son. Later that night, after Rick had fallen asleep drunk, Jackie went to Robert's room to comfort him. He had stopped crying and looked more like a man than she had ever recalled.

It was in that moment that Jackie realized her silent suffering hadn't been protecting her children after all. To the contrary, she had only served to bring them into her nightmare.

"When I'm old enough, Mom," Robert had said with steely-eyed determination, "I'm going to kill him. I swear I will."

After that she went to see a divorce lawyer. He told her that at the end of the day—that was the phrase she remembered the lawyer used to set up nearly every sentence he uttered—she'd get half of their marital assets, which were relatively meager, composed mainly of the equity in the house that would result from the forced distress sale.

He also said that New Jersey matrimonial law entitled her to twenty-five percent of Rick's income as child support, but only until Emma turned eighteen. As for alimony, that was a maybe, but if she got any, it would be relatively little and not for very long. The bottom line was that—*at the end of the day*—she'd get somewhere in the neighborhood of fifty grand and maybe a few hundred dollars a month for a couple of years, and she'd have no place to live.

The lawyer not only couldn't guarantee that she'd get sole custody of Robert and Emma, but opined that it might be a bit of a long shot. He pointed out that even the abuse was going to be hard to prove, the proverbial he-said/she-said situation, as she had never filed a police report or sought medical attention. Jackie's counter that Robert and Emma could corroborate Rick's violence was met with a shrug and a "Do you really want to put your children through that?" remark, as if making her children testify to the truth was more damaging than subjecting them to living part-time with an abusive father. Perhaps recognizing that Jackie was willing to do anything to keep her children away from Rick, the lawyer said that no matter what the children said at trial, Rick's side would find an expert to explain that children can easily be manipulated into testifying to abuse that never actually happened.

Leaving the lawyer's office, Jackie fully grasped the grim picture he'd painted. And yet it was still Shangri-La compared to being married to Rick. So she went home and told her husband she wanted a divorce.

He laughed in her face.

"I won't give you a penny. I'd sooner go to jail."

"I don't care. I just want to be rid of you."

"I'll fucking take the kids," he said.

She knew that was just an idle threat. Not only would a judge never take children away from a loving mother, but Rick wouldn't even want the kids full-time because it would impinge on his drunken skirt chasing.

"No you won't!" she shouted back. "If you're lucky, you'll get visitation every other weekend like any other asshole divorced father."

It was what he said next that stopped her cold, however.

"Then I'll fucking kill you, Jackie. Guaranteed."

She knew that wasn't just talk. Jackie had become an expert in knowing when Rick was lying. About this he was speaking the stone-cold truth.

So she stayed. And things got even worse because now Rick knew she was trapped. The cheating became more open and the beatings more vicious. All she was left with was the dream that Rick would someday die and then her family would be free. Like when Dorothy threw the bucket of water on the Wicked Witch of the West. Even her children would rejoice over the death of the monster that terrorized them.

Tonight, however, she had to live a different dream. Not hers, but the one that the people she went to high school with a thousand years ago believed: that the prom queen married the high school quarterback and they both lived happily ever after.

3

April

*K*urtosis and *heteroscedasticity*.

These are the words that Haresh Venagopul is saying over and over into the other end of the phone. In between are words that Jonathan *does* understand, but they don't help him comprehend what Haresh means. What is abundantly clear, however, is that Haresh is very agitated.

Jonathan is sitting in the middle of Wolfgang's, a high-end steak restaurant on Park Avenue and Thirty-Third Street, and the entrée—steak for three, medium rare, extra char—has just arrived. His dinner companions are the hedge fund's two biggest investors: Michael Ross, who heads the capital investment group at Maeve Grant, the sixth-largest investment bank in the world, and Isaac Goldenberg, the octogenarian casino magnate, who views investing with Jonathan as just another form of gambling. Neither of them is going to want to hear that the guy who monitors the fund's position is in a full-blown panic.

"Can I call you right back?" Jonathan says to Haresh.

"I'm sorry," Jonathan says to his dinner companions, getting up. "It's my wife. I'll only be a minute."

Ross raises a fist and flicks his wrist while making the pussy-whipped sound. Goldenberg chuckles at that and helps himself to more steak.

It's raining outside. Not a driving storm, but more than a drizzle, so Jonathan takes shelter under Wolfgang's awning. The combination of the wind and the fact that the overhang is not very wide results in Jonathan getting pretty wet, so he's hoping that this will be a short conversation, and that the steak will still be warm when he returns.

"Okay, Haresh. I can talk now. What's the problem?"

His second-in-command says the gibberish words again. *Kurtosis* and *heteroscedasticity*.

"Goddammit, Haresh. I get that there's a volatility issue. What I don't get is why you're calling me about it. There's always volatility somewhere in the position."

Jonathan can hear Haresh sigh. "You know what a tail is, right?" he says.

Jonathan hates it when Haresh talks to him like he's a second grader, although he likely deserves it for talking to Haresh like he's an idiot, which he most certainly is not.

"Yeah," Jonathan says sharply. "What normal people call the variation of risk, you guys in the bull pen refer to as tails."

"Right," Haresh says, apparently with no recognition that Jonathan is being short. "It's because that's how the position shows up on a chart as deviating from the mean. We expect a small amount of deviation, but it should be negligible. Maybe .03 percent. But when the distribution is farther away from the standard deviation, it shows up on the chart as the tail getting fatter."

"Haresh, I've got a hundred billion bucks sitting inside eating steak, and I'm standing here in the rain, so I'd really appreciate it if you get to the point already. And *in English*, please."

"Our tail is fat as fuck."

Haresh had these Chicken Little moments from time to time. Jonathan had come to believe that his second fancied himself as the lookout man on the *Titanic*, the last set of eyes that could avoid catastrophe on the horizon.

Jonathan, however, prides himself on being a man who exhibits grace under pressure. The one who keeps his head while those around him are losing theirs.

"So . . . the gap is widening," Jonathan says with an air of calm. "Big fucking deal. It'll close eventually. I mean, the sun is still rising in the east, right? We increase our position and then we'll maximize our profit when the alignment hits?"

Silence on the other end, which means that Haresh disagrees. Finally, Haresh says, "We're overleveraged, Jonathan. It's already nearly three to one."

This slows Jonathan down. The fund can only generate its outsize returns if it borrows heavily, leveraging the cash on hand so that it can put far more capital in the market than the money actually entrusted to the fund by its investors. The problem was that borrowing more than three bucks for every one dollar invested exceeded the model's protocol, rendering the fund overly susceptible to interest rate movement—namely, the cost of such borrowing.

"What's the CMT?" Jonathan asks.

The constant maturity tables. They're more commonly referred to as the Treasury yield curve, but on Wall Street it's known by its acronym.

"Almost inverted," Haresh says.

Jonathan doesn't know why Treasury yield curves become inverted any more than he understands the chemical reaction that causes water to freeze. But what he does know is that water freezes when it's thirty-two degrees Fahrenheit, and the Treasury yield curve becomes inverted when an economy is slowing, and that, in turn, means there's a good chance that interest rates will stay low.

That's at least one bright spot. The cost to the fund to borrow a few hundred million dollars more won't be prohibitive.

"Go to four to one on the leverage," he tells Haresh.

"That'll exhaust our credit."

Jonathan looks into the restaurant, where he can see Ross and Goldenberg yukking it up. "Just do it, Haresh, and let me worry about where the money comes from, okay?"

"Okay. You're the boss."

Back in the restaurant, Jonathan sees that either Goldenberg or Ross has taken it upon himself to order another bottle of the four-hundred-dollar Amarone that Jonathan will be paying for. It's just as well, as he'd prefer these guys get good and drunk tonight.

* * *

Jonathan stumbles home close to one in the morning. Natasha is asleep. Or pretending to be so she doesn't have to engage her husband in his inebriated state. Jonathan doesn't care which; he'd rather be alone, too.

After dinner, Ross thought the revelry should continue, so after they put Goldenberg in his limousine, Ross and Jonathan ended up at the St. Regis Hotel's King Cole Bar, drinking overpriced scotch. Jonathan had watched his wine intake at Wolfgang's, as he never liked to get too drunk with clients, but the scotch had pushed him over the edge. He'll be good and hungover tomorrow, but it was worth it to keep Ross happy.

Before Ross's speech became slurred, he clearly articulated the words that Jonathan had longed to hear: that he was open to staking Jonathan in his own fund. This had long been Jonathan's ultimate dream, to be free of the Vincent Komaroffs of the world and to reap one hundred percent of the profits he earned. What impeded this fantasy from becoming reality was that he'd need somewhere near two billion in cash to start the fund, and in order to do the type of trading that would give his investors the returns they demanded, he'd also need to borrow close to six billion more. That's what had long tethered Jonathan to Harper Sawyer: they have that type of borrowing power, and he doesn't.

Jonathan realizes that given the amount of alcohol Ross had consumed, he might not remember anything about what he'd said tonight, or might pretend as if he didn't if he thought better of his offer in the clear light of day, but if he was serious about putting a billion or so in a fund under Jonathan's banner, that would go a long way toward convincing other big-shot CEOs to follow suit. The banks, in turn, might see that kind of blue-chip clientele as a reason to loosen the purse strings and give Jonathan the credit he'd need.

With the fantasy now a little closer to reality, Jonathan returns to one of his favorite parts of this daydream: the naming of his would-be fund. He's considered honoring his humble roots (Carlisle Investments); or a Greek god (Ares Management); or going with a pop-culture bent (Gotham Partners). But in the end, he knew he'd never be able to resist the self-congratulatory ring of Caine Capital. It was just too good to pass up.

Right behind the name game is an even greater fantasy: his final showdown with that self-inflated egomaniac Vincent Komaroff. Jonathan envisions them walking toward each other like gunslingers in the Old West, in a final battle for supremacy. When they came face-to-face, Jonathan would tell Komaroff that if he had only been less stingy at bonus time, things would never have come to this, but now there's no turning back. He imagines Komaroff begging—offering him a twenty-million-dollar bonus just for staying for a few more years—and Jonathan laughing as he literally turns his back on the boss on his way out the door.

Sometimes Jonathan even took the daydream to the trading floor of his self-imagined Caine Capital. Fifty thousand square feet of open space with helicopter views of New York City. Now a hundred traders occupy the X-shaped desk, with Jonathan still at its center.

His home is different in this fantasy, too. It's now the penthouse of some new construction overlooking Central Park that he's undoubtedly purchased for a record-breaking sum, and, of course, he summers in that oceanfront mansion in East Hampton.

It's not lost on Jonathan that although he envisions his fantasy life with striking clarity, he never sees Natasha in these glimpses of his future. He doesn't imagine that she's divorced him, for he's certainly upheld his part of their marital bargain by providing her the life of opulence she craves. And he doesn't envision that he's left her, either, as that would require alimony, and he'd rather not weaken this fantasy by depleting his net worth by half.

No, for it to truly be a fantasy, Natasha must meet some type of sudden end. Preferably one that makes Jonathan seem even more heroic for having endured such suffering.

4

Eight Months Later/December

As soon as he gets out of his car, Jonathan hears the Divinyls' "I Touch Myself" and he's firmly back in 1990. He surveys the other vehicles in the East Carlisle High School parking lot. A lot of economy cars, most of them domestic, scattered among the SUVs and minivans.

His Bentley looks very out of place, and Jonathan smiles.

When the invitation to his twenty-fifth high-school reunion arrived in the mail two months ago, Jonathan could not envision any confluence of events that would have led him to attend. It had long been something of a point of pride that looking back had never held any interest.

And yet here he is.

"Hey, you're Johnny something, right?" says an obese man sitting on a bench in front of the high school, a plume of smoke around his face.

Even with the man's extra hundred pounds and bald head, Jonathan recognizes Pauley DiGiacomo. The smell of pot is also a trigger. Pauley was a first-class burnout in high school, although in East Carlisle, and apparently nowhere else on earth, the stoners were called ginkers. He's wearing jeans and a black T-shirt with some type of writing on it that's obscured by the gray hoodie he has half-zipped over it, which immediately makes Jonathan think that his decision to wear his Brioni suit was a mistake, even if he did forgo the tie.

"I go by Jonathan nowadays. Jonathan Caine."

Jonathan extends his hand for a shake, like grown-ups do, but Pauley puts up his palm, inviting a high five. "Fuck yeah," Pauley says, after Jonathan slaps his hand. Then apparently realizing that he's being ungracious, Pauley says, "Hey, you want a hit?"

Pauley pushes the joint that's clutched between his stubby fingers toward Jonathan. The irony isn't lost on Jonathan that he could have easily had this exact same conversation with Pauley DiGiacomo senior year.

"No, I'm good," Jonathan says. "So what have you been doing with yourself, Pauley?"

"You know me, still kickin' it with the drums."

Jonathan suddenly recalls that Pauley was in some type of band in high school, and now that he's accessing that part of his memory, a pretty decent version of "In the Air Tonight" performed at the senior variety show with Pauley on the skins comes back to him.

"So you're in a band?"

"Yeah. We're called Caravan. We just did the open mic night down at the Grove. We play at my church sometimes, too."

"Hey, that's great. Married? Kids?"

"No way, man. Got Nixie, though. She's a black Lab mix. Just the two of us against the world. You know how it is, right?"

Even though Pauley obviously meant the question to be rhetorical, it throws Jonathan. The last thing he wants is to be able to identify in any way with Pauley DiGiacomo's life. And yet, he *does* know how it is, and he doesn't even have a dog.

"You going to make it inside?" Jonathan asks.

"I'm just chillin' here for a few. Sounds rockin', though."

"Okay," Jonathan says, glad to be able to extricate himself from a stoned ghost of the past. "I'm going to head in now."

Pauley takes a toke. "Great talking to you, man."

* * *

The signs inside the high school direct Jonathan toward the gym, which he could have figured out on his own because that's where the music comes from. Now it's Roxette's "It Must Have Been Love."

In front of the gym is a row of tables, manned by middle-aged people who should be teachers, but Jonathan recognizes them as his former classmates. Dana Mason's hair is as blond as he remembers it, almost white, but God does she look old. He wonders whether it's possible that the mirror has been lying and he looks that old, too. At work, he's surrounded by people in their twenties and thirties, and Natasha is still two years shy of the big three-oh. Somehow he had convinced himself that they were all contemporaries.

"Johnny Caine—no way!" Dana says brightly. "Well, you look great. You didn't come to the other reunions, right? And you're not on Facebook. Or if you are, I can't find you. I've looked. Wow, Johnny Caine. So . . . tell me?"

"Tell you what?" he says.

"Married? Kids? Job? Where do you live? You know, twenty-fifth high-school reunion stuff?"

"I'm married, but no kids. I work on Wall Street and live in New York City."

"I knew it. I knew it," Dana says with a giggle. "I always used to say that Johnny Caine is going to be a millionaire someday."

He smiles to confirm her assessment. "Your turn."

Although he didn't think it was possible a moment earlier, Dana's expression lights up even more. She reaches into her purse and pulls out her phone.

"I should keep this out because I keep showing people. This is Jackson, he's my baby, and a high school senior now. And my oldest . . ." She scrolls through the pictures. "She looks terrible here, but this is Mandy. She's a sophomore at Rutgers."

Jonathan feels like a dirty old man when he thinks about the fact that Mandy looks almost exactly like Dana did back in high school. "Wow. Your daughter's in college."

"Karen Thompson is a grandmother already! And I don't think she's the only one. Is your wife here? I'd love to meet her."

"Unfortunately, I'm here by my lonesome. My wife had another engagement."

"Oh, that's too bad," Dana says. "But I totally get it. My husband is tired of the old stories, too, which is why I'm also flying solo tonight." Then, looking over Jonathan's shoulder, she says, "Hey, it's Patty Tiernan. You remember Johnny Caine, don't you?"

Jonathan turns around. "Hi," he says, even though he doesn't recognize Patty Tiernan at all.

"Hi," she says back, sounding as if she can't place him, either.

"Well, you're all set, Johnny," Dana says. "Go have fun. I'm going to be done here in another forty minutes or so, and then I'll come find you. Okay?"

"Sure," he says. "One thing, though, I go by Jonathan now."

"Good choice," Dana says, nodding. "Fits you better."

* * *

The same thought recycles again and again in Jackie's brain: How could she have ever been friends with these people? Vain and insecure. Mean-spirited to the point of nasty. And above all else, stupid as the day is long.

Barbara DeSapio was Jackie's best friend in high school. The number of nights they slept at each other's house likely qualified each of them for legal residence.

They lost touch in college, but not for Barbara's lack of trying. It was Jackie who broke away, wanting to put as much distance as possible between the vapid beauty queen she was in high school and the person she wanted to be. And for a while, it worked. She had long considered it her greatest failing that she'd returned to Rick and to East Carlisle. In the end, Jackie had no excuse other than that she'd been afraid. Instead of relying on her intelligence, which she'd never been quite confident would support her, she fell back on her beauty, which had never let her down, and she ran back to the land where she had once been queen.

Facebook did the rest, reacquainting her with the old high school crew. Barbara lived on Long Island, and even though she was only two hours away, their contact over the past years had been limited to liking one another's status and the annual birthday call.

When she sees her former BFF in the flesh, it's even more apparent than from photographs that Barbara has kept up her looks, so much so that she could still manage a passing resemblance to Heather Locklear, her senior yearbook separated-at-birth partner. Jackie assumes that some of that must come with money—as Barbara's Facebook feed was a never-ending stream of photos with her personal trainer. On top of which, Jackie assumed that a nip or tuck had been done, too, or at the very least, a healthy amount of Botox. Barbara didn't have a wrinkle or crease on her.

Michelle Sackler, née Abromowitz, and Melissa Romero, née Farella, completed the quartet of high school royalty that ordinary students referred to as the Cliquesters. They both attended college at University of Miami and then moved in together after graduation. Their parents willingly picked up the rent because they viewed an apartment in a complex that was next to the medical school as a better investment in their daughters' future than graduate school. Turned out they were right. Before the two-year lease ran out, Melissa married an anesthesiologist who lived on the sixth floor, and Michelle tied the knot with a plastic surgeon resident on nine.

The M&Ms, as Michelle and Melissa called themselves, now live within five minutes of each other in Boca Raton. They're both stay-at-home moms, even though the youngest of their children is in high school, which leaves a lot of time for them to have lunch, shop, and go to the gym together. One of those lifelong friendships straight out of a multiplex rom-com, Jackie thinks.

"I can't believe that you and Rick never left East Carlisle," Melissa says.

"Yeah," Michelle chimes in. "It must be so strange to go to the same places where we used to hang out as kids."

"Have you driven down Route Eighteen?" Barbara laughs. "I doubt that there are five stores still around from back then."

"The mall's still there," Michelle points out. "Remember, Jacqueline, when we'd go into the dressing room of . . . what was the name of that store with the really short skirts? And we'd stuff the miniskirts into our bras and then walk out like we were Dolly Parton or something?"

"G&S," Melissa says.

"Right, G&S," Michelle says.

Jackie recalls precisely this dynamic from over two decades ago, and hated it then. The M&Ms finishing each other's thoughts, as if combined they might have a normal-size brain, and Barbara trying to drive a wedge between them and Jackie, so she could protect her position as Jackie's best friend.

"It's actually very nice," Jackie says. "Living in the same town you grew up in, I mean. There are still a lot of teachers around from our time, and there's something—I don't know what the word is, gratifying, maybe?—to see your kids doing the same things you were doing. Our youngest, Emma, she's a gymnast over at the Weider school, and Robert plays quarterback for the Bears."

"I bet that makes Rick happy," Barbara says.

There's something about Barbara's tone that Jackie finds unsettling. A familiarity that shouldn't be there. Jackie's often wondered whether Barbara slept with Rick, maybe when they were in college and she and Rick were on one of their many breaks. Maybe in high school, for all Jackie trusted either of them.

"Out of all of us," Melissa says, "I think Jacqueline's life is the closest to what I would have imagined in high school."

It's about as bad an indictment as Jackie can imagine, even though she can certainly see why Melissa would have planned this for Jackie twenty-five years ago.

You'll marry Ricky and live in a house on Farmington Lake, and you'll have a boy and a girl, and the boy will be a football player, and the girl will be beautiful.

How much did Jackie not want that to be the way her life turned out? And yet, maybe she protested too much. She didn't have to move back to East Carlisle after college. She could have turned down Rick's marriage proposal and gone on to graduate school, like she'd originally planned.

She had never imagined the price she'd pay for her insecurity would be so unbearably high. A life of abject fear with no end in sight.

* * *

Alex Miller is the first person Jonathan encounters whom he was actually friendly with in high school. They weren't in the same core social circle but in the same general sphere of high school life at least: smart boys with ambition. Alex had done all right for himself too. A couple of years back, Jonathan ran into Mitch Glassman at a restaurant in SoHo, and Mitch mentioned that Alex Miller was a partner at Cromwell Altman, a top-tier New York City law firm.

Alex is looking good, which gives Jonathan a boost that he might not be as run-down as the others he's scanned from a distance. Alex's hair remains full, albeit half-gray now, and he doesn't seem to be a completely different shape than he was in high school.

In the time it takes Jonathan to approach, Alex has been joined by Stephen Hirshman, who was a world-class geek in high school. The years have not been kind to Hirshman. A bean pole with a huge Jew-fro back in the day, he's now swung in the opposite direction, close to three hundred pounds and bald as a cue ball.

"Finally, men in suits," Jonathan says.

Alex chuckles. "Yeah, really. Did an e-mail go out that everyone was supposed to dress like teenagers?"

"Only among the guys," Hirshman says. "The girls seem to have gone all out. Some social scientist should make a study about why the female of the species preserves itself so much better. Look over there—Jacqueline Lawson and the Cliquesters. I swear, it's like time has stood still for them."

Cliquesters, Jonathan repeats in his head. He hasn't heard that term in twenty-five years.

"Okay," Hirshman says excitedly, "this definitely falls under the category that there is no karmic justice in the world, but I heard that Jacqueline married that douche bag Ricky Williams. The prom queen and the quarterback of the football team. Clichés are clichés for a reason, I guess."

Alex is apparently uninterested in high school classmates who never gave him the time of day, so he asks Hirshman, "What's your post-ECHS life been like, Stephen? You went to MIT, right? If I had to guess, I'd bet you hit it big with a tech start-up."

"I wish," Hirshman says with a nervous laugh. "No such luck. Sometimes I think I'm the only guy who got a computer degree from MIT in 1995 who *isn't* a millionaire. But I had the foresight to turn down a job at Microsoft because I didn't feel like moving to Seattle. And so instead of being retired at thirty and now spending my time running my own charitable foundation, I was just canned from the place where I've worked for the last twenty years."

Jonathan tuned out of this discussion the moment he caught sight of Jacqueline Lawson. She was still breathtakingly beautiful, that was for damn sure. Dark shoulder-length hair, not that frosted dye so many women in their forties go to; and the same sparkling emerald eyes he remembered so vividly from a quarter century ago still shimmered from across the room. She must also work out every day, as she seemed tight in all the right places.

Every boy in ECHS had a thing for Jacqueline Lawson. Jonathan sure as hell did. How many nights did he spend alone in his bedroom fantasizing about her?

I want what I want, he thinks to himself.

"Stephen," calls out a heavyset woman with short, spiky gray hair.

Jonathan can't place her from high school, although that didn't necessarily mean that they weren't classmates. He hasn't recognized most of the attendees tonight.

Hirshman does the introductions. "This is my wife, Allison. Allison, this is Johnny Caine and Alex Miller, two really good guys."

"Hi," she says, but obviously is uninterested in them. "Stephen, the sitter just called. Max is throwing up. We need to go."

"He'll be fine, Allison. He probably just has a stomach bug. There's nothing we're going to be able to do for him at home, and we just got here."

"Can I speak to you about this privately?" Allison says in a way that makes clear that *no* is not a possible answer.

"Good talking to you guys," Hirshman says, sighing. "If we stick around, I'll try to catch up with you later."

"My God. Poor bastard," Jonathan says after Hirshman's wife yanks him away. "How about you, Alex. Do you have an equally lovely wife at home?"

Alex laughs. "Well, without comparing the two, the answer is yes, I'm married. Elizabeth is home with our children tonight. A boy and a girl. Charlotte's eleven, and Owen is about to turn five. And you?"

"Married, no kids. My wife—perhaps wisely—suggested that I'd have more fun if I relived my not-so-glory days without her."

There's a sudden awkward silence, the small talk having run its course, before Alex says, "I hope I'm not talking out of school, Johnny," and then, realizing the play on words, he quickly adds, "which of course I'm not, because I'm talking *in* school. But . . . I know a little of what's going on with you . . . This obviously isn't the time or the place and, believe me, I'm not pitching for business, but . . . I always liked and respected you, at least back when we actually knew each other . . . and so if you need someone to talk to . . . Well, the truth is that I've kind of been there a little bit myself, and I offer my friendship with the added benefit of the attorney-client privilege."

Jonathan feels like he's been caught naked. He hadn't expected any-one at the reunion to know anything about his life other than what he bothered telling them.

Alex reaches into his suit jacket pocket and pulls out a business card. Jonathan glances at the firm name.

"Peikes Selva & Schwarz?" Jonathan says. "I thought you were at Cromwell Altman."

"I was, but I've been at Peikes for the last couple of years. Long story, but like I said, it gives me some frame of reference for what you're going through."

"Thanks," Jonathan says. "Do you mind? I need to make a call. But I do appreciate the offer, Alex. Truly and seriously."

* * *

Jackie pries herself away from her supposed best-friends-forever under the guise that she needs to call home and check on the kids. As she walks out of the gym, she spies Rick whispering to Diana Mata-razzo. He looks barely able to keep his tongue in his mouth. Jackie can't make out what either one of them is saying, but she knows her husband well enough to surmise that she'd be disgusted if she heard two words of it.

There's some refuge in the fresh air, although the moment Jackie steps outside, she wishes she had stopped to grab her coat. In the slinky dress she's wearing, she won't last two minutes out here before she begins shaking from the cold. Still, that's two minutes that she doesn't have to be inside with any of them.

She has the overwhelming impulse to scream. Just shout at the top of her lungs how much she hates her life, and everyone and every-thing in it. But she stifles that thought, fully knowing it's misdirected.

The person she hates is herself. She's to blame for her life, no one else—

"Hey."

The sound of someone else's presence actually causes Jackie to jump.

"Oh, I'm sorry. I didn't mean to scare you. I just came out here to get away from it for a little bit. But if you did that, too, then I guess my presence defeats the purpose. At least for you."

Jackie squints. "You're Johnny Caine, right?"

Jonathan smiles. "Jonathan now, but yes. I often wondered if high school royalty knew the names of their loyal subjects."

She tries to conjure an image of Johnny Caine in high school, but all she can remember is that he was one of the smart kids back when she didn't realize that mattered a lot more in life than being able to throw a tight spiral. From the looks of him, Jackie concludes that Johnny Caine figured out a way to monetize his intelligence. Lawyer, maybe. Or a doctor?

The Cliquesters made it something of a Friday-night activity to rank the hottest guys, usually getting up to twenty before they decided that no one else was worth the effort. Johnny Caine never made the cut. He would now, though.

"That was a very long time ago, you know," she says.

"It was indeed," he says. "Twenty-five years, if you believe the banners hanging in the gym. You look cold." Jonathan takes off his suit jacket. "Is that okay?" he asks, offering it up.

Jackie smiles at him. In a different life, she thinks, she might have ended up with someone like Johnny—no, Jonathan—Caine. Smart. A gentleman. Not an alcoholic, cheating wife abuser.

"Do you mean is my husband going to kick your ass because you kept his wife from freezing to death?"

"I'm less concerned about that than that you'll find me too forward."

Jackie takes the jacket from Jonathan and wraps it around herself. She can tell it's expensive from the way it slips onto her shoulders.

"No. I appreciate a gesture of chivalry now and then. So are you having fun?"

"Now I am," he says with a grin. "You should know I made it my mission tonight to say hello to you."

Jackie can't deny she's flattered. She still gets a lot of male attention, but nowadays it's from Rick's asshole buddies and the occasional guy with a MILF fetish.

"Oh really. And why is that? Did you ever say hello to me in high school?"

"See, that's just it. I was afraid to talk to you in high school, so maybe now we could be friends."

"Uh-huh. Call me crazy, but I get the sense that I just might be an item on your bucket list. You know. Buy a Porsche. Have sex with the prom queen. That kind of thing."

Jonathan chuckles. "I guess I shouldn't have worried so much about being too forward."

"Tell me it's not true," she says with a smile.

He stares hard at her, no smile on his lips. "It's not true. Sorry if I made you think that." Then he waits a beat. "But if I'm being totally honest with you, I should probably confess . . . that I already have a very nice car."

They share a laugh.

"If you want to know the truth, the reason I've accosted you like this is because my father's dying over at Lakeview, and I'm going to be spending some time in East Carlisle. I heard you still live here, and so I thought I should at least come and say hello because I don't know anyone else who still calls East Carlisle home except you and your husband, and he's the guy who gave me wedgies all through middle school, so I thought you were the safer bet to seek out as a potential friend."

"I'm so sorry to hear about your dad."

"Thanks. It's tough, but . . . circle of life, I guess. We're at that age when our parents are going to get sick and die. I went through it just last year with my mother. This time, I decided to take some time off from work so I can spend it with him. I figured it's now or never."

"You poor thing. Your mother, too? My father died . . . oh, it's been more than twenty years now—when I was in college—but I still miss him. My mother is still alive, so I guess I'm lucky there. She lives in Baltimore, but we still see each other a lot. If you don't mind my asking . . . what's wrong with your father?"

"The doctors aren't exactly sure. There's definitely a dementia component, which makes it hard in a different way than it was with my mother. She died of cancer, and so she still had all her marbles, right up until the end. With him . . . sometimes he's there and other times . . . not so much." He holds up his ring finger. "And besides, I'm married. So, milady, you can take comfort in the fact that my intentions are completely honorable. But I was still hoping that we might be friends."

He smiles at her. It reminds her of the smile she once had.

On impulse, she says, "Give me your phone."

Jonathan does as directed, unlocking and handing her his iPhone. Jackie presses the buttons for her own phone number, at which time her purse begins to sing Sara Bareilles's "Brave."

"Now you have my number, and I have yours. Call me if you want to get coffee or lunch or something."

"Thank you, Jacqueline," he says. "I'd like that."

"You're very welcome, Jonathan. But I go by Jackie now."

She hands the phone back to him, and in the exchange their fingers brush together. Is she imagining it, or has he let their touch linger? What she knows for certain is that she's hoping Jonathan Caine's interest in her is not as honorable as he professes.

5

May

Jonathan always orders the filet mignon at Sant Ambroeus, as he does tonight. Natasha opts for the Dover sole, which means that they can't agree on a bottle of wine, so they order by the glass.

"Harrison called me today with a house that he says we have to see," Natasha says after the entrées arrive.

Harrison is Harrison Kaye, the universally regarded best real estate broker on the East End, which is how those in the know refer to the Hamptons. He's in such demand that he initially resisted taking Jonathan and Natasha on as clients because their thirteen-million-dollar budget wasn't worth his time. His exact words were that he doesn't work with HENRYs—those who are "High Earners, Not Rich Yet." He changed his mind upon meeting Natasha, a result she effected in most men, including, apparently, those who are gay, as she claimed Harrison to be.

"Is it on the ocean?" Jonathan asks.

Oceanfront real estate in East Hampton is the latest status marker Jonathan is determined to possess. It has been an ever-expanding list through the years, along with exponentially increasing price tags. Six-thousand-dollar Brioni suits gave way to the need for a fifty-thousand-dollar Lange & Söhne chronograph wristwatch, and then a $250,000 Bentley (which he leased because cars are a depreciating asset). More recently, he's required an eight-million-dollar penthouse and expensive artwork to put on its walls. And now he simply cannot live without an oceanfront home in East Hampton.

"No, but he says that it has an amazing view, and a pool and a tennis court."

"Uh-uh. If we're going to buy, it's got to be on the ocean."

I'm sorry, but I want what I want.

"Then you're going to have to buy in 2008," Natasha says, "because Harrison says that there's no way we're going to see the ocean in our price range. Not in East Hampton, at least. If we go more west, maybe . . ."

"No, I don't want to do that. East Hampton is where we need to be."

"Please. Will you at least just see the house that Harrison is talking about?"

Jonathan sighs. He knows he's not going to win this fight. "When?"

"Sunday."

"Okay," he says. "But no compromising."

* * *

Harrison Kaye's Rolls-Royce actually has vanity plates that read *Brkr2stars*.

"So, this house that we're going to see. It's being sold by a close personal friend of mine," Harrison says, looking in the rearview mirror to catch Jonathan's eye. "I'm not at liberty to say who it is, but she's an Emmy Award–winning actress. Hell, you'll figure it out by the pictures, anyway. Claire Danes. You know, from *Homeland*? There, I said it. Anyway, Claire and Hugh Dancy—that's her husband, and he's an actor, too. He did something on Broadway a few years ago, and he's been in some movies, but I can never remember which ones, which is kind of embarrassing because, you know, I see them like all the time. Well, long story short, they already closed on something else and they want to sell before the summer because last summer they rented this place out and they had, let's just say, a less than ideal experience."

Jonathan's more than happy that Natasha is riding shotgun, because it allows him to tune out Harrison's babbling. Natasha was clearly right about Harrison's sexual orientation. Jonathan can't imagine any straight man being caught dead wearing a pink shirt with matching pink pants, which is Harrison's getup today.

"So, Jonathan," Harrison continues, "like I told Natasha, this place won't hit the market until next week. But then it's going to sell in one day. That's why this is such a great opportunity. You can snatch it up before it's even officially for sale."

The driveway is lined with white pebbles that rattle around the underside of the Rolls. In the distance sits a modernist structure, all glass and angles, even though Jonathan had made it clear he wanted something traditional.

When they alight from the car, Jonathan signals his displeasure to Natasha with a scowl. Natasha has apparently gotten this message, because she leans into him and whispers, "Oh, come on. Just keep an open mind. Okay?"

"How much?" Jonathan says to Harrison, who is a step ahead of them, unlocking the home's front door.

"Twelve-nine. And I'll tell you something funny about the real estate market. Nobody prices their home at thirteen million. Just like the way hotels skip the thirteenth floor. Triskaidekaphobia, it's called. So, if you're unfortunate enough that the comps indicate that your house won't fetch fourteen, you have no choice but to price it at twelve-nine. What that means for you is that it's a real investment opportunity. If the market goes up two percent next year, it can be listed at fourteen million, and so it's an easy way to flip it and make a cool million for yourself."

Jonathan is tempted to correct Harrison's math, but instead he smiles as if he fully understands. What Jonathan hears loud and clear, however, is that Harrison is conjuring the same type of smoke and mirrors that Jonathan pushes on his clients.

"This place was built five years ago by Bachman Architects,"

Harrison says as they enter the large foyer, which has black-and-white marble square flooring that seems to go on for a hundred feet. "Kat Bachman is the gold standard for modern houses on the East End. He's done about five or so out here, and now he's involved in much bigger projects, which is only going to increase the value of his homes. It's still top secret, so don't tell anyone, but he's going to do the new building for the New York City Ballet, and when that happens? The sky's the limit."

Inside, the place is absolutely beautiful, but in a minimalist way. The color scheme is neutral, with virtually all-white furniture.

"It's being sold furnished," Harrison says, "but I tell you, it would go for exactly the same price unfurnished. They just don't want the hassle of having to empty it out."

Harrison leads them toward the back of the house, where the Long Island Sound comes into view. "We'll look through the whole house in a minute—and I know you're going to love it," he says. "Five bedrooms, four fireplaces, you know, all the bells and whistles. But Natasha told me it was very important that you wanted a view, so I thought it made sense to start out back."

It's ten degrees colder on this side of the house, with the wind whipping up from the water. A sandy beach about ten yards wide runs the length of the property, beyond which gray-green water stretches as far as the eye can see.

"That the Sound?" Jonathan asks, although he knows it is. He's asked the question simply to register out loud that it's not the Atlantic Ocean proper.

"That's right," Harrison answers. "And it's the best piece of property on the Sound because, as you can see, the view goes on forever. With some properties, you can see the North Fork on the other side. It's a matter of preference, of course, but Natasha told me that you expressed a desire to be on the ocean, and so I thought that this would be appealing because it captures that same sense of infiniteness."

"Or we could get something, you know, actually on the ocean," Jonathan counters.

Harrison smiles and takes a step toward Jonathan. For a flicker, Jonathan reacts as if it's an aggressive gesture, but when Harrison gets within arm's length, rather than taking a swing at the client, he puts his hand on Jonathan's shoulder and says, "Look, I want you to understand something, just to manage your expectations. I'm as good as there is out here, so the last thing I would try to do is tell you that a house on the Sound is the same as a house on the ocean. It's not. No way, no how. So, if you *only* want a house on the ocean, and you *only* want East Hampton, we should leave this place right now, and let me show you some inventory I have that meets your specifications. But let's be real here, something on the ocean . . . in East Hampton . . . is going to cost twenty million, easy. And at that price, it's a teardown. So, if that's what you want, I got two or three to show you. If you want *this* particular house but on the ocean, you're looking at thirty million plus. I got some inventory like that, too. I can get you in today. Just say the word."

What Harrison Kaye lacks in physical menace he more than makes up for in psychological warfare. He has just managed to hurt Jonathan more acutely than any punch to the face could by openly shaming him for only being able to afford a $12.9 million summer home.

* * *

"I really think we should put in an offer on that house," Natasha says that night while they're in bed. "Harrison says it's a steal."

Jonathan snorts at the thought of a thirteen—sorry, *twelve-nine*—million-dollar house being a steal. "I think he's the one committing larceny here. You do know that he's going to net an eight-hundred-grand commission for an hour's work."

"Don't think about him, Jonathan, think about us. Relaxing in that hot tub, looking out onto the water . . ."

She nuzzles next to him. He allows her to nibble his ear, but when she reaches down to his boxers, he knows he's being played.

"You mean the water that is *not* the ocean, which is the one thing I said I wanted," he says bluntly. "No, that's not right—I also said I wanted a traditional, which that house is *also* not."

Natasha rolls away from him. Whatever sexual energy she had a moment ago is gone. So much so that she actually hikes the blanket up a bit, bringing it to just below her shoulders.

"Jonathan, we can't get an oceanfront house in our price range. Not in East Hampton, anyway. It's that simple."

"Fine. So we'll rent this summer on the ocean and we'll buy next year."

"Jonathan, renting something on the ocean in East Hampton is going to cost four hundred thousand for the summer. At least."

"Then that's what we'll pay. You know . . . I want what I want, Natasha."

"That's a ridiculous amount to spend for eight weeks."

"You say that like you earned it."

She lets out a loud sigh, feeling no obligation to hide her disappointment. After a moment, in which she looks as if she's measuring her words, Natasha says, "Jonathan, someday you'll see that you can't always get exactly what you want."

He raises his head and looks at her as if she's just uttered the worst form of blasphemy he can imagine.

"Of course I can, Natasha. I have for my entire life, and I have no intention of stopping now."

6

Seven Months Later/December

Jackie wishes she could sleep. After tossing and turning a few hours, she's awake for good by six.

There's a silver lining to her insomnia, however. On a Sunday morning, she'll have the run of the house for several hours. Emma is sleeping at a friend's, and Robert never wanders out of his room before noon on the weekend. Based on how much Rick imbibed, he likely also won't show his face until afternoon.

Diana Matarazzo or somebody else last night must have gotten Rick all hot and bothered, because when they got home after the reunion, he was like a dog in heat. She didn't protest, having long since realized that her resistance only revved him up more. And so she endured, thankful when he turned her over, so she didn't have to look at his goddamned face. That he was drunk made him last longer than usual, which only gave her more time to think about how much she absolutely hated her husband.

After making herself a pot of strong coffee, she takes a seat on the corner of the living room sofa, staring out the large bay window onto Farmington Lake. Clasping the mug with both hands, she allows the coffee's warmth to enter her.

Jackie knows that right now, clad in her flannel pajamas, taking in the view of the serene lake from the comfort of her home, she looks like an actress in a commercial depicting the idyllic suburban life. But her existence is far from a fantasy. As she does most mornings when she finds herself in this position, she wishes she were dead.

* * *

Jonathan doesn't feel the same sense of dread when entering Lakeview for the second time. He walks through the hallways and says hello to the African American nurse from yesterday. Today he notices she's wearing a name tag that says *Yorlene Goff.*

"I'm Jonathan Caine," he says. "How's my dad doing today?"

"I remember you, Mr. Caine," Yorlene says with a warm smile. "He's good, but why don't you go on in and ask him yourself?"

As if he was expecting his son's visit today, William Caine is sitting up in bed, watching television, when Jonathan enters his room. That it's figure skating and not playoff football is enough for Jonathan to surmise that one of the nurses selected it.

"Hi, Dad. How are you feeling today?"

"Johnny!" his father says rather brightly, as if he hasn't seen him for months.

"I was here yesterday, don't you remember?"

His father looks lost for a moment. "You were?"

"Yeah. I told you that I'd be back today because I was going to be staying at the house."

There's no sign of recognition from his father, but he accepts the truth of Jonathan's statement without further inquiry, and a silence falls between them as thick as any wall. Jonathan wishes his father would say something—anything—if only to prove that he's still connected to the world. But by the way he stares at the television, Jonathan knows that, at least for the moment, there's nothing for William Caine except figure skating.

Jonathan takes a seat in the recliner under the window. A Russian skater is performing to Taylor Swift's "Shake It Off."

"Do you like figure skating now, Dad?" Jonathan asks.

"I like the costumes. They're pretty. Especially the ones with lots of colors. I don't like the ones that are either all black or all white as much."

Jonathan always found his father to be a weak man. Part of that was because for as long as Jonathan was sentient, he knew that his mother called the shots. But Jonathan pinpoints the exact moment when he lost all respect for his father to be during a Fourth of July barbecue when he was fourteen. It was a small gathering at their home. The guest list was limited to his one living grandmother, his aunts and uncles on both sides, and their kids, as well as his mother's childhood friend Joan Samuelson, her husband, Barry, and his father's closest friend, Phillip Levinson, and his wife, Gayle.

At some point, Jonathan went inside—he can never remember why—and went upstairs to his bedroom. At the top of the steps, he heard something from his parents' room, and when he found the door open, he entered.

From behind the closed door to the master bathroom, he heard the unmistakable sound of his mother groaning. Even at fourteen, Jonathan knew why.

He ran downstairs, and then outside to the yard with the other guests, his stomach in knots. The first person he saw was his father, who was busy manning the grill, a stupid-ass grin on his face.

Jonathan figured out who was with his mother by a process of elimination, but he nevertheless kept a careful eye on the door. Not more than five minutes later, his mother returned to the backyard. A minute after that, Dad's buddy Phillip Levinson exited the house.

Burned into Jonathan's brain to this very day is the self-satisfied look on Levinson's face. Like he'd just won a medal for valor or something.

The Levinsons were the last to leave the party. When they made it to the doorway, Mrs. Levinson air-kissed his mother and then turned to make actual cheek contact with his father, at which time Mr. Levinson moved in to kiss Jonathan's mother good-bye. He most likely was planning to kiss her on the cheek, but at the last moment Jonathan's mother's head shifted so she caught him full on the lips, and then she lingered there. It couldn't have been more than a tenth of a second, but it was long enough for Jonathan's eyes to shoot over to his father. His gaze was still turned to Mrs. Levinson, however, so Jonathan was the only witness to the transgression.

And then the absolute worst part happened—the part that still makes Jonathan wince when he thinks about it. Phillip Levinson, his father's best friend, turned and said, "Bill, as always, I thoroughly enjoyed your hospitality."

Jonathan understood in no uncertain terms that for Phillip Levinson, cuckolding his supposed best friend was far more pleasurable than having sex with his supposed best friend's wife. Jonathan also knew that the proper response would have been to direct his anger toward his mother. She was the one, after all, who had betrayed their family. And yet, since that day, he always laid blame solely at his father's feet. None of this would have happened if William Caine had been more of a man. Able to satisfy his wife, and capable of putting the fear of God in the hearts of the Phillip Levinsons of the world, so that they knew they took their lives into their own hands if they even thought about interfering with what was his.

Jonathan was far from an introspective person, but even he knew that the experience was formative, not only in creating the distance between him and his father that persisted to this day, but in shaping the man he had become. In the end, it was Phillip Levinson—a man who took what he wanted—who became his role model, and Jonathan's father was reduced to a cautionary tale.

When the skater's routine is completed, the elder Caine turns away from the screen. Jonathan views it as his cue to speak.

"So I went to my high school reunion last night."

"Yeah?"

"I told you about it yesterday. Do you remember?"

"Um. Okay."

Jonathan assumes that his father has no recollection of the previous day's discussion, and that rattling off names of his long-lost classmates will only confuse him. But when the next figure skater takes the ice, his father's focus stays with Jonathan, as if he's trying to engage and is looking for help.

"Do you remember Jacqueline Lawson?" Jonathan asks.

"No," his father says. "Is she your friend?"

"I went to high school with her. We weren't friends back then, but she was the prettiest girl in the class. Prom queen and all that."

"Your mother was the prettiest girl in my class," he replies.

This isn't true. Jonathan's parents didn't attend high school together. He sees no reason to correct his father, however, so he continues about Jackie.

"She still lives in East Carlisle, so we may see each other for lunch while I'm here. She's married to this guy who was a real jerk in high school and, by all accounts, hasn't changed much since then."

Silence ticks by, which Jonathan has by now realized doesn't necessarily mean that a response will not be forthcoming. But this time, none comes. William Caine has since retreated into the black hole that is his illness.

* * *

Two hours later, Jonathan is back at his house—his parents' house, more accurately—composing a text message.

So nice seeing you, Jackie (I remembered, not Jacqueline). Do you want to get lunch tomorrow?

He reads it again. His main concern is that he'll frighten her away, and he almost mentions again that he's married, but that's protesting too much, he thinks. After checking his handiwork one more time, he presses the send button.

She answers almost immediately.

Love to. Just tell me where and when.

How about that? *Love to.*

He gives fleeting thought to waiting until later to respond, but then decides he'd just as soon not play such games.

1 pm. Does the Chateau still exist?

LOL Sure does. C u there.

7

June

The e-mail came at 10:00 a.m. on the dot. It was from his key investor, Michael Ross at Maeve Grant, although Jonathan had little doubt it was drafted by someone else. A lawyer, most likely. The subject line read simply: Redemption.

Pursuant to section 8(a)(1)(i) of the agreement between Maeve Grant Capital Fund Inc. (defined herein as the "Investor") and Harper Sawyer Derivative Currency Fund (defined herein as the "Fund"), Investor hereby provides notice of redemption in full of all monies invested by Investor currently held by the Fund. As set forth in section 16(d)(1)-(3), such payments should be made as follows:

$250,000,000.00	Within 7 days of this notice
$250,000,000.00	Within 30 days of this notice
Balance	No later than 60 days from this notice

A spike of pain drives into Jonathan's head. He pushes it aside, telling himself that every second counts now, and he starts to think through a strategy.

Maeve Grant has nearly three-quarters of a billion invested. Paying that back would be bad enough, but it's the fund's nearly four to one leverage that makes the situation critical. It means that in addition to coming up with Ross's money, the fund will have to reduce its borrowings in order to remain within the collateral parameters imposed by the banks. The bottom line is that by redeeming Ross, more than $3 billion is going to go out the door in the next sixty days, and that's enough of a hit to bring the entire fund down.

* * *

"Please hold for Mr. Ross," an administrative assistant says.

At least Ross isn't ducking his call, which is the first bit of good news of the day. It means he doesn't think that Jonathan's already dead in the water.

Jonathan has left the trading floor—and the building entirely, for that matter—to make this call. He almost never leaves the desk, particularly first thing on a Monday morning, so his underlings must already suspect that something's amiss, but he figures that's better than their overhearing they all may be unemployed by the end of the day.

"Good morning, Jonathan," Ross says into the phone.

"Not for me, Michael. What the fuck?"

The other end of the line is completely silent, as if he's been put on mute. Jonathan assumes Maeve Grant's general counsel is right there beside Ross.

"I take it you received my e-mail, then?" Ross asks, back on the line.

"Yes," Jonathan says, trying to keep his anger in check. "I have to say I'm very surprised, Michael. The fund is doing great, and just a month or so ago, when we were at Wolfgang's, you said you were very pleased. You talked about backing me in my own fund, or don't you remember?"

"I remember drinking a lot that evening, is what I remember," Ross says with a laugh.

Jonathan lets the remark pass. He hopes that his silence is enough to convey that he doesn't find this to be a laughing matter.

"Bottom line is that I really don't understand why you're now considering pulling out," Jonathan says.

Ross answers quickly. "We're not *considering*, Jonathan. We *are* pulling out. The timetable was in the redemption notice so there'd be no misunderstanding there."

"Look, Michael . . . I think this is a discussion we should have face-to-face. I'm willing to meet you wherever you want. Right now."

The mute sound again. This time the silence is longer, almost half a minute.

"I don't see the point, Jonathan," Ross finally says. "Everything I had to say is in the redemption notice."

"The point . . . ! Michael . . . ! The point is that we've known each other for some time now, and I think you understand what kind of major Category Five shit storm is going to rain down on me over this."

Calm down, Jonathan says to himself. He's got to project that he's in total control if he's going to talk Ross out of redeeming.

Jonathan takes a deep, cleansing breath and tries again, this time from a different direction. "Michael, a *gentleman* would have the decency to meet with me. I thought you were that type of man. Are you?"

Jonathan can only imagine that the lawyer is shaking his head vehemently to tell Ross that there's no way he should agree to a face-to-face. Jonathan knows Ross is too vain not to grasp the gauntlet Jonathan has thrown down. Ross prides himself on being a man of honor, as if he were some type of medieval knight, rather than an obscenely paid paper pusher.

"Okay. I'll meet you in fifteen minutes at . . . the Pulitzer Fountain, in front of the Plaza Hotel," Ross says. "I've got an eleven at the Plaza, so I can give you a few minutes before that."

"I'll be there."

* * *

It's less than a ten-minute walk from Jonathan's office to the Plaza. As he's approaching his destination, it starts to drizzle. Even in his dispirited state, Jonathan finds humor in the rain cloud that seemingly hangs over him. He considers ducking into the Plaza for shelter but fears he'll miss Ross, so he stands there in the rain, which is only increasing in intensity. He's well on his way to being drenched when a stretch limousine pulls up.

The glass is tinted. When it comes to a stop, the back window rolls down.

"Get in," Ross says.

Jonathan hesitates. He has the feeling that he's about to be kidnapped, like in a Mafia movie. But at this point, that would be a good development, so he climbs into the back of the car.

The partition is up, but Jonathan has no idea whether that means the driver is blocked from hearing what is about to unfold. Not to mention that Jonathan assumes the car is equipped with recording devices. At least Ross came without a lawyer.

"Thanks for seeing me, Michael. I'm not going to beat around the bush here. The fund's position is very precarious at the moment, and I'm afraid that if we have to liquidate to redeem you, the whole thing might collapse. But if you hang in there for . . . I don't know, a year, maybe less, I personally guarantee we'll redeem you then, and you'll be twenty, twenty-five percent richer."

Ross's expression is worse than anything Jonathan could have anticipated. It's not rejection, but pity.

"I know I've put you in a spot," Ross says, "but I've got government regulators so far up my ass that, I swear, I tickle their noses when I take a shit. They do periodic inventories of our positions, and they told me that your capital structure is out of whack. Four to one? C'mon, Jonathan, that's too much leverage, even for your fund."

"It's not four to one, Michael. It's . . . it's the same leverage it was last year." This is a lie. The fund is actually carrying twice the leverage of a year ago, and even though Jonathan thinks he's sold it well enough, he decides to gild the lily a bit. "Besides, it's the leverage that allows us to deliver such outsize returns. And correct me if I'm wrong, but last year we provided you with a thirty-five-percent ROI, which I believe contributed to that hefty payday you received from your board of directors."

"And it was very much appreciated, Jonathan. But last year was last year, and this is now. And now my regulators are telling me that we need to raise capital because our investment in your fund puts us on the wrong side of some regulation. I'm not willing to dilute my stock by taking on fifty billion dollars in debt, so I'm going to exercise my contractual right to unwind my position with you. No tears. We can do business again—just not right now."

Jonathan's mind is racing. He ping-pongs back and forth between sucking up and playing hardball. He decides to try the carrot one last time, largely because he has only one stick and that's a last resort.

"How about if we offer you a kicker to stay in? Favored nation status with Harper Sawyer? Name your price."

"Sorry, Jonathan. No can do. I'm out."

The fact that Ross didn't even make a counteroffer means there's no give there. This isn't a negotiation, and never has been. Ross wants his money, end of story.

Which means that Jonathan has to go with Plan B. Delay.

"Okay, Michael. You win. We'll cash you out. But we simply can't do it in the time frame you want. I'm going to need at least ninety days to make the first payment."

Jonathan manages to say this with a straight face. He's hoping that Ross at least meets him somewhere in the middle. Even if Ross demands the first payment in thirty days rather than the seven called for in the redemption notice, it would be a godsend.

"Ninety days? Oh, no, I'm sorry, Jonathan. You're going to have to honor the timetable in the offering docs."

Jonathan can no longer hold it together. "I'm not going to crater the fund," he says sternly. "No way. That'll cost a lot of people a lot of money. And for what? So you can satisfy some bureaucrats? Michael, let's be real here."

Whatever civility existed between them has now ended. Ross shakes his head, as if to say that Jonathan clearly has no idea who he's dealing with.

"How's this for real, Jonathan? Seven days from now, I'm expecting two hundred and fifty million dollars to be wired from your shop to mine. If that doesn't happen, my lawyers are in federal district court within twenty-four hours."

Jonathan has only one play now, and it's the nuclear option. He's never pressed that button before, but then again, no one had ever threatened the survival of the fund before.

"Michael, all it takes is a single phone call from me to the *Journal* to say that the fund is insolvent, and thirty seconds after it's online, every single one of my investors will want out, too. You won't get your money because there won't be enough to go around. Like you said, we're at a four-to-one leverage here. And I swear to God, that's exactly what I'll do. I'd rather go out in a blaze of glory and have all my investors share the pain than fucking redeem you and then *still* go under two or three months from now."

Michael Ross at first seems like he's considering Jonathan's ultimatum. But then he lets out a deep-down guffaw that leaves no doubt that Jonathan has overplayed his hand.

"Jonathan, you need to think through what you say sometimes. You really think I give a flying shit about losing what I got with *you*? We're paying seven billion in fines next week to settle some oil disaster fuck-up. Even if we lost every nickel in your little pissant fund, it doesn't rise to the level of our disclosure requirement. So please, don't delude yourself. This isn't a situation where we both have guns to each other's head. If I pull the trigger, your fucking head explodes. You pull it? At most, it's like a mosquito bite." Ross clicks the lock on the car door. "Now, why don't you run along. Get the fuck out of here."

* * *

Jonathan literally runs the five minutes back to the office. The rain is now coming down even harder than before, so by the time he reaches the trading floor, Jonathan has no misapprehension that he's a sorry sight, sweat drenching him as much as the rain.

He makes a beeline to Haresh Venagopul's cubicle.

"Jesus. What the hell, Jonathan? You look like . . . crap, actually."

"Come with me."

Jonathan doesn't wait for an answer and strides purposefully toward the men's room. Nor does he turn around to confirm Haresh is following him.

Once inside, Jonathan bends down to check under the four stalls. After verifying he and Haresh are alone, he walks over to the sinks and turns on all three faucets. Then he positions himself up against the door, blocking anyone else's entry.

"Whoa, okay, Jonathan, now really, what the hell is going on?"

Jonathan replies just loud enough to be heard over the running water. "Michael Ross wants to redeem. The whole fucking position."

Haresh's eyes widen. "Seriously? What's the timetable?"

"He's not giving us any break on the terms. Bottom line, we need to raise two hundred and fifty million dollars by this time next week, and that much again in thirty days, with the balance of his investment due in full at sixty."

Haresh noticeably slackens, as if he's just taken a body blow.

"Options," Jonathan snaps. "What happens if we unwind the position?"

"That's not possible," Haresh answers. "Actually, let me be more specific. *Possible* . . . but the position is about as bad as it could be right now. The ruble is trending down, and a redemption of this size will trigger the banks' rights to demand a pay-down of the credit line, which means we'll need to liquidate even more of the fund. Redeeming Ross means a loss of at least . . ." Haresh's eyes go back in his head, as if he's calculating. "Could be ten billion."

Ten billion dollars. Might as well be ten trillion. Either way, it means the end of Jonathan's career.

Jonathan nods. He already knew this, but hearing it from Haresh makes it certain. "Okay, how about raising the cash," he says.

"Seven hundred million? From where?" Haresh quickly answers.

"Baby steps. Right now, two hundred and fifty million buys us a month. We'll worry about the rest later. What's our borrowing power?"

"Uh, nothing. When we increased the leverage the last time, we exhausted the credit line. If anything, we're already overextended."

"Really nothing? Or not two hundred and fifty million nothing?"

Haresh shrugs, now leaning against the sink. "I don't know, Jonathan. It depends on where you mark the position . . . I mean, with some creativity . . . maybe thirty million. Maybe."

Jonathan allows himself a small smile. Progress. "Okay, so we're two hundred shy, give or take."

"No, more like two twenty-five. Besides, what difference does it make if we owe Ross two hundred million or two twenty-five?"

"Don't worry. I'm going to raise the difference and pay him off," Jonathan says matter-of-factly.

Haresh looks over at the running faucets half filling the basins, Jonathan's crude effort to avoid being recorded. "You need to be careful," Haresh says. "You're entering Madoff territory here."

*   *   *

Five minutes later, Jonathan is back in the rain, although at least this time he's brought an umbrella. He moves away from the assistants taking a smoke break, and although he's not quite alone, he assumes he's put enough distance between them that he's not going to be overheard.

His first call is his best shot—Isaac Goldenberg.

It's eight forty-five in Las Vegas. The phone rings five times, and for a moment Jonathan worries that no one is in yet, but finally Goldenberg's assistant answers.

"Hi, Marilyn, it's Jonathan Caine. Is Mr. Goldenberg in?"

"Oh, hi, Jonathan. No, I'm afraid not. He's in Macau."

Damn. "What's the time difference there?"

"Fifteen hours ahead," she says quickly. "So it's . . . eleven forty-five at night."

Now Jonathan worries that Goldenberg is asleep. The guy's eighty-three, after all.

"Okay, I'll try him on his cell. Thanks."

Surprisingly, Goldenberg picks up on the second ring. The man always sounds like he's got a mouth full of marbles, so Jonathan can't tell whether he's woken him. Not that Jonathan cares. He's thanking his lucky stars that this call won't have to wait until morning in China.

"Isaac! Jonathan Caine here in New York. I'm so sorry to bother you this late on the other side of the world, but I have this really tremendous opportunity and I'm calling my investors in order of magnitude, and I wanted to make sure that you had the first swing."

Goldenberg chuckles, which causes Jonathan's heart to sink. He's pressing too hard. *Dial it back*, he tells himself.

Jonathan says more deliberately, "There's been a market uptick and we want to quickly capture all the profit we can on the position, and that requires additional capital. Harper Sawyer is putting up two hundred and fifty million, with a one-billion target commitment. I'm calling to test your appetite for some or all of that last seven hundred and fifty mil."

Jonathan now waits. The next words out of Isaac Goldenberg's mouth will seal his fate.

What he hears is another laugh, and then Goldenberg says, "Well, let me check my coat pocket and see if I got that kind of change rattling around."

"I got to be honest with you here, Isaac. You're going to hate yourself if you pass on this."

This earns a much louder laugh from Goldenberg. One that Jonathan knows has nothing to do with Goldenberg actually being amused.

"Jonathan . . . first of all, we both know that you're definitely *not* being honest with me. I may be in China, but I hear that desperation in your voice loud and clear. I really don't want to know why, because, frankly, I figure you'll lie to me anyway . . . but I know that you wouldn't be asking unless you were pretty deep in it."

Shit. It's all over.

"But here's the good news. I like you. I really do. And I say that even though all you Wall Street pricks think you're a helluva lot smarter than some guy like me who doesn't have a fancy MBA but just built a business from nothing. So here's what I'm going to do for you. The moment I get a guarantee, in writing, that you're going to double my investment in one year, I'm going to wire you one hundred million dollars. What do you say to that?"

Jonathan wants to scream *YES!* but he's got to play hard to get, or Goldenberg will know that Jonathan's troubles are twice as bad as he surmises.

"I'm sorry, but I just can't do that, Isaac. You know the bureaucracy here. It'll take me three months to get that kind of request through . . . and even then, I don't know if it'll get approved. Hell, I don't even know if what you're suggesting is legal."

"Ah, I can see you're not getting it, Jonathan. I'm not negotiating. Either I get a written confirmation from you in the next sixty minutes that you're guaranteeing me a two-hundred-million-dollar payout next year, or I go with my gut, which is telling me to get out of the fund while the getting's good. And I bet that makes your problems ten times worse."

The phone goes dead.

Jonathan's all smiles, however. He's now a hundred million dollars closer to averting disaster.

His next call is to Norm Solomon.

"To what do I owe the pleasure, Mr. Caine?" Solomon says.

"Why don't you just call me Mr. Opportunity, because I'm a-knockin', Norm. I have the inside track on a position, and we're offering it only to our biggest investors. Between us—and I'll deny it if you tell anyone—Goldenberg and Ross are both in big, as is Harper Sawyer. I've got a sliver left, and thought you might want it."

"So, I'm third, huh?"

"I don't think it's so bad to be behind the guy who's number five on the *Forbes* list and the head of Capital Investments at Maeve Grant. And not to burst your bubble, but I gotta tell you, you're nowhere near being our third-biggest investor. But there's a window that's about to shut, and I know you can move money fast and without a lot of commotion. I don't want my other investors' panties in a twist about why I didn't come to them first. So discretion matters here. A lot."

"I see. And how much is this opportunity going to make me?"

"Two hundred million now, and you'll see at least three hundred in six months."

Jonathan knows that Solomon can't raise two hundred million dollars. At most, he's good for half of that. Jonathan's only asked for more because he wants Norm Solomon to be the beggar here.

Sure enough, Solomon bites. Jonathan knew he would—the guy's greedy as hell.

"You putting that in writing?"

Jonathan decides to play along. In for a penny, in for a pound, and he's got to fabricate something official-looking for Goldenberg anyway, so what's another fraudulent document in the big scheme of things?

"Already drafted. I just need to know what name to put on the signature line."

"That's Solomon, like the king. Only thing is that I'm afraid you're going to need to put me down for a hundred only. That's all I can do."

Jonathan now has him on the hook. It was time to reel Solomon in.

"I wish I could, Norm, but I'm really looking at doing this in just a few big tranches, so my inclination is just to say no and go down my list. If I have to break up the opportunity, it'll cost me more. That last piece always does. God knows what I'm going to have to offer just for the tail."

"Oh, c'mon," Solomon pleads. "Do me a solid on this one, I really need a win."

"You're breaking my heart, Norm." Jonathan pauses for dramatic effect. "Here's the best I can do for you. If you wire a hundred mil by COB, you're in, but I'm not papering it. For that little, it's not worth the legal fees. But you have my word on the upside. Guaranteed."

"You're a prince," Solomon says.

"Damn right I am," Jonathan replies.

Then he hangs up without saying good-bye. Goddammit, he's almost there.

* * *

Jonathan calls three more investors, but none of them are as gullible as Norm Solomon or as rich as Isaac Goldenberg. There are still others Jonathan could ask to put up the last fifty million, but he assumes that he'll get the same excuses—timing issues, liquidity problems, taxes, blah-blah-blah. Besides, the more people who know he's trying to raise cash fast, the greater the risk.

At twelve thirty, he and Haresh Venagopul are once again in the men's room. Like before, Jonathan checks the stalls and turns on the water before he says a word.

"You know, people are going to start talking about us if we keep meeting like this," Haresh says.

Jonathan ignores the quip. "I've got two hundred million. Now I just need you to look the other way so I can get the last fifty."

Haresh is obviously pained by the suggestion. He should be. Jonathan is asking him to aid and abet in securities fraud. A felony punishable by prison time.

"What's the long-term strategy here?" Haresh asks. "I mean, why put your head—I should say *our* heads—on the chopping block to get this first round over and done with when our heads are definitely going to get lopped off when you miss the second payment in thirty days?"

"You know as well as I do that thirty days is an eternity in this business. If the market moves in our direction, all my problems are solved."

"That sounds more like a prayer than a plan, Jonathan."

"I have no other option, Haresh."

Haresh nods. He's too much of a gentleman to remind Jonathan that there is another option. The correct one: admit defeat and face the consequences.

"Okay," Haresh says. "If you mark the position to show steady profit, and do it slowly so as not to raise any flags, and if you can get the fund's NAV up fifty or sixty million by next Monday, then I can loosen up fifty million in borrowing power, and I'll pretend I didn't notice that our net asset value is inflated."

Jonathan puts his hand on Haresh's shoulder. "Thanks, Haresh. I really owe you."

Haresh looks at him askew. "Don't thank me yet. Compliance might still see it on their own."

This is a risk Jonathan is willing to take. The folks in Compliance don't understand the first thing about his trading, and even if they did know enough to ask a question, he could talk circles around them. It was Haresh's support he needed, and now he had it.

"No, really. I owe you, big-time, for this," Jonathan says.

"Uh-huh. Just understand that I don't want you repaying me with cigarettes when we have adjoining cells in prison."

8

Six Months Later/December

East Carlisle, New Jersey, is not known for its fine dining. Its neighbor to the west, which for some reason is called New Carlisle rather than West Carlisle, is a college town, so what passes as good food in this area of the state is located there. The best of a mediocre lot is the Château, or at least it was back when Jonathan called East Carlisle home. The kind of place reserved for anniversaries and Valentine's Day, or when you are trying to impress the prettiest girl from your high school after twenty-five years.

In recognition of the season, a large Christmas tree is beside the door, a smaller menorah beside it, and a framed poster advertising the restaurant's New Year's Eve extravaganza—a hundred dollars for seven courses and all the champagne you can drink. In Manhattan, the same prix fixe would be a grand, maybe more. The poster also proudly proclaims that the musical accompaniment will be provided by Lou Cross and Cathedral. Jonathan tries to recall whether that was the band that ginker Pauley DiGiacomo referenced at the reunion, but he can't remember.

The lunchtime crowd is sparse, comprised mainly of men who Jonathan speculates must be businessmen by virtue of the fact that they're wearing ties, even though none are in full suits. There are two tables of women in the back who appear to be well into their sixties, and Jonathan tries to imagine what event brings together a group of that age. A birthday party, maybe?

All thoughts leave his head when he sees Jackie, however. She's seated next to the window, the sun streaming through, backlighting her to angelic effect. That she's wearing a white silk top reinforces the point. It strains against her perfect breasts, exposing the outline of her bra. Twenty-five years later, and he's still imagining whether Jacqueline Lawson's bra is lace. Some dreams never die, apparently.

"Hey there," she says, getting up. She kisses Jonathan lightly on the cheek, and he breathes in her scent.

When he met Natasha, Jonathan thought she might just be the most beautiful woman he had ever seen, but even then his hesitation was due to his recollection of the teenage Jacqueline Lawson. Sitting beside Jackie now, he knows that Natasha would turn more heads—after all, a fifteen-year age gap is too much for any fortysomething woman to overcome, no matter how beautiful. Still, Jonathan doubts that Natasha will look this damn good at forty-three.

"I haven't been here since . . . wow, forever." Jackie laughs.

"I gather the Château isn't the in-spot anymore. Had I known, I would have picked someplace else."

"Oh, it's not that. I . . . I guess I just don't go out much anymore."

Jonathan hears some sadness in the disclosure, a trace of marital discord. Jackie Lawson must feel she's being taken for granted by her husband, which Jonathan considers a very good thing for him.

The waitress asks whether there's anything they want to drink, but they give her their full orders. For Jackie that's a glass of white wine and a salad Niçoise, and Jonathan selects the old standby of a burger and a beer.

"I'm so glad that you reached out to me," Jackie says when the waitress leaves. "To be honest, I wasn't exactly sure what to make of our little conversation the other night, and there was a part of me afterward that thought maybe I'd imagined it. So, when you texted, at least it confirmed that I'm not going completely insane."

Jonathan can tell she's nervous. Her eyes dart all around the restaurant and seem particularly attuned to the front door. He understands her concern, of course. If anyone saw her with a male stranger, word would get back to her husband.

He sees her paranoia as yet another hopeful sign. It means she hasn't told Rick that she's here, and that suggests she's thinking that this may lead somewhere. Same as he is.

"Didn't you tell me at the reunion that this was *my* fantasy?" he says with a laugh. "Why then would you imagine it? Is it every prom queen's dream to have dinner with the king of the high school nerds after twenty-five years?"

"Now you're just fishing, Johnny . . . I mean, Jonathan. I know you've done very well for yourself. International man of mystery, as it were. There was talk at the reunion that reminded me of that scene in *The Great Gatsby*. You know, when the party guests are speculating as to how Gatsby earned his fortune."

"Did anyone think I was a bootlegger?"

She laughs. "No, but I did hear a lot of different theories. So, why don't you tell me the truth?"

The truth. No, Jonathan's not going there. That's for damn sure.

"I'm an arbitrageur," Jonathan says matter-of-factly, although he knows that will prompt her to request further clarification.

Which she does, right on cue. "And that means what, exactly?"

This gives Jonathan license to launch into the cocktail-party explanation he's used a thousand times before. "It's a fancy term for saying that I'm a money manager. My fund invests in different currencies. Rubles. Dollars. The euro. This is obviously an oversimplification, but remember the transitive property from third-grade math? If a dollar equals two euros, and two euros equals three rubles, then three rubles should equal one dollar, right? Well, in the financial markets, it's usually off a bit, so two-point-nine rubles will equal one dollar. They have to come into alignment at some point, and so I invest heavily on that event happening. It doesn't matter how the alignment occurs—if the dollar goes down or the ruble goes up; so long as the alignment happens—which it always will eventually—my fund makes money."

"Sounds to me like you're a professional romantic," she says. "Investing in the belief that the world will return to the way it's supposed to be."

Jonathan is impressed. "I never thought of it that way. Huh. I may just have to change my business card now."

She smiles, and Jonathan feels the full force of Jackie's power. It's as if he is basking in a warm, bright sun. He can't believe that he's actually sharing a table with Jacqueline Lawson. The It Girl of East Carlisle High School, class of 1991. The girl every boy wanted to have and every girl wanted to be.

"And how about you?" he asks. "Bring me up to speed with how the last couple of decades have treated Jacqueline Lawson Williams."

She smiles again, but this time it's as if it emanates from a different person altogether. It tells Jonathan more than words ever could that the past twenty-five years have not treated Jackie kindly.

"Well, my psychology degree turned out to be exactly the waste of forty thousand dollars that my father had predicted," she begins. "I was accepted to a few master's programs, and the plan was to become a child psychologist, but my dad died, which made grad school beyond my budget, and Rick wanted to get married and . . . I know, it's the old story . . . but I have two beautiful children. They're both students at good ol' ECHS. Robert is a senior and the quarterback of the Bears, and Emma is my baby. She's a freshman, although she prefers the term *freshperson*."

Jackie forces one last smile. It's the saddest Jonathan's ever seen on Jacqueline Lawson. "So tell me about your wife," she says.

"Her name is Natasha. She's Russian by birth, but has been living in the States since she was around five. Grew up in Texas, of all places, but went to college and grad school on the East Coast. Tall, blonde, blue-eyed." He shrugs.

"I hate her already." Jackie laughs.

"And I'm slightly embarrassed to say I'm nothing if not a cliché." He gives her a sheepish grin. "She's young, too. Twenty-eight."

"Now I really hate her."

Jackie says this with her old smile back in place. It tells Jonathan that despite her words, she doesn't perceive Natasha as a threat.

The food arrives, and the waitress asks whether they'd like another round of drinks. Jackie says, "I'm game if you are," and Jonathan quickly agrees. The wine has seemingly relaxed Jackie. She's no longer looking toward the door each time a new diner arrives.

Their banter is easy, and more than a little flirtatious. Jackie's certainly making all the right body movements—the flip of her hair, the soft laughter at his jokes, the light touches of his arm when she speaks. Jonathan wonders how far she's going to let this go, and he's come to the conclusion that the sky's the limit.

When the check comes, Jonathan grabs it.

"We should split it," Jackie says.

"No. I asked, so I pay. If you ask the next time, then you can pay."

Jackie doesn't hesitate. "How about Wednesday night? Rick plays poker and he's usually out late."

"Perfect," Jonathan says.

He waits a beat, then decides to throw caution to the wind. "Hey . . . crazy thought here. Would you mind terribly . . . if I cooked for you? The only reason I bring that up is that you seem a little nervous about being out in public."

Jackie's slow to answer, and Jonathan is tempted to withdraw the offer, or reiterate that his intentions are strictly honorable. But he tells himself to wait, to trust his judgment. How many times on the trading floor had others been yelling for them to sell or they'd lose their shirts, and he had held it together knowing that the position would hit? It was the same thing here. He had read Jackie correctly. He knew it. She wasn't concerned about his intentions; she welcomed them.

"Honestly, that would be . . . really wonderful," she says. "Thank you."

And then she gives him a smile to die for.

* * *

After they say good-bye with another exchange of cheek kisses, Jonathan heads to Lakeview for his daily visit with his father. He greets Yorlene by name and asks how she's been before segueing to inquiring about his father's condition.

"He was very talkative this morning," Yorlene says. "I really think your presence has been therapeutic for him. He seems . . . happier, I think."

"How can you tell?" Jonathan says. "I mean, the happier part?"

"Because he's smiling, which he didn't do much when he first got here."

"Yeah, well, he didn't do it much my whole life," Jonathan remarks.

Yorlene's smile vanishes, her way of telling Jonathan that she doesn't approve of his disrespecting his father. "Well . . . he's smiling now. Go see for yourself."

William Caine is sleeping when Jonathan enters his room. He looks more disheveled than in prior days, something akin to a homeless man; Jonathan realizes that's because Dad's sporting a few days of gray beard stubble. It prompts Jonathan to consider other personal hygiene issues, so he checks his father's fingernails and satisfies himself that he's being reasonably groomed.

"Can I ask how often is he bathed and shaved?" Jonathan asks Yorlene when he comes back into the hallway.

"Every three days," Yorlene says. "It should have been done today, but . . . perhaps they were running late or something. I'll make sure it happens tomorrow. Don't worry."

"Thanks. And does he get any exercise? So far, I've just seen him in bed."

"No, not really. It's hard for him to stand. But maybe when he wakes up, you can take him outside to the patio. It would do him good to get some fresh air."

Jonathan returns to his father's room and settles into the vinyl recliner beside the bed. He turns on the television and flicks past the business channels that once so consumed him. He couldn't care less about the market's fluctuations these days. Instead he selects an old movie, the name of which he doesn't know, and the cable service at Lakeview unfortunately doesn't come with an on-screen guide. It stars Steve McQueen as a race-car driver.

About an hour later, William Caine awakes and declares himself hungry.

"Why don't we have a snack outside?" Jonathan says.

His father doesn't look the least bit surprised that he had been alone when he fell asleep and is now in his son's company. What seems to throw him, however, is the concept that anything exists beyond this room.

"Outside . . . ?"

"Yeah. The nurse, you know, Yorlene, she said it was okay if we went outside for a little bit. Get some fresh air."

Jonathan thinks he sees assent in his father's eyes, but words don't follow. That's good enough for Jonathan, however, and he attempts to resurrect his father from his hospital bed. It doesn't take long for him to realize that the maneuver requires professional assistance. He calls for Yorlene's help and, a few minutes later, a large man in blue scrubs enters the room and engineers the lifting of William Caine's fragile body from bed to wheelchair.

"Do you want to stop for something to eat?" Jonathan asks as he rolls his father down the corridor.

"Something to eat?" his father asks, apparently failing to remember his request from several minutes earlier.

"You said you were hungry."

"Oh. Okay. What do they have?"

"I don't know. We'll ask the nurse."

It's not Yorlene, but a different woman, one whom Jonathan hasn't encountered before, who is now manning the nurses' station. She tells them that they're in between meal service, and dinner won't be available for another hour or so.

"You can get something in the vending machines, though," she adds.

"Is that okay for him?" Jonathan asks.

"Yes, of course. Potato chips are good for the soul. But if you plan on going outside, I would recommend taking a blanket or something." Her head disappears behind the desk, and she emerges holding a blue swath of cloth, which must be what accounts for a blanket at Lakeview.

Jonathan thanks her and tucks the corners around his father's legs and arms. He pushes the wheelchair down the corridor, passing the open doors of the other residents' rooms. As he peeks in, he sees that most are bedridden and alone. Jonathan feels a sense of satisfaction in the conviction that he stepped up and did the right thing by his father, and then that pride runs away as he recognizes that his reason for being here is far from pure.

In the visitor room, he asks his father what kind of chips he'd like, fully expecting his inquiry to be met with a childlike response. *What are chips?* Or *Rainbow flavor.*

Instead his father says, "Do they have salt and vinegar?"

To Jonathan's surprise, they do. "Yeah."

"Sometimes they're out," his father says. "And, Johnny, could you get me a Coke, too?"

Snacks and beverage in hand, Jonathan follows the signs for the patio while pushing his father along. Although Jonathan had been expecting little more than a small slab on cement, the space is landscaped with large trees on either end, and at last he sees the elusive lake that gives the hospital its name.

They come to a stop in the center, to take full advantage of the sunshine. Jonathan opens the bag of chips for his father, and then screws off the soda bottle's top. Even though it's cold outside, the sun is strong, and Jonathan finds the experience far more pleasant than being cooped up in a hospital room.

"Are you cold, Dad?" he asks.

"No," his father says, reaching in for a chip. "You want one?"

"Sure," Jonathan says, and reaches into the bag.

It's an actual father-son moment, Jonathan thinks to himself. He certainly can't remember the last one they shared.

9

July

The first two-hundred-and-fifty-million redemption occurred without a hitch. As Jonathan had predicted, there wasn't a peep out of Compliance. The money that came in from Goldenberg and Solomon undoubtedly assuaged whatever concerns registered from the watchdogs at Harper Sawyer, none the wiser that the fund was teetering on the brink.

Jonathan wrote the agreement with Goldenberg himself, and no one else at the firm had even reviewed it. The shit wouldn't hit the fan on that one for another year, when Goldenberg demanded his two hundred million, and by that time, Jonathan hoped he'd have the profits from which to pay. And Solomon's hundred-million investment came in without raising any eyebrows at all. Just another longtime investor trying to get more.

As luck would have it, a late-week rally in the Indian markets had even smoothed over Jonathan's mismarking of the position. As a result, paying Ross the first two hundred and fifty million had hardly even decreased the fund's net asset value.

It was the next quarter-billion tranche that would test Jonathan's mettle—and Harper Sawyer's oversight functions. Raising new money wasn't an option any longer, as Jonathan had tapped his only ready sources. He now had no other choice but to sell off the part of the position that hedged the ruble against further decline. Each day a little more, careful not to liquidate so much as to raise flags with Compliance (or even the other traders on the desk) that the fund was now exposed to market risk.

At the beginning of the second week of this strategy, Haresh unexpectedly follows Jonathan into the men's room—their safe house, as it were. This time, it's Haresh who checks the stalls and turns on the faucets.

"This is your plan?" Haresh says.

"It's working, right?"

"Yeah, so long as the ruble keeps rising. But what happens if it goes the other way?"

"It's a calculated risk, Haresh. The ruble is down way below its fifty-two-week low, and the MICEX is up. The odds must be seventy-five percent or better that the position is going to align with the ruble rising. When that happens, we'll have more than enough to put the hedge back on, and pay off Ross in full."

Haresh's response is a tight grimace. Clearly he wishes that there was another way. Then, again, Jonathan does, too.

Without the hedge, Jonathan was just another gambler. He was betting everything that the currencies would align because the ruble rose, but now he was doing so without making the contra-investments that hedged the position. In other words, he was all in, without a net to save him. As long as the ruble ascended, he was golden, but if it dropped much further, the entire fund would be wiped out.

"And if you're wrong?" Haresh asks, even though he undoubtedly knows the answer.

"Then I'm barely more fucked than I am now," Jonathan says.

* * *

Two weeks before Ross submitted his redemption demand, Jonathan made the $450,000 up-front payment on an oceanfront rental in East Hampton, "from MD to LD," meaning from Memorial Day to Labor Day. Jonathan sometimes wonders whether he would have been so quick to plunk the money down if he'd known how precarious his world was going to turn. But he always concludes that of course he would have. It's the motto he lives by—you ride her until she throws you, or you don't ride her at all. That and *I want what I want.* In this case, the two credos merged perfectly.

The house is a five-bedroom, six-bath traditional with a wraparound porch. Of course, that was four bedrooms and five baths more than the two of them needed, but every house with a panoramic view of the ocean was similarly proportioned.

The previous summer, Natasha had commuted with Jonathan, spending the weekends on the East End, and Monday through Friday in Manhattan. This summer, however, she is living on the island full-time, with Jonathan joining her on weekends.

On one particularly sunny day in mid-July, Natasha suggests that they make the pilgrimage to the Montauk Lighthouse, which is located on the easternmost tip of Long Island.

"I don't want to drive all the way out there to see the same ocean I can see from our backyard," Jonathan says.

"Jonathan, don't be such an asshole all the time, okay?"

He gives in, and they drive the forty minutes or so to Montauk's easternmost point, which from the United States is about as far out in the Atlantic Ocean as you can get. When they finally arrive, the air is moist, and refreshing enough on Jonathan's face that it prompts him to inhale deeply, filling his lungs. The vista is breathtaking, nothing but open sea for miles.

"I'm cold, Jonathan," Natasha says a few seconds after stepping out of the Bentley.

"Didn't you bring a sweatshirt?"

"I didn't realize it was going to be hot as hell in East Hampton and freezing a half hour away."

"Well, you're going to have to tough it out, cowboy, because it looks like there's quite the line to make it up to the top of the lighthouse."

"Then let's just bag it and head back."

"Seriously? You dragged me out here and you don't even want to do what you came here to do?"

"Are you serious? You didn't even want to go in the first place and now you're telling me you don't want to leave?"

"Now that we're out here, I want to see the lighthouse."

"And I see it," she says, pointing. "Right there. The building with the long line in front of it."

"I bet the view at the top is amazing."

"You're unbelievable, Jonathan. Didn't you tell me an hour ago that it was the same view as from our house?"

"No, you're unbelievable, Natasha. Didn't you tell me an hour ago you wanted to come here? Now that we're here, I'd like to go to the top. If you don't want to come, you can just wait in the car. Turn the heat on, and I'll see you in half an hour."

Her look should be beside the word *disgust* in the dictionary. "Silly me. I almost forgot that what I want has never mattered to you, Jonathan."

Neither of them says anything for a second. Then she puts out her hand palm up. "Give me the key," she says.

* * *

There are at least forty people on line to enter the lighthouse, and a sign indicates it's a twenty-minute wait from the place Jonathan is standing. Under other circumstances, he would have turned back, but given that he took a hard-line approach with Natasha, he has little choice but to wait his turn to climb the 137 stairs to the top.

Rather than the twenty minutes the sign promised, it takes more than an hour to reach the summit. Once he's there, the wind is even stronger than it was at the beach, but damn, the view makes it all worthwhile. Infinite and awesome.

Jonathan has always loved the ocean, not only for its beauty but for its power, and its mystery. So long as you stayed above it, you were its master, but beneath the serenity were unfathomable depths to plummet.

Two weeks ago, Jonathan felt as if he were being pulled to the very bottom. But now, he's certain that he will not only avert disaster but enjoy his greatest triumph.

The ruble is rising, as he expected it would, while the other currencies had begun to descend. With each tick, the fund nets nearly a million dollars, which, if it continues for just another few weeks, will earn a profit that's more than enough to cover the second and third payments to Michael Ross. Best of all, he'll have done it without anyone at Harper Sawyer being the wiser.

It's enough for Jonathan to actually believe he might just be infallible.

* * *

On the last day of July, Jonathan's sister, Amy, calls from Florida. "I just spoke to Dad," she says. "He doesn't sound good at all."

Jonathan has no response. It's been long enough since the last time he spoke to his father that he no longer has any frame of reference as to what constitutes *good*.

"Jonathan, you only live an hour from him. You should visit."

Amy is the only person who calls him Jonathan and makes the name sound false. As if she knows that the persona he had created for himself since high school was a sham.

"We're in the Hamptons every weekend, Amy."

"So don't go one weekend and visit your father instead."

"I'm not paying four hundred and fifty grand for a summer rental to spend a weekend in East Carlisle."

"You're paying what?!"

"That's what it costs, Amy."

"I could . . . I could retire and live out the rest of my life in luxury for what you're spending on . . . what, eight weekends?"

Jonathan resists telling her that it's not eight weekends. It's Memorial Day to Labor Day, for chrissakes, and he and Natasha take the two weeks leading to Labor Day for vacation. But Amy wouldn't understand. She lives the life of their parents, while his existence is on a totally different scale.

"I thought you called to tell me about Dad. Now you're complaining about how I spend my money?"

"It's about priorities, Johnny. Yours are totally out of whack."

She didn't just casually slide the "Johnny" in there. Amy is too smart not to know when to use that leverage with him. She was making it quite clear that although to the rest of the world, he might be the high and mighty Jonathan Caine of Wall Street, barking orders at his minions, she knows him better than that.

"I'll visit him right after Labor Day. I promise," Jonathan says.

She sighs, which tells him not only that she disagrees but that she's resigned to the fact that she will not change his mind. "There may not be much of him to see after Labor Day, Jonathan."

"No reason to be so dramatic, Amy. He'll be the same then as he is now. How much of a difference can a month make?" Jonathan hears how that sounds, so he decides to adopt a more concerned tone. "What makes you think he's not doing well, anyway?"

"For starters, he asked if Mom was visiting me."

"At least he's not imagining that she's in the house with him."

"Not funny, Johnny," she snaps. "This is a real problem."

"What does . . ." Jonathan searches for his father's private nurse's name but can't come up with it. "What does the nurse say?"

"You mean Theresa?" Amy says with an obvious edge.

"You've made your point, Amy. You're the golden child. All I do for him is pay all the money for *Theresa* so Dad can stay in his home. But of course, none of that counts for anything. All that matters is that I don't remember her goddamned name."

"Jonathan, I'm not Mom, trying to guilt you here. You're crazy if you think I don't appreciate the financial support you give to Dad. I'm just worried that you're going to regret not spending more time with him while you still can. Once he's gone, that's it."

Jonathan likes to say that it's an occupational prerequisite for a trader to live without regret. Opportunities present themselves for an instant, and they're taken or not . . . but there's never any going back. Ever. That's true whether you're about to make a billion-dollar investment in response to some market fluctuation you don't fully understand, or you're asked to give up a weekend in the Hamptons to sit on the crappy furniture in your father's den in East Carlisle, New Jersey.

You decide, and then you move on. Always without regret.

"I'm really busy right now. I'll go in September. I promise," he says.

10

Five Months Later/December

Jackie pauses to consider just how much of a message she wants her clothing to make. Her closet has half a dozen ensembles that are appropriate for a married woman meeting a friend for dinner. She eschews them all in favor of what she considers to be her sexiest dress, a silver number with a plunging neckline. She pairs it with black thigh-high tights and three-inch heels.

Her kids, true to form, are oblivious to what she looks like. Their faces are buried in their screens. For once, she's pleased by the self-absorption of teenagers.

"I need to go out for a few hours. A friend is having a Christmas party," Jackie says. Neither Robert nor Emma so much as lift their heads. "Robert," she says, which at least makes him look up. "Here's twenty dollars. Order a pizza and make sure your sister gets to bed at a reasonable time. I should be back before midnight. If for some reason your father gets home before me, which I seriously doubt will happen, just tell him that I had to go out, and that I'll be back by midnight at the latest."

After taking the money, Robert buries his head back into the screen. "Earth to Robert. Please confirm that you heard and understood."

"Uh-huh," he grunts. "Pizza. Emma asleep. You out."

Close enough, Jackie thinks.

* * *

The butterflies flutter in Jackie's stomach the entire drive over to Crowne Road, and intensify when she sees Jonathan's car parked in the driveway. She doesn't know its make, although she can tell even at a distance that it's expensive. When she gets out of her car, she bends over to read the nameplate. A Bentley. She's never seen one for real, only in movies. Of course Jonathan Caine drives a Bentley, she thinks to herself.

Jonathan greets her at the door, kissing her on the cheek as he did at the Château, but this time he hugs her a little tighter, holding his hand in the center of her back, so he must have discerned that she's not wearing a bra.

"It's so nice to see you," he says, welcoming her inside. "You really look beautiful. I'm kind of embarrassed that I'm so underdressed."

Her eyes take him in. No reason for him to be even a little bit self-conscious. He looks great. Jeans, a button-down blue shirt, and, it appears, the same expensive suit jacket he had lent her at the reunion. Handsome, successful, not overdoing it, but not just throwing on sweatpants like some men she knows.

"It smells great in here," she says. "What did you cook for us?"

"Cassoulet."

"Sounds delicious."

Jackie looks around the house. Hardly out of *Architectural Digest*, that's for sure, even if it was a forty-year-old issue. Lots of orange and brown, a matted-down shag rug in the den. But she quickly realizes that she can't ascribe any judgment to Jonathan because he doesn't really live here.

"Can I offer you any wine?" Jonathan asks.

Jackie smiles. Yes, wine is exactly what she needs to calm her nerves.

"That would be great," she says.

She follows him into the kitchen. She had expected a similar period piece, but the kitchen, while certainly not modern, at least isn't a relic. Early *Seinfeld* era, she figures.

The wine is a dark purple in color. When Jonathan hands Jackie her glass, their fingers touch, and she flashes on that moment at the reunion—the lingering when she handed him back his phone, even though she's since wondered whether she'd imagined it. This time, however, she's certain that the contact is intentional.

"Come here, take a look," he says, motioning toward the stove. She follows, and he places his hand on the lid of a large simmering pot, as if he's a magician, about to flourish the big reveal.

"So when I remove it, lean in and take a deep breath."

Jackie does as directed, and it smells truly amazing. A mélange of sausage and duck, stewed with white beans, and a toasted bread-crumb crust at the top.

Jackie takes a swallow of wine for courage, and then puts out there what she's been meaning to ask Jonathan since they arranged this get-together.

"What does your wife think of all this?"

Jonathan doesn't appear the least bit off balance by the question's implication. He cocks his head to the side and says, "You mean what does my wife think of my cooking dinner for a beautiful woman whom every person at East Carlisle High School was crazy about back in the day?"

"Yeah. That."

"To be honest, I haven't told her."

"Rick is in the dark, too."

Jonathan nods. Jackie takes the gesture as evidence that they've entered into a tacit agreement that whatever goes on tonight remains only between them.

"The cassoulet has been simmering for six hours," Jonathan says. "I think it's more than ready to eat. Shall we?"

He takes Jackie by the hand and leads her to the dining room. Like the other spaces in the house, it has a bit of a grandparent feel to it. A heavy mahogany table fills the room, with six wood-carved chairs around it. There are two place settings—one at the head and the other catty-cornered to it—and in the center of the table are a pair of candles in tarnished silver holders. Jonathan certainly has gone all out for this. She can't deny that she likes that.

Jonathan lights the candles, and then he dims the overhead chandelier. Jackie is tempted to comment that it's all very romantic, but she decides not to say a word, for fear it will spoil the moment.

In addition to the cassoulet, Jonathan prepared a salad and string beans sautéed with butter and almonds. She tells Jonathan that it's all delicious, and by that she means that she's having the best time she's had in years.

Jackie isn't much of a drinker and can't remember the last time she's had a third glass of wine. But the high she's experiencing now is too wonderful to let go, so all other considerations—like the fact that she's about to be drunk in the home of a man whom, for all intents and purposes, she's just met—fall by the wayside.

"How long will you be staying in our humble little town?" Jackie asks.

"I'm not sure, exactly. A lot depends on how my father is doing."

"Your wife . . . is she okay with you being away from home?"

"Yeah. I travel a lot for work anyway, so I think Natasha just views this as another business trip."

"And your job doesn't mind?"

"I've actually taken a leave of absence. It's not like I'm going to be able to spend time with my father when it's more convenient for me to be away from work. I figured it was now or never."

"I really think it's amazing that you're doing this. Your father is very lucky."

"I don't know about that," Jonathan says with a shrug. "I do know that I'm lucky to have this time with him. I wish . . . you know, the usual, that I'd done some things differently. Do you ever feel that way?"

"Every day and twice on Sunday," Jackie says.

Jonathan raises his wineglass. "Well, then. To fewer regrets in the future."

Jackie clinks her glass to his. There is nothing she wants more than fewer regrets in the future.

* * *

Jonathan knows that dinner is going very well. He's seen that look in a woman's eyes before, the one that suggests there's no place on earth she'd rather be. She threw him a bit when she asked about work, but he thinks he covered well enough.

"Can I ask you something stupid?" Jackie asks.

"Of course. Stupid questions are the best ones."

Jackie laughs, a nervous giggle. "What did you think of me in high school?"

"Ah," Jonathan says with a smile. "Let me ask you this first. Why would you care about what I thought of you twenty-five years ago?"

"Because I think it influences what you think of me now."

"So maybe I should just tell you what I think of you now."

"If you'd prefer."

"You're obviously still very beautiful. You don't need me to tell you that, I'm sure. But you're also now sadder than I remember you being in high school. It's almost as if you're unsure about who you are, and back then, everyone knew you were queen of the Cliquesters."

She laughs, but its shaky tenor confirms Jonathan's assessment was spot-on. "I was just as insecure back then. Believe me."

He does believe her, although he never would have thought so when they were in high school. Back then, she seemed to be all confidence. But isn't that always the way? The popular girl forever fearful because her power is so ephemeral?

"You sure hid it well," Jonathan says. "But that still doesn't tell me what fills you with regret now."

Jackie looks at him impassively, as if she's letting his words come to a resting point before she responds. Finally, Jackie says, "I don't know how my life ever got so . . . I don't know . . . far away from what I wanted it to be? Does that make any sense?"

Make sense? Jonathan could be Exhibit A for that sentiment. He's not ready to share that with Jackie, not yet, but he is willing to dispense the advice he repeats in his head every morning. The words that keep him alive for one more day.

"I'll tell you something you learn early when your life is tied to the financial markets. It's never as bad as it seems at any given moment because it can always get better." He waits a beat. "And worse."

"I so want it to get better," she says quietly.

He views that as his opening and slowly leans over to kiss her. He gives her enough time to pull away, but if anything, he senses that she's moved closer.

He feels an actual tingle when their lips meet.

"Jackie . . ." Jonathan says in a whisper, his face close enough to hers that he can feel the warmth of her breath. "Do you think we can go upstairs?"

She doesn't hesitate. "Yes."

He stands and takes her hand. They walk together up the stairs, and at the top he has a decision to make. Jonathan turns into his childhood bedroom, rather than the master.

"Sorry about the twin bed," he says, "but I promise I'll make it up to you in other ways."

*   *   *

Jackie wakes with a jolt and a sense of complete disorientation. It takes her a moment to realize that she's in Jonathan's house—his parents' house, actually—and then a second more to comprehend that she's lying naked beside him. She feels like she's in that scene in *Big*. She's a grown woman in the bedroom of a thirteen-year-old boy.

Nineteen years of marriage to an alcoholic, cheating wife abuser and she'd never before strayed. She should feel some level of remorse for breaking one of the Ten Commandments, but her only emotion right now is elation. She hasn't felt like this in . . . has she ever felt like this?

Then reality sets in. Rick. What would he do to her if he knew?

She quickly checks her phone, panicked that Rick has been trying to reach her. But there's no missed call or text. He's undoubtedly found something more interesting to do tonight than check up on her.

As Jonathan snores lightly beside her, she slithers out of the bed, careful not to wake him. Her clothes are strewn around the room, reminding her of their dance—her dress on the floor near the door, her stockings on the chair beside the bed, her panties in the sheets.

Once she's clothed, she walks around to his side of the bed and kneels beside him. "Jonathan," she says. His eyes open and he smiles. "Thank you. Tonight was wonderful."

She kisses him on the mouth, and then allows herself to be pulled on top of him. Even though she knows she should leave, she decides to indulge in one more round.

11

August

The rain in East Hampton is hard enough that it's clear the entire Sunday will be a washout. By two o'clock, Natasha has had enough.

"Why don't we just drive back into the city now? That way we might beat the traffic."

"You're not going to stay out here this week?" Jonathan asks.

"I've got some things to do at home. Besides, you promised you were going to take off the last two weeks of August, and so this is my last chance to do some shopping in the city before Labor Day."

As it turns out, Natasha was not the only person on the East End with hopes of avoiding the traffic. It's bumper-to-bumper through Route 27, and the Long Island Expressway is even worse. A trip that would take less than three hours without traffic takes nearly five, all the while the rain pounding off the car. To make matters that much worse, Jonathan realized too late that he forgot his phone charger in East Hampton, so by the time they're on the LIE, he's out of juice.

A little before seven, Jonathan pulls the Bentley into the garage under their apartment building. Natasha had previously suggested that they go out to dinner, but it's raining even harder in the city, and that's enough to dissuade her from venturing outside again.

"Why don't we just order in from Mr. Chen's tonight?" Natasha says as they enter their lobby.

Jonathan doesn't answer. Instead he stops short, startled by the sight of Haresh Venagopul sitting in his lobby and staring intently into his phone.

"Haresh?" Jonathan says. "What's going on?"

"I'm sorry to bother you on a Sunday evening," Haresh says in his deliberate way, "but there's something important I need to talk to you about. I tried calling, but couldn't get through."

Something bad has happened, that's for sure. Haresh doesn't just show up unannounced on a Sunday night to impart good news.

Jonathan's kicking himself about his phone, and about the fact that he let Natasha listen to her music playlists. If he'd had the radio on, he might at least have some idea of what the hell has Haresh so spooked.

"Natasha, can you give me some time alone with Haresh?" he asks calmly. "I'll be up in a few minutes."

Natasha has no interest in Jonathan's business, so she doesn't look the least bit concerned. "Sure," she says. "I'm going to order dinner, though, so don't be too long."

"It'll be ten minutes, at most."

Haresh nods, telling Jonathan the estimate is accurate. As soon as Natasha starts toward the elevator, Jonathan and Haresh go in the other direction, leaving the building to distance themselves from the doorman's oversight.

They take cover under the small awning of a non-doorman building, which is not nearly wide enough to keep them dry. The teeming rain sounds like a march, and Jonathan looks to his number two to explain why they're getting soaked.

"So I gather you haven't heard," Haresh says.

"No. I've been on a news blackout the last four hours in the car. My cell was dead. What's up?"

"Your cell's not the only thing that's dead. So is Alexeyev." Haresh says this as grimly as if the Russian president were a member of his family. "The news is spotty. Some reports are that he died of natural causes, but others are suggesting that he was assassinated. Either way, the hard-liners seem to be using it to grab power. It's two o'clock

Monday morning in Moscow, and the reports are that the MICEX isn't going to open."

"Fuck," Jonathan spits out.

"Yes. To put it mildly."

Jonathan's mind turns to fantasy savior scenarios—the news is wrong and Alexeyev is alive. Or his successor is chosen quickly and the markets open tomorrow as scheduled . . . but he knows better than to voice any of this. No matter what actually unfolds, it's going to be days, and much more likely weeks or even months, before the situation is stable. And for money wizards like Jonathan, instability is often just as bad as the worst-case scenario.

"So what do you propose we do?" Jonathan asks.

"Nothing," Haresh says. "The ruble is going to plummet, and all we can do is hang on for dear life."

*   *   *

As soon as Jonathan enters his apartment, he rushes to the desktop computer and pulls up his personal account at Harper Sawyer.

The firm's rules require that employees maintain all of their brokerage accounts under Harper Sawyer's control. The stated reason is so that the firm can monitor any insider-trading activity. Jonathan, however, has long believed it was really so they could squeeze people like him in situations like this.

He's got $7.3 million in his brokerage account. It's managed by a guy Jonathan's never met other than over the phone, who invests it according to Harper Sawyer's standard guidelines. Another $8.4 million is in unvested Harper Sawyer stock, the part of his compensation each year that the firm holds hostage to keep him from leaving.

On top of that, his ownership percentage of the fund is worth ten million, at least it was when Alexeyev was alive. But Harper Sawyer won't let him pull any of it out of the fund until the fund's termination date—five years from now.

His checking account is at Citibank, and that's outside of Harper Sawyer's reach, at least without their first obtaining a court order.

But transfers to Citibank in excess of twenty thousand dollars in any thirty-day period need to be approved. Which means that while on paper he's worth more than twenty-five million, twenty thousand is likely all he'll have to his name when everything hits the fan.

He's just finished inputting the transfer when Natasha enters the study.

"I didn't even hear you come in," she says. "What did Haresh want?"

"The Russian president died while we were stuck in traffic on the LIE."

"Is that bad for the fund?"

Jonathan recognizes the opportunity the question presents. A chance to come clean. To share with his wife what's been going on and bring her in as an ally in the fight that's surely to come.

He decides to go the other way.

"No . . . the fund's hedged just for that reason. So when something like this happens, we're fine. Haresh was just concerned that investors would be jittery and he wanted to nail down some talking points."

Jonathan has now firmly boxed himself in. He'll be alone in what happens next, and he'll have to continue to lie to keep Natasha in the dark.

Although every aspect of his life is up in the air right now, the one thing he is certain about is that he's made the right decision not to confide in his wife. He also knows that it's about as damning a statement he can make about his marriage.

* * *

The next morning, as Jonathan is in the elevator going up to his office, he's thinking about the scene in *Wall Street* where Charlie Sheen is arrested. The way he walks in and everyone looks away, and then he asks his friend, the guy who was later on *Scrubs*, "Someone die?" and his buddy answers, "Yeah."

Jonathan steps off on the eighth floor expecting the worst, but Rita, the receptionist, says, "Hello, Jonathan," just like she does every day. Everything seems status quo on the trading floor, too, the usual buzz of activity afoot.

"Morning, Jonathan," Haresh says as Jonathan walks by his cubicle. "Crazy about the Russian market, right?"

"Yeah," Jonathan says, not quite sure what to make of the off-handed comment.

Jonathan types his password into the computer. He fully expects to be locked out, but the screens indicating the fund's current trading position and value come right up.

As Haresh said would occur, trading has been halted on the MICEX, and the Russian Central Bank had announced it would hike interest rates to prop the ruble. Despite this, the currency had still fallen more than twenty-five percent against the dollar. The European markets are down across the board, as was the New York Stock Exchange, and oil and gold, the normal hedges against economic collapse, were trending up.

The fund's stated net asset value was down nine percent. This naturally prompted the usual frantic calls from the fund's most nervous investors. Norm Solomon predictably was having a fit, and he'd already left three messages. Jonathan couldn't care less. The next redemption period wasn't until December. As far as Jonathan was concerned, that was a lifetime from now.

Of course, neither Norm Solomon nor anyone else knew how dire the situation actually was. The net asset value was meaningless because it was based on mismarked positions—a hedge that did not exist. To cover Michael Ross's redemption, Jonathan had removed the position that protected against the ruble's decline, but on the books it still existed. As a result, the net asset value reflected the ruble's decline and also the offsetting gains of the hedge—gains that actually didn't exist other than on paper.

In point of fact, more than half of the fund—somewhere around twenty billion dollars—was now gone.

12

Four Months Later/December

I need to see you.

Jackie's text comes four days after their cassoulet date. Jonathan called her (texted, actually) the next day, and they met the following afternoon for a repeat performance, this time without any pretense that they'd be sharing a meal. The day after that, yesterday, was the same. Jackie's invitation means that today will be their fourth rendez-vous.

When?

Now!

Jonathan assumed that *now* still meant he had ten minutes, so he jumped into the shower. It turned out that she must have been close by when she texted, because as soon as he steps out of the shower, he hears a knock on the front door. He grabs his father's fraying bath-robe off the hook on the back of the door, and jogs downstairs.

"I'm sorry," he says. "I hope you weren't waiting too long."

"No, I just got here. But I owe you an apology. Seems like I pulled you out of a shower. Is there anything I can do to make amends? Anything at all?" she says with mock innocence.

"Oh, I don't know. It was a pretty great shower, but if you follow me, I'm sure we can figure something out together."

Jonathan takes her by the hand and leads her upstairs, back into his bedroom. It's almost surreal to him. Twenty-five years ago it was his greatest teenage fantasy that Jacqueline Lawson would be making her way to his bedroom—with the blue wall paneling and ABA basketball globe light.

It reminds him that not only does he want what he wants, but he gets it, too.

*　*　*

After, as they lay quietly bathed in sweat, Jonathan's cell phone rings. He reaches over and sees that it's his sister calling.

"I've called you three times," Amy says.

He'd heard the phone ring, but of course didn't know it was Amy. Not that it would have mattered—the calls had come in while he and Jackie were in the throes, so he wouldn't have answered the phone even if it was God on the line.

"Sorry. I was . . . What's up?"

"I just got a call from the hospital. Dad took some type of turn. They said he's stable, but they moved him to the ICU."

Amy sounds controlled, as always, but Jonathan can hear the fear in her voice. It reminds him of the time he convinced her to ride the roller coaster at Great Adventure with him, when he asked her whether she was scared and she said no, even though she was white as a ghost.

"What happened?"

"I don't know, exactly. Something about his blood pressure dropping. I asked if this was the beginning of the end or whether he'd recover. They said . . . you know, what doctors say. Could be, but maybe not."

"Why'd they call you? I'm at Lakeview every day."

A stupid question. They called Amy because she checked their father into Lakeview, so she listed herself as his emergency contact.

"I don't know, Jonathan. They must have my number in the file.

Look, you're going to need to talk to a doctor face-to-face to get a straight answer about what's going on."

Jonathan recalls getting the phone call from his mother in which she informed him that she had only six months to live. At the time, he thought she was being melodramatic. She was about to embark on chemotherapy, which he knew they didn't do when there was no hope of remission. In the end, it turned out she had been off by only a few months.

He considers that Amy's call, like his mother's, is the beginning of the end. How long to the end, though? A year? Six months? Weeks? Could it be days?

Jonathan places the phone on his night table and considers that he's not ready for his father to die. The irony isn't lost on him that he's had years to forge a relationship with his old man, and now when the clock is running down, he feels that he doesn't have enough time.

"Everything okay?" Jackie asks, even though she heard enough of Jonathan's side of the phone call to know the answer.

"They transferred my father to the ICU. That was my sister, Amy. I should get over to Lakeview and see what's going on, I think."

"Do you want company?"

Jonathan knows that Jackie's offer isn't sincere. Actually, that's not right. He assumes that there's nothing Jackie would like more than to hold his hand as he sits beside his father's bed. But she can't. Not without risking her husband's wrath.

"Thank you, but I'll be okay," he says. "Just knowing you offered means a lot, though. So, thank you."

* * *

The nurse stationed at the ICU explains to Jonathan that before he's permitted entry to see his father, he's required to wash his hands thoroughly and put on a paper cap, like the kind fast-food employees wear, and a disposable hospital gown. After Jonathan does as directed, he finds his father sleeping in the fourth bed of a row, the one closest to the window.

William Caine doesn't look much different than he had any of the other times Jonathan had come across him during his stay here at Lakeview, except that now he sleeps with wires connecting him to a monitor and a breathing tube under his nose.

The other beds are all filled. Their occupants are also connected to tubes and appear lifeless. Beside each of the beds is a chair, but it's not like the big recliner that his father's room has downstairs. These are unpadded. The ICU obviously doesn't encourage long visits.

"Hi, Dad," Jonathan says.

For a moment Jonathan waits, hoping for a smile, or maybe a wink, like would occur if this were a movie. His father doesn't stir, however.

*   *   *

Jonathan leaves his father and returns to the nurses' station. There's now a different nurse sitting behind the desk. She's a bit younger than Jonathan, in her late thirties. She's got a fleshy quality about her, although she's not exactly overweight.

"My father is William Caine," Jonathan says. "He was brought down here a few hours ago."

The nurse nods but doesn't smile. Jonathan assumes that ICU nurses don't get emotionally attached to patients or their families.

She pulls out a clipboard from a rack beside her. "He experienced a sudden drop in blood pressure. Stable now. The doctor was just here."

"Can I talk to him?"

The nurse hesitates for a moment. "The doctor? *She's* on rounds at the moment. You can leave a message with her service."

"When do you expect her to return?"

"Not until morning."

"Can you tell me anything else about my father's condition? Any prognosis for when he might leave the ICU?"

"I'm sorry, but I can't. I'll leave word for Dr. Goldman that you'd like to speak to her."

Jonathan thanks the nurse and pulls out his cell phone, only to have the nurse tell him that cell phone usage is strictly prohibited, while she points to a sign saying the same thing. Without protest, he walks out into the corridor and then calls his sister.

"The doctor won't be back until tomorrow and the nurses don't know anything," he says. "I heard the word *stable* thrown around, but when I asked for more information, I was told I needed to talk to the doctor. And like I said, she won't be back until tomorrow morning."

"How does he look?"

"He's hooked up to lots of monitors, but other than that, he looks like he's just sleeping."

"Okay," Amy says. "You need to promise me something, Johnny."

The use of his nickname signals that she's about to ask for something that his first instinct would be to reject.

"What?"

"Stay with Daddy tonight."

"Amy, he's in the ICU. There are nurses everywhere and there's . . . there's not even a decent chair in there."

"Please, Johnny. I . . . I feel guilty enough not being up there. If it weren't for the fact that Kevin's away on business and there's no one to watch the kids, I would have gotten on the first plane up there and I wouldn't need to ask. I really don't want Dad to be alone."

When their mother passed, Jonathan was at his trading desk. Amy had called earlier in the day and reported that the doctors believed the end was near, but Jonathan thought there would be more time.

Sometimes Jonathan thinks that's what they're going to inscribe on his own tombstone: *He always thought there'd be more time.*

"Okay," he tells his sister. "I'll stay."

13

September

The rain is hard enough that Jonathan decides to forgo his morning run, which allows him an extra hour of sleep. The downpour hasn't abated when he leaves for work, which means that getting a cab is going to be difficult, even at six thirty in the morning.

"Taxi, Mr. Caine?" Ruben, the doorman, asks.

"Yes, thank you," Jonathan replies.

Ruben heads out into the storm. He uses a silver whistle as well as his hand to flag down oncoming cabs. After five or so minutes of standing in the rain, Ruben blows the three rapid-fire whistles indicating he's finally landed one.

Jonathan jogs out into the storm and wordlessly slaps ten dollars into Ruben's hand before grabbing for the cab's door. As he opens it, Jonathan hears a voice beside him.

"Going uptown?" asks a well-dressed man. Despite the fact he's holding a large umbrella, the stranger is still getting wet.

Jonathan hates sharing cabs. "I'm only going to Fifty-Ninth and Park," he says.

"Then this must be my lucky day, because I'm heading there, too. Fifty-Seventh and Park, actually, so I won't even take you out of your way."

"Okay . . . sure," Jonathan says through a thin smile.

Jonathan scoots over to the far window, and the man slides into the back of the cab beside him. After he carefully shakes the excess water from his umbrella onto the cab floor, the man extends his hand to Jonathan.

"I'm Jeremy Woodrow," he says.

Getting a better look, Jonathan realizes that his cab-mate is none other than the son of the real estate scion Archibald Woodrow, who owns more than half a dozen office buildings in Manhattan. Jonathan recalls recently reading a magazine article about how the family was now diversifying the family portfolio into other investments.

Jonathan can't believe his luck. It's as if God himself has sent an angel from heaven. The Woodrows could drop a few hundred million into the fund without batting an eye.

"Jonathan Caine," he replies with a grin, pumping his new best friend's hand.

Jonathan bides his time waiting for Jeremy to ask what he does for a living, but that question doesn't come. Instead the taxi rolls along, making nearly every light until the red signal stops them at Forty-Second Street.

Jonathan figures that it's now or never. "What line of work are you in, Jeremy?"

"Real estate."

"Interesting. I work with a lot of people in that space. I head up the currency derivative desk at Harper Sawyer."

Jeremy Woodrow nods. Jonathan is hoping that he'll express greater interest than that, but he remains silent as the cab begins to move forward again.

At Fifty-Sixth Street, the light goes against them. Jeremy Woodrow calls to the driver. "I'll get out here. That way you don't even have to stop just for me."

The building directly across the intersection is one Jonathan's passed a million times. Above the doors is the Woodrow name in large gold letters.

Jeremy Woodrow pulls out a twenty-dollar bill, even though the meter only says seven dollars. Jonathan waves away the gesture.

"No, no. My pleasure, Jeremy."

"Oh. Okay. Well . . . thank you so much for the ride, Jonathan. Call my office and maybe we can get lunch sometime."

* * *

Jonathan enters the Harper Sawyer trading floor with an extra spring in his step. In Jonathan's world, the only reason men have lunch is to discuss terms of a business transaction. That means that Jonathan's first and only order of business this morning is to learn everything he can about the Woodrow empire, with an eye toward how large an investment he might be able to pry out of Jeremy Woodrow.

He types his password into the computer. Instead of his normal screen displaying the current trading prices of various world currencies, he sees the message *See Tech Desk*.

Jonathan's stomach clenches. It's not that he's never seen this message before. Once or twice a year, there's some snafu when passwords have to be changed and this type of thing happens.

You're just being paranoid, he tells himself. He's in the midst of a hot streak—Ross has been fully redeemed, the crisis in Russia was short-lived, and the ruble is now rising steadily, winning back most of the losses previously suffered. The chance meeting with Jeremy Woodrow only confirms that Jonathan is once again in control of his own destiny. It can't be over now. It just can't.

He picks up the phone, but it isn't the tech desk he calls.

"Were you able to log in?" he asks Haresh.

"Yeah. Why?"

"I got a message that I should contact the tech desk."

Haresh sighs. In that breath, Jonathan's worst fears are confirmed. It's over for him. Harper Sawyer knows.

"I'm sure it's just a password thing," Haresh finally says.

Jonathan has always known Haresh to be a lousy liar. For the first time, he sees that as bad news. Haresh won't be able to convincingly tell Harper Sawyer anything but the truth. In fact, he probably has already told them everything.

"Yeah, that's what I figured, too," Jonathan says, knowing his own lie sounded more convincing. "I'll call them right now."

He doesn't have an opportunity to call anyone, though. His other line is ringing before he puts down the phone.

"Jonathan Caine," he says.

"Mr. Caine, this is Joy Brown, in Vincent Komaroff's office. Mr. Komaroff would like you to come immediately to the forty-seventh floor to meet with him."

"What's this about?" Jonathan asks, knowing he won't get an answer.

"I honestly don't know, Mr. Caine. Mr. Komaroff just asked me to call you. They're waiting for you."

They? Komaroff has called in others for this. That's got to mean lawyers. Or worse, cops.

Jonathan's trying to think of something to say, but there's only one response that's acceptable when the CEO summons you. After a few seconds, he provides the expected answer.

"I'll be right up."

Before leaving the trading floor for what he knows will be the last time, Jonathan takes a moment to survey his soon-to-be former kingdom. It's no different than any other Monday morning. The traders are screaming into their phones, the runners are scurrying about, the lights on the big board are flashing.

Jonathan had dedicated his life to the numbers on that board. When they went in his favor, he felt invincible. A god. And when they moved against him, he became a gladiator, ready to take up the fight to regain his standing.

What will he be now without any of it? Will he even be himself anymore? He thinks not. He'll be nothing. A nobody.

He briefly considers making some type of valedictory statement, or even just saying good-bye to Haresh. He knows better, however. Anything he'd say now would later be used to incriminate him.

As he walks off the trading floor, Jonathan considers the fact that the next time he'll see any of these people will likely be from across a courtroom.

* * *

Even though he was expecting it, Jonathan is still taken aback when he steps off the elevator to see Harper Sawyer security. Four of them, to be exact. Big men wearing rent-a-cop uniforms. At least Jonathan doesn't see any firearms.

But then he realizes that their presence is actually a good thing. Building security, at least, can't arrest him.

Vincent Komaroff's assistant, the woefully misnamed Joy, is a woman in her fifties whom Jonathan has never seen smile. She stands in front of the wall of security men; her job is to escort Jonathan back to Komaroff's office. Joy doesn't say anything aside from "Follow me, please," and they walk silently in what Jonathan feels is a death march.

Inside the chairman's office, it's a full house. Attending the party is Komaroff and Fran Lawrence, as well as Harper Sawyer's general counsel, Calvin Caldwell, and three other men, none of whom Jonathan recognizes. The oldest of the three might as well have a tattoo on his forehead that says *outside counsel*—gray hair, horn-rimmed glasses, three-piece suit, high-shine, cap-toe shoes, the works.

They are all seated—the lawyers grouped together on the sofa, and Komaroff and Lawrence in chairs on either side. An empty chair is opposite them. There's little doubt from the configuration of the furniture that Jonathan is the enemy here.

"Have a seat, Jonathan," Komaroff says. "You know Calvin, the firm's general counsel. And I've asked Benjamin Ethan to join us today. He's with Taylor Beckett, and represents us in various regulatory matters. As you might have surmised, we have something of a problem here."

So that's the older one's name, Benjamin Ethan. Jonathan's heard of him. A big gun. This is CYA time for Harper Sawyer.

Jonathan doesn't say a word. Not even hello. No handshakes are offered. Just the empty chair, which Jonathan reluctantly places himself in. Then he waits for the guillotine to drop.

Benjamin Ethan has apparently been charged with running the meeting. "Mr. Caine, we know that back in June, Michael Ross at Maeve Grant sent in a redemption notice seeking the immediate withdrawal of over seven hundred million dollars," he says.

Ethan comes to a full stop. He and Jonathan stare at each other. Jonathan is determined not to be the one who blinks first.

"That's . . . correct, isn't it?" Ethan asks.

Jonathan knows that saying nothing is the smartest move. On the cop shows, only idiots try to talk their way out when they're guilty. Then again, he figures that there can't be much harm in admitting to what they already know.

"Yes. Mr. Ross redeemed in June. The redemption was not immediate, however. It was pursuant to the terms in the docs. There's paperwork on that."

"How'd you cash him out?" Ethan asks.

"There's paperwork on that, too," Jonathan answers flatly, this time looking at Vincent Komaroff.

Fran Lawrence takes up the mantle. He normally plays the heavy in these situations.

"You need to adjust your attitude, Jonathan. You'd do yourself a lot of good if you understood the seriousness of your predicament and cooperated with us."

Cooperating is the farthest thought from Jonathan's mind. He knows it won't do any good. He's already fired; they just haven't told him yet.

"Compliance never said a word to me that anything was off," Jonathan says. "What's the problem?"

"Compliance," Lawrence snorts. "Compliance will be dealt with, too, I promise you that. But this is about you. I'll give credit where credit is due. You almost pulled it off. Bad luck about Alexeyev, though. Even someone as deceptive as you couldn't cover up a loss of that magnitude."

"I'm sorry, I still don't understand," Jonathan says, managing to maintain his poker face. "The fund is down a bit, but not materially so. And like you said, Alexeyev's death was a real market mover."

"Fuck you, Caine!" Lawrence barks. "You could have single-handedly bankrupted a company that's been in existence for five generations!"

"But I didn't. The fund is doing fine and I've made you millions!" Jonathan shouts back.

Komaroff puts up his hands. "I don't see any reason to prolong this," he says to no one in particular. Then he turns his focus on Jonathan. "You are hereby suspended from Harper Sawyer, without pay, effective immediately. We will be conducting a thorough investigation. During the pendency of this matter, you are not to come to the office or attempt to contact anyone at the firm, or to access any corporate data remotely. We have revoked all of your passwords and frozen all of your accounts."

They froze all his accounts. Komaroff might just as well have shot him in the head. That would have ended his life more efficiently than denying him every penny he has in the world.

"Whoa, whoa, whoa, I've got over twenty million dollars in that account," Jonathan says as if in a daze. Then more forcefully, "That's *my* fucking money!"

"That's a matter for the courts to decide, Mr. Caine," Benjamin Ethan says calmly. "And until they do, every penny is staying right here."

"Yeah, well, we'll see if my lawyers agree with that," Jonathan snaps, even though he doesn't have lawyers. And now that he doesn't have any money, the chance of his getting lawyers—or even a single lawyer—is not very high.

In fact, he has nothing now. No job. No money. Zero. Nada. Zilch.

"Security will escort you out of the building," Lawrence says. He's obviously not the least bit intimidated by Jonathan's threat of a battalion of attorneys descending on Harper Sawyer to unfreeze his accounts.

Lawrence rises and makes his way to the door. He pushes it open to reveal the four men who had greeted Jonathan at the elevator upon his arrival. Security must have been standing guard just outside Komaroff's office the whole time, ready to come in if Jonathan needed to be subdued.

If Jonathan had still been employed, he would have earned more in two weeks than all four of them combined make in a year. Now these lunkheads are showing him the door.

"This isn't the end of this," Jonathan snarls. "Not by a long shot."

"For your sake, I hope it is," Komaroff says, more in sadness than in anger. "Because I have the feeling it's only going to get worse for you."

* * *

"You're home early. Did something happen at work?" Natasha says when Jonathan enters the apartment at six o'clock.

He's stayed out as long as he could—sitting in a near-empty movie theater watching two showings of some film he now can't even remember. Apparently, he should have stayed for a third show if he wanted to sidestep the comment Natasha just made.

Even though Natasha has presented him with another opportunity to come clean, he rejects it out of hand. Admitting failure is not something Jonathan's prepared to do. Not now. Maybe not ever.

"Everything's fine at work," he says. "I think I ate something at lunch that didn't agree with me. I'm going to lie down for a little bit."

He enters his bedroom and takes a step toward the window, staring out into the Hudson River. One thought swirls in his brain: How will he survive?

The co-op would likely sell for close to ten million, but it's worthless to him, at least in the short term. It would take six months at least to close on the sale. In the meantime, he can't even access the equity, because the co-op board rules prohibit home equity loans.

The Bentley is a prepaid lease, and although he might be able to sell it, Natasha would want to know why and he isn't ready to cross that particularly treacherous Rubicon. The artwork might fetch some cash, and Natasha's jewelry is probably worth in the neighborhood of $250,000, but, once again, he can't sell it without alerting her to the mess he's made. Besides, art and jewelry of that quality has to be sold at auction. A pawnshop would give him, at most, twenty cents on the dollar. He looks down at the Lange & Söhne chronograph on his wrist, remembering that he paid fifty thousand for it. The good folks at Tourneau might give him half that now.

Natasha wouldn't know if they stopped paying the mortgage or maintenance, so between his Amex card, the twenty thousand he'd moved to his checking account last month, and pawning the watch, there might be enough to get them through year's end. But then what?

Outside his window, Jonathan sees whitecaps on the Hudson, a ferry circling the Statue of Liberty. A second option occurs to him. He could just throw himself out the window. Better yet, hightail it out of here and start his life over.

"Not yet," he says aloud, albeit in a whisper. Even though all he can see right now is defeat, as long as he stays in the game, there's still a chance he can win it.

14

Three Months Later/December

Jonathan spends the evening in the ICU, sitting beside his father in an uncomfortable chair. At around midnight one of the ICU nurses shows him that there's a family lounge on the floor, complete with a television and sofa. Thereafter he divides his time between watching his father sleep and a *Rocky* marathon on Spike.

Jackie texts that she's thinking about him and wishes she could be there. He imagines she sent it while holed up in her bathroom, with the door locked, and then erased the message immediately after hitting send so Rick wouldn't find it.

Still, he appreciates the gesture. For a moment, it makes him feel slightly less alone.

* * *

Jonathan falls asleep in the lounge midway through *Rocky V*, and then awakes at seven in the morning in a panic, consumed by the same sense of dread that his father was dead that fell upon him when he entered Lakeview for the first time.

He races to the ICU, failing to abide by the protocol of washing and putting on the paper clothing. Nothing has changed, however. His father continues to snore quietly into his breathing tube.

"You can't be in here like that," a nurse scolds.

She's the youngest one he's yet encountered, early twenties, he figures. Something like a frat-boy fantasy of a nurse. Long, curly reddish hair, pale, freckled skin, and a uniform that fits snugly.

"I'm sorry," Jonathan says. "I . . . I just got scared for a second."

He allows her to lead him back to the nurses' station. Once he's there, relief slowly begins to settle in. As his other senses return, he realizes that he's in serious need of coffee.

"Where's the cafeteria here?" he asks.

"Second floor," the nurse says.

"I shouldn't be more than ten minutes. I'm just going to go down there, get some coffee, and come straight back. Here's my cell number." Jonathan reaches over and grabs a pen and a pad off the desk. "If the doctor shows up, please call me and hold her here. I've been waiting all night to talk to her, so please, please don't let her leave."

The nurse smiles at Jonathan, almost as if she's taking pity on how pathetic he sounds. "The earliest Dr. Goldman will get here is eight, and she usually arrives closer to nine. But if for some reason she comes earlier, I won't let her leave. Promise."

Jonathan thanks her and heads to the second floor. The Lakeview cafeteria is decorated for the holiday, complete with a large tree covered in ornaments and a four-foot-high menorah beside it. Cardboard cutouts of Santa and reindeer adorn the walls side by side with Jewish stars. The overall effect, at least to Jonathan's mind, is that the displays make the place even more depressing.

The cafeteria sign proclaims that they proudly brew Starbucks coffee, and just the thought of caffeine perks Jonathan up. In addition to the largest coffee available, he buys an almond croissant that actually doesn't look half-bad.

True to his word, he's gone less than ten minutes. Upon his return to the ICU, the redheaded nurse assures him that the doctor hasn't shown up yet. Jonathan tells her that he's going to be in the family lounge and asks her to come find him when the doctor arrives.

Back in the lounge, Jonathan has the crushing need to call someone. To share that his father is near death, to share the experience so he knows it's real, and feel less alone.

Jackie is whom he'd really like to call, but at this hour she's likely in bed next to Rick. He could call Amy, but she's either asleep or in a frenzy getting the kids out the door for school. Besides, he still has nothing to report, which means he'll spend most of the conversation trying to comfort her. Better to call his sister after he speaks to the doctor, when he has some information to impart. The only other person in his life is Natasha, but she's the last person Jonathan wants to speak to.

He honestly doesn't remember when he stopped having friends. There were guys in college and, later, business school whom he kept in touch with for a while, and then work colleagues became what passed as his social acquaintances.

The reality is that for the past few years, Haresh Venagopul has been Jonathan's best and only friend. Jonathan knows that this is a call he simply should not make. He has that same feeling that goes through your mind right before drunk-dialing an ex. And just like most people do when confronted with the warning, he ignores it.

Harper Sawyer disconnected Jonathan's company cell phone when they kicked him to the curb, which means that Haresh won't recognize the new phone number. Jonathan's reasonably sure that if caller ID revealed his identity, Haresh would let the call go to voice mail.

Instead, Haresh answers on the second ring.

"Haresh," Jonathan says.

It takes a few seconds for his former colleague to place the voice. "Jonathan . . . ?"

"Surprised?"

"I am, actually. You know that they told me I can't talk to you. No one here can. In fact, I'm sure my phones are tapped, just in case you called."

"I know, and I'm sorry you're in that position, Haresh. And, truthfully, I wouldn't have called if it weren't important. And it's not about the fund or the investigation."

Jonathan laughs to himself at the irony of his last statement. He's calling about something important, not that other trifling stuff like the twenty-five million of his assets that Harper Sawyer has frozen or whether he's going to go to jail, which until a few weeks ago Jonathan had viewed as the most important things there were, much more so than mere life and death.

"The thing is . . ." Jonathan continues, "I'm sitting here in a hospital in East Carlisle, New Jersey—that's where I'm from, and my father is in the ICU. You remember my mom died in March? Anyway, my father's been out of it for a while, dementia of some type, and I've been living at his place so I can spend time with him. I'm waiting for the doctor to get here and give me a sense of what's actually going on, and I felt like . . . I don't know, that I just wanted to tell someone about it. So . . . I didn't feel so goddamn alone."

The silence is long enough that Jonathan actually checks his phone to see whether Haresh hung up somewhere during his speech. But the call is still connected.

"Hey, I'm sorry," Haresh says, sounding sincere. "I really am. I . . . I didn't know."

"Thanks, man. It's actually a little tougher than I thought it'd be. He's been sick for a while, but the thought that he's going to be gone soon . . . maybe today, and that's it. Forever."

"Is Natasha with you?"

"No . . . oh, that's a whole other story."

Jonathan considers whether to confide in Haresh about his marital woes, but decides better of it. The purpose of this call is not to prove how far he's fallen since being canned by Harper Sawyer.

"You gotta stay strong, Jonathan. I know you've hit a rough patch, and your dad . . . that's tough even if everything in your life was going great. I wish . . . I wish I could say something to help. Or better yet, I wish I could come out there and hang out a little . . . but I'm afraid I just can't."

Jonathan knows that Haresh can't do or say anything helpful without risking his job, maybe even prison. Even this phone call will likely be construed by Komaroff & Co. as Haresh giving aid and comfort to the enemy.

"Thanks, Haresh. I didn't expect you to come visit. I totally get what must be going on there with you. I . . . um . . . I really just wanted to tell someone. I've always liked and admired you. Not sure if I told you that enough when we were working together." Jonathan clears his throat, trying to shake away any chance that he'll choke up. "Okay. I gotta go see some doctors and I imagine I ruined your day, on account that you're now going to spend it with Legal. But it's real good talking to you, Haresh."

"You too, Jonathan. Stay strong, okay?"

* * *

Jonathan is sitting beside his father's bed when Dr. Goldman finally enters the ICU. She's African American, and he assumes that very few people aren't surprised by that, given her surname. Like Whoopi Goldberg, he muses. She's also younger than Jonathan had expected, probably not more than a few years out of med school.

Dr. Goldman spends about fifteen seconds at each of the first three beds, doing little more than glancing at the clipboard that hangs off the footboard. She does the same thing at William Caine's bedside, but after reading his chart, she looks at her patient, and then at Jonathan.

"You the son?" she asks.

"Yes. I'm Jonathan Caine. How is he?"

She scrunches her face, as if she stepped on something that's hurt her foot. "His pressure is very depressed, which has put him in a semi-comatose state."

"Why did this happen?"

Dr. Goldman's facial expression doesn't change. "A patient's blood pressure dropping means that blood isn't moving through the veins at a normal rate. That can occur for any number of reasons, and with an elderly patient who's already in poor health, like your father, it could truly be at least ten different causes. As a result, I'm less concerned with understanding why this happened than with how to increase the blood flow so that his condition improves."

"Okay, how do you do that, then?"

"We're still in the process of ruling out various things. Hopefully his BP will come back to normal on its own in a few days, but you should prepare yourself that he's going to be like this for the next day or two, at least."

"But eventually he'll get back to . . . I know he's not normal, but the way he was before, right?"

"We're just going to have to wait and see."

Jonathan is struck by two questions at once. "What's the best-case scenario?" he asks first.

"That he's more or less like he was right before this episode, but for shorter periods. So, whatever his cognitive state was last week—and I understand that wasn't great, either—but the hope is that he returns to that level. He's likely going to need more rest in between his periods of alertness, however. And before you ask, the worst-case scenario would be that he doesn't really improve from how he is now."

That wasn't Jonathan's other question.

"How long can he live this way?" Jonathan asks.

"It's hard to tell. And I hate to answer that question because most family members believe that I have some type of crystal ball, and then they're very upset if I'm wrong, which I quite often am. But, if you're asking for my best medical opinion, and you're willing to understand the margin of error involved in this type of analysis, I would say that, short of a superseding event, I don't think he's in any immediate danger."

* * *

After the doctor leaves, Jonathan calls Amy to tell her the news. She says "Thank God" when Jonathan tells her that Dr. Goldman didn't believe their father's death was imminent. Then she adds, "Thank you so much for staying with him, Jonathan. I'm sure it meant a lot to Dad."

"He never opened his eyes, Amy."

There's a pregnant pause. Jonathan assumes the silence is because his sister is weighing her next words.

"Can I ask you something, Johnny?"

"Sure," he says tentatively.

"Why are you so angry at him?" she asks.

She asks this without betraying any judgment. As if it was a perfectly valid question, the answer to which she's long wondered about.

"I'm not angry at him, Amy. I just don't . . . care as much as you do."

"In a way, that's almost worse. Being indifferent about your father. And I just don't get it. I mean, if you guys had some huge falling-out over . . . I don't know, money or something, or if he didn't like Natasha—which he didn't, by the way, but he never told you that, I bet—then I might be able to understand. But you kind of just gave up on him. Like you gave up on all of us. I know you don't think you need your family, Johnny, but we're good to have."

"Why?" Jonathan asks. He's surprised he's been so blunt with Amy, but his sleep deficit has brought it out.

"*Why?* Because . . . because family loves you forever. Stands by your side no matter what. Because we have a shared history. What do you even mean, *why?*"

"I didn't mean it that way, Amy," he says, although he very much did mean it that way. "I'm just exhausted. I was up all night with him, like you asked, and that should at least earn me some slack from you."

"Okay," she says. "I'll let you deal with whatever is going on between you and Dad on your own. I just hope that you figure it out while he's still here. For both your sakes."

Jonathan is thankful that it will end there, because he knows that the truth is that she was right. He *did* give up on their father. And not just because of Phillip Levinson. Jonathan had long ago recognized that the whole episode at the barbecue was a symptom, not the cause of their estrangement. It was his father's weakness that Jonathan despised. The weakness that allowed Phillip Levinson to encroach on his best friend's marriage in the first place. The weakness that, to Jonathan's mind, made his father a failure.

To avoid a similar fate, Jonathan was determined never to be weak. He would be a rich and powerful master of the universe, so that no one could take what was his.

And, of course, the irony is now staring him right in the face. He's allowed others to take everything. Even his failure of a father owns a home, had a wife who loved him, has children who are caring for him. What does Jonathan have? Nothing. Which makes Jonathan Caine the weakest man alive.

15

October

In the investment-banking world, suspended without pay is a purgatory that only leads to hell. Jonathan knew he'd be fired soon enough, but Harper Sawyer would dangle the possibility of reinstatement, or at least the possibility of unfreezing his accounts, to squeeze whatever they could from him before they finally cut him loose.

The first step in that dance came a week after security had escorted Jonathan out of Vincent Komaroff's office, in the form of a call from James Jefferson.

Jefferson identifies himself as an attorney whom Harper Sawyer has retained to represent Jonathan free of charge. Considering that his assets are frozen, Jonathan knows he's looking a gift horse in the mouth, but he's obviously more than a bit suspicious of this arrangement.

"Why would I want those guys picking my lawyer?" Jonathan asks.

"You heard me say free of charge, didn't you?" Jefferson replies with a tone that indicates Jonathan wasn't the person to pose the question. "That's why. And believe me, I don't come cheap to them. A thousand bucks an hour, to be exact. So, at the very least, why don't you meet with me for an hour and cost your former employer a grand?"

A few days later, Jonathan is sitting in a well-appointed conference room near the top of a Midtown Manhattan skyscraper. Jefferson reminds Jonathan a little of a drill sergeant. A no-nonsense guy who doesn't suffer fools lightly.

"Here's how it works," Jefferson begins. "If you decide to hire me, I'll represent you and nobody else but you. I do not represent Harper Sawyer, and I have never represented Harper Sawyer in any capacity whatsoever. They're paying me to represent *you* to the best of my ability because they've made the calculation—the correct one, in my opinion—that *they*, meaning the good people at Harper Sawyer, are better served if you are well represented, at least at this stage of the process.

"Our relationship is covered by the attorney-client privilege," Jefferson continues. "That means that anything you say to me will never be shared outside this room without your consent. Doesn't matter what it's about. You stole from Harper Sawyer. Sure, whatever. You engaged in the worst form of securities fraud this side of Charles Ponzi. Oh my, how could you? You're the mastermind behind 9/11, you goddamn traitor. I don't care. It's our secret. Unless you instruct me to disclose it, I take it with me to the grave."

Jonathan allows Jefferson to give his little speech, but as soon as he's finished, Jonathan says, "So what's the catch?"

Jefferson doesn't miss a beat. "The catch is that Harper Sawyer expects that you will instruct me to share our attorney-client communications with them. That's what they get out of it—knowing what you're going to do before you do it. Don't get me wrong. They're definitely going to claim you acted alone here, Mr. Rogue Trader. Like the London Whale and the guy in Singapore. But that doesn't mean they don't fear the firm being hit with a failure-to-supervise charge. Or worse, that you're going to claim you told the higher-ups all about it, and they looked the other way, hoping you could trade your way out of it."

Against his initial impulses, Jonathan actually likes Jefferson. He seems like a straight shooter, if you overlook the fact that his entire professional life is built on the dubious premise of being wholly independent from the people who actually pay him.

"Well, that's going to be a problem because there's nothing I'd like to do more than hurt them. Bad. I'll say whatever it takes to get those bastards to unfreeze my twenty-five million."

"That right there is the other reason that Harper Sawyer thinks it's a good idea to have me represent you," Jefferson says with a smile. "They know, human nature being what it is, that your greatest impulse will be to hurt them. Might even cloud your judgment about your own self-preservation. My job is to protect you, not hurt them. And the two don't align here. Don't get me wrong. I know the value of a buck, especially when you're unemployed and your assets are frozen, but you need to understand that money is worthless in prison. And admitting you engaged in securities fraud in the hope that Harper Sawyer pays some kind of fine that's chump change to them anyway is the surest way to wind up spending some time as an involuntary guest of the federal government."

Jonathan feels sufficiently chastened. Jefferson's right. He needs to get his priorities straight.

"So how do I stay out of jail?" Jonathan asks.

"First, by hiring me, and then once you do, by doing exactly what I tell you to do."

* * *

When he comes home on Halloween, Jonathan's greeted by a nearly six-foot-tall Cinderella, the bodice of the costume straining to contain Natasha's ample bosom. It's only then that he remembers they have a benefit masquerade party to attend.

"There's a Prince Charming costume lying on our bed," Natasha tells him.

Jonathan knows that Batman would be a far better choice for him, given that he's been living a double life that would make even the Caped Crusader proud. It's now been six weeks since he was fired, and Natasha still doesn't have the first clue that the world as she knows it is over.

The surprising thirty grand his Lange & Söhne timepiece fetched and the twenty thousand he moved to Citibank on the day President Alexeyev died were enough so that the ATM continues to spit out fifties whenever Natasha inserts her bank card. As long as that continues and her American Express card isn't declined, or the bank padlocks their penthouse, Jonathan is determined that she remain in that blissful state of ignorance.

The other part of the deception was laughably easy to pull off. Natasha never called Jonathan at work, as it was Jonathan's inviolate policy not to take personal calls at the office, long ago telling her if she had anything that couldn't wait, she should text. Fortunately, she didn't think twice when he told her he'd lost his cell phone—which had been paid for by Harper Sawyer back when they employed him—and had to get a new number.

The only part of the charade that was any challenge for Jonathan was deciding where to spend his days. Sitting in Jefferson's conference room going over his old trading records occupied some of his time, but that still left a lot of hours with nothing for him to do and no place for him to be. Jonathan's been passing the time in movie theaters and museums, and drinking scotch at hotel bars, where he figured there was less of a chance he'd run into someone either he or Natasha knew.

Jonathan knows that a better man would come clean to his wife. But he's putting it off, hoping that he'll be able to counter the bad news with something more positive. *Don't worry, I have another job lined up.* Or, *Money isn't going to be an issue because Harper Sawyer agreed to unfreeze our accounts.* Even, *My lawyer says that there won't be any criminal action brought against me.*

Of course, he has no illusions that anything he were to say or do would save his marriage. It was over the moment he was escorted out of Harper Sawyer.

*   *   *

As they enter the Neue Galerie, Jonathan is still somewhat unclear about the organization that's sponsoring this fete. It's been something of a mission of Natasha's over the past year to ingratiate herself to the well-heeled benefactors of one cause or another. Jonathan laughs to himself that these people won't give his wife the time of day once they realize she's penniless.

"So what is this little soirée about?" he asks. "Daughters of the czar? Vodka preservation?"

Natasha looks at him sideways. "Neither, actually. It's for juvenile diabetes. A friend introduced me to the executive director, and he invited us."

"And what did we pay for this invitation?"

"It's all for charity, Jonathan."

Jonathan knows that this must have been set up months ago. They didn't have enough in their checking account to cover the cost of tonight's dinner. He laughs to himself that Harper Sawyer is actually footing this bill. After all, if Natasha hadn't made the twenty-thousand-dollar or whatever contribution that brought them to this place, those funds would now be frozen along with the rest of their money. Much better it goes to sick kids than to those rat bastards.

The Neue Galerie is located in the center of Museum Mile, in a landmark mansion built by the robber baron William Starr Miller, whose only true contribution to the world was his house. It's now the pride and joy of another billionaire, Ronald Lauder, and serves as the place where he stores his collection of German and Austrian twentieth-century art.

The raison d'être of the Neue Galerie are the Klimts that adorn the first floor's walls. Jonathan never cared much about art, other than the cachet that comes with owning it, of course. But the Klimts—almost life-size portraits glimmering in gold—are an arresting sight, even for him.

"Natasha, my beauty," says a man sidling up to Jonathan's wife.

He's wearing an overblown military uniform and a funny hat. From the costume alone, Jonathan would guess that he's dressed as

Cap'n Crunch, but there's something about his demeanor that suggests he takes himself far too seriously for that kind of frivolity.

"Ferdinand!" Natasha says as they air kiss each other on both cheeks. "This is my husband, Jonathan."

"The pleasure is mine," Ferdinand says, in a way you'd imagine a man named Ferdinand to say it. "Wonderful, aren't they?"

At first Jonathan thinks he's referring to Natasha's breasts, given that's where his eyes are fixed, but then realizes he's referring to the art.

"Yes," Jonathan says. "Very impressive."

"*The Kiss*," Ferdinand says, "is of course the most famous of Klimt's works, but I believe that the *Portrait of Adele Bloch-Bauer* is his true masterpiece."

Ferdinand doesn't point to indicate the work that is the *Portrait of Adele Bloch-Bauer*, which Jonathan assumes is some type of pretentious game of one-upmanship men in this world play. Jonathan has no interest in engaging, but Natasha says, "I'm sorry, Ferdinand, which one is that?"

"Oh, my apologies. It's this one here," he says, now pointing. "There are actually two Klimt works of the lovely Mrs. Adele Bloch-Bauer. She's the only person to have such an honor, at least in a full-length portraiture. The one to which I am referring is the first one, which was painted over three years and completed in 1907. It is the first of Klimt's so-called Gold Period. Look at how the fabric shimmers on her gown, and then contrast that with the background gold."

Natasha nods as if she's never heard anything so fascinating. This apparently emboldens Ferdinand to continue his lecture.

"But what is most striking about the work," he says, now looking only at Natasha, "is how Klimt depicts his subject as a thoroughly modern woman. Prior to this, females were represented in art only as sensual vessels, apart from the Virgin Mary, of course. But in this work, the artist captures her intelligence. Look at how her hands are folded. In reality, she suffered from a deformed finger, but it's concealed in this work, and yet I think that the positioning gives her a sense of power. Don't you agree, Jonathan?"

The sound of his name momentarily startles him. Jonathan has no idea what question has been asked of him, so he dodges it.

"You certainly seem knowledgeable about your Klimts," Jonathan says.

"I should be," Ferdinand replies, "given that I'm the chief curator of this museum."

"Oh, I'm sorry," Natasha says. "I should have made that introduction."

"And here I thought my Kaiser Wilhelm outfit would have been enough to indicate my affiliation with the gallery," Ferdinand says, laughing.

Jonathan has no idea why a Kaiser Wilhelm costume would cause anyone to assume that Ferdinand was with the museum, or how anyone could tell that his getup was of Kaiser Wilhelm to begin with. But Jonathan also really doesn't care. He looks nervously around the room, hoping not to see anyone who might know him, and who therefore would be aware that he has absolutely no business being here.

"And you two . . . right out of a fairy tale," Ferdinand says, again looking directly at Natasha's chest.

A fairy tale, Jonathan repeats in his mind. Not exactly. More like a business deal that had gone south, and all that now remained was its rescission.

16

Two Months Later/December

On Christmas Eve, Jonathan goes to the Carlisle Square Mall. In high school, it was the epicenter of the social scene. The place to be and to be seen. Little has changed in the past quarter century. It's still anchored on one end by a movie theater that was the Saturday-night destination, and on the other by Macy's, which Jonathan still thinks of as Bamberger's, even though the name changed almost thirty years ago.

Walking through the mall, Jonathan passes a montage of his teenage years: the video arcade (still here!) where he spent more time than he could remember playing Frogger and, later, Tetris; the pizza place that went through various names—American Pie (long before the teen comedies co-opted that name), La Bella, Mr. Pizza—and whatever the name, you could get a slice and a Coke for a dollar, but now its current occupant, Anthony's, is running the same promotion for five bucks; the gift shop where he bought his parents a god-awful fake fish tank that is still proudly displayed on the baker's shelf in his parents' living room; and Spencer's Gifts, where he bought the Christie Brinkley poster that hung in his bedroom well into his college years.

On the store directory, Macy's refers to the lingerie department as *Intimate Apparel*. It's located on the third floor. A woman who looks to be on the far side of seventy approaches Jonathan as soon as he crosses the imaginary line that puts him in her department.

"Can I help you with something? A present for someone special, perhaps?" she asks.

The last time Jonathan had shopped for lingerie was when he bought Natasha a baby-doll nightie the first Valentine's Day they were together. For that, he went to Agent Provocateur on Madison Avenue and paid close to six hundred dollars for less than half a yard of fabric.

"I'm not entirely sure what I'm looking for," Jonathan says. "A nightgown that's pretty and not . . ." He wants to say *slutty*, but speaking to a woman who reminds him of his mother, he says instead, ". . . trashy."

"Of course," she says with a smile. "We have some very beautiful items. Do you know her size?"

"I'm not sure, exactly. She's about five-five, maybe five-six. Thin."

"And in the chest area?"

"What?"

"You don't need to know her exact bra size, but . . . would you say she's small busted, medium, or large?"

"Medium, I guess."

The saleswoman apparently has enough information. She excuses herself, then returns a minute later holding several hangers.

"This is a very pretty nightgown," she says, placing a white garment in front of her torso. "It falls past the knee, which I think is a bit more romantic, and it feels silky on the skin. Very luxurious."

Jonathan fingers the material, trying his best to erase the mental image of the septuagenarian saleswoman wearing this nightgown. It feels cheap to him. Then he flips over the tag. Sixty-five dollars and it's a hundred percent polyester. It *is* cheap.

"There's this pretty lace design across the chest," the saleswoman says. "It also comes in red and black. I recommend the matching robe as well, because . . . this material isn't very warm. As a set, it's ninety-nine dollars."

"Okay," Jonathan says. "I like the white. And I'll take the robe, too."

Jonathan slaps down his American Express black card.

The saleswoman looks at the card as if it's an exotic animal. "I've never seen one in black before."

Jonathan is tempted to tell her that it's the highest echelon of the credit-card world, and it's offered by invitation only. Instead he says, "It's called the Centurion card. It's actually made out of titanium."

She smiles and swipes the card at the register. Then she frowns.

"I'm sorry, sir. It's saying that your card is declined. Do you have another one?"

Jonathan feels the same sense of dread as when he was locked out of the Harper Sawyer computer system. He wants to tell the saleswoman that his overcoat cost more than eight thousand dollars goddammit, but what's the point? So he pulls out a crumple of bills, which add up to seventy-eight dollars.

"How about I'll take just the nightgown," he says.

* * *

"I love it!" Jackie exclaims when she opens the Macy's box later that afternoon. She came over to Jonathan's house at his invitation, but told him she had to be back home in two hours.

"I'm sorry that it's as much a gift for me as for you," he says. "Maybe more for me, come to think of it. But I was concerned about getting you anything that Rick would see, and so I thought you could just keep it here."

"Thank you," she says. "And . . . since I didn't get you anything, let me make my gift to you trying it on at least."

Jackie bounds toward the bathroom and emerges a few moments later in all of her glory. She has an unsure look, as if maybe making a big show of herself in lingerie wasn't such a good idea after all.

"Do you like it?" she asks tentatively.

"Very much. You really are very beautiful, Jackie."

"And you're very kind, Jonathan."

She steps closer to him, then kisses him deeply. Under other circumstances, Jonathan would have removed the nightgown as soon as they'd gotten into bed, but since he had just given it to her as a gift, he works around it.

* * *

"Oh my God, Jonathan," she pants when it's over, and she rolls off him.

"I feel exactly the same way," Jonathan says.

The afterglow is short-lived, however. When Jackie looks at her phone, panic sets in. There are three missed calls from Rick, and one voice mail.

The message is short and to the point: *Jackie, where the fuck are you? Call me back the second you get this message.*

She doesn't want to call Rick back ever, and certainly not from Jonathan's house. But for all she knows, he's calling to say he'll be late, which means she won't have to leave right away.

"Rick called," she says to Jonathan, to explain why she was quickly getting out of bed. "And he's not a happy camper. I'm going to call him back from downstairs, okay?"

"Sure. Whatever you want. I'll leave if you want to stay here and have some privacy."

"No. I need to have some time to think, anyway." She's suddenly feeling much more self-conscious wearing only the lingerie, so she grabs Jonathan's shirt from off the floor and throws it over her shoulders.

"Do you mind if I borrow it?"

"I only mind that you look so much better in it than I do," he says.

As Jackie makes her way downstairs, she runs through various excuses to explain why she was not immediately available when Rick called. She sits on the sofa in the den and takes a moment to compose herself. Then she calls Rick's cell.

"Where the hell are you?" is the first thing her husband says, without so much as a hello.

Nice to talk to you too, asshole.

"I'm at the gym."

"You always answer your phone when you're at the gym."

This is true. She keeps her phone beside her when she works out because she knows she'd get this precise reaction from Rick if she didn't.

"I'm in the locker room," Jackie says. "I took a long shower and spent some time in the steam room. I can't bring my phone in either place, so I'm sorry I wasn't there to pick up the instant you called."

"Oh," he says. "Uh, I'll be home by five."

I hope you never come home.

"Okay. Thanks for the news flash. Was there anything else?"

"No . . . I just didn't know where the hell you were."

As if you care. Go back to screwing Brittney.

"Well, now you do. Thanks for your concern," she says, and hangs up.

* * *

Jackie's clothes are in the downstairs bathroom, from when she changed into the nightgown. She reverses the process from before, putting her clothes on and leaving the nightgown on the hook behind the door. Then she goes back upstairs, where she finds Jonathan sitting on the bed, a bare leg sticking out of his bathrobe.

"Rick was looking for me," she says, sighing. "He was pissed that for once I wasn't there at his beck and call." She shakes her head, wondering whether she should say what's on her mind, and then before she's actually decided, she hears herself speaking the words.

"He's going to find out about us. Sooner rather than later, probably. He'll hire a private detective or put some type of tracker on my car. And when he does find out . . ."

She can't even say the words. *He'll murder us both.*

"Is that your way of saying you want to stop?" Jonathan asks.

The words feel like an actual blow to Jackie. A sharp pain at first, and a duller ache as it recedes. *Stop?* That's not what she meant at all.

"No," she says with a small shake of her head. "I never want to stop, Jonathan. What I want is for us to live happily ever after."

She's finally said it. Laid it all out for Jonathan. He must think she's insane. They've known each other for a few weeks, and he has a beautiful young wife in New York City and a powerful job in finance, and she's . . . stuck in East Carlisle married to a sociopath.

She fully expects him to pull back. To tell her that this was just a fling for him. Soon he'll have to return to his real life, so maybe now isn't such a bad time to end things. Before either of them gets in too deep.

But instead Jonathan leans closer to her and places his hand on top of hers. "That's what I want too, Jackie," he says softly. "I know it sounds crazy, but I've been unhappy for a long time, and with you . . . I feel like I've always wanted to feel."

"I know. I know," she says softly.

"So, let's just be together. Life's too short not to be happy."

"I . . . I can't," Jackie says.

"Of course you can."

"No, I really can't. Don't you think if it was that easy I would have left Rick long ago?"

"It is that easy, Jackie. It's what I'm going to do."

He didn't understand. For her it wasn't a choice. It was a matter of survival.

"As awful as my life is now, it'd be a thousand times worse if I tried to divorce Rick. For me and for my kids."

"How can that be? People get divorced all the time. It's hard, but then we can be together. If that's what you want—like you said— then that's the only way."

"Rick will never let us be together."

"He doesn't have any choice in the matter. It's what we want that counts."

"No, you don't understand. Rick is a vindictive son of a bitch. Two years ago, I told him I wanted a divorce. He laughed in my face." She chokes up, but wills herself to finish. "He said that I'd either be his wife or I'd be dead."

"That's just a threat, Jackie."

"For anyone else, I'd agree, but not for Rick. He'll kill me. I know he will. And if I leave him for you, he'll kill you, too."

"Then call the police."

"And tell them what? I'd like to leave my husband but he's threatened to kill me?"

"Yes," Jonathan says with deadly seriousness. "That's exactly what you say."

She shakes her head in defeat. When Jonathan catches her eyes, he sees that she's begun to cry.

"And then what?" she says. "What can the police do to protect me? Or my kids? I have no proof of his violence. And even if I did, and even if they arrested him, he'd get out someday and then he'd kill me. No, unless I'm willing to go into witness protection, I'm never going to be rid of him."

"There's always a way, Jackie," Jonathan says.

"Well, when you figure out what it is, please tell me."

17

November

In the nearly two months since he was so unceremoniously escorted off the Harper Sawyer premises, Jonathan's had a standing appointment with attorney James Jefferson on Tuesday and Thursday mornings at ten o'clock. He spends the days sitting in the conference room reviewing the last six years of trading records, which had been provided courtesy of Harper Sawyer. Jonathan repeatedly told Jefferson that the only trades that mattered were the ones that began in June, after Michael Ross pulled out of the fund, but Jefferson was adamant that they had to go back six years, because that was the time period within the statute of limitations for securities fraud. As a result, Jonathan has been wasting hours upon hours scrutinizing older trades that were meaningless, knowing that Jefferson was only undertaking the exercise so that his billable-hours meter ran at full throttle.

Jonathan didn't much care. Jefferson's bill was the only way he had to soak Harper Sawyer.

It wasn't until they'd been going at it for more than a month—which by that time meant that Jonathan was enough of a regular that the security guard downstairs didn't ask to see his building pass before permitting him entry—that Jefferson and his three associates entered the conference room en masse, each holding a three-inch black binder that had the word *June* on the cover.

Here we go, Jonathan thinks.

"It's time for the main event," Jefferson says. "But before we get into the trees, let's spend a moment talking about the forest. I just got off the phone with your good friend Benjamin Ethan. He's getting slightly impatient with me. I can't blame him, to be honest. If I were him, I'd be annoyed at the pace with which we're going through these records, too. Now, he's no fool, and so he knows that I'm playing slow ball because my expectation is that we're *not* going to cooperate with Harper Sawyer . . . and as soon as we tell Mr. Ethan that we're shutting him out, he's going directly to the US Attorney's Office, at which time he'll pledge Harper Sawyer's full and complete cooperation to build a case against you in the hope that it's enough to get Harper Sawyer out from under any type of supervision charge."

"Why haven't they already done that, then?" Jonathan asks.

"Because the first rule of litigation is that it's always best to do nothing and get more information. That's why they've been waiting for me to finish with you, and why I've been taking so long to do that. But I'm afraid the string on that ball of twine has pretty much run out. Look . . . we've been through the June records and, of course, I want to get your take on everything, but our analysis is that after Michael Ross gave notice of redemption, you began to deviate from the fund's model and exposed the fund to market risk. Then when the Russian president croaked, you mismarked the position to hide the extent of the losses."

"In other words, exactly what I told you on day one?"

"Yeah, but the records leave no other story to tell. And, unfortunately for you, that's just not a story you can tell Harper Sawyer."

"Why not? They're going to fire me if I don't cooperate with them anyway, right? So why not tell them the truth?"

Jefferson purses his lips and blows out a long sigh. Then he shakes his head the way you might when disagreeing with a three-year-old.

"Do I need to draw you a picture, Jonathan? There are a hell of a lot of things worse than being fired. If you tell them the truth, you admit to criminal conduct. Benjamin Ethan takes your admission down to the US Attorney's Office with a ribbon around it and, pardon the mixed metaphor, serves you up on a silver platter. So unless you really, really want to find out what prison food tastes like, it's my advice that you decline to be interviewed by Harper Sawyer. Without a live witness, it's a technical case for the prosecution, which means it's a winnable case for you. The trading positions are very complicated. You live and breathe this stuff, and . . . let's face it, if prosecutors could understand it, then they'd be bankers themselves and make real money. And that's not saying anything about those fine folks on the jury. Trust me, if God forbid you find yourself in a courtroom, I can guarantee that you will not be judged by a jury of your peers. You always got out of jury duty, am I right?"

Jonathan nods. He's never once served.

"Yeah, like I said, try explaining to a bunch of cabbies and plumbers why removing a collared call on the downside trajectory of a ruble option contract is considered a crime. You'll see lots of eyes glaze over. But that calculus changes in a big hurry if you admit that you intentionally unhedged the position and then fraudulently marked that position to avoid detection. Then it's shooting fish in a barrel for even the most dim-witted prosecutor."

"Okay. You sold me. You can tell Harper Sawyer thanks, but no thanks."

"Right. That's the only call. But that doesn't mean there won't be collateral damage here."

"Like?"

"Like the moment we shut it down, Harper Sawyer is officially going to fire you and me both. And right after that, they'll go down to the FBI and say that they've conducted a full investigation and concluded without a shadow of a doubt that you were a rogue employee whom they want prosecuted to the full extent of the law."

Jonathan takes this in. It's true, of course. The part about his being a rogue employee. Still, that doesn't make it any less distressing an outcome.

"So . . . how long before it all hits the fan?" he asks.

As the words leave Jonathan's mouth, he's struck by how much it sounds like he's asking for a medical diagnosis. *How much time do I have left, Doc?*

"I told Benjamin Ethan that I'd give him our position on the interview before Thanksgiving. You'll likely be fired that same day, maybe the next, depending on how they want to manage the press."

"And then what do I do?"

"You hunker down and wait to see if the US Attorney's Office has enough evidence to indict you."

Damn. Waiting has never been Jonathan's strong suit.

* * *

True to his word, James Jefferson stalls until the day before Thanksgiving to tell Benjamin Ethan that Jonathan would not cooperate with Harper Sawyer's internal investigation. And just as Jefferson had predicted, a few hours later, Jonathan is officially fired by Harper Sawyer via an e-mail from Ethan to Jefferson.

Jefferson breaks the news to Jonathan in a phone call later that evening.

"It's not unexpected," Jonathan says.

"This is the end of our relationship, too," Jefferson replies. "Benjamin Ethan made that very clear. They're not paying my fees any longer. Not even for this telephone call."

"Also not unexpected."

"Best of luck to you, Jonathan. I mean it."

"Thanks, James. Really."

* * *

Jonathan's termination from Harper Sawyer will not be front-page news, but it will make the business section. Which means that he has to come clean with Natasha tonight, or run the risk that she'll find out on her own.

After hanging up with Jefferson, Jonathan finds Natasha sitting in front of the fireplace, reading.

"Hi. Um, there's something I need to tell you," he says.

He should have thought through how he wanted to convey this information, because it sticks in his throat. He forces the rest of it out without further preamble.

"Harper Sawyer fired me."

Jonathan's not sure exactly what type of response he expected, but he had anticipated at least some heightened emotion. Natasha didn't get angry often, but when she did, she wasn't above throwing things or profanity-laced diatribes.

But the only reaction his confession evokes is a look of utter disgust. As if this is old news, and his greater sin is that he's withheld it for so long.

"When did this happen?" she finally asks.

It's further indication that perhaps she already knew he was unemployed. He had expected her first question to be why, not when.

"It was just made official today," he says.

Even though she seems not to care about the cause of his termination or, more likely, already knows all about it, Jonathan adds, "There was an issue with some of the trading."

"Okay. I guess I should do this now, then, so you don't think it's because of your job," she says.

"Do what?" he asks.

Natasha walks over to the dining room, where her purse sits on the table. She fishes around inside for a moment and then removes something from her wallet.

"I was going to wait until after Thanksgiving, but perhaps it's better if we just get it over with."

She hands Jonathan a business card. *Peter Stambleck, Attorney at Law.*

"My divorce lawyer," she says. "Have your lawyer call him . . . and that way we don't have to talk to each other about it, all right?"

"Uhhh . . . what the fuck, Natasha? How long have you been planning this?"

"*Planning* is not the right word, Jonathan. But I've been thinking about it for a while."

"And when did you finally decide to stop thinking and go out and get a fucking lawyer?"

"About a month or so ago."

The sentence hangs in the air. He was tossed from Harper Sawyer two months ago, and he didn't believe for a second that wasn't the impetus for Natasha retaining a divorce lawyer.

"I'm going to go to my brother's for Thanksgiving," she continues in a controlled voice. "I'd like you to be moved out when I come back on Sunday. Like I said, our lawyers can talk about how to finalize everything."

Natasha doesn't look the least bit conflicted about ending her marriage. Truth be told, Jonathan isn't, either. He has little desire to face his current difficulties with someone like Natasha at his side. He'd rather go it alone.

"I don't think you understand, Natasha," he says. "Harper Sawyer froze all of our assets. That means we don't have any money. *You* don't have any money."

He says this for no other reason than pure spite. He wants Natasha to know that she's not the winner here. Her life, at least as far as she knows it, is also coming to an end.

But the thought that she might soon be destitute doesn't appear to faze Natasha in the least. "There's still the apartment," she says, "and whatever is in the Harper Sawyer account is half mine. Even if they can freeze *your* money, they'll have a harder time freezing my half of it because of something *you* did."

Jonathan wonders whether Natasha will be able to wrest from Harper Sawyer half of the frozen accounts. Maybe. James Jefferson had told him that divorce is often a legal strategy in these situations, the spouse claiming an equal right to the assets as the firm. Both of them equal victims of Jonathan Caine's wrongdoing.

"I guess you have it all figured out, then," he says.

"I'm sorry, Jonathan," she says, and shows as much empathy as she's probably able to muster, before she adds, "I know how important your work was to you."

He stares hard at the woman he married. Like everything else in his life, his marriage wasn't real. It was all just an elaborate stage set, something to trick an audience viewing from a distance.

"Fuck you, Natasha. Feel sorry for yourself. I'll be fine. I'm staying in a hotel tonight."

He slams the door behind him on his way out, proud that he didn't lose it completely in front of Natasha. But when he hits the street, he realizes that he now truly has nothing.

* * *

Jonathan returns to the apartment on Thanksgiving Day. Natasha is nowhere to be seen. At dinnertime, when everyone else in America is carving up turkey, Jonathan orders Chinese food because Mr. Chen's is the only place in the neighborhood that's delivering. Over some greasy General Tso's chicken, he ponders where he will go come Sunday.

The next day, Jonathan's sister calls. He assumes it's because Amy is going to once again plead with him to visit their father. A week before the holiday, Amy literally begged Jonathan to join her and her family in East Carlisle for Thanksgiving. Jonathan said that they couldn't make it on account of the fact that Natasha's family was coming up from Texas and the entire clan was going to convene at her brother's place in Boston. He realized he could have reversed course after his marriage ended, but that would have meant explaining things to Amy, and he just wasn't ready to do that. So he opted to spend Thanksgiving with General Tso rather than his father and sister.

"Did you have a good Thanksgiving with Natasha's family?" Amy asks.

"Yes," Jonathan lies. "And you?"

"Not so much. I'm calling to tell you that Dad passed out last night. He's okay now, thank God. Alert and responsive. I called 911, and they took Dad over to Lakeview Hospital. They're still running tests, but they said it's time for him to move into their assisted-living facility full-time. He needs more care than Theresa can provide."

Jonathan's first thought is that he can't afford putting his father in assisted living. Theresa's agency had required a year's payment up front, so she was a sunk cost.

"How much is that going to run?"

Amy's silence reveals her surprise. Jonathan's never once asked about the cost of anything.

"It's covered by insurance that was part of Theresa's agency's deal," Amy says. "They told me that there won't be any out-of-pocket to us."

Jonathan's relieved. At least his financial collapse won't affect anyone besides him and Natasha.

"I guess we should do that, then," he says. "I mean, if that's what the doctors say."

"All right. I'll handle all the admittance stuff."

"Thanks."

"We're booked on a flight out tonight. I've used up all my vacation days at work, and Jack has a cello recital, and the kids have school, and I just can't spend any more time here."

"Amy, don't worry about it. I appreciate that you were with him this weekend."

"I'm not asking for your permission to leave, Jonathan. I'm telling you that I'd like you to come to East Carlisle and see Dad. He shouldn't be in the hospital alone."

"Okay," Jonathan says.

"Okay you'll go?" she asks, as if she can't believe she's gotten him to agree.

"Yeah. I'll go."

"Thank you," she says, sounding both relieved and confused. "I can't tell you how much better I feel knowing that you're going to be with him."

"Of course," Jonathan says. "It's been too long since I've seen him. In fact, things are slow for me at work right now anyway, and so maybe I'll see if I can take a little time off and spend it in East Carlisle, so I can see him on a . . . you know, regular basis. I guess I'll stay at Dad's house. My twenty-fifth high-school reunion is tomorrow night anyway. I wasn't going to go, but now I suppose I will."

"Um . . . okay," Amy says.

Clearly she knows something's up, but that's the least of Jonathan's concerns at the moment. What matters is that he won't be homeless come Sunday night.

18

One Month Later/December

"What are you going to do to ring in the New Year?" Jackie asks.

They're scrunched together on Jonathan's twin bed. Jackie's head rests on his bare chest. He can feel her breasts along his midsection.

"I thought we weren't supposed to talk about our spouses," Jonathan answers.

"I'm willing to make an exception this one time. I want to imagine what you're doing tonight when I think about you. Which, I hope you know, will be every second of the evening."

It's another opportunity for him to come clean with Jackie and tell her all that he's been hiding—about his job, his marriage, his life. He could tell her that he's ringing in the New Year with his father, that his marriage has been over for a month now, far longer than that in reality, that he's unemployed and homeless, without a penny to his name.

He's not ready to come clean. Soon, he hopes, but right now Jackie's love is his only hope of salvation, and he can't bear to think about what life would be like if she also found him to be a failure. To paraphrase what Jack Nicholson famously said, Jonathan simply can't handle the truth.

And so rather than answer, he glides his fingertips down the length of Jackie's spine and says, "You go first."

"Well, our New Year's Eve tradition is glamour all the way," she says with a laugh. "Do you remember Tony Gallucci?"

"I think so. Big guy. Football team. Not very bright."

"Yeah, him. We go to his house and spend the night in his basement. He is so goddamm proud of that basement because he remodeled it a few years ago, with an oak bar and stools, a dartboard, and, I kid you not, a *Playboy* pinball machine. It's like the basement every sixteen-year-old boy wishes he had, but Tony actually installed it when he was forty, so . . ."

"That doesn't sound that bad," Jonathan says.

"Oh, believe me, it's awful. Everyone will be drunk by eleven, and disgusting by midnight."

Jackie lifts her head up so she's looking in Jonathan's face. She seems pained by merely having to think about the evening that awaits her.

"Now it's your turn," she says.

Jonathan is spared from lying by Jackie's ringtone.

"Do you want to get that?" Jonathan asks.

"No, I really don't," Jackie says. "It's like what they say about two a.m. phone calls, right? Nothing good ever happens at two a.m. Well, I think nothing good ever happens when you're a married woman in bed with another man and the phone rings. I should just head home. After all, a new year awaits."

She kisses him deeply. "Happy New Year, Jonathan."

* * *

Although Jackie would have thought it was impossible, she finds Tony Gallucci to be an even bigger asshole now than he was in high school. He's on his third marriage, this one to a woman who served him beer at the Grove while he was only a few months into his second. Instead of going on a honeymoon, he bought his new bride D-cups.

Jackie and Rick arrive a little after ten, and the basement already smells like lager. Tony's wife, Cheryl, who calls herself Cher, is busy making sure that Tony gets his money's worth on his investment in her chest. Rick seems all too happy to take in the view.

"I hope we didn't miss too much, Cher," Rick says. "I couldn't get this one out of the bathroom," he adds, pointing to Jackie with his thumb.

"My man!" Tony calls out from behind the bar. "Belly up here, Ricky, have a brew, or three. You're way behind, my man."

Rick makes his way to Tony. Their palms make a loud cracking sound as they slap together in a high five.

"Boys," Cher says cheerfully. "Am I right?"

Jackie thinks that *idiots* is more accurate.

She looks around the basement, thinking that a little alcohol might go a long way tonight. She knows Rick is going to be too drunk to drive home, but she concludes that she's not going to get through the evening without at least some wine.

After pouring herself a glass of chardonnay, Jackie makes her way over to Lori Abbey, who was two years behind Jackie and Rick at East Carlisle High. Her husband, George, was their year, and shares the football connection with Rick and Tony.

"Happy New Year, Jackie," Lori says as they kiss each other's cheeks. "You look beautiful as always. I love that dress."

"Thank you," Jackie says. "You look lovely as well. How have you been?"

"So busy. The boys are playing ice hockey now, and so we're up at the crack of dawn every day to get them to the rink, and then Sophie's violin concert was last night, and that was a big event, with my parents and George's parents all there." She looks at her wineglass. "So Momma is very happy to be here tonight getting her drink on."

Jackie shares the plastic smile she's perfected over the years for such interactions. "Did you have fun at the reunion?" she asks.

"Oh God, yeah, so much fun," Lori says. "You know, with Facebook, reunions aren't such a big deal anymore. I already know what everybody looks like, and how many kids they have and what ages. But it was still so great to talk to everyone in person."

Lori scans the room, and then conspiratorially leans in to Jackie. "And I saw you hanging around with Johnny Caine. I didn't think you two were even friends in high school."

Jackie feels a sense of panic take hold. Does Lori know more than just that she and Jonathan were talking at the reunion? How about jumping into bed with him every chance she got since then?

She tells herself she's being paranoid. If Lori knew about her and Jonathan, it would be a nanosecond before she'd tell George and less than that before he'd alert Rick. And if Rick knew, he'd be sure to let Jackie know. No doubt with the back of his hand. Or worse.

"It's funny," Jackie says with what she hopes is a convincing expression, "because that's what he said, too. I went outside to call home and check on the kids and he came out for a second to make a phone call, and so we said hello, and he said something like, 'You know, we went to high school together for four years and never said a word to each other, and now here we are talking twenty-five years later.' Anyway, he seemed nice. Told me that he's married and works on Wall Street."

Jackie reflexively turns toward Rick, who is on the other side of the room, still anchored to the same bar stool. Sometimes she fears he can read her mind. But if Rick knew what Lori was suggesting, he'd be beating the crap out of her right now, and not yukking it up with Tony Gallucci.

"Well, here's to a New Year," Lori says, raising her wine above her head in a toast.

Jackie clinks her glass, but the sentiment sounds more like a prison sentence than the promise of good tidings ahead. She can't stay married to Rick another year. She just can't.

* * *

William Caine's recovery differed from the worst case by only about ten minutes every few hours. In the past ten days, Jonathan had seen his father awake only twice, and both times he was groggy to the point of being even more incoherent than usual.

As if he realizes that this will be the last time he ushers in a New Year, William Caine stirs at ten minutes to midnight. His eyes pop open, and rather than seeming drugged, he looks as if he's awoken to a brand-new day.

"Johnny," he says.

His speech is labored, much weaker than before he was moved to the ICU, but at least now his father's voice bears a passing resemblance to its prior tenor. Jonathan takes his father's hand, something that he never does, but tonight he feels like he needs the extra connection.

"Hey, Dad. I'm glad you're awake," Jonathan says.

"Me, too," his father says, and then smiles as if he gets the joke he's just made.

"It's almost a New Year."

"That's nice," his father says.

"Do you have any New Year's resolutions?"

"What?"

"New Year's resolutions. Things you want to do in the upcoming year. Changes you want to make about your life. That sort of thing."

"No. My life is good," he says.

Jonathan considers the answer. His father, likely only months away from death, doesn't want to change anything, and Jonathan desires that everything be different. Jonathan knows that there's only one way the next year will be better, though, and that's if he's with Jackie. He can hardly believe how hard he's fallen for her. Him, a man who never believed in love, truly believes that even with all the troubles swirling around him, even if he never makes another dime, if he's with Jackie, he'll be happy.

Of course, there remains a major impediment to that plan. Jackie's made it quite clear that so long as Rick's alive, he'll never let her ride off into the sunset with Jonathan.

Jonathan had told Jackie that he'd find a way. And indeed he has. Rick Williams needs to die in the New Year.

That is his New Year's resolution. Not to lose weight or read more, but to figure out a way to murder Rick Williams, so he and Jackie can live happily ever after.

I want what I want.

* * *

Jackie hasn't spoken to Rick since they arrived, and Rick hasn't moved off the stool at the corner of the bar in all that time. A minute before midnight he shouts "Jackie!" across the room, the way you might summon a dog.

Ryan Seacrest is on the big-screen television, going on about how the countdown is about to begin. The camera switches to a close-up of the crystal ball that drops from the tower in Times Square.

Jackie does as commanded, taking the bar stool beside her husband, but Rick ignores her until the countdown to the New Year officially begins on TV, at which time he pulls her stool closer. She knows that she's only there for him to have someone to kiss at midnight, after which time he'll go back to drinking with his buddies.

Ten. Nine. Eight. Seven. Six. Five. Four. Three. Two. One.

"Happy New Year!" the room shouts.

All except Jackie, who takes a long sip of wine instead.

Rick pulls her into him, nearly knocking her off her own stool. Without warning, he jams his tongue into her mouth. He tastes like foul beer, and then he drunkenly puts his hand on her ass, without any consideration that they're in a room full of people they know.

Next year, as God is her witness, she'll be kissing Jonathan at midnight.

* * *

Jonathan hears the countdown to New Year's begun by the nurses outside, and he joins in. His father looks confused, as if something is going to happen that might be frightening, so Jonathan halts his count at six.

"People count backward from ten to indicate the end of the old year and the beginning of the new one," he explains.

"Happy New Year!" is heard from the nurses' station.

"Oh," his father says, despite the fact that he's most likely experienced more New Years than anyone else on the floor.

Jonathan leans over and kisses his father on the forehead.

"Why did you do that?" William Caine asks.

"Because it's a New Year's tradition to kiss whomever you're with at the stroke of midnight."

"Did anyone kiss your mother?"

"She's in heaven, Dad. I don't know if they have New Year's there."

"Oh."

Jonathan offers a sad smile. "Do you think there's a New Year's in heaven?" he asks, solely so there's something to talk about.

"I don't know. But I'm sure I'm going to find out soon, and then I'll tell you."

* * *

As expected, Rick passes out during the ten-minute car ride home, snoring loudly. Jackie was determined to let him sleep it off in the car, but the moment they pulled into the garage, he came to.

"Heyyyyy, I'm going to start this New Year right," he growls at her when he climbs into bed.

His breath actually smells like vomit, even though Jackie is reasonably sure he hasn't been sick tonight. Perhaps it's a foreshadowing of things to come.

"I'm not feeling that well, Rick," Jackie pleads.

"Don't worry, I'll do all the work. You just gotta lay there. You know, like you usually do."

Jackie shuts her eyes tight and lets Rick start his New Year right. Trying her best to hold back tears for fear they will just set him off.

It only ends with Rick dead. That's the mantra that replays in her head, punctuating his every grunt.

It only ends with Rick dead.

Part Two

January

19

Jonathan awakes to the realization that the New Year is starting no different than the one just ended. He remains unemployed, penniless, and homeless. His father still lies dying. The only comforting thought Jonathan can conjure is that things cannot possibly get worse.

And then, of course, they do.

It begins with an incessant ringing of the doorbell. The chimes are followed by two loud knocks.

Jonathan can't imagine who the hell would call on him at ten o'clock on New Year's Day. His first thought is the worst one. Maybe Lakeview sends a representative to pay a personal visit when a patient dies. He pushes that from his mind in favor of a happier image. Perhaps it's Jackie, come to tell him how much she missed him last night.

From the master bedroom window, all Jonathan can ascertain is that whoever it is arrived in a late-model, four-door black sedan. Not Jackie's car, which is a minivan.

Jonathan throws on his father's bathrobe and walks downstairs. On the ground floor, he peeks through the side-panel glass. His callers are two male strangers almost identically dressed—dark suit, white shirt, dark tie. They even look somewhat alike—big men, with the physique of high school linebackers who have let themselves go over the past decade, but they are otherwise sharply groomed with closely cropped hair and smooth shaves.

"Good morning and Happy New Year," Jonathan says after opening the door.

"Good morning to you, sir," one of the men says back.

"Are you Jonathan Caine?" the second man asks.

The question sets off alarm bells. Only a limited number of people know that Jonathan's living in his parents' house. His sister, maybe some of the nurses at the hospital, his father (assuming he remembers on any given day), and Jackie. Even Natasha doesn't know, as they haven't spoken since he left.

All of a sudden, Jonathan realizes that these men may have been sent by Rick Williams—to teach a lesson to the man fucking his wife. He takes his hands out of the pockets of his robe, just in case he has to block a punch.

"What's this about?" Jonathan asks, fully realizing that it's non-responsive to their request for him to confirm his identity.

The first man says, "I'm Special Agent Aaron Pratt, and this is Special Agent Luis Montoya. We're both with the Federal Bureau of Investigation." Pratt thrusts the envelope he's been clutching at Jonathan, and by instinct Jonathan takes it. "You have been served, sir."

The FBI? How'd they know where to find him? Then Jonathan remembers he told Haresh he was staying at his father's place. Harper Sawyer must have been tapping the phones. That, or Haresh is co-operating with the FBI.

"Served with what?" Jonathan says, looking down at the envelope, the outside of which provides no clue.

"It's self-explanatory," Montoya says.

Jonathan is annoyed at the way they speak in tandem. Tweedledee and Tweedledum.

"Is there anything I need to do?" Jonathan asks. "I mean, right away? It's New Year's and my dad's very sick . . ."

Jonathan has no idea why he's said this, especially the part about his father. He knows that these FBI agents don't give a good god-damn about his troubles.

"It's self-explanatory," Pratt repeats, seeing as it's his turn to speak.

"There's also a number to call if you have any questions," Montoya adds.

"Happy New Year," Pratt says, without any hint as to whether he's being sarcastic. Montoya nods, apparently denoting that he, too, wishes Jonathan the same.

* * *

Jonathan tears open the envelope, just as he hears the FBI agents' car pulling out of his father's driveway. It's two pages, and very official looking.

UNITED STATES DISTRICT COURT

for the

Southern District of New York

SUBPOENA TO TESTIFY BEFORE A GRAND JURY

To: Jonathan Caine

YOU ARE COMMANDED to appear in this United States district court at the time, date, and place shown below to testify before the court's grand jury. When you arrive, you must remain at the court until the judge or a court officer allows you to leave.

Place:	Date and Time:
United States Attorney's Office One Saint Andrew's Plaza New York, New York 10005	January 29; at 10:00 AM

You must also bring with you the following documents, electronically stored information, or objects *(blank if not applicable)*:

All documents referring to any trading activity in the Harper Sawyer Derivative Currency Fund. The time period for this request shall be January 1, 2015 to the present.

The subpoena is robo-signed by someone claiming to be the clerk of the court, but underneath his signature is a phone number. It's for the assistant United States attorney in charge of the investigation: Elliot Felig.

Even though it's a national holiday and he's quite sure Elliot Felig is not waiting by his office phone for Jonathan to call, Jonathan is tempted to call the number on the bottom of the subpoena and demand to know what all this is about. But he knows what it's about. The federal government has officially opened a criminal investigation into Jonathan's trading at Harper Sawyer. Just as the attorney James Jefferson predicted, after Jonathan shut out Harper Sawyer, the firm's lawyers went straight to the FBI.

As with his father's mortality, Jonathan had known that this day was coming. And as with that, too, he thought he had more time.

* * *

During his lifetime, William Caine played the role of father without distinction, but also without any fatal defect. Like a midlevel employee working for a paycheck, lacking any real passion for the job.

Jonathan always treated that reality with an *it could be worse* shrug, but now he feels like he needs some good old-fashioned fatherly advice. The irony isn't lost on him that he doubts his father would have had much to offer when he was at his best, and now he is asking an addled mind to provide sage counsel.

Jonathan finds his father fast asleep in a wheelchair that has been rolled out into the reception area.

"Hey, Dad," Jonathan says in a voice loud enough to wake him.

His father's eyes open slowly. First one, then the other.

"Johnny," he says, and then his lips form an asymmetrical smile.

"How you doing today, Dad?"

"Still alive."

"I see that. C'mon, you want to get some fresh air. It's cold out, but with the blankets, you should be okay."

His father nods somewhat noncommittally, but it's enough for Jonathan to start wheeling him away. When the automatic doors open in the front of the building, a blast of cold air hits them, and Jonathan's father actually says, "Brrrr."

Jonathan wheels them over to a place in the sun. The light shines on William Caine's face, as does the grin he wears at receiving its warmth. Jonathan rearranges the blankets, tucking them under his father's legs, and then pulls his own overcoat more tightly shut, raising the collar so the shearling comes above his ears.

"I wanted to talk to you about something. I'm not sure how much of it you're going to understand, but I just felt like I needed to talk to my dad about it, you know?"

Beyond a squint brought about by the sunlight, William Caine doesn't react to Jonathan's preface. Jonathan has the sinking feeling that this is going to be a waste of time for both of them.

"I feel like . . . I don't know, like my whole life has fallen apart, and I just want to go back and start over again. But make better decisions this time."

"Can you do that?" his father asks, as if time travel were a realistic possibility.

Jonathan laughs. "No. I can't."

"Then that's not an option, is it?" his father says, with every indication he means it seriously.

Jonathan can't imagine what he was thinking. His father can't usually recall whether his own wife is alive. How on earth did he think his father would be able to help him sort out the mess he'd made of his life?

But then William Caine says, "Johnny, you need to stay positive. Believe in yourself."

"What if I don't? Believe in myself, I mean. What if I'm worried that I'm never going to be happy? That as bad as things are now, they're only going to get worse?"

More silence. Jonathan assumes that somewhere along the line of his pouring out his deepest fears to his father, the old man lost interest. It's just as well. It's not like his father has any frame of reference for what he's facing right now.

But then his father shifts in his chair, and his brow furrows, as if he's deep in thought. "That's the wrong way to think about it," his father finally says. "You can always make things better. You can do things to make yourself a better man."

The bluntness of his father's words momentarily throws Jonathan. It's as if his father, who had made so little sense over the past month, had reached down deep to dispense with some fatherly advice that actually was sound. But was it? Could Jonathan actually be a better man?

William Caine shuts his eyes, as if he's trying to vanish. When he opens them again, he smiles at his son, his reaction no different than if he was seeing him for the first time today.

There's more Jonathan wants to say, but that feels greedy. His father looks tired.

He kisses his father on the top of his head and says, "Thanks, Dad."

20

The Monday after New Year's, Jonathan takes the bus into New York City, leaving the Bentley in the driveway of his father's house. He hasn't taken this hour-long ride since the summer after his first year of college, when he commuted into the city for an unpaid internship. The reason is the same now as it was then—he doesn't want to pay the thirty dollars for parking. He's been hoarding every penny ever since his Amex card was declined.

After arriving at the Port Authority, Jonathan navigates the subway downtown because a twenty-dollar cab ride is also a nonstarter. His destination, the Equitable Building, is three blocks east of the World Trade Center site, and a block north of Wall Street. The landmarked thirty-eight-story neoclassical structure maintains its prewar grandeur with a sand-colored, marble entrance that stretches the length of a city block, and a thirty-foot-high coffered ceiling. Nevertheless, it's now considered a second-tier address, occupied largely by government agencies.

Jonathan stops at the security desk and momentarily forgets the name of Alex Miller's law firm. He pulls the business card Alex gave him at the reunion out of his wallet.

"I'm going to Peikes Selva & Schwarz," Jonathan says.

"Fourth floor," the guard tells him.

Of course, Jonathan thinks. *A floor without a view.*

Jonathan meanders around different pathways on the fourth floor until he finally finds Suite 414, which has the name PEIKES SELVA & SCHWARZ on the door in cheap gold letters. Jonathan can't remember the last time he was at any place of business that didn't occupy an entire floor.

The receptionist is a pretty, twentysomething Asian woman with stick-straight shiny black hair and an easy smile. Jonathan gives her his name and tells her he's here to see Alex Miller. She tells him to have a seat in the reception area, which is little more than two fabric-covered armchairs beside her.

"Mr. Miller," she says into the phone. "Jonathan Caine is here to see you."

A minute later, Alex Miller appears. He's wearing a navy suit, blue striped shirt, and no tie.

"Jonathan, hey, good to see you!" he says, shaking Jonathan's hand. Then he turns to the receptionist. "Julie, I've known this guy since high school."

Julie smiles politely. At her age, Jonathan assumes she still sees her high school friends all the time.

"Mr. Miller, I'm sorry," Julie says, "but Mr. Selva is in the conference room. He didn't reserve it, but . . ."

Jonathan recalls all too well the petty power plays that are a mainstay of corporate life. Back when he wore a suit and tie, he was usually the one taking conference rooms without a reservation, and if someone at Harper Sawyer ever did it to him, there would have been hell to pay.

Alex doesn't seem the least bit upset by the boss pulling rank, however. He turns to Jonathan and says with a smile, "Why don't we just meet in my office, then?"

He leads Jonathan down a short hallway and directs him into an office two from the corner. Jonathan's first impression is that Alex Miller's office is small. Very small, in fact. Barely large enough so that the door doesn't hit the one guest chair that's opposite a modest, built-in desk. Nothing at all like the kingdom that James Jefferson practiced out of, which was large enough to hold not only a baronial-size desk but also a sofa and sitting area.

"I'm glad you called me," Alex says as he settles into the chair be-hind his desk. "Although I have to say that your cloak-and-dagger attitude on the phone gave me some cause for concern."

"Sorry about that, but I didn't want to say anything on the phone. I don't know, paranoia, I guess. I take it that you already know that I was fired from Harper Sawyer, right?"

"Yeah. I read about it in the legal press. That's why I said what I did at the reunion."

"Well, you'd think that was the worst of it, losing your job, but I guess it can always get worse. The other day, I got this hand-delivered to me."

Jonathan reaches into his inside coat pocket and pulls out the grand jury subpoena. He hands it to Alex without further explanation.

Alex says "Oh" as he begins to read. When he's finished scanning the document, he lifts his eyes back to Jonathan. "Okay, then. And your testimony is scheduled for January twenty-ninth."

"So . . . what does it all mean?"

"The truth?" He doesn't wait for Jonathan to confirm he's seeking veracity. "It's not good. A grand jury subpoena is something of a life-altering event, I'm afraid."

Jonathan, of course, had realized that being subpoenaed to testify under oath before a federal grand jury wasn't cause for celebration. Nevertheless, hearing Alex confirm that this was *not good* hits him hard.

"Should I go on the lam now?" Jonathan says, through a pained smile.

"Well, it's not that dire," Alex says with what appears to be an equally strained expression. "All types of people get grand jury sub-poenas. Some are victims or just witnesses to a crime. Others are people who the government thinks might have engaged in criminal conduct. They use the term *subject* for those folks. And, once the government has a present intention to indict someone, they use the designation *target*."

"Any way to know which one I am? Witness, subject, or target?"

"Sure. I can call the assistant US attorney—you'll hear the acronym AUSA as the jargon—and ask him or her." Alex looks down at the subpoena. "Um, I guess him. This guy named Elliot Felig."

"And he'll tell you?"

"Yeah, but don't expect too much insight from a phone call. Most prosecutors divide the world into two types of people: those who *might be* indicted and those who *have been* indicted. And based on the very little I've read about your situation, I'm fairly certain that I'm going to hear the word *subject*, and that's only because they know if they tell me that you're a target, then I'm going to advise you to shut down. I'd also bet real money that the AUSA is going to ask me if we'll save the grand jury the time and submit to a voluntary interview."

"After I got tossed from Harper Sawyer, they hired a guy named James Jefferson to represent me. That is, until I refused to cooperate with them, and then they cut him loose. But while he was being paid, Jefferson told me that I'd be crazy to talk to anyone, anywhere, about anything."

"I know Jefferson. He's a good lawyer. And he gave you sound advice, especially in the pre–grand jury phase of this investigation. The choice is a bit starker now, though. The only way you get out of a grand jury subpoena is to invoke your Fifth Amendment right against self-incrimination—"

"And if I do that, they immediately conclude I'm guilty."

"Right. But, on the bright side . . . they probably already think that."

Needless to say, Jonathan does not see that as a silver lining. In fact, his circumstances seem as dark as he can fathom.

"Okay. So how does this work?" Jonathan asks.

He means, how does he defend himself? How does he stay out of jail?

Alex apparently understands all that subtext, because without further prompt, he says, "First we talk about a retainer amount, and then we discuss the facts. After I'm up to speed, I devise a defense strategy, and then, if you agree, you sign off on it."

"Well, that first part . . . the retainer, uh, that's going to be a problem for me. Harper Sawyer froze everything I have, and my soon-to-be-ex-wife has everything else."

"I'm sorry . . . about your wife."

"Thanks. I guess this was a ride she didn't want to take. You know, the way up was fine, but the crash . . . Anyway, she's living in our co-op, which is worth about ten million, but I suspect that's going to be a foreclosure, as I don't see her making the mortgage or maintenance payments. And I have about twenty-five million frozen at Harper Sawyer. If that gets unfrozen, I'll be able to pay whatever I owe you."

Alex has been around the block enough to know that Jonathan's blowing smoke. They both know that Harper Sawyer is never going to unfreeze the money, and no court is going to allow Jonathan to access millions so long as there's any possibility that he's caused billions in damages.

Alex gets up and walks over to close his door. "Let's start again," he says as he makes his way back to the desk. "I'm not worried about the fee. Don't get me wrong, I'd like to get paid, but right now there isn't going to be much time devoted to this, and so I'm happy to try to help you out a little. If it becomes more serious . . . an indictment, for example, or a civil suit against you by Harper Sawyer, or their investors, then my partners are certainly going to have a problem with my doing this pro bono. But until then, I can keep them at bay. So let me reach out to the AUSA. I'll tell him that I'm representing you, and ask him what's going on, and then we'll take it from there."

"Thanks, man. Really."

Alex nods. "I'm reasonably certain that this investigation is focused on you, and so even if they say you're a subject only, not a target, you still need to be in full lockdown mode. And that means it's my strong advice that you refuse the request for an interview and empower me to inform them that you'll invoke your Fifth Amendment rights if called to testify before the grand jury. If that makes them look at you harder, so be it. It's still a lot better than telling them something they don't know."

Jonathan nods that he understands. But what he grasps more than anything else is that this is yet another beginning of the end for him.

"For how long will I be in lockdown mode?"

Alex hesitates, as if he's only now formulating the answer to the question he must have known was coming. "The short answer is that the government could bring an indictment tomorrow . . . or the last day before the statute of limitations runs—which in a securities fraud action is six years from the stated date of the fraud. Or, God willing, they may never indict. Prosecutors hate these cases because there is a lot of complicated trading that they need to explain to the jury, and the"—Alex air quotes—"victims are people who can afford the loss and are reluctant witnesses because they'd rather not have the bad press that lets their clients know that they were defrauded. No offense."

"None taken," Jonathan says. "But Christ, six years?"

"Yeah, I hear you. It's a long time. And I know you're thinking that the wait is going to be a living hell, but it's actually the opposite. Every day you're out of jail—even if it's with this hanging over you like the sword of Damocles—is a gift, because you're free. So my advice to you is to go live your life. Pretend like this"—Alex waves the subpoena—"never happened."

"Could you do that?" Jonathan asks. "Live your life like this isn't hanging over you?"

"Me? No, I'd be scared shitless," Alex says with a grin. "But that's why I'm a risk-averse lawyer. I always thought you guys who were masters of the universe weren't scared of anything."

* * *

Jonathan had given fleeting thought to arriving without warning, just to see Natasha in her natural, postmarriage state. It would have been easy enough to do. Even though he hadn't set foot in the building since the Saturday after Thanksgiving, none of the doormen, all of whom Jonathan had always tipped lavishly, would deny him entry to his own home. But in the end, he decided that type of surprise might be worse for him than for Natasha. The way his luck was going these days, he'd find her in bed with someone, or she'd shoot him, thinking he was a prowler. So he called to tell her that he was in the neighborhood and was going to stop by to get a few things.

It didn't occur to him until after he got off the phone that his warning might cause Natasha to make herself scarce. She didn't say that she was going out, but she was probably so surprised to hear from him that she didn't know quite what to say.

If Natasha is here, she doesn't rush to greet him at the elevator when the doors open to the penthouse apartment he'd called home for the last three years. Then again, she didn't do that even when they were living together.

"Hello?" Jonathan calls out from the entry foyer. "Anybody home?"

There's no answer back. He's already made it to the living room before he sees her.

Natasha's sitting in front of the fireplace, but she's not reading or listening to music. Her only activity appears to be staring into the flames. Jonathan has the strong suspicion that she staged her appearance in just that way. Her clothing also strikes him as something of a costume. Black yoga pants that are as tight as Jonathan can imagine clothing can be, and a formfitting white tank top, with a lightweight cardigan over it, so she doesn't look completely obscene.

She stands and makes her way over to Jonathan, at which time she does not kiss him hello but does explain her attire. "I was on my way to the gym when you called, and so I pushed back my session with Stefan an hour, but I'm going to need to leave in about twenty minutes, so . . ."

Jonathan doesn't know what offends him more: that Natasha is still seeing her personal trainer or that she's treating her husband like he's the cable guy, unwilling to leave him unmonitored in her home—the home he bought—for fear that he'll steal something.

"So nice to see you too, *honey*," Jonathan says.

"C'mon, Jonathan, you're not here to see me. And even if you are, you don't find it *nice*. You're here . . . actually, why the hell are you here?"

"Like I said on the phone, to pick up some things."

"Well, you're in luck, because I haven't thrown your stuff out yet. But since you're here now to . . . *pick up some things* . . . I'm giving you fair warning that I'm getting rid of everything you don't take with you today."

"Ah. Finding the three thousand square feet here a little cramped, are we?"

"With you standing in it, yeah, I sure am."

Jonathan takes a step back. Then he allows his lungs to fill and attempts to start anew.

"Natasha, look, I didn't come here to fight, and so I'm not so sure why you're ready for battle. I just came by to grab a few more pairs of underwear and some other stuff, because, as you know, when I left, I took virtually nothing with me."

Natasha shakes her head in disgust. "Jonathan, I haven't heard one word from you since the day you left. Don't get me wrong, I wasn't expecting it, but I don't know why you'd think I have any interest in seeing you now."

"I hope I don't have to remind you that after you told me to leave *my house*—which left me homeless at the same time I was also penniless, by the way—you handed me your divorce lawyer's business card and mentioned that I should have *my* lawyer call him so that we didn't have to talk to each other."

"And have you done that?" she says, now making direct eye contact, with a look of anger flashing across her face.

"Have I done what?"

"Had your lawyer call my lawyer?"

Jonathan can't believe just how much in her own universe Natasha lives. Does she not understand what he's going through? Not even care?

"Natasha, I don't have the money to hire a divorce lawyer. I don't know what you're living on these days, but my criminal defense attorney is working for free, goddammit. Don't you get that? I don't know what the hell you're paying Stefan with, but I'm pretty sure a divorce lawyer is going to want money. And I don't have a fucking nickel to my name."

"And whose fault is that?"

"I suppose the same person who earned the money in the first place. Do you have any clue who that might be? I'll give you a hint. It sure as shit wasn't you."

Neither of them say anything, their body language doing all the talking. Natasha with her arms folded across her breasts, and Jonathan with both hands balled into fists.

"This is why I didn't want to talk, Jonathan," she finally says. "I knew nothing good would come of it. I don't want to hear how awful your life is because you're meeting with lawyers and worried about money because, guess what? Me, too. You don't think I'm wondering what's going to happen to *me*? The only difference between your circumstances and mine is that you at least know it's your own goddamn fault."

This time Jonathan doesn't let any silence persist between them. "You know something? Fuck you, Natasha. Fuck *you*. I'm done. I'm not going to take anything. I don't want a single thing that reminds me of the phony life I had with you. *Nothing*."

He storms back to the foyer. She follows him there, but he's pressing the elevator button before he hears her voice again.

"Phony? And who's the bigger phony?! You are! You always were!" she shouts at his back. "Good, get the hell out of here! All your precious things are going straight into the garbage the second you leave. I don't want a goddamn reminder that I was ever married to you, either!"

He considers correcting her by snidely pointing out that she's only going to be giving his belongings away, and that everything she owns would always be a reminder of their marriage. He even hears himself asking whether that means she'll be moving out of the apartment, too, but realizes that this comeback is all in his head.

The elevator doors open, and Jonathan steps inside. Once there, he turns back toward the apartment and places his hand over the side of the door to prevent it from closing, to allow him one last look at Natasha.

Her appearance disgusts him. He now sees her perfect face as nothing but an ugly mask, hiding the monster that is beneath the skin. How could he not have seen that before?

For a flash, he wishes she were dead. No, not just dead. He wishes that she had never existed at all.

His rage quickly gives way to shame, however. It doesn't take much for him to imagine that through Natasha's eyes, he's even a more repulsive image. Certainly not the master of the universe, which is always as he imagined she saw him. He's nothing more than a homeless man. Like one of those beggars on the street asking for pity and loose change.

Without saying another word, he removes his hand, and the elevator doors close in front of her. When she is shut out of his life, he imagines Jackie on the other side of that door.

21

Jackie calls Jonathan at five and tells him that Rick had just told her he had a business dinner. From her tone, Jonathan knows she doesn't believe him, but he also knows that she doesn't care where he spent his nights, as long as she can spend hers with Jonathan.

"I won't be able to stay long, though," she says. "I don't want the kids going to sleep without my being home. But I can get away for two hours or so, if you'll have me."

"Of course I'll have you," he replies. "More than once, if you'll let me."

* * *

Jackie arrives a half hour later, and they immediately go upstairs to Jonathan's bedroom. Jonathan has learned that Jackie likes to be in control when she climaxes, so when she's almost there, she turns him onto his back. He watches her approach the threshold—first her breathing gets fast and loud, then she shuts her eyes tight, losing herself in a rapturous smile, as if she's reveling in a delicious secret that only she knows, and then lets go a scream of pleasure. Perfection.

After, Jonathan listens for Jackie's breathing to slow back to normal. As it does, she pushes herself closer to him, laying her head on his bare chest.

"Can we just lie like this for a little bit?" Jackie says. "I wish we could stay like this forever."

He strokes her hair. He, too, dreams of a life where he and Jackie can be together. But unlike Jackie, who fears for her life if she tried to be with Jonathan, his concern is that she won't want to have anything to do with him once she knows the truth.

His father's words ring in his ears. If Jonathan is to be a better man, now is the time to start.

"There's something I need to tell you," he says.

She lifts her head up from his chest to catch his eyes. "Nothing good ever starts off that way," she says.

"Well, why don't I tell you and then you can decide how to categorize it."

"Okay," she says tentatively. "But you're scaring me."

"It's two things, actually. Two things that I haven't been honest with you about. I . . . I don't know, I was embarrassed and thought this was a fling and so it didn't matter, but now I know I feel much more strongly about you than that, and I don't want there to be secrets between us."

"Jesus, Jonathan, tell me already."

"Okay. It's about work."

He can see her body relax. She apparently doesn't care about Jonathan's job. Of course, she doesn't know what else he's about to disclose.

"I'm not on a leave of absence. I was fired. It had to do with trading issues."

Jackie smiles at him. "I'm sorry about your job, Jonathan. But you'll get a new job, I'm sure of it."

"I don't think so, Jackie. Wall Street isn't exactly a place known for handing out second chances. My career there is finished."

She nods that she understands. "Then you'll find a new career. You're smart—that's really what matters. And if I can be selfish about it for a second, this is actually good news for me, right? It means there's now one less reason for you to go back to New York. More time that you'll be able to spend with me."

Jackie kisses him and then, apparently assuming his disclosures are complete, returns to her position on Jonathan's chest.

"There's more," he says.

She doesn't move. "Like what?"

"When they fired me, they froze all my assets, and so I'm not just unemployed, but penniless. And worse still, there's a criminal investigation into my trading."

This gets her to re-engage. She sits up, but her face still shows no hint of concern.

"Remember Alex Miller from high school?"

"I don't think so," she says.

That doesn't surprise Jonathan. He doubted that Alex registered with the Cliquesters any more than he did.

"He's a criminal defense lawyer in the city. I met with him yesterday. He says this is going to hang over me for a while. Years maybe, and without any guarantee it ends happily. But he also said I should just go about living my life as if it weren't a factor, because he's hopeful it won't be."

"That sounds like good advice," Jackie says.

"While I'm in full-disclosure mode, there's one more thing," Jonathan says.

"Natasha and I have been separated since right before Thanksgiving. So, I guess on this one I'm confessing that I'm not actually having an affair with you."

"Why didn't you tell me any of this before?"

"I'm sorry. I guess it was because I didn't want to scare you away. But now I don't want there to be any secrets between us. I want to make a life with you, for us to be together for real."

His revelation about Natasha has apparently distressed Jackie more than the specter of criminal prosecution. Or maybe it's the totality of the disclosures that has changed her mood. Whatever the cause, she no longer looks unconcerned that everything is going to be fine between them.

"Sometimes I wonder what our lives would be like now if we had dated in high school?" Jackie asks softly. "Or even if we'd met right after college or something. Before Rick and Natasha. Do you ever think about that?"

"You wouldn't have been interested in me then. You had a certain type back in the day . . . handsome and not-too-smart jocks. And that wasn't me."

"No, that's not right—"

"I'm not criticizing you, Jackie. Believe me, as much as I was crazy about you from afar in high school, just like every other guy in our class, all I cared about back then was getting out of East Carlisle and making as much money as I could, and then showing everyone what a success I'd made of myself. I'm embarrassed to admit it, because I know how it sounds, but Natasha was no different than my penthouse co-op or my Bentley. Just another symbol of all that I'd accomplished."

"And are you any different now? You just said that you want a life with me. Will you be happy with that life? Think about it, Jonathan. I have kids who don't know you, and you just told me that we'll have very little money. Our lives together won't be all sex. We'll have to exist in the real world. I'm fine with that. The question is, are you?"

"I am," Jonathan says, and in that moment he believes it with all his soul. If he's with Jackie, he'll be happy. Everything else that once mattered to him—cars, houses—they're all just *things*, and the insatiable acquisition of things is a part of his past. The woman in front of him is his future.

I want what I want.

* * *

They decide to keep the real world at bay for a little while longer and engage in another romp in the sheets. After, they fall asleep, but the slumber is broken by the buzzing of Jonathan's phone.

"Damn," Jackie says, likely because she realizes that she's fallen asleep and needs to head home right away. Jonathan shares the sense of dread, but not for the same reason. It's Amy who's calling, and she never tries to reach him after dinner, the time of day she's completely consumed by the needs of her family.

"Hi," he says.

His sister's silence reinforces that she's called to tell him something bad. When she sniffles, he knows it's something really bad.

"The hospital just called," she says. "Dad died."

"What . . . ? I was just there yesterday, and everything seemed good. I was on my way back there now."

"What can I tell you, Jonathan? He's dead now."

His sister doesn't say anything else. Like she said, their father is dead, no matter how he seemed when Jonathan last saw him.

* * *

Jackie knows that something life-altering has occurred, because all color has drained from Jonathan's face. If it weren't for the fact that he'd just told her that Natasha is no longer in the picture, she would have assumed that they'd been found out by his wife. For a fleeting instant, she thinks that she has the right idea but the wrong spouse. But if it was Rick that Jonathan had been talking to, the conversation would have lasted longer, and been a hell of a lot louder.

Besides, he'd said something about having been there yesterday. That means the bad news was about Jonathan's father.

"Everything okay?" she asks, even though she knows it's not.

Jonathan rubs his eyes. "That was my sister. She just got a call from the hospital that my father died."

"Oh God. I'm so sorry, Jonathan," Jackie says. She places her arms around him and feels him squeeze her back. "Is there anything I can do?"

"Do?" he says, as if he doesn't understand the meaning of the word.

"You know, call people? Arrangements. That kind of thing?"

"Oh . . . no. Amy said she'd handle that. She's flying up tomorrow and mentioned something about the funeral being . . . Thursday, I think."

"I'd like to come," Jackie says. "To the funeral."

After the words spill out, she realizes the utter hell she'd have to pay if Rick found out she attended the funeral of Jonathan Caine's father. Rick doesn't even have a clue that she knows Jonathan, much less what they've been doing together. If he knew that she felt the need to be there for Jonathan in his time of grief, Rick could be counted on to make it a funeral for two.

For a moment, she hopes that Jonathan will decline her offer. But then he says, "I'd like that. To feel like there's someone there for me," and she feels nothing but elation.

22

The next morning, Jonathan is sitting in the kiss-and-fly waiting area at Newark Airport when his phone rings. He assumes it's his sister calling to tell him that she's just landed, but is happily surprised to see that it's not Amy's phone number but Jackie's on the screen.

"Hey, you," he says.

"Who is this?" an obviously angry male voice barks.

Jonathan pulls the phone away from his ear and rechecks the number. It's from Jackie's cell, all right, which means that the enraged party on the other end is none other than Rick Williams.

"Is this the asshole fucking my wife?!" Rick shouts.

"I'm sorry, I have absolutely no idea who you are or what you're talking about. You must have dialed the wrong number."

"Oh, really, dipshit. Here's the way it is, motherfucker. I'm going to find out who the fuck you are, and then I'm going to fuck you up. But first, I'm going to deal with my fucking slut of a wife."

The line goes dead just as Amy's phone number flashes on the screen.

"Just landed," Amy says. "It'll take me . . . I don't know, ten minutes to make it out of the terminal. Okay?"

Jonathan still has the other phone call in his mind. When he doesn't answer his sister, she says, "Jonathan, did you hear me?"

"Yeah. Okay. I'm here now, so I'll pull up."

Jonathan doesn't see any way that he can warn Jackie that Rick knows about them. Calling her cell phone would lead him right back to Rick, but doing nothing means that Jackie will be at Rick's mercy, and God knows what he'll do to her. The only other option is to call the police, which means that he'd be confirming Rick's suspicions, at least to the extent that Rick will realize that the man he'd just threatened to fuck up knows his wife well enough to send the police to his home.

Still. Jackie.

After a deep breath, Jonathan calls 411 and asks to be connected to the East Carlisle Police Department.

* * *

Amy is standing under the Jet Blue sign. She laughs when Jonathan's Bentley rolls up.

"Oh my God, you've got to be kidding me. Nothing like being picked up in style," she says before kissing her brother on the cheek. She places the suitcase handle in his grasp and then gets into the front seat.

Jonathan hasn't seen his sister for nine months, not since their mother's funeral. Her hair is about two inches longer than it was then, and it's straighter than he remembers it from when she was a girl.

His sister's resemblance to their mother is unmistakable. They both have dark complexions, large brown eyes, and dimpled noses. Jonathan wonders whether the similarities between them are more than skin deep. He thinks not. His sister seems sincerely happy, whereas in this regard he takes after his mother—always longing for more, never content with his lot in life.

"Does this thing have an autopilot?" Amy asks, running her hand along the soft-as-butter leather upholstery.

"It's a lease," Jonathan says, although he's not sure why. He is quite certain that the amount he paid for the privilege of three years of driving was more than the mortgage on Amy's house. "So, did you have a good flight?" Jonathan asks, to change the subject from the price of his car.

Amy begins to tell him something about the large man who was seated next to her, but Jonathan has tuned out after the first few words. He's imagining what must be unfolding at Jackie's house.

"Jonathan," Amy says, a touch louder than conversational tone. "I asked you a question."

"I'm sorry. I zoned out for a moment. What did you say?"

"I said that I assume it's okay if we all stay at Dad's."

"Oh. Yeah, sure. You and Kevin can take Mom and Dad's room. I've been staying in my old room anyway. The kids can share your bedroom downstairs. How's that?"

"Fine. The same funeral home that did Mom's can do Dad's too. They said that they could do the funeral tomorrow morning, which I thought made sense. Kevin and the kids land tonight at eight thirty. Sorry to make you have to do a second airport run, but Kevin only gets ten vacation days a year."

"It's fine."

Indeed it is. The least of Jonathan's worries at the moment is that he has to go to Newark Airport twice in one day.

Amy begins to discuss the logistics. She was always good at planning, which was how she ended up with exactly the life she'd always wanted: solid husband, two kids, one of each gender, exactly two years apart, a comfortable house in a nice neighborhood with a good public school system, and a pure-breed dog.

"I was trying to think who we needed to call," Amy says. "You know, with Mom, there were people she knew from work and she had some friends, but I don't have the first clue as to whether Dad had any people. I Googled Robin and Randi and got a number for Robin that might be her. She still lives in upstate New York somewhere, right?"

Jonathan has no idea where their cousin Robin lives. He hasn't seen her since he was in high school, so he just shrugs.

"Well, I left a message on the number I found for her online. The voice mail greeting was one of those electronic ones that just repeats the number you've called, so I'm not even sure if the person I called is a man or a woman. Randi's totally off the grid. I mean, no Internet presence at all. I figure that if Robin calls me back, I'll ask her to get in touch with Randi. And that's all of Dad's family that I know about. I've heard him mention that he had cousins living someplace in Arizona, but I don't have any idea where, or even what their names are."

"Yeah, I don't know," Jonathan says.

"I was also thinking . . . remember the Levinsons? They didn't come to Mom's funeral, but I'm not sure anyone told them about it. Mr. Levinson was Dad's best friend, right? Maybe you could do some Googling and find him."

Jonathan knows he's not going to lift a finger to find Phillip Levinson. He considers sharing with Amy why he does not want that man at their father's funeral, but decides there's no reason for him to sully her memory of their parents.

"He was Dad's friend like forty years ago, Amy. He's probably dead himself now. Besides, they moved to California a long time ago, didn't they? I don't see him flying across the country to attend Dad's funeral tomorrow."

Amy considers this. "I guess you're right. And it might be better if it's just our family. But I think you should tell him anyway. Just so he knows."

"Okay," Jonathan says, seeing it as a harmless lie. "So how are the kids?" he asks to change the subject for the second time.

If Amy realizes that it's out of character for Jonathan to inquire about her children, she doesn't let on. Instead she says, "They're good. Really good, actually. They were upset about Dad, which is ironic because they both thought he was kind of scary. But that's the way kids are, I guess. Molly was funny. She now thinks that whenever she's going to see an older person, she needs to bring a black dress. Remember when Mom died? We came up here to make that good-bye visit, but I thought Mom was going to linger a little longer and we'd go back home and then I'd come back for the funeral without the kids. But then Mom passed while we were still here, and I didn't have a black dress for Molly. So now whenever we visit Kevin's mother, which we do, you know, once a month or so, Molly asks, 'Is she going to die?' And I tell her no, that it's just a visit, but Molly still always says, 'I think we should bring a black dress. You know, just in case. Like what happened to Grandma Linda.' So at least this time I could tell her that she gets to bring a black dress."

As Amy talks about her children, Jonathan's mind returns to Jackie. It's now been about ten minutes since he called the East Carlisle police. At the time, he imagined that Jackie was at home when Rick had called him, but now he realizes that may not have been the case. Maybe she left her phone behind, and that gave Rick the opportunity to scroll through it. If Jackie isn't home when the cops arrive, Rick will say that their tip was just a crank call. *No disturbance here, Officers. I'm all alone.* Which means that when Jackie does come home, Rick will be there, likely even angrier than he was on the phone with Jonathan.

"Jonathan, you're doing it again," Amy says in a singsong voice. "What's up with you, anyway? I'm tempted to think it's Dad, but I know you better than that."

"I'm sorry," Jonathan says.

"I asked you if the lovely Natasha was at Dad's house."

Amy never made any secret that Natasha was far from her favorite person on earth. Jonathan could hardly blame her. Few women liked his wife, so there was no reason for Amy to be any different.

"No . . . well, I guess I might as well tell you. We're separated now. Since right before Thanksgiving. And I haven't told Natasha about Dad or even where I'm living these days."

"Oh. I'm sorry."

"No, no, you're not," he says with a laugh.

"No, I am. She's your wife, and you're my brother, so I am really sorry."

He's still wondering whether it's true when his phone rings. It's Jackie's number. His first instinct is to let it go to voice mail, to avoid a second confrontation with Rick Williams.

Then again, it might be Jackie. He can't risk missing her, so he answers.

"Hello . . . ?"

"Jonathan . . . what the hell happened?"

It's Jackie, thank God. His relief is short-lived, however. He'd just as soon not have this discussion in front of his sister.

"Are you okay?" he says.

"Not really. The police got an anonymous call that there was a domestic disturbance at my house. Did you call them?"

Jonathan can feel his sister's stare. "I just picked up my sister at the airport. Can I call you back in about an hour?"

"No," Jackie says in a whisper. Jonathan imagines that she's secreted herself in the bathroom, and is cowering in fear. "I don't think you understand what's going on. Rick's downstairs with the police right now. I need to go in a second and talk to them, too. I realized that I forgot my phone, and when I came back, I saw that a call to you was made while I was out. I figured that Rick called you and then you called the police. Tell me what's going on."

He doesn't have much choice. He needs to tell Jackie that her husband knows about them. Having his sister hear about his sordid life is now of secondary concern. Jonathan's worried first and foremost about the retribution Rick will exact against Jackie.

"Yes," Jonathan says. "It was just like you said. I'm sorry, but I felt like I had no choice."

"Jesus, Jonathan."

"Can you leave?" Jonathan asks. "I mean when the police do. I don't want you alone with him."

"I don't know," she says. "I'll try, and then I'll call you."

Jonathan quickly looks over at his sister, and then back to the highway. "I'm sorry if I made things worse, but he was making threats, and I didn't know what else to do."

There's a long pause. "I know," Jackie says, and then she ends the connection.

* * *

Jonathan hopes that by acting as if nothing unusual has occurred, his sister will not see the need to ask him about the call. So he tosses his cell phone into the cup holder and continues to stare straight ahead, as if he's transfixed by the beauty of the New Jersey Turnpike.

His sister isn't going to let it go without further comment, however.

"What the hell, Johnny?" she says.

"It's complicated."

"Yeah, it sure sounds like it. Are you in some kind of trouble?"

"What?"

"You said the word *police* and something about threats being made."

There are just so many lies he can keep track of. He might as well tell his sister what's going on. Some of it, at least.

"Do you remember Jacqueline Lawson?"

"From high school? Queen of the Cliquesters?"

Jonathan laughs. "Yeah. That one."

"What about her?"

"Well . . . let's just say that we reconnected at the reunion."

"Ah. Is that why you and Natasha separated?"

"No, the thing with Natasha happened first. And it was her idea. So, at least that's not my fault. Well, not entirely. But I take total blame for having the brilliant idea to start a relationship with a married woman. I suppose you also remember Ricky Williams, right?"

Amy was two years behind Jonathan at ECHS, so a different generation of Cliquesters and football gods ruled her senior class. Still, Ricky Williams was the big man on campus in Amy's sophomore year, so Jonathan assumed she'd recall the name.

"Vaguely," she says. "Wasn't he a football player?"

"Yes. Another acceptable answer would have been a Class-A douche bag. Anyway, he's her husband, and right before I picked you up, he called me. Apparently he knows about Jackie and me, and made it quite clear he was going to take it out on her. Long story short, after I drop you at Dad's, I'm going to meet up with Jackie to see how much damage I caused."

"Is that why you decided to move into Dad's? To be closer to Jackie?"

The question confuses Jonathan. As he processes it, he realizes that of course that would be his sister's assumption, but that's only because her chronology is off.

"No . . . Natasha kicked me out first. I went to Dad's because . . . well, the truth is that I didn't have any place to live."

Amy still looks confused. "I figured you'd take a suite at the Four Seasons or something. To be closer to work."

It's as if Jonathan's whole life is unraveling again, this time in a single conversation with his sister. It wasn't how he envisioned their reunion beginning. He feels enough shame to lie to her, but then recalls his father's plea to be better than that.

"I've also been let go from my job," he says. "If it's okay, I don't want to get into all the gory details right now. Suffice to say, when it rains, it pours. And sometimes it pours down shit."

"I'm sorry," Amy says. "Just know that I'm here for you, if you ever want to talk. Okay?"

"Thanks, Amy. Really."

Amy puts her hand on her brother's shoulder and sighs. "Well, I got to say this, Johnny—your life isn't boring, that's for sure."

23

Jackie comes out of the bathroom and down the stairs to see the two police officers still talking to Rick. She can tell that Rick is trying his best to remain calm. He's wearing what she thinks of as his lying face. The one she sees whenever he tells her that he was out at a business dinner when he comes home reeking of perfume.

"No," Rick is saying with that face right now, "everything is fine. In fact, my wife was out until about a minute before you both arrived." He sees Jackie making her way down the stairs. "Isn't that right, honey?"

"Isn't what right?" she says, stalling.

"Your husband just told us that you weren't home this morning," one of the cops says. He's closer to the age of her son, Robert, than to her own, and so thin that his uniform hangs off him. "Where were you?"

"At the gym," she says.

The other police officer looks to be slightly older than his partner and has twenty pounds on him. "Which gym?" he asks.

"Bally's."

"The one off Hardenbrooke Lane?" the skinny cop asks.

"Yeah. The kids leave for school at seven thirty, and then I go to the eight a.m. Pilates class."

Jackie's tempted to just explain everything—well, maybe not everything, but some of it. She could tell them that her husband went through her phone and found a number he didn't recognize, and even though Rick chases every skirt he sees, he's also a jealous prick, so he called that number and threatened the man who answered, who was a friend, nothing more, but who was understandably concerned for her well-being, so he called the cops.

She sees no good coming from that scenario, however. For starters, the police would ask for the man's name to verify her story, and that'll involve Jonathan, which she'd rather not do. On top of which, she'd be lying about her relationship with Jonathan, and she wouldn't even be accusing Rick of doing anything illegal. Not really. These two male cops aren't going to arrest Rick because he called the phone number of a guy he thought was sleeping with his wife.

"Can we speak for a moment in private?" the larger officer asks.

"Sure," Jackie says, "we can talk in here."

She leads him into the den. When they are behind closed doors, the cop looks at Jackie with concern, then says in a low voice, "Okay, ma'am, you need to listen. If your husband has gotten physical with you, he's not going to stop, no matter what he says or how sweet he acts right after. And that means you need to get out of here. Right now. For your sake, and for the sake of your kids. And if you have concerns about your safety, we can protect you. You and your kids. I guarantee it."

The cop hands Jackie his business card. Officer Craig Sinoway.

Jackie knows that she should take the police up on their offer of protection and get the hell out of there. But no matter what the police promise, she'll never be safe from Rick.

"Thank you, Officer Sinoway," Jackie says, reading the name off the business card. "I really appreciate your concern. But I'm fine."

"If you say so," the officer says, now looking even more worried than before. "But if anything happens, or if you have any worries that something will happen, please call me. Day or night. My cell phone number is on the card."

"Nothing is going to happen," Jackie says with a smile that she hopes will put the cop at ease. "Really. I'm so sorry that you had to come out here for nothing."

* * *

Rick doesn't even wait for the police cruiser to pull out of the drive-way. When he hears the second car door slam shut, he turns on Jackie.

His lying face is gone. Now it's the face she fears most. The monster.

Jackie pulls out her phone. It's her only defense to keep her husband at bay, and she brandishes it as if it's a weapon.

"I have their phone number on speed dial, Rick. You take another step toward me, and they'll be back in two seconds."

"Who is he?!" Rick screams.

"What are you talking about?"

"Who are you fucking?!"

"No one, Rick. What is wrong with you?"

He reaches into the bookcase beside him and pulls out a framed picture. He doesn't appear to notice that it's of the kids and not her before he hurls it against the wall, shattering the glass.

"I'm goddamned serious, Jackie! I want to know that cocksucker's name, and I want to know it right now!"

"I don't have anything to tell you, Rick. I don't know what's set you off, but you're scaring me. Just go to work. We can talk about this when you get home. Hopefully you'll be calmer and understand that it was just a crank call. That's it."

Jackie is sure that Rick's going to hit her. He's got that same crazy-eyed look he gets the moment before striking. But this time, Rick's fist slackens. His restraint can only be because he fears she'll make good on her threat, and the cops will return in a heartbeat.

"This isn't over. Not even close," he announces.

He stomps out of the house, slamming the front door hard to punctuate the point. She watches him leave through the living room window, her hand still clutching her cell phone, just in case he comes back for more.

Rick's SUV tears out of the driveway and then shoots up the street.

It's not until he's out of sight that Jackie releases her grip on the phone.

Then she slumps on the floor and begins to cry.

* * *

Bicentennial Park was erected, as the name suggests, in 1976. It's not more than a baseball field connected to a picnic area, but it's one of the few parks in East Carlisle. Given that everyone in the town has their own backyard, and the town used the ball fields at the various schools for recreational sports leagues, erecting parks has never been a civic priority.

Jonathan figured it was a good meeting place for people hoping not to be noticed, especially in winter. Sure enough, he hasn't seen anyone since he arrived five minutes ago.

He places his phone beside him on the bench, just in case he gets a frantic call or text from Jackie. A minute later, it rings. It's a New York City number, but not Natasha's, or at least not any number he recognizes as belonging to her.

"Hello?"

"Jonathan, Alex Miller here. Did I catch you at a bad time?"

"Does anyone ever answer that question honestly when their lawyer calls?"

"I guess that's right," Alex says with a chuckle. "Sometimes I feel like the Grim Reaper. No one ever wants to hear from their lawyer. But I wanted to bring you up to date with my call with the US Attorney's Office. Bottom line, I told them that you'd invoke your right not to testify before the grand jury, and the AUSA said that your refusal to cooperate with the investigation would result in greater scrutiny."

"So, just what you said would happen, in other words."

"Yup. They're following their standard operating procedure. But I wanted to keep you in the loop and talk about next steps."

"I appreciate that, Alex. I do, but . . . my father died yesterday, and so I've got my hands full with arrangements. I understand how important this is, but can we put a pin in it? Just for a few days. Until after the funeral, at least? That's tomorrow."

"God, Jonathan . . . I'm sorry. I didn't even know your father was sick."

"Yeah. The other reason I was in East Carlisle. You know, aside from not having a place to live and no money."

Jonathan says this with a laugh, but Alex doesn't join in. He must not see this as a time for false levity.

"I'm so sorry that I bothered you at a time like this," Alex says.

"No, I understand that you're doing your job. And doing it for free. So I'm very grateful. It's just that . . . I can't focus on it right now."

"Understood. One more thing, though. Again, I'm sorry, but they asked and it'll slow down the US Attorney's Office if you voluntarily turn over your passport."

Jonathan laughs again, this time for real. Running is probably the smart move, all things considered. Still, he isn't going anywhere.

*　*　*

Jonathan watches Jackie approach from her car. She looks in every direction twice before venturing into the park, doubtless to make sure no one sees her. It reminds him of their first "date" at the Château. So much has happened since then, but the one thing that hasn't changed is that Jackie is still deathly afraid of what her husband would do to her if he knew about them.

Jackie takes a seat next to Jonathan on the bench. She wraps her arms around herself, a nod to the chilly weather. After looking around once more to ascertain that they're truly alone, Jackie puts her hand on top of Jonathan's.

"I'm so sorry, Jonathan. The last thing you should be worrying about now is my deranged husband making threats."

Jonathan smiles. "Comes with the territory, I suppose. Small price to pay, actually."

She smiles back. "I wish I came without any price at all."

"So what did you end up telling Rick?"

"That I didn't know what he was talking about. That there was no one else."

"Do you think he believed you?"

"No, I'm sure he didn't. He told me in no uncertain terms that it wasn't over yet." She shakes her head and forces back the tears she can feel trying to burst free. "I'm so sorry, Jonathan. I always—*always*—keep my phone with me. And I always erase your number from the call list. I . . . must have forgotten this one time and he saw a number he didn't recognize. I guess he was suspicious already . . . I've been out a lot lately . . ."

"It's not your fault. And it sounds like Rick still doesn't know that it was me he called."

"He's going to find out, Jonathan. I know he will. And . . . when he does, he's going to kill us both."

"Don't worry," Jonathan says soothingly. "I won't let that happen. I promise."

She looks at him with uncertain eyes. An expression that suggests there's nothing she'd like more than to believe him, and yet she can't.

"Trust me, Jackie. We're going to be together soon."

Jonathan's tempted to tell Jackie how he's so sure that they're going to live happily ever after, but then thinks better of it. He'd rather she believe that Rick's death was an accident.

24

Amy's husband, Kevin, and their two kids, Jack and Molly, land at Newark Liberty International Airport right on time at 8:30 p.m. Kevin has Molly in one arm and Jack's hand on his other when Jonathan pulls the Bentley up to the Jet Blue terminal for the second time that day.

The kids hug their mother, and Amy kisses her husband on the lips. The very embodiment of a happy family.

This was nothing Jonathan recalls from his own childhood. He has no sense that his parents were ever in love. For a while after that family barbecue, Jonathan had imagined that Phillip Levinson was his mother's true soul mate, but as he began to see the world through more adult eyes, he came to the conclusion that Phillip Levinson was likely one of many men who cuckolded William Caine. His mother's insecurity and narcissism was a particularly harmful combination to the maintenance of marital fidelity. And for his father's part, Jonathan's old man always seemed barely to be keeping his head above water, mere survival superseding any thoughts of happiness.

As Jonathan watches his sister re-engage with her loving family, he realizes that *happiness*—contentment, joy, fulfillment—was not something to which he even really aspired. He simply didn't think it was real, and so, just as the atheist pursues earthly desires, Jonathan's ambition was to obtain the one thing he believed in—money. And with it he would acquire the life he envisioned, which to Jonathan's mind included a beautiful wife, just as it did a penthouse apartment and a summer home on the ocean. Being happy as an end in itself was never part of the equation.

He sees the error of his ways now. He only hopes it's not too late to rectify the situation.

*   *   *

When they arrive back at the house, Kevin volunteers to put the kids to sleep, which apparently entails reading three stories and some singing—at least for Molly, as Amy explains that Jack has declared himself too old for the singing but not the reading.

After Kevin heads upstairs, Jonathan offers Amy some scotch, and to his surprise, she accepts. Yet another thing he didn't know about his sister—she's a scotch drinker.

"You know when Dad got this bottle?" he says as he hands the tumbler to Amy.

"Yes. I actually had a sip of it with Dad on my wedding day. He told me he bought it on his honeymoon, with the expectation that someday he'd drink it with his children when they got married."

Jonathan laughs. "He told me he bought it the day I was born, to drink with me when I came of age. I guess he couldn't wait until I turned twenty-one, because I had a glass with him on my eighteenth birthday."

Amy laughs, too. "Well, whatever the truth is, I bet Dad's smiling down on us right now. So, cheers."

Jonathan's not a believer in the afterlife. And yet he can't help but allow for the possibility that his father *is* somehow smiling down on his children, drinking his crappy blended scotch together.

"To William Caine," Jonathan says, clinking his glass to Amy's.

"To William Caine," she concurs.

They both take a sip. Jonathan lets the alcohol roll back into his mouth, the way his father advised him that very first time, twenty-five years ago.

"You know, I never really felt like I got Dad," Jonathan says. "Mom was kind of easy."

"Yeah, because narcissistic borderline personality is an actual thing."

Jonathan can't deny that. "And what's your diagnosis of Dad, Dr. Freud?"

"He was just a guy who tried his best. Living with Mom was no picnic, and I think he was happy just to have any oxygen to breathe."

"What kind of a life was that?"

"I don't know. I always thought Dad was happy. Didn't you?"

"I have no idea. That's kind of what I mean about not really under-standing what he was all about. But I know that I couldn't be happy with that kind of life."

"No offense, Jonathan, but I'm not sure *any* type of life that didn't involve millions of dollars could make you happy. The rest of us, we get by with far less."

Jonathan knows Amy didn't mean to hurt him with the barb, but it still stings. Amy must sense that she's crossed a line, because she tries to backtrack.

"What I mean," she says, "is that he loved Mom, and so he was happy because he was happy with her. And I think, in her own way, she loved him, too. After all, they were married a very long time."

He considers sharing with his sister that their mother was unfaith-ful, but stops himself. If she wants to believe their parents were in love until death did them part, he won't stand in the way, even if her version is pure fiction.

"My last conversation with Dad . . . I had a real heart-to-heart with him," Jonathan says. "It's funny because over the last . . . I don't know how long, he sounded like he was talking gibberish for all the sense he made, right? But this was only a few hours before he died, and he was completely lucid. Like he understood that I needed to talk to him, and maybe on some level he understood that he had to do it then because . . . because he wouldn't be around to do it later."

Amy rearranges herself to sit up straighter. "What did he say?"

"He said that I should start my life over, and do it better this time."

"That seems like good advice," she says.

Jonathan takes another swallow of the scotch. Another sentiment rolls around in his head, but he decides not to voice it.

"What?" Amy says, apparently sensing he's holding something back. Jonathan smiles. "You don't want to know."

"No, I do. I know we haven't been very close, and I hope you know that I wish it wasn't that way. And it doesn't have to be that way in the future. Especially if you and Natasha are really over. With Mom and Dad gone, for better or worse, I'm your only family left."

Jonathan hadn't thought about it in those terms before, but Amy's right. Like the failings of his other interpersonal relationships, the blame for his estrangement from his sister fell squarely on his shoulders. He'd always been too busy mastering the universe to take much of an interest in Amy or her growing family. She had tried, though. Always making a pilgrimage into New York City when she visited East Carlisle to see their parents, inviting Jonathan to come to Florida for every holiday. It was Jonathan who never made any effort.

He could change that now, however. By opening up to her.

"The truth of the matter is that I'm afraid I won't be able to do it. Be a better man, I mean. Sometimes I think I'm just hardwired to be who I've always been."

Amy's face shows nothing but understanding. She puts her hand on top of his, and Jonathan recalls Jackie's identical gesture to comfort him at Bicentennial Park.

"I don't believe that, Johnny. Not for a second. I think you can be the kind of man you want to be. Just because you spent the last . . . I don't know how many years being one type of person, doesn't mean you don't have the capacity to change. Maybe . . . I don't know . . . maybe you're meant to be with Jackie. Maybe with her, you'll be the kind of person you want to be."

Jonathan takes another gulp of scotch. More than anything else, he hopes that his sister is right. That he can be with Jackie and that she can be his salvation. Even though he knows he'll first have to commit a mortal sin to get there.

He still wants what he wants. Now, however, the stakes are much greater than ever before.

* * *

Rick comes home before five, a first for him. Jackie's decided to adopt a strategy of pretending that this morning never happened.

"I'm in the kitchen," Jackie announces. "Making spaghetti and meatballs for dinner."

When she sees Rick, she knows at once that he's not in the mood to forgive and forget. He's removed his winter coat but not his work boots, which make him a good two inches taller, so he towers over Jackie by that much more.

The look in his eyes indicates he has murder on his mind.

Jackie spies all the things in the room that she can use to defend herself: iron skillets, knives, even the boiling water. And then she realizes that these things are equally accessible to Rick.

She decides to try another tack.

"Please, Rick. Let's not start this again. I'm sorry that someone apparently thought they heard something and called the police, but I was at the gym, so you can't blame me for it. And I don't know why you think that I'm having an affair, but I'm not, and so I wish you'd just let it go already."

"There's one thing I can promise you, Jackie, I'm not letting this go. No fucking way."

He attacks her so fast that she doesn't even know it's happened until she's on the floor. When she locks eyes with Rick, there's not even a hint of remorse staring back at her. Instead, Rick looks like a fighter ready to go in for the kill.

He won't hit her again if she remains on the floor, she tells herself. She's dead wrong.

His boot smacks up against her backside, and the kick is hard enough that she cries out. The momentum of the blow flips her onto her stomach, and she turns to see Rick hovering above her.

He drops to the floor like a cat and grabs the back of Jackie's head.

His fingernails bore into her scalp and he presses her face into the marble floor. It's cold and rough, and she thinks that this is what it would feel like if her head were caught in a vise. It's as if Rick is trying to push her face through the solid surface.

"Get off me!" she screams. "Get off!"

She can no longer see Rick, her field of vision completely blocked by the floor. Even the blackness is now playing tricks on her, with light that she knows to be imaginary dancing in front of her eyes.

He laughs at her demand. It's a deep, guttural sound that says she's delusional if she thinks she has any control in this situation.

"I'll get off you when you tell me what I want to know, Jackie. What's his goddamn name?"

"Rick, you're hurting me. Please. Please stop!"

"You're fucking doing this to yourself. I'll stop the moment you tell me the truth. Who have you been fucking, Jackie?!"

The pressure on the back of her head increases and is joined by Rick's knee crushing down on her spine. She wonders how much her body can handle before something breaks.

And then, all at once, she feels a lightness that is the absence of pain. Jackie's afraid to look up, fearful that Rick has relented only so that he could grab a weapon to finish the job.

"Mom?" she hears from the foyer. "Anybody home?"

When Jackie finally opens her eyes, she's alone. A moment later, she hears Rick greet their son at the front door.

She scurries upstairs and takes refuge behind the locked bathroom door so that she can tend to her wounds. Looking in the mirror, she sees the side of her face growing redder. She knows it'll get worse in the next two hours, but for now, it's nothing she can't hide with some makeup.

She shudders with the thought of what would have happened if Robert hadn't come home when he did. Rick would have killed her. With his bare hands. No doubt about it.

A few minutes later, she's regained enough composure to face her son and make her way past Rick. She races downstairs, where she sees Robert sitting at the kitchen counter, Rick standing behind it.

"Hiya, sweetheart," she says to Robert, careful to remain out of her husband's reach. "You need to come with me . . ."

"Where?"

"Robert, just come!"

She grabs her son by the arm and drags him toward the door.

"Just give me a second," Robert says. "I need to go to the bathroom."

Jackie's afraid to let him out of her sight, but she doesn't see any way she can deny Robert time to pee without alerting him to the fact that something is seriously wrong. She sighs and lets go of his elbow.

"You got two minutes," she says.

Robert jogs toward the stairs, leaving his parents alone, staring at each other.

Jackie shakes her head at Rick, telling him to not even think about it. "Not in front of Robert," she says.

He looks at her like a snarling bull, his stare beating into her with the promise that a more physical retribution will follow.

"You think you're so fucking clever," he says. "But you're living on borrowed time, honey. And if I find out that you're heading to that cocksucker boyfriend of yours . . . Well, he's not going to have a cock to suck when I'm done with him."

Robert appears at the top of the stairs. He looks like he's lost.

"Let's go, Robert," Jackie says firmly. "We're late."

Her son looks too afraid to even ask what they could possibly be late for. He's frozen in place, but then Jackie starts toward the stairs, and Robert slowly moves down them. When they meet, she again grabs him by the elbow and begins to pull him toward the door.

The moment she crosses the threshold and leaves her home, Jackie feels like an escaped convict. She's made it out alive, but she's not safe yet.

She won't truly be safe until Rick is dead. She's surer of that now than ever before.

* * *

Once they're in the car and on the road, Jackie tells Robert that she's going to be visiting her mother, and that his father might be traveling for business, so it's best that he stay at Jeremy's house for a few days.

"Why can't I stay home? I'm eighteen."

"Please don't argue, Robert."

"I don't have my clothes or any of my stuff."

Damn. She hadn't thought about that.

"I'll stop at the mall and we'll grab you and your sister something."

"Where's Emma going to be?"

"She's going to stay at Hannah's."

"When will you be back?"

"Sunday."

She can feel her son's gaze zero in on her bruised cheek. Now Robert knows full well the true reason he's staying at Jeremy's and his mother is leaving town.

* * *

After a quick pit stop at the mall, where Jackie buys essentials for her children to survive the next few days—toothbrushes, underwear and socks, two T-shirts and a wool sweater (they can re-wear their jeans, she figures)—she arrives at Jeremy's house. Jackie spins the same lie to Jeremy's mother that she told Robert. She puts her thumb on the scale a bit by claiming that her mother is ill, which is why she can't wait for the weekend to visit, and promises to return by Sunday.

Sharon has no reason to disbelieve the tale. She's known Jackie since their kids were in Pop Warner together and is always happy to help a fellow mom in a jam. "Of course—Robert's always welcome here," she says cheerfully.

From there, Jackie drives to East Carlisle High School to pick up Emma, who had stayed after school for gymnastics practice. Like Robert, Emma doesn't question her mother's explanation as to why she needs to stay at a friend's for the rest of the week, and as with

Robert, Jackie assumes that's because Emma knows the truth behind her mother's hasty departure. Indeed, it's as plain as the swelling on Jackie's face.

Jackie repeats the lie about her own mother's illness to Hannah's mother. Donna appears more suspicious of Jackie's explanation, but that seemingly makes her more receptive to the request. "Jackie . . . if there's anything I can do . . . anything at all, please tell me."

"Thanks," Jackie says. "This is a big help. I'll be back on Sunday, at the latest. I really appreciate that Emma can stay with you."

* * *

Her children in a safe place, Jackie now seeks shelter for herself. She drives to the Hilton hotel, which is located just off the New Jersey Turnpike. It's probably the only building in East Carlisle more than six stories high and has gone through various hotel iterations over the years, but the Hilton designation seems as if it's going to last.

The front desk is manned by a mousy-looking girl. She's the type who likely was teased mercilessly by the popular crowd in high school. Jackie once pitied these girls, but now she'd trade places in a heartbeat.

Jackie asks for a room, but when she seems unsure about how long she's going to stay, the mousy girl looks concerned. Although she's trying to avoid staring, Jackie knows that she's zoomed in on the side of her face that Rick had pressed into the floor. When Jackie says she doesn't have any luggage, she assumes that the clerk has figured out what's going on.

"Can I have your driver's license?"

"I'm going to pay cash," Jackie says.

"It's hotel policy. I need to keep a copy of your driver's license. Also, a credit card . . . you know, for incidentals. In-room movies, phone, room service."

Jackie reaches into her purse and hands over her American Express card and her driver's license. "I'd really rather that no one knows I'm staying here," she says quietly.

"Of course," the clerk says. "We don't give out that type of information."

Jackie's given a room on the fifth floor with a view of the parking garage. Nevertheless, her accommodations are nice enough, with a large flat-screen television and a marble bathroom with a full-size tub.

She puts on only the hot water and squeezes some of the hotel-label body wash into the running faucet. It begins to foam, and she enjoys the floral scent that takes over the room.

Jackie lowers herself into the hot water. It's too hot, and she should run some cold water to temper it, but she welcomes the feeling of pain. First the burning on her feet, then her legs, and then all over as she submerges herself.

Rick has already called her a half dozen times. She didn't answer any of the calls, letting each one go to voice mail. Rick hasn't left any messages. He must not want to leave any evidence of a fight. There's only one reason why he'd care about that: because he was planning on doing something very bad to her.

She didn't care anymore. She was planning to do something bad to him, too. Soon. Very, very soon.

25

For the first time since New Year's Day, it's not cold enough for snow, so a freezing rain falls. Jonathan can't help but see some symbolism that today is going to be as uncomfortable as possible, without any beauty to it.

The Caines lacked any religious affiliation growing up. Jonathan's father wasn't just a nonbeliever but affirmatively opposed religion in any form. Jonathan's mother used the phrase *culturally Jewish* to describe the home in which she'd been reared, by which she meant that her family lit Hanukkah candles and attended someone else's Passover seder.

Amy's husband, Kevin, however, came from an Orthodox Jewish family, and while Amy's family wasn't that observant, they were still more Jewish than any other family Jonathan knew. Amy had handled all of the arrangements for their mother's funeral, as Jonathan had told her he was too busy at work to help, so she had picked a Jewish cemetery and purchased a double plot. Which meant that William Caine was being laid to rest for all of eternity in a Jewish ceremony, too.

At the cemetery, Amy and Jonathan are led into a small room off the main chapel. It's well appointed, with four overstuffed leather armchairs for one sitting area, and behind it a sofa and two other matching chairs. On every hard surface is a box of tissues.

The funeral home director is roughly Jonathan's age, with a bald head and a full beard. Jonathan recognizes him as the same person who handled their mother's arrangements, and nods, but the man displays no similar familiarity.

"Mr. Caine and Ms. . . . . Thacker," he says, looking down at his clipboard to ascertain Amy's married name, "my name is Mr. Stasiak. I am so very sorry for your loss."

He sits in one of the armchairs and immediately gets down to filling in the blanks on the sheet attached to the clipboard. "Your father went by William? Or did his friends know him as Bill or something else?"

"No. William," Amy says.

"And his wife, Linda, she passed . . ." Mr. Stasiak looks back down at his cheat sheet. "Oh, I see it was just this past March. I'm so very sorry again. You'd be surprised how many times I see that pattern. Spouses who have essentially died of broken hearts."

"Well, actually our father had been sick for some time, even before our mother died," Jonathan says.

"Of course," Mr. Stasiak says. His tone conveys he didn't mean the broken heart thing literally. "But when a longtime spouse dies, the survivor sometimes loses the will to live. Now, that may manifest itself in various diseases that become the immediate cause of death, but I truly believe it's the loss they've suffered that's the underlying cause."

Jonathan would just as soon get this part over with, so he doesn't counter the undertaker's romantic notion of death. This allows Mr. Stasiak to ask what William Caine did for a living.

"He owned a furniture store," Amy says.

"I see," Mr. Stasiak answers. "So, he devoted himself to the comfort of others, then?"

"Exactly," Jonathan says, "and at twenty percent less than the competition."

"Jonathan," Amy says.

Neither Jonathan's quip nor Amy's rebuke gives rise to any reaction from Mr. Stasiak. He goes through a few more questions and gets short answers from Amy. When he finally puts down his pen, he asks whether either of them would like to see their father before the service begins.

Amy looks to Jonathan and then says, "No. I don't think I need to see Dad that way."

"I would, please," Jonathan says. "Just for a moment."

"Very well," Mr. Stasiak says. "Follow me, please."

He leads Jonathan through a corridor that ends at a door with a sign that says *No Entry*. Without hesitation, Mr. Stasiak opens the door, and then motions for Jonathan to enter first.

The room is small, with stark white walls and no windows. It's empty, other than a plain pine box on a gurney in the center.

The coffin seems small, too small to hold William Caine. Jonathan's stomach turns at the thought of his father trapped inside that box. Perhaps he's made a mistake, and seeing his father crammed inside is not such a good idea after all.

A large man in dirty jeans and a faded blue work shirt is standing beside the casket. A gravedigger, Jonathan assumes, although he wonders whether that's what they call themselves these days. Mr. Stasiak asks the man to slide down the lid.

"We'll give you a moment," Mr. Stasiak says after the coffin is open.

When he's alone, Jonathan peers into the box. Other than a flimsy, white burial sheet, William Caine wears a quizzical expression, as if he's not sure what to make of being dead. It's the face his father sometimes made after taking the first bite of his entrée in a restaurant, when he was considering whether he'd chosen well.

"Hiya, Dad," Jonathan says. It reminds him a bit of his hospital visits, including the fact that he doesn't expect a response. "I wanted to take one last time to say . . . I'm sorry. Sorry that I wasn't a better son. But I'm very grateful for the last few weeks we had together. I'm trying to follow your advice. To be a better man."

Jonathan leans over and kisses his father's forehead. The moment he touches his lips to his father's flesh, he wishes he hadn't. His father's skin is waxy, and cold to the touch, highlighting that his father is not actually there at all.

* * *

The sanctuary could hold fifty or so people, but there is no one present besides Amy and her family when Jonathan takes his seat beside his sister. Apparently Jackie thought better of coming after all. Jonathan can't deny that he's disappointed, even as he tells himself that she's safer staying away.

"How'd he look?" Amy whispers.

"Peaceful," Jonathan says, because he assumes that's what Amy wants to hear.

A rabbi who doesn't introduce himself, and as best as Jonathan recalls did not officiate at his mother's funeral, begins to chant some prayers in Hebrew. He transitions to English to say something about God's will, and then segues to summarize in thirty seconds William Caine's seventy-four years. He spends the same amount of time confirming that Mr. Caine died of a broken heart, longing to be reunited with his wife.

"Would anyone here like to say a few words?" the rabbi asks, looking at Jonathan and Amy.

Amy turns to Jonathan. "You should say something," she whispers.

Jonathan had not thought about delivering any type of eulogy, especially because he'd essentially be talking solely to Amy and her family. But with his sister prodding him that it was part of the responsibility of being the firstborn, and the rabbi now expecting a family member to deliver some remarks, he feels as if he has no choice in the matter and heads to the stage.

Standing behind the podium, Jonathan sees Jackie in the back of the room. She must have entered after the service began, perhaps because she wanted to minimize the risk that someone would spot her here.

He can feel his heart expand. Just seeing Jackie has that effect on him.

There are three rows of seats vacant before her, but she has apparently decided not to occupy any of them. Instead, she leans against the wall as if she were just walking by and decided to watch a little.

She's wearing a black dress, but even in mourner's garb, Jackie looks spectacularly beautiful. Jonathan pushes away the impure thoughts that Jackie stirs in him and focuses on his father. Not the weak man he always saw him as, or the dementia patient Jonathan's spent the last few weeks with, or the one who didn't know about good scotch, or the cuckold from the family barbecue, but the man he remembers once idolizing.

"I want to tell a story about my father. It's one I've never really told before, and so it should be new even to you, Amy. But it remains one of my earliest memories of him. And Jack and Molly, I think you might like it, too, because it happened when I was four or five, on a day my father took me to the park. Nothing eventful occurred while we were there, but as we're leaving, a man flagged us down, waving his arms over his head." Jonathan acts this part out, his arms swinging as if he's calling for a rescue party. "The man told Dad that there was something wrong with his car, and I could see that it was stuck in the middle of the road. Not in a space or anything, but blocking traffic. As if the car was riding along and then just stopped dead. So Dad tells me to wait on the sidewalk, and that I shouldn't move. I even remember he said that I should hold this tree branch like it was his hand, so I didn't wander off. And he tells the other guy that he'll push the car into a parking space."

Jonathan pauses and smiles. He's brought back to that day in the park so thoroughly that he can actually feel the branch in his hand, the wind in his hair.

"And all I can think is . . . *What?* How on earth is he going to push a car? Does he think he's Superman? So, the other man gets in his car and after rolling down his window, he calls back to Dad, 'Okay, ready.' And my father rubs his hands together and then places them down on the car's trunk and starts to push."

Jonathan allows himself a light chuckle and shakes his head in disbelief. "When that car started to move, it really was like . . . I don't know, but it was no different in my mind than if my father had just lifted off the ground and begun to fly. My father *was* a superhero. End of story. And it didn't take me long to think to myself, This is great, because I'd inherit his superstrength, and maybe other stuff, too. X-ray vision, superspeed, who knows what else? You know . . . I don't recall talking to him about it. Not on the car ride home or after, even. Maybe we did and I just can't remember, but I don't think so, because this idea that my father was a superhero persisted for some time after. I just thought . . . I knew what I saw."

Jonathan begins to choke up but wills himself to say more. "I don't remember when I realized it wasn't true. I remember believing it, and then at some point, I didn't anymore, but I don't recall when it changed from one to the other. Kind of like Santa Claus, I guess."

Jonathan had been alternating his gaze between Amy in the front row and Jackie along the wall in the back, but now his eyes fall to the floor. Everyone is blocked out of the room. And it feels, for a moment, that he's alone with his father again.

"Anyway, for much of the time after I realized my father actually didn't have any special abilities . . . well, I didn't want to be like him at all. He seemed to me to be weak, unsuccessful, just . . . average."

Jonathan clears his throat, to give himself a chance to regain some composure, but it doesn't work, and he begins to break down. The rabbi walks over to the podium and hands Jonathan a small plastic cup with water. Jonathan swallows it in one gulp.

"Thank you," Jonathan says in a quiet voice. "I think I can finish. I'll just be another minute."

The rabbi takes a step back but doesn't return to his seat. Apparently he thinks he'll soon be called on again to assist Jonathan.

"I'm so ashamed that I ever felt that way," Jonathan says, his voice cracking. "But now I know, in a way I sadly did not for so many years, that William Caine *was* a superhero. Even though he couldn't run faster than a speeding bullet or leap tall buildings in a single bound, and even though he wasn't a millionaire or famous or some of the things that back when I was younger I thought mattered, he was a man who was married to the same woman for over forty-seven years. He built a business that kept his family sheltered, clothed, fed, and educated. And in his last breath of life on this earth, he was still teaching his son how to be a better man. What's more heroic than that?"

* * *

After Jonathan returns to his seat, the rabbi concludes the service with a few more prayers, before saying, "The family should follow the casket out of the chapel and toward the burial site, which is a short walk from here. Take an umbrella, because I think it's still raining. There is an awning beside the grave site and so we'll be covered during the short interment ceremony."

Jonathan waits until Amy's family is out of the chapel before kissing Jackie hello. He'd overheard Amy telling her kids that their aunt Natasha was visiting her family back in Russia, which was why she couldn't come to say good-bye to their grandfather, and he'd just as soon not put his sister through the trouble of explaining why there was a new woman holding their uncle Jonathan's hand.

"Thank you for coming," he says to Jackie.

The moment the words come out, he stops short. Her makeup hid the red mark on Jackie's face from a distance, but up close it's obvious. A rage flushes through him.

"Oh my God, Jackie!"

"Yeah, well, it looks worse than it feels."

"That fucking animal!" he says.

"Don't," Jackie says through clenched teeth. "Not here, and not now. I came here for you. Because . . . I don't know, I just wanted to see you and so you'd know that I'm here for you."

"Let me be here for you, too. Don't go back home. Stay with me. We'll figure this out together."

"Thank you, but you have your hands full right now with your sister and her family. And I've got my situation under control. I've made arrangements for the kids to stay with friends for the next few days. I told the mothers that I had a family emergency to attend to, which I guess isn't really a lie. So Robert and Emma are in a safe space while I figure out what to do next."

"And where are you going to stay?"

"I spent last night at the Hilton off the turnpike. I was going to call you, but I knew your sister and her family were staying with you . . . and, I just didn't want you to worry about me."

"I like worrying about you, Jackie. And whether you want me to or not, I'm doing it now. Are you staying at the hotel again tonight?"

"No, I'm going to go see my mother in Baltimore for a few days. I know this may be a lot to ask, but I was hoping I could see you one more time before I left. I kept the room for the night."

The way she says it makes Jonathan think that he's never going to see her again after tonight. He's fearful that she's decided to do something drastic, but figures that this is not the time or the place to enter into such a heavy discussion. He's got to get to the grave site, and he can talk to Jackie tonight.

"I'd love to," Jonathan says.

"Thank you," she says. "I'm in Room 519."

26

After returning to the Hilton, Jackie watches some cheesy daytime television and waits for Jonathan's arrival. She's actually enjoying herself, momentarily forgetting about her troubles, when her phone rings.

Rick's picture comes up on the screen, which makes her too afraid even to touch the phone, for fear that she'll inadvertently answer it. When the ringing stops, she breathes a sigh of relief, but then the phone pings to indicate she has a voice mail.

It's the first message Rick has left since she walked out of their house nearly twenty-four hours ago. She's reluctant to listen to it, paralyzed with the ridiculous fear that Rick could somehow glean her location if she hears his voice. But then reason prevails, and she hits play.

"Jackie," he says, "I'm just calling to tell you that I love you. I really meant what I said last night and I can't wait to see you."

His syrupy voice only adds to the terror of his words. It's a threat and a defense. She now knows with utmost certainty that Rick has decided to kill her. That's the only reason he'd leave this type of message. So that after she's dead, when the police question him, he'll point to this voice mail as proof of how happy they were together. *Of course there was no problem with my wife before she suffered that horrible accident,* she can hear him telling the police. *In fact, we were very much in love. You heard my voice mail message to her, right?*

She smiles with the thought that she's going to turn Rick's message around. *No, Officer, things were fine between Rick and me before his horrible accident. Didn't you hear the sweet message he left for me right before he died?*

* * *

Jonathan arrives at Jackie's hotel room a little before four. He pulls Jackie in to him, but she winces when he touches her in the spot where Rick had used his boot.

"I figure you could use a drink," she says, breaking their embrace. "What if I order us a nice bottle of wine?"

Jonathan's smile tells her that he's not going to reject the idea. She grabs the phone. "Hi, this is Jackie Williams in Room 519. Do you have a really nice bottle of cabernet? . . . Yes. That sounds lovely . . . No, nothing else. Thank you."

"Ten minutes," she says after hanging up the phone.

Jonathan laughs.

"What?" she asks.

"That's too little time for sex," he says.

"We could talk, you know."

"My second-favorite activity with you."

"You pick the topic: politics, art, music, movies?"

"Actually, there was something on my mind. At the funeral, you asked me to come over tonight as if I was never going to see you again. It . . . frankly, it worried me that you might be thinking about doing something drastic."

Jackie laughs, but she can tell at once that her dismissiveness hasn't assuaged Jonathan's concern. To the contrary, by the way Jonathan's jaw clenches she knows she's actually exacerbated it.

"Jackie . . . I'm being serious," he says.

"I know you are, and I love you for it, Jonathan. But no, I haven't gone completely off the deep end. I just wanted to see you tonight. I'm sorry if I worried you. But I'll be coming back from my mother's. I promise."

Jackie considers sharing her plans but concludes that won't do anyone any good. Better for her that Jonathan have plausible deniability about what is to unfold.

Then, as if he could actually read her mind, Jonathan says, "What's the plan, then?"

She feels like she's been caught. "What do you mean?"

"You've bought yourself a few days' reprieve from Rick. Then what?"

Relief settles in. Jonathan has no idea what she's going to set in motion.

She's about to say something about seeing a divorce lawyer again, but before she can get the words out, there's a sharp knock at the door.

"Saved by room service," she says with a laugh.

"That was quick," Jonathan says, jumping up.

He walks across the room and opens the door. It's then that Jackie sees her husband standing in the doorway.

"Mother*fucker*," Rick snarls.

Rick swings hard, smashing his fist into the side of Jonathan's head. Jonathan crumples to the floor, and Rick follows him inside the room, kicking him, the way he'd done to Jackie the day before.

"Stop it!" Jackie screams. "*Stop it!*"

Rick doesn't hesitate, however. He's kicking Jonathan again and again. Screaming at Jackie with each blow.

"I thought you said you weren't fucking around!" he shouts at her. "That must mean that I'm not kicking the living shit out of anybody!"

Jonathan has rolled into a defensive position, but the kicks continue to rip into him. Jackie rushes toward them, trying to stop her husband's onslaught. Rick smacks her across the face with the back of his hand, as if he were taking a swing at a tennis ball, knocking her onto the bed.

Jackie expects to be hit again, this time harder, when she hears two raps on the partially open door.

"Room service," a high-pitched voice says, and then a head belonging to a skinny boy wearing a white hotel uniform sticks into the room.

This freezes Rick, which allows Jonathan time to come to his feet. For a moment, everyone hangs in place, almost as if in suspended animation. Without notice, Rick bolts for the door, pushing so hard past the hotel steward that he knocks him into the wall. Once outside the room, Rick sprints away.

* * *

Jackie can't understand what the hell Rick was thinking with that stunt, except then she realizes the obvious: he *wasn't* thinking. No, he was being his usual hotheaded self. How did he find out where she was? He might have figured out that she was at the Hilton by a process of elimination, or by tracking her car, but how in the hell did he know what room she was in? She flashes on the mousy girl. Did Rick bribe her? Threaten her? If not her, maybe he got another clerk to do his dirty work. And doesn't he know that hotels have security cameras? He'll be on tape now, fleeing out of there.

This last part concerns her. Not only has she created a record of checking into a hotel, which can only mean marital discord, but now Rick will be on the security cameras running from the room. Then she thought about the room service guy. How was it that he didn't hear the fight? Maybe those guys are just programmed to deliver food and not ask questions. Or maybe he thought it was the television or something and didn't realize what he'd interrupted.

The busboy is not more than twenty, tops. He looks shell-shocked. Probably afraid that he's going to get blamed for this. Still, she had to ensure that he didn't tell anyone what he saw. That would ruin everything.

Jackie signs the room service bill with a shaky hand, leaving a thirty-dollar tip for an eighty-dollar charge, even though an eighteen percent service charge was already included. Then she reaches into her purse and pulls out all the money she has—$120—and hands it to him.

"I would greatly appreciate it if you didn't tell anyone about this," she says, still holding the money even though it's also in his grasp. "It would mean a lot to me. Can I count on you?"

"Y-yes," he stammers.

Jackie studies him closely. From the look of abject terror on his face, she discerns that he's more than willing to keep this entire episode to himself rather than become embroiled in her soap opera.

"Good. Thank you. I put a nice tip on the receipt, and this is for you, too," she says, and releases the money into his grasp.

He leaves the room almost as quickly as Rick had a few minutes earlier. When the door closes behind him, she says to herself, *Nothing has changed. Stick with the plan. Rick will be dead soon, and everyone will think it was an accident.*

* * *

Jonathan emerges from the bathroom with a hand towel applied to his mouth. Its corners are speckled with blood.

"I'm so, so sorry, Jonathan," Jackie says. "Do you want some ice?"

What he wants, first and foremost, is to kill Rick Williams. But since that option is not immediately available, he decides that he'll soothe himself with some alcohol.

"Can you see if there's any scotch in the minibar? If not, I'll take whatever is the closest thing."

Jackie opens the fridge and pulls out two small bottles. She pours them both into the glass next to the bar.

"Here you go," Jackie says, and hands Jonathan a glass of brown liquid, the color a deep copper. "I poured you a double."

With the first sip, Jonathan winces. He feels the sting of the alcohol when it seeps into the gash in his mouth.

He didn't see it coming. If he had, he's sure the outcome would have been different. But he opened the door expecting their wine, and when he turned back to Jackie to allow the steward to enter, Rick laid him out with a sucker punch.

His ribs were sore, but he was relatively certain that they were only bruised and not broken. So he brushes off Jackie's request that they go to the hospital.

"How the hell did he find you? You didn't tell him you were here, did you?" Jonathan asks.

"No, of course not. But . . . I don't know, how many hotels do you think there are in East Carlisle? Knowing Rick, he bribed or tricked the desk clerks at all of them until he found me. Or he had me followed."

"I'm going to fucking kill him," Jonathan says.

As the words come out, he recognizes them as the truth, and not just some fantasy playing out in his mind. He *is* going to kill Rick Williams. No doubt about it. The sooner the better.

*   *   *

They decide that staying in the room for a while is the safest course, just in case Rick is lying in wait. At five thirty, Jackie packs up her meager belongings. They leave together, both of them looking around every corner for Rick.

"Give me your keys," Jonathan says once they're downstairs in the hotel lobby. "I'll get your car and pull right up to the front."

She nods that she understands why that's the safest course. "I parked about three rows back, to the left," she says, handing him the keys.

As he walks through the parking lot, Jonathan's on careful watch. He's not going to get sucker-punched twice by that bastard. That's for damn sure.

There's no stir of activity, however. So he pulls Jackie's minivan up to the hotel entrance, and Jackie and he switch positions. Outside the vehicle, Jonathan leans into the open window.

"You be safe, and call me when you get to your mother's," he says.

"I will. You be safe, too."

And then she kisses him on the mouth, and he winces.

27

I t shouldn't take more than four hours to drive from East Carlisle to Baltimore. Even allotting for time if Jackie stopped somewhere on the road for a snack, she still should have arrived at her mother's no later than ten.

It's now eleven, and Jonathan still hasn't heard from her.

Each of his phone calls has gone straight to voice mail. Her phone must be off, or she's in a place with no reception.

At least that's what he hopes is the explanation. He can't rule out that she decided to stop at home first. To pick up clothes or something, and that Rick finished what he started.

* * *

Before she even enters her mother's house, Jackie calls Jonathan from the driveway. "I'm so sorry" is the first thing she says. "I turned my phone off because . . . I know this is crazy, but I was worried that Rick might be able to find me if it was on. So I bought a prepaid one at a rest stop on the highway. It's got like two hundred minutes on it, so I should be good for a while with this number. And then I hit traffic at the toll before the Delaware Bridge, and it was bumper to bumper for like an hour before the Harbor Tunnel."

"I'm just glad you're safe, Jackie. I was starting to freak out a bit."

"I'm so sorry, Jonathan. I didn't . . . I just didn't think. To be honest, it's been a very long time since anyone worried about me, and I'm out of practice about what that means. But thank you. Really. It means a lot to me. I haven't even seen my mom yet, so let me go talk to her. I'll call you in the morning, okay?"

"Okay. I love you, Jackie."

These are the words she's longed to hear. And they couldn't have come at a better time.

"I love you, too," she says.

* * *

Jackie sometimes told people that she and her mother had a complicated relationship, but as Jackie got older, and her own children grew, Jackie wondered whether maybe the fault was hers. Perhaps she had been too demanding.

Her mother divorced her father thirty seconds after Jackie left for college, which only reinforced Jackie's perception that her parents' marriage had been miserable for years. After Jackie's maternal grandmother died, Jackie's mother inherited her house outside Baltimore and relocated there to start her life anew.

At the time, Jackie resented that her mother didn't sell the house and stay in East Carlisle, but Jackie understands now what she did not then. Her mother wanted to be free to live her own life, and that meant she had to go back to where people remembered her for being *her*, and not solely as a wife and mother. She sees the irony now all too clearly: her mother went home to come into her own, while Jackie's return to East Carlisle snuffed out whatever chance she had of being the person she aspired to be.

That was sixteen years ago. Jackie still thought of this place as Grandma's house. And a lot of it hasn't changed from when Jackie was a girl. The kitchen still looks like it's out of *Mad Men*, and she can still see remnants of the stain on the rug from when she kicked over a glass of wine when she was six. But there's a charm to the place that Jackie didn't appreciate when she was younger, when it just seemed like an old lady's house.

Jackie called her mother on the drive down, asking whether she could come to visit for a few days. Her mother asked what was wrong, and Jackie had simply said that she and Rick had a fight, and she needed some time to decompress. Her mother let it rest there, but

Jackie knew there would be a more thorough cross-examination to come.

As soon as Jackie enters her mother's home, her mother's eyes go straight to the side of Jackie's face on which Rick had inflicted damage.

"Oh my God," her mother says.

"It's not as bad as it looks," Jackie says.

"Did Rick do this to you?"

Jackie nods.

"That bastard. You can't stay with him."

"I know, Mom. I know. That's why I'm here."

"Are the kids okay? Does he hit them?"

"They're fine, too. They're with friends for the rest of the week."

Jackie has never felt so ashamed. Her mother's look is the one Jackie recalls from high school when she came home an hour after curfew. Complete and utter disappointment.

"Did you call the police?"

"No."

"Why the hell not?"

"It's complicated, Mom."

"It isn't, Jackie."

"I want to think through my options before I do anything that I might regret, okay? I've just driven five hours, and it's late, and I'm exhausted. I promise we can talk about this as much as you want tomorrow, but right now I really just want to crawl into bed and go to sleep."

Her mother's response is a frown, followed by a disappointed shake of her head. This gesture, too, Jackie recalls from her high school days.

"Okay," her mother says. "Sleep well. But tomorrow, we are definitely going to talk about this."

Jackie is thankful for the reprieve, so she capitulates to her mother's terms. After hugging her mother good night, Jackie heads upstairs to the room she stayed in whenever she visited, her mother's childhood bedroom. Jackie always enjoyed sleeping here as a child, imagining her mother at her age, playing with her dolls on the floor, sleeping in the same bed.

Tonight she hopes that she'll fall quickly asleep, but she's not that lucky. Instead she lies awake, thinking about the life she has and the life she wants. They're so far away right now, but she's hoping that soon, maybe very soon, they will merge.

28

Rick Williams wasn't at all happy about not being able to reach his wife, although that disappointment was nothing compared to his anger that the fucking room-service guy interrupted his kicking the shit out of that scumbag Johnny Caine. The guy was an absolute nothing in high school. Didn't even register. Unless you were on the chess team or into astronomy. It was just like Jackie to go for that type of asshole. Thinks he's worth fucking because he went to some college with ivy on the walls.

Rick soothes himself with the thought that his bitch of a wife can't hide forever. She's going to have to come back for the kids, and for the time being, he's just as happy to have the house to himself. In fact, after the fireworks at the hotel, he decided to give Brittney a good fuck in his marital bed. And he's got no interest in changing the sheets, either. Let Jackie do it, the whore.

Rick's even thinking that maybe he'll bring Brittney back again tonight. Nothing he'd like more than to have his wife walk in on them going at it.

The one thing Rick knows for certain is that when his slut for a wife does show her face, she's going to be in for a world of pain. He no longer cares about leaving a mark. In fact, he wants to brand her so the world will know that she couldn't get away with the shit she was doing. After Jackie has been dealt with, he'll turn his attention to cutting the balls off Johnny Caine. He wishes he'd saved the scumbag's cell phone number from when he called him last week because at least then he'd be able to let little-boy Johnny know what was going to befall him.

He figures that he can find out where the guy lives easily enough, though. His Google search indicated a New York City address, but Rick doubts that this prick is coming through the tunnel to fuck his wife. He must be local now. If need be, he'll call Caine's old man and pretend he was Johnny's asshole buddy from back in the day and he's trying to reconnect.

First things first. Jackie is the top priority. So that morning, on his way to work, he dials her up. Of course, he fully expects Jackie's going to let the call go to voice mail, just like she has every other call.

After four rings, that's what he gets.

"Hey there, sweetie. I just wanted to hear your voice. I love you."

He's laughing out loud after he disconnects the call. Jackie will know the coded language. Only an idiot would threaten his wife before beating the crap out of her. Jackie will find this message twice as terrifying as any threat he could make.

Rick steps out of his truck with a self-satisfied smirk on his face. Nobody but nobody gets the better of Rick Williams, he thinks to himself. And those who try . . . well, they regret it in a hurry.

Rick doesn't see the weapon that ends his life until it's already speeding toward him. By the time it registers as a threat, it's too late. The truck closes in within a second. No time to even move one way or the other. It's just barely enough time for the thought to register that he's seriously underestimated his wife in the worst way.

Part Three

29

Jackie woke to see that she'd received yet another voice mail from Rick. Same modus operandi as before.

"Hey there, sweetie. I just wanted to hear your voice. I love you."

She didn't delete it. It may come in handy.

* * *

When Jackie comes downstairs, she follows the aroma of the coffee and finds her mother sitting at the kitchen table. She doesn't have a newspaper or other reading material beside her, just a mug of coffee. It's as if she's been waiting patiently for Jackie to come down and explain to her why she's still married to a wife-beater.

"Good morning, Mom," Jackie says brightly.

"Did you sleep well, sweetheart?"

"I did."

Jackie helps herself to a cup of coffee, but she can't find the sugar in her mother's kitchen and has to open several cupboards before her mother says, "It's the one over the sink."

"Thanks," Jackie says, and then opens the refrigerator and pulls out the milk.

"Are you ready to talk now?" her mother asks as Jackie sits down at the table.

"As ready as I'll ever be, I suppose."

"So, tell me."

Jackie shrugs. "There's really nothing to say that you don't already know, or couldn't have guessed. Rick's a son of a bitch. He drinks too much, he chases anything in a skirt, and he's got a temper. The trifecta.

The other day we got into a fight about something and he hit me. And I decided enough was enough. I arranged for the kids to be with friends for the rest of the week, and I ran away to see you. End of story."

Her mother takes in this information without showing much reaction besides offering a soft nod of support. But when Jackie's finished with her tale of woe, her mother takes her hand. Jackie enjoys the warmth of her mother's touch, which was intensified because her mother had been cradling her own coffee cup in her hands.

"I'm proud of you, Jackie," her mother finally says.

Jackie laughs. "It doesn't take much to get hit. You just need a face."

"You know what I mean. I'm proud of you because you realize that you're worth more than that. I'm proud of you because you're able to fix things when they need to be fixed. And I'm proud of you that you're not going to take Rick's shit anymore."

"I'm glad you're proud. I'm just ashamed. How did I ever let things come to this?"

Jackie's mother offers a sympathetic smile. "I think that's what everyone says before things get better, right? There's no shame in finding yourself in a bad situation, Jackie. The shame is in being in that situation and not doing anything to fix it."

Jackie nods that she understands. She wonders whether her mother will still be proud of her when she realizes how Jackie had decided to fix this problem.

* * *

Jackie's mother's favorite place to eat breakfast is the Flashback Diner. They go there every time Jackie visits. Sometimes more than once. It's about a five-minute car ride away from her mother's house and is hard to miss from the street on account of the fact that it has mirrored siding. There's a life-size cutout poster of Elvis beside the door, and to the King's left is a case full of desserts of every conceivable variety.

The hostess tells them to take any seat they'd like, and they find a four-top near the window to call their own. They both ask for coffee, and the waitress returns with a small coffeepot for them to pour themselves. Jackie's mother orders a Greek omelet, which has been her standard diner breakfast for as long as Jackie could remember. Jackie is not one to throw stones on this issue, as she selects egg whites with tomato, her invariable selection.

As soon as the waitress leaves, Jackie's cell phone rings. She expects to see Rick's number on her caller ID, but instead it reads: *Unknown Caller*.

"Hello," Jackie says tentatively.

"May I speak to Jacqueline Williams, please?"

It's a man's voice. Very serious sounding.

"This is she."

"Mrs. Williams, my name is Detective Quincy Martin. I'm a police officer with the East Carlisle Police Department. Are you currently at home?"

"No. I'm at my mother's in Baltimore. Is something wrong? Are my kids okay?"

It's enough of a cue that her mother whispers, "What's wrong?" but Jackie shakes the question away.

"Yes, ma'am, they're fine," the detective says.

"Okay . . . so what is this about?"

"I'm sorry to have to tell you this over the phone, Mrs. Williams, but there was an accident at your husband's workplace and he's been killed."

She's silent, uncertain of what to say. Finally she manages, "How?"

"Your husband was crossing the street in front of his place of business, and he was struck by an SUV. Unfortunately, the driver fled the scene."

Jackie exhales deeply. It feels like she's in a dream. So much so that she's tempted to pinch herself, but she doesn't because, if it's not real, she has no desire to wake up.

"Mrs. Williams, are you still there?" Detective Martin says.

"Yeah. I'm . . . I'm sorry."

"We would greatly appreciate it if you came back to East Carlisle right away. Please come directly to the police station."

"Um, okay. I'll be there as soon as I can."

She disconnects the call and places the cell phone on the table beside her. Her mother is saying something, but Jackie has tuned it out. She's completely and utterly focused on the fact that Rick is finally dead. It's no longer a fantasy. Her nightmare is over. She's free.

*   *   *

"Who was that? Where will you be as soon as you can?" Jackie's mother says.

The words pull Jackie out of her trance. After taking a deep breath, she says, "That was the police. Rick . . . he's dead. A hit-and-run accident, they said."

"Oh my God, Jackie," her mother says.

Jackie suspects her mother doesn't believe it was an accident. The odds of Rick being killed by a random motorist only the day after he struck Jackie seem astronomically high not to find the two connected. Still, abusive husbands are sometimes the victims of fatal accidents, so who is she to say that her mother's initial impulse must be to assume murder?

"I need to go back to East Carlisle."

"I'll come with you," her mother says.

"No," Jackie says quickly. Then more softly, "Thank you, but . . . I'd like to do this alone. I need to go straight to the police station, and then after that, I'll need to tell the kids, so . . ."

"You're going to talk to the police?"

The question's tone implies the correct answer—Jackie should not talk to the police. The reason is self-evident: Jackie's mother believes Jackie is a murderer.

Will the police be equally quick to reach that conclusion? Jackie thinks not. They won't know that Rick was the kind of guy who should have been killed long ago. So there's no reason for them to see this as anything but a random hit-and-run accident.

"They asked me to come in," Jackie says. "I can't say no."

"Maybe . . . I don't know . . . maybe you should call a lawyer."

It was a good idea, obviously. Yet Jackie knew it was going to be tucked away with all the other advice her mother had dispensed over the years that she'd rejected. Number one on that list was not to marry Rick in the first place.

"No, I can't do that. How many wives of victims of hit-and-run accidents do you think immediately get a lawyer?"

Her mother sighs deeply, apparently understanding the logic of Jackie's position, if not accepting its correctness. "Just be careful, Jackie," she says.

This advice Jackie plans to take fully to heart.

*   *   *

Jonathan recognizes the number of Jackie's burner phone. He answers immediately. "Hello."

"God, it's good to hear your voice," she says.

Jonathan can tell at once that something's off. Jackie sounds scared.

"Are you okay?"

"I'm fine. But Rick's dead."

For a moment, Jonathan's not sure he heard her right. Could it actually be true? Rick dead?

"Hit-and-run accident," Jackie says without inflection before Jonathan can form a question. Although if he had been given more time, *How?* would not have been what he asked.

"I'm going to the East Carlisle police station now," Jackie continues. "But I wanted to call you right away. You need to be careful now."

You need to be careful?

Why would she say that? Does she think he ran down Rick?

Maybe she does. After all, at the hotel he promised to kill Rick. And he meant it, too.

But he didn't kill Rick. He assumed she did, but if she's not taking credit for it, then maybe Rick was really the victim of a random hit-and-run.

And then a darker explanation comes into focus. Maybe Jackie did the deed but is now trying to pin the murder on him.

"Jonathan," she says, as if it's a completed thought.

"Yes."

"It's going to be hard to stay away from you, but we shouldn't be seen together for a while. We can still talk—just call me on this number, okay?"

Jonathan wonders whether he should get a burner phone, too. That would make him look guilty, he thinks. Besides, if his contact with Jackie is hidden through her burner phone, he doesn't need one.

"Okay," he says.

"And Jonathan . . . I love you."

He doesn't want to confirm that he's in love with Jackie, for fear that if she is recording him, it would be an admission. Then again, he doesn't want to give her any reason to distrust him, either.

"Me, too," he says.

30

Jackie's last visit to the East Carlisle police station was on a fourth-grade field trip. It's still located in the same complex of buildings as it was back then, across the pond where she ice-skated as a girl, with the public library right beside it.

A female officer introduces herself, but Jackie doesn't catch her name. The officer leads Jackie through the squad room, where the detectives sit in cubicles on the perimeter of the room with an oval conference table in the center. The cinder-block walls are a dingy gray and badly in need of a touch-up, and the smell of stale coffee permeates the air.

Jackie's taken to a small, windowless room. Pushed up against the wall is a metal table surrounded by three metal chairs. A video camera is perched midway up the corner of the wall, which is enough to identify that the space is used for interrogations.

She looks to see whether the camera is on. No red light, but that doesn't mean anything. Do the police have to tell her whether they're taping? Is that a question an innocent person would ask? Even if they are taping, it's not as if she's going to leave or change her story. *Just act as if it's on*, she tells herself.

The officer leaves her alone, shutting the door behind her. A moment later, Jackie's solitude is broken by a loud succession of knocks on the door. Before she can say "Come in," the door swings opens. That must be the police's way of saying that she's in their house, and they don't need her permission to enter.

The man who enters first introduces himself as Detective Quincy

Martin. Jackie remembers the name as belonging to the cop who told her on the phone that Rick was dead.

Her initial impression is that Detective Martin is a former jock, a conclusion she reaches simply by the swagger with which he approaches her, and yet she's nearly certain of its validity. Former high school gods now in their forties is something of a specialty of hers. It gives Jackie a feeling that she might have a slight advantage over him, until she realizes that he's probably equally well versed in the psyches of fortysomething former homecoming queens.

She further assumes Detective Martin's sport was basketball. He has a tall, lanky frame that wouldn't lend itself to success on the gridiron; dark, round eyes that leave no doubt he sees things that others don't; and a thoughtful mouth, which is surrounded by a beard flecked with gray. His scalp is shaved smooth. He must have gotten tired of going bald and just decided to be done with it.

Beside Detective Martin is a younger man wearing the policeman blues. His face is so innocent that Jackie can imagine him blushing if he heard an off-color joke. The name tag beside his shield says *Officer Romatowski*.

The detective sits closer to Jackie, and his more junior colleague across from her. Romatowski takes out a pad. It's one of those big leather-covered ones, like the police use to write tickets.

"Mrs. Williams, I'm very sorry for your loss," Detective Martin says.

"Thank you," Jackie says.

She wishes she could will herself to cry, but she's not that talented an actor. Instead she rubs her eyes, hoping the gesture conveys the same sense of grief as actual tears.

"We really don't know very much about what happened," Detective Martin says. "Your husband was struck by what witnesses identified as a black SUV. There's some discrepancy about the model. None of the witnesses could recall any of the numbers in the license plate, although one of them told us they thought it had New Jersey tags."

Jackie nods, considering what the proper reaction to this news would be if she was actually in mourning. She decides that a loving wife would accept this explanation at face value and not inquire any further.

"Is there any way I can help?" she asks. "With the investigation, I mean."

In her head, this sounded better. To her ear it's a non sequitur. What could she possibly do to help with the investigation of a hit-and-run accident?

Detective Martin either didn't pick up on anything being amiss or he has a world-class poker face, because his expression shows no negative reaction to Jackie's offer. Instead he gives her a warm smile and says, "Thank you. That's a very kind offer. And we may need your help down the road. But right now, what we need for you to do, unfortunately, is to make an identification of your husband."

A moment of panic overtakes Jackie. Could it be possible Rick isn't dead? That it's some type of mistaken identity?

As if he can read her thoughts, Detective Martin says, "The identification is something of a formality because we know it's him. His employees identified him at the scene, and he was carrying his driver's license. But we need a family member to do it officially. Before I do that, however, I need to ask you a few questions. Standard inquiries, but it's a box I need to check, I'm afraid."

Jackie hadn't expected the police to question her about a hit-and-run accident that occurred when Jackie was close to two hundred miles away. She plays out in her head an attempt to decline. *I'm so sorry, but I can't answer any questions now . . .* No, that won't work. *Focus,* Jackie commands herself. *You're supposed to be a grieving spouse in shock. Just play that part.*

Jackie rubs her eyes again. "Okay."

Detective Martin asks a flurry of basic background questions: date of birth, address, marriage date, names and ages of her children. Jackie provides short answers to each, seemingly to Detective Martin's satisfaction, because after the preliminaries are completed, he says, "Okay, then. Why don't we head on over to the morgue."

* * *

Jackie had expected that the morgue would be downstairs in the basement of the East Carlisle Police Department, but Detective Martin tells her that the facility is actually a ten-minute ride away. She turns down his offer of a ride, telling him that she'd prefer to follow him in her car so she can go straight home afterward to break the news to her children.

The identification is just like the ones she's seen on television. Detective Martin leads her into a sterile-looking room with cement floors and a drain in the center. There's a single gurney in it, with a body—Rick's body—in a blue bag lying on top.

Jackie rubs her biceps, more out of nervousness than because she's chilly, although the morgue is at least ten degrees cooler than normal room temperature. The air smells like some type of disinfectant, but the odor isn't as unpleasant or as strong as she'd imagined it would be.

"Ready?" Detective Martin asks.

Jackie nods, all the while thinking that this is her star turn. Should she break down? Turn away? Play the stoic?

He unzips the bag down to the base of Rick's throat. Rick doesn't look like he's sleeping, which is how she had imagined this scene unfolding. He's bluer than she had anticipated, the color of a vein almost. He must have been bleeding from the scalp, because his hair looks matted. Rick was nothing if not meticulous about his hair.

She looks at Detective Martin as she tries to will herself to cry. No dice. The tears aren't coming, so she falls back to the eye rub again, while turning away from Rick's corpse for effect.

"Yes, that's Rick," she says. "That's my husband."

* * *

Jackie considers picking her kids up at school to break the news, but decides to allow them to finish their day so she can tell them in the comfort of their home. She texts them that she's back from their grandmother's house, and asks them to come straight home after school.

As soon as Robert and Emma arrive home, Jackie asks them to sit down in the living room. "I have something I need to talk to you both about," she says.

From the looks on their faces, they appear to be expecting bad news. It occurs to her that they likely think the news is about their grandmother. After all, that was Jackie's pretense for shipping them off to their friends—that her mother had taken ill.

"Your father was killed today," she says softly. "A hit-and-run traffic accident near his office."

She leans over to hug Emma, and out of the corner of her eye spies Robert. He doesn't seem the least bit distressed. Even Emma, who still cries over animated movies, hasn't been moved to tears and pulls away from her mother after a few seconds. Her eyes are bone dry.

"I'm going to hold the wake at the church, and then the funeral will be the day after tomorrow," Jackie explains. "You should tell your friends so you have your own support network. You'll stay home from school the rest of the week, but next week I think you should go back. When my father died, I wasn't all that much older than you two, and I found it really helpful to get back to my regular routine as soon as possible."

Neither Robert nor Emma says anything. Jackie can't discern whether that's because they are trying to hold it together or because they feel no sense of grief over their father's passing. She strongly suspects it's the latter—Robert and Emma knew full well the horrors of living under the same roof as Rick Williams.

"Are you guys okay?" Jackie finally asks.

Robert speaks first. "Yes," he says in a strong voice.

Jackie turns to Emma.

"I don't think it's going to be for us like it was for you when your father died," Emma says. "And not because it's going to be worse because we're younger. I mean, you and your father were really close, and . . . I don't know."

Jackie pulls her daughter back in to her. "The three of us, we're going to be better now. I promise."

Robert leans in to participate in the group hug. Jackie can hardly believe it, but her main emotion is disappointment. She's sorry she didn't murder the son of a bitch years ago.

* * *

Jonathan hasn't left the house since Jackie called that morning to tell him that Rick was dead. He's spent the day watching television and eating Domino's Pizza—and waiting for Jackie to report on her visit with East Carlisle's finest. That call—from Jackie's burner phone— finally comes at ten that evening.

"I was starting to worry," he says.

"I'm sorry. I didn't want to call until the kids were in bed."

"So . . . how did it all go today?"

"Fine." She lets slip out a small laugh. "That sounds so awful, right? It went fine. Identifying Rick's dead body went fine. Telling my kids that their father was dead went fine. But it did. I actually think that they were as relieved as I was. Christ, can you imagine? That's what I should put on that asshole's tombstone. His wife and kids were relieved that he was finally dead."

Jonathan weighs his next words, hearing them in his head before committing to them. "Jackie . . . did you kill him?"

She doesn't hesitate. "Yes. Not directly, of course. But I hired a guy who did it, so . . . yes, I killed him."

Even though Jonathan knew that was what had happened, hearing Jackie say it still rocks him. In his wildest dreams, Jonathan hadn't imagined Jackie capable of murder.

"I'm not going to say I did it for us," she continues, "but now we can finally be together. If you'll still have me, I mean."

He's slow to answer, grappling to get his mind around the change of circumstances. It's a question he never thought he'd ponder: Can he love a murderer?

"Jonathan, I'm scared. And not just about the police. But about you too. For the next . . . I don't know how long . . . we won't be able to see each other, and I . . . I know it's a lot for me to ask, but I need to know that you're with me."

Jonathan exhales loudly. It is a lot to ask. Then again, not so much when it's being asked by someone you love.

"Yes. Yes. I'm with you," he says.

31

Jackie attributes the large turnout at the funeral more to the fact that Rick never lived anywhere other than East Carlisle than that he was actually liked by any of the attendees. Rick didn't have much family. He was an only child. His mother died before Emma was born, and he hadn't spoken to his father since long before that, despite the fact that the elder Mr. Williams lived only one town over. Rick always claimed their estrangement was because his old man was an abusive alcoholic asshole, and Jackie believed him; something in the gene pool, she figured. Rick's father didn't attend the mother's funeral, so Jackie had no reason to think that he'd appear to say his final good-bye to his son, either.

Most of the people she recognizes, although every time she sees a halfway attractive woman, she assumes it's one of Rick's mistresses. Brittney's there, in a middle pew wearing a too-tight little black dress. The whore.

During the service, Jackie sits between her children, holding their hands, as the priest talks about a man she never knew. A kind man. A loving husband and father.

She told Jonathan to stay away, explaining that it was too risky for him to come. He agreed, and when he did she felt a pang of disappointment. She had hoped he'd put up a fight, arguing with her that many people from their high school graduating class would be there, so his attendance would not give rise to any suspicion. When he so quickly accepted the logic of her position, it occurred to Jackie that Jonathan may have his own reasons for keeping his distance. Perhaps he'd reconsidered a life with her. After all, it wasn't the smartest move to marry someone who had committed mariticide.

After the service, there's a procession to the cemetery. It's only twenty minutes away, but someone had the idea that it would be a fitting tribute to Rick if the hearse passed by the East Carlisle football field, and Jackie was in no position to disagree, even though it means extending this charade another ten minutes.

The ceremony at the grave site is mercifully short. Finally, the priest utters the closing benediction, and Rick's casket is lowered into the ground.

It is all Jackie can do not to smile.

*   *   *

Detective Martin wasn't at the service. Jackie's almost certain of it. Rick didn't have any African American friends, and she feels confident she would have noticed him among the sea of white faces. He must have been waiting until after it was over to corner her, because there he was standing in front of the cemetery's business office, blocking the only way to the parking lot from the grave site.

"Mrs. Williams, I'm very sorry for this intrusion," Detective Martin says as she approaches.

Jackie is flanked by her children, with her mother a step behind. Although Jackie would prefer not to, she has no choice but to engage Detective Martin.

"How are you?" she says, careful not to call him by title.

"I'm fine, thank you. I realize that today is a difficult day for you, but I was hoping that you could give me just a few minutes. I've spoken to Mr. Graham, and he said that we could use his office."

Jackie doesn't know who Mr. Graham is, although she assumes he's connected with the cemetery, and he apparently has an office. Office or no, Jackie knows that Detective Martin's tracking her down is not a good sign.

"I need to get back to the house," Jackie says. "People are going there after the service."

"This will only take a few minutes, Mrs. Williams, and I wouldn't be here if it wasn't very important that we get some information right now."

Jackie understands Detective Martin's subtext. He's not really asking. If she declines, he'll make that clear, perhaps by placing her under arrest. With her children beside her, that's the last thing Jackie wants.

"I'll only be a minute," Jackie says to her children. Then, turning to her mother, she adds, "Will you take the kids and wait in the car?"

Robert looks at his mother, his face full of concern. Emma, who hadn't cried once during the service, has been brought to the verge of tears by the thought her mother will be detained.

Jackie turns to Detective Martin, willing him to confirm her estimate of the delay, and hopefully bring some comfort to her children.

"It'll just be a few minutes," he says.

* * *

Mr. Graham's office is tastefully decorated—leather-bound books on the shelves, a grand mahogany desk with a green shaded lamp, and a chesterfield sofa in brown leather. Detective Martin turns around one of the guest chairs facing the desk, so that it's now in the direction of the sofa. He gestures with his arm that Jackie should have a seat on the sofa. After a moment's hesitation, she complies.

"Thank you for giving me a few minutes, Mrs. Williams. Something has come up, and we wanted to address it as soon as possible."

"Okay," Jackie says. She does the eye-rub thing again. Even she assumes this act is getting old by now.

"We know there was a domestic disturbance call that brought the police to your house a few days before your husband's death. I got to be honest with you, I'm very concerned that you didn't mention that when we met. I would have thought you would have found that rather important."

Jackie can feel panic set in, but she quells it. *Stay in character*, she tells herself.

"I . . . I don't really understand what difference it would make if there was a crank call or whatever sending the police to our house right before a hit-and-run driver killed Rick."

"The significance, Mrs. Williams, is that you didn't tell us about this crank call."

Detective Martin says this like a disappointed parent. There was something in the way he said the word—*crank*—that told her loud and clear that he didn't believe it was a crank. He has *her* in his sights. She just knows he does.

"I'm sorry, Detective. I honestly didn't think the call had anything to do with Rick's accident. Probably I was in more than a little bit of shock when we spoke, and I wasn't thinking clearly. But now that you connect them, of course. Maybe someone was out to get Rick, and so they called the police to have him arrested, and when that didn't work, they killed him. So, again, I'm very sorry for not sharing that with you. There's nothing else that comes to mind right now that I think you should know, but I will go over the last few weeks and rack my brains to see if there's any other information I can provide. Unfortunately, at this moment I really need to take care of my children. They're waiting for me, having just laid their father to rest, and so I really have to get back to them. I'm sure you understand."

Without waiting for Detective Martin to confirm that he understands Jackie's maternal obligations, Jackie rises and walks toward the door. With each step, her entire body trembles. She wants to look over her shoulder to see Detective Martin's reaction, but she knows that she shouldn't. She feels like a tightrope walker, her eyes on the goal—the door. If she makes it there, she can shut him out.

Even so, she knows he's onto her. Now he's going to start digging, and when he does, he's going to find out about Jonathan.

* * *

That evening, after everyone had finally left her house, Jackie's mother asks about the man Jackie was speaking to after the funeral. The "nice-looking black man," her mother calls him.

"Just a friend of Rick's," Jackie lies. Before her mother can cross-examine her further, Jackie says, "Mom, I'm going to go for a little walk. Just to clear my head."

Her mother's face reveals that she finds this as believable as the nice black man being Rick's friend. Among his other fine qualities, Jackie's mother knew Rick to be a racist.

"Are you sure? It's freezing outside."

"I need some fresh air," Jackie says. "I won't be more than ten minutes. One lap around the block."

* * *

Jackie bundles herself up, but more important than her scarf and gloves is her burner phone. As soon as she's two houses over, she calls Jonathan.

The sound of his voice is a balm, soothing her frazzled nerves. None of her problems seem insurmountable when she's with Jonathan, even if only on the phone.

"I only have a few minutes," she says, "but I wanted to tell you right away that after the service, a police detective cornered me." She pauses, allowing Jonathan to prepare for what she's about to disclose. "He knows about the domestic disturbance call at my house."

"What about it?"

"That it happened."

"Does he know that I'm the one who called?"

She wishes his first response had been concern for her well-being, rather than for his own self-preservation. "I don't think so," she says. "He didn't mention your name."

"Okay, okay. That's good. So long as they don't know about us, you don't really have a motive. They don't know about the abuse, right? You never reported it or told anyone. So that's a dead end. But if they find out about us, everything changes. Our affair gives you a motive."

Jackie knows that's right, but it's also incomplete. If the police discover the affair, it gives Jonathan a motive, too. He may be trying to sound calm, but she can hear the fear in his voice.

And that leaves her with a question for which she doesn't know the answer: What will that fear make Jonathan do?

32

The doorbell wakes Jonathan. According to his cell phone it's nine o'clock, and he hasn't slept that late in months. Then again, he hadn't drifted off until well after four.

Jonathan knows the chimes foretell bad news. No one ever visits him other than Jackie, and she's made it clear that they shouldn't be seen together for a while. If she's paying him a visit now, that can only mean trouble.

He peers out the upstairs window. It's not Jackie, but that doesn't change his initial impression that trouble has come calling. His guests are two men in suits who have arrived in a dark, four-door sedan. He flashes on the FBI agents who visited him on New Year's Day.

It's not them, but these guys also reek of law enforcement.

When he opens the door, Jonathan can see that the men are wearing their badges front and center, affixed to the lapels of their overcoats. Jonathan takes that as yet another bad sign. Uniform cops, at least, would mean that someone had determined that this visit required a lower degree of attention.

"Jonathan Caine?" the older of the two men asks.

He's got a full head of salt-and-pepper hair and a bushy mustache of the same color combination. He's wearing a camel-colored overcoat that goes well past the knee, which means it's at least five years old, and might even be ten.

"Yes," Jonathan says.

"Good morning, sir," the salt-and-pepper man says. "My name is Detective Gerald McGeorge. This is Lucas Swensen."

Swensen looks to be under thirty. He has a vacant expression that suggests he's not the sharpest knife in the drawer, but at least his overcoat stops at the knee.

"Do you mind if we come in?" Detective McGeorge asks. "We'll only take up a few minutes of your time."

Jonathan knows the answer to this question should be a resounding no. And yet he says, "What's this about?"

Detective McGeorge scrunches up his face. He might as well have just said that people with nothing to hide don't ask questions, they invite the police in.

"It's about Rick Williams. You went to high school with him, didn't you?"

Jonathan smiles. "Yeah. A million years ago."

"It's cold out here, Mr. Caine. Do you mind if we come in?"

The moment of truth. It doesn't take a mind reader to figure out that they're sniffing around for whether he and Jackie were having an affair. If he shuts them out, they'll know the answer for sure. Jonathan decides it's worth the risk to take a shot at disabusing them of that notion.

"Sure, come on in," he says.

His parents' house is what's referred to as a split-level, which meant a four-stair climb to the living room, but the den was adjacent to the foyer. Ever since Jonathan can remember, guests were always brought to the living room. Jonathan, however, shows the police into the den. The furniture in that room is less comfortable, so Jonathan's hoping that means their stay will be shorter.

An early indication that the police intend to stay longer than Jonathan would prefer is that the younger cop, Swensen, takes off his overcoat, placing it on his lap as he sits down. Detective McGeorge, at least, leaves his on and takes the spot next to his partner.

Jonathan stands above them, not wanting to settle in. Detective McGeorge says, "Please, sit down, too, Mr. Caine," as if he's the host in this situation. With little choice, Jonathan takes a seat in the armchair that had the best view of the television.

"So, what can I help you with?" Jonathan asks with as much of an *I have no idea why you're here* smile as he can muster.

"You can tell us about your relationship with Jacqueline Williams," Detective McGeorge says flatly.

Jonathan continues to wear the same stupid expression that suggests he's completely in the dark. "Uh, not too much to tell. We went to high school together, but barely talked back then. Not in the same social circle. We got reacquainted at my class's twenty-fifth reunion, which was about a month ago. I had just moved back to East Carlisle to tend to my father, who was a patient at Lakeview at the time, but he recently passed. Anyway, we had lunch once or twice, talked on the phone a few times. That's about it."

"You know her husband was killed a few days ago?"

"Yes. I heard. As you said, Rick Williams was also in my high school class at East Carlisle."

"Who told you about Mr. Williams's death?"

Jonathan hadn't anticipated the question. "I don't remember," he says. "I think I read it online somewhere."

Jonathan has a momentary fit of panic. Maybe it wasn't online anywhere.

No one says anything for a good thirty seconds. Then Detective McGeorge breaks the silence.

"You sure you want to stick with that story?"

Jonathan tries not to look thrown. "I'm sorry . . . ?" he says.

"I think maybe you should be sorry, Mr. Caine. You see, we think that there's more to your relationship with Mrs. Williams than you're telling us. I'm not saying you were involved in Rick Williams's murder, but that's the conclusion I'm going to reach if you insist on lying to my face."

Damn. The police know that Rick Williams was murdered, and they know Jonathan was having an affair with Jackie. And now they know he's lying to cover it up.

"I don't understand," Jonathan says, hoping it sounds like he really doesn't.

"It's not rocket science, Mr. Caine. Rick Williams was murdered. You were screwing the man's wife. Put two and two together, okay?"

Jonathan's mind is racing. Part of him is screaming in his brain to shut this whole thing down and call Alex Miller. The other part is telling him that he needs more information about what the police know. That side wins. For now, at least.

"You think Rick Williams was murdered?" he says.

This pushes the younger cop to speak. "Why don't you just cut the crap. You do yourself a whole lotta good if you tell us the truth. Starting. Now."

Jonathan has little choice but to continue to play dumb. "I want to help in any way I can," he says, "but I really don't know how I can. Jackie and I were . . . friends. Nothing more."

"Mr. Caine, if that's the case, we'd like to examine your phone. That way, we can look into the frequency of your contact with Mrs. Williams, see any text messages, and the like. If it all checks out as the two of you just being pals, so be it."

Jonathan has been careful to delete Jackie's voicemail and text messages, but he can't be certain he never missed one. Besides, he has no idea how easy it is to retrieve deleted messages off an iPhone 6. What he is certain about is that anyone who listened to even one of Jackie's messages would know that they were much more than friends.

"Like I said, I want to help, but one of our classmates over at ECHS is a lawyer that I'm friendly with. Alex Miller." Jonathan stops to ascertain if the name means anything to them. It doesn't seem to. "Anyway, let me call him and see what he thinks. Just leave me your business cards, and I'll call you back."

"We're more than willing to wait while you call your lawyer friend," Detective McGeorge says.

"Thank you, but I usually don't get him on the first try, and I actually have something else to do right now, so I'm not sure if I can call him for another hour anyway. So if you'll excuse me, I'll do what I need to do and I'll call you back very soon. I'm sure you understand."

As they get up to leave, Detective McGeorge says, "You know, Mr. Caine, we do understand. All too well. Yours is the reaction we get a lot from guilty people. Folks with nothing to hide, they don't lawyer up."

Jonathan watches the cops pull out of the driveway. His heart is beating so loudly he thinks it's going to jump out of his chest. He wonders whether Detectives McGeorge and Swensen's next stop will be Jackie's house. He should warn her, but what if she's put all of this in motion? What if she told the police that he killed Rick and that's what sent them to his house in the first place?

He decides to call Alex Miller before doing anything else.

* * *

Jackie's sixth sense tells her that the knock on her door is not opportunity. A quick view out her window tells her the rest. Detective Martin is calling, this time with a female partner.

They are coming to arrest her. Why else would he need a woman to chaperone? Probably to protect him from her screaming *rape* or something.

Jackie gives fleeting thought to pretending she isn't home. Her car is in the garage, so how could they know? But she decides that type of low-rent deception is too risky. They could have been watching the house. She braces herself to face the music.

"Good morning, Mrs. Williams," Detective Martin says when Jackie opens the door. "This is Erica Murray."

She is also African American. Thirtysomething, pretty, with straight hair, tinged with a little red.

"Mind if we come in?"

Of course I mind. Who wouldn't mind being interrogated by the police about her husband's murder?

"No, of course not. Please, come in."

Jackie leads them to the living room, and they settle around the coffee table, Jackie on the sofa under the window, the police in the armchairs directly across from her.

Once everyone's in position, Detective Martin wastes no time.

"The reason we're here, Mrs. Williams, is that the domestic-disturbance call we talked about at your husband's funeral is really just the tip of the iceberg. We've uncovered some very troubling evidence, and we wanted to give you the opportunity to do yourself a lot of good by admitting to some of the things we already know."

He stops. Jackie knows she should be quiet, but the silence becomes too much, and she says, "I . . . I don't know what you're expecting me to say, Detective."

"Well, let's start with the easy one. I'm expecting you to say that you are having an affair with Jonathan Caine."

"Who said that?"

"I'm asking you, Mrs. Williams."

"No, you told me."

"Are you saying it's not true?"

She scrolls through her mind, wondering what evidence the police could have to prove the affair. Did someone see something? That seemed unlikely. She and Jonathan haven't been in public since that time at the Château. That was weeks ago, and there wasn't any public display of affection. Phone records from before she got the burner phone would only reveal one or two calls a day. That wouldn't be frequent enough to prove the affair, would it? They must have listened to her voicemail messages or read her texts. That's the only way anyone would know about her and Jonathan.

But she immediately deletes every message Jonathan sends or she receives from him. Maybe Jonathan doesn't. And even if he does, that doesn't necessarily mean they're really gone. The damn cloud, whatever the hell that even is, might still have them.

If the police have even a few of the messages, they'd know about the affair. Not the murder, but the affair. No doubt about it.

Then a dark thought forces itself into her brain. Maybe Jonathan told them about the affair.

"Mrs. Williams, yes or no?" Detective Martin says with an obvious edge. "Were you having an affair with Jonathan Caine?"

"No. It's not true. We're friends. Nothing more. I don't understand why you would think otherwise, and I think the least you can do is tell me what you think you know."

"I know your husband was murdered," Detective Martin says.

His big reveal might as well be followed by scary music. *Da-da-duuuum.*

Jackie's entire body goes numb. It's as if she's watching someone else, and wondering why on earth that person is talking to the police when they so clearly believe she murdered her husband.

"Do you know a man named Ariel Kishon?" Detective Martin asks.

"No."

"Are you sure?"

"Yes. Who is he?"

"So you never communicated with him by e-mail?" he presses.

"No. Never. Why would I?"

There's a long pause. Then Detective Martin answers Jackie's question. "Because he was hired to kill your husband."

Jackie's about to say *Hired by who?* when the female cop, Murray, says, "Mrs. Williams, I'm with the FBI. I've been assigned to the case because it's a murder-for-hire. That also makes it a federal crime, so the FBI has concurrent jurisdiction with the East Carlisle PD. And even though New Jersey has abolished the death penalty, it's alive and well in the federal system. Now, we know that Ariel Kishon ran down your husband. And we know that someone paid him ten thousand dollars to do it. And the way we see it, this went down one of three ways. You hired Kishon, Mr. Caine hired him, or you did it together. Bottom line for you is that if you tell us how it happened, you might just spare yourself a date with a lethal injection."

Lethal injection? Jackie's heart is hammering in her chest to such an extent that she clutches at it, almost as if to ensure it doesn't burst through.

She's got to end this. Now.

"I think you should leave," Jackie says, trying to sound forceful but acutely aware that she sounds scared more than anything else. "And please don't bother me again."

Detective Martin doesn't budge, although the FBI agent, Murray, rises. Jackie has a momentary panic that they're going to arrest her right then and there.

"You're playing this wrong, Mrs. Williams," Detective Martin says, finally coming to his feet. "All wrong."

*   *   *

Alex Miller answers his own phone, and does so on the first ring. Jonathan wonders whether Alex has any other clients. He must, because Jonathan isn't paying him, so there are undoubtedly other clients who keep the lights on at his law firm.

"Hey. What can I do for you, Jonathan?" Alex says.

Jonathan gives him an uninterrupted narrative. As part of the download, he confesses the affair with Jackie, but adamantly denies that he had anything to do with Rick's murder. He withholds from his lawyer that Jackie admitted to committing the crime. He's not entirely sure why, but decides that such information should be dispensed solely on a need-to-know basis, and right now, at least, Alex Miller doesn't need to know.

When he's finished, Jonathan hears the familiar sigh of disapproval from his lawyer. "Well, I suppose you already know that talking to the police was a big mistake," Alex says.

It's one of the things that Jonathan finds so frustrating about dealing with Alex. It's easy to pass judgment after the fact, with greater knowledge than was had at the time a decision had to be made. But in life, like on the trading floor, immediate action is required based on imperfect knowledge.

"I do now. At the time, it seemed more like a calculated risk."

"All right, I guess what's done is done. No more talking from now on, though. Understood?"

"Yeah. Got it. So, tell me, what do I do?"

"The next step is to have Jackie lawyer up. I can't represent both of you, but I'll reach out to a buddy of mine who practices criminal law in New Jersey. Let's all meet at my office tomorrow. Five o'clock?"

"Okay. Sounds like a plan," Jonathan says.

"One more thing," Alex says. "You need to remember that your conversations with Jackie aren't privileged, and for all you know, she's recording you. So don't say anything to her that you don't want to hear again over the speakers in a courtroom."

Alex has clearly come to the conclusion that Jonathan is trying mightily to resist: Jackie might turn on him to save herself.

"I understand," Jonathan says.

* * *

Jonathan calls Jackie right after he gets off the phone with Alex. He gets her voice mail and decides to heed Alex's concern enough not to leave a message. She'll see a missed call and call him back. He's been anxiously waiting that return call for the last twenty minutes.

Jonathan's first interpretation of the silence is that it means Jackie has already turned. After some reflection, he takes odd comfort in the fact that the cops wouldn't play it that way. If Jackie's cooperating with them, they'll want her to call back. Like Alex said, when she does, she'll be taping the call.

When the ringtone finally sounds, Jonathan prepares himself for her betrayal. But as soon as he hears Jackie's voice, he realizes that she's been crying.

"They know," she says through the sobs.

That doesn't make sense. They certainly would have shared with him if they had evidence that Jackie killed Rick. All the cops indicated to Jonathan was suspicion about the affair.

Jonathan can still hear Alex's admonition not to have any substantive discussion with Jackie—that she might be taping him—ringing in his ears, but his curiosity overwhelms him. He needs to know what the police know.

"Know what?" he asks.

"About Ariel Kishon."

The name means nothing to Jonathan. "Who's that?"

"I'm assuming he's the guy I hired to kill Rick," Jackie says. "The guy I found on the Internet didn't tell me his name, but the ad said he was a former Israeli commando. And now the cops are asking about a guy with an Israeli-sounding name, who claims he was paid to kill Rick."

Jonathan swallows hard. "What did you say?"

"What could I say? That I didn't kill Rick. That I didn't have the first clue who this Ariel Kishon guy was. That you and I are friends, nothing more. I lied about everything."

Jonathan is trying to process this information. If the police know that Rick was murdered, and they know this Ariel Kishon was hired to do it, that can only mean that they've arrested Kishon. But Kishon must not know Jackie hired him. If he did, they would have already arrested her.

"It may not be so bad," Jonathan says, trying to sound comforting. "The police obviously can't connect this guy to you or they would have arrested you. And they were here, too, and they didn't arrest me."

"They were at your house?"

"Yeah. I guess they coordinated this to question us both simultaneously."

"What did you tell them?"

"It sounds like the same thing you did. I said we were friends, nothing more. They didn't ask me about any Israeli commando guy. But they did ask to see my phone. That's when I told them that I wanted to talk to a lawyer first. Then I called Alex Miller."

"Who?"

"You remember, I told you about Alex. He went to ECHS with us.

He's a criminal defense lawyer in New York City. He was helping me in the securities thing, and so I called him."

"What did he say?"

"That you need a lawyer."

Jonathan realizes that sounds like he's distancing himself from Jackie. *You* need a lawyer. It reminds him of her comment that *You need to be careful.* He wants her to believe that they're in this together.

"I mean, Alex will be my lawyer, and so he contacted a friend who can represent you," Jonathan says.

"Okay," Jackie says, in a way that suggests that she understood what Jonathan meant the first time. That *she's* the one who needs a lawyer.

33

At three o'clock the next day, Jackie pulls her car into Jonathan's driveway. His Bentley, which has been a fixture since she's met Jonathan, is not there, and Jackie wonders for a moment whether she's mistaken about the time they had agreed to meet to go to the city.

A moment later, Jonathan exits the house. He jogs over to her car and climbs into the passenger seat.

"Would you mind driving?" he asks.

"Sure. Where's your car?"

"It was in my driveway when I went to sleep, and when I woke up there was a certified letter from Harper Sawyer on my doorstep that repeated the word *repossessed* several times."

"I thought it was a prepaid lease?"

"Apparently Harper Sawyer believed it was *their* prepaid lease," he says.

"I'm sorry," Jackie says. "I know you loved that car."

Jonathan shrugs. "I did once . . . just like I loved my penthouse and the East Hampton oceanfront house I was going to buy. But it was all in the same kind of way. I loved what I thought they said about me. That I was successful, I guess. That I mattered."

"You matter, Jonathan. You matter to me."

He looks into Jackie's face. He's still not sure what's going through her mind. Does she love him, or is he being played for a fool? The one thing he does know is that he certainly loves her. And that is enough for him to take a leap of faith.

* * *

Jackie stares up at the skyscrapers like the tourist she is as they walk the few blocks from the parking garage on Williams Street to Peikes Selva & Schwarz. Upon entering the firm, Jonathan says hello to the receptionist and introduces her to Jackie. Alex Miller comes out a minute later, with another man following close behind.

"This is Mark Gershien," Alex says. "He's a friend of mine from law school, and a top-rate criminal defense attorney."

Even though Mark Gershien was Alex's classmate from law school, Gershien looks a good ten years older. He's a handsome man, with kind eyes and a strong chin, but there's a weathered quality about him that's more in keeping with someone who has already crossed fifty.

"Very nice to meet you," Mark says, shaking Jackie's hand, and then Jonathan's. "Although I'm sorry it's under these circumstances."

"I've given Mark a very superficial understanding of what's going on," Alex says, "in part because I don't fully understand it myself. So I thought it would be the best use of our time today, Jackie, if you meet with Mark in the conference room, while I chat with Jonathan in my office."

Jackie looks at Jonathan with concern. She apparently doesn't want them to be separated, even if it is only to meet their respective lawyers.

"It'll be okay," Jonathan says.

"Okay," Jackie says, sounding less sure.

* * *

Once they're in Alex's office, Jonathan says, "So, your buddy, is he any good?"

"He is. Good enough that I can guarantee you that his advice to Jackie is going to be that she should turn on you."

Jonathan at first thinks Alex is kidding, but he hasn't cracked a smile. "I told you, I didn't have anything to do with Rick's death."

"I know," Alex says, which sounds more like *I hear you* than *I believe you.* "But that doesn't mean that she's not going to *say* that you killed him. I hate to break the fantasy, but the truth doesn't always set you free in the American legal system, and love doesn't always conquer all anywhere."

"She's not going to say that I killed Rick," Jonathan says.

"Are you willing to bet your life on it? Because this is really one of the few times when the question is actually meant literally. If she turns on you, your life is over. And I got to tell you, I've seen couples who were married thirty years, couples with six children together, turn on each other to avoid prison. So, are you sure—and I mean really sure, bet-your-life-on-it sure—that Jackie isn't going to turn on you to save herself?"

The truth is no, he's not. How could anyone be sure what someone else is willing to do to save herself?

"I don't know," Jonathan says, fully knowing that it means she might.

"In that case, I need you to listen to me, Jonathan. Keep an open mind, and hear what I have to say. Will you do that?"

Jonathan knows what's coming. "Yeah."

"Just like I told you that Mark's a good enough lawyer to advise Jackie to turn on you, I'm that good a lawyer, too. And my very strong advice is for you to turn on her. Empower me to seek a deal where you get immunity in exchange for testifying that she admitted to killing Rick. I may even be able to get the immunity deal to cover the securities fraud, too. A complete get-out-of-jail-free card for you. The one caveat is that you have to do it ASAP—before she tells them that you confessed to her."

As with his fears about whether Jackie would turn on him, Jonathan has also considered this counter-option—saving himself by giving her up. At least he'd be telling the truth. He hadn't even considered that he could get out from under the securities fraud charges, too. If the specter of a criminal indictment went away, he could start his life over. Maybe stay in banking, even.

Nevertheless, he shakes his head as if it's not even a consideration. "No, I'm not going to do that."

Jonathan wonders whether Alex believes him. He's sure that many people declare that they're never going to turn, and then they do, when all other options evaporate.

"No judgments, Jonathan. You know me better than that. But this is a serious fucking thing here. Not to say that a potential securities fraud conviction isn't, but you have an excellent shot of beating that one, or at the very least pleading it down to a sentence that's doable. Three years, maybe. Short enough that you'll still have a full life afterward. But this . . . this is a full-on murder charge we're talking about. Worse than that, actually. It's a murder-for-hire. That makes it potentially federal, which brings the death penalty into play. And like I said, the clock is ticking. If she makes the deal first, it's all over for you."

* * *

Jackie's first impression of Mark Gershien is that he seems too happy to be there for her liking. She suspects that defending an attractive woman in a murder trial brings out the hero complex in a male lawyer, and so she decides to give him the benefit of the doubt for a little while longer.

"I've had lots of introductions under these circumstances, and I know how hard it can be," Mark says after he and Jackie enter the conference room. "For what it's worth, you're holding up pretty well. At least from what I can discern."

She's tempted to correct him. She's not holding up well. She's about to jump out of her skin. He has no idea how hard it can be thinking about spending the rest of your life locked in a cage. But she doesn't see the point of telling him that what she's experiencing is well outside his comprehension. If Mark Gershien likes to pretend that he knows something about what she's going through, so be it.

So she says, "Thanks."

"I thought we'd start off with a reading from the Gospel of Criminal Defense according to Mark L. Gershien."

Jackie smiles. She knows that he's trying, so she might as well throw him a bone.

"I can't wait to hear it."

"Good. I'll let you in on a little secret. The best criminal defense lawyers do not win at trial. Winning at trial costs a lot of money and a lot of sleepless nights. Not to mention that the odds of acquittal are very long. The prosecution wins . . . I don't know, ninety percent of the time. That's why the very best lawyers win *before* trial."

Jackie bites. "So, how do I win before trial?"

"By cooperating against Jonathan," Mark says matter-of-factly, staring intently at her.

Jackie immediately looks away. She wonders whether her lawyer will think the worst of her if she turns on Jonathan, or whether that judgment will only apply if she doesn't.

"Jackie . . . listen to me. If Jonathan is responsible for the crime . . . or even if the two of you did it together, I can go to the DA and see what type of deal I can get for you. They're going to demand jail time if you were in on it, but I may be able to get them down to something that is livable. Not easy, mind you, but survivable. Maybe ten years. I think you already know this, but I gotta say it anyway. If you lose at trial, the best case is life without the possibility of parole."

"They said that I could face the death penalty. Is that right?"

Mark cocks his head to the side. "It probably won't be a capital case. Most of the time, spousal homicides, even when they're murders-for-hire, are charged as state crimes, and New Jersey abolished the death penalty about five, ten years ago. But, yes, to answer your question, they could charge it as a federal murder-for-hire and ask for the death penalty."

Jackie feels as if she's going to pass out. That, or throw up.

"When will we know?"

"Unfortunately not until—and if—you're arrested. If FBI agents do it, it's federal. If it's East Carlisle cops, it's state. Even if it goes federal, they may not charge it as a capital offense. There are a lot of factors that go into it and the decision to seek the death penalty ultimately needs to be approved by the US Attorney General."

Jackie doesn't find this comforting. In fact, she's lost in the despair that a cabinet-level official will actually be tasked with deciding whether she's put to death.

"Which brings me back to the initial point," Mark says. "The best way for you to protect yourself is to seek a deal in exchange for testimony against Jonathan. Is that something you're willing to do?"

"No," Jackie says flatly, as if that's all the response the question required.

"Can I ask you why not?"

"Because Jonathan had nothing to do with killing Rick."

"How can you be so sure?"

"Because I hired that guy to kill Rick."

There, she said it. Told her lawyer the God's honest truth. She wonders how many people admit they're murderers to their lawyers, especially during the initial meeting. Does Mark Gershien respect her candor? Or is he repulsed by the sight of her?

"Okay," Mark says after a long pause. "I'm not going to lie to you, that limits our options. Does Jonathan know it was you?"

"Yes."

Jackie's admission is met with a scowl. It's as if her lawyer is more troubled that she confided in Jonathan than that she's a murderer.

"How much does he know?"

"Everything."

"What about details? Does he know . . . how you made the payments or communicated with the hit man?"

"Yes. I told him everything."

Mark's concern is now undeniable. He's holding his hand over his mouth, as if he's physically trying to hold in his response.

"I hate to say this, Jackie, but Jonathan is far and away the greatest danger to you. All he needs to do is tell the police you confessed to him, and then corroborate that confession with some of the particulars of the crime, and they're going to give him immunity in exchange for his testifying against you."

"He's not going to do that," Jackie says.

As the words come out, Jackie hears how silly she sounds. The cold reality is that she's known Jonathan for all of a month. She can't believe it's been that short, but the calendar doesn't lie. And if she considers Jonathan with even a modicum of objectivity, she knows he's a man who possesses a finely honed self-preservation instinct.

34

When they leave the lawyers, Jackie suggests they take advantage of being away from East Carlisle and try to enjoy a nice dinner. Jonathan's experience over the last few hours has eliminated his appetite, but Jackie insists (making it clear that she's picking up the check), and Jonathan ultimately suggests a French restaurant in Tribeca that's about a ten-minute walk.

Jonathan is initially concerned that they won't be seated without a reservation, but the model-beautiful hostess tells them to follow her, and they are placed at a table in the front of the house. The space has been renovated since the last time Jonathan dined here, and now the room has an open floor plan, with murals of romantic images on the walls. Flowers are everywhere, and the waitstaff move around as if they're on roller skates.

"So . . . what did Alex say to you?" Jackie asks once they each have a glass of white wine.

"Nothing I didn't already know," Jonathan answers. "This is a serious charge. The police are going to be able to prove our affair. That type of thing. Why, what did your mouthpiece say?"

Without missing a beat she says, "He told me to make a deal and save myself by telling the police you killed Rick." Then she offers him that classic Jackie smile.

Jonathan's been caught in a lie of omission. Jackie must know that Alex made the same appeal as her lawyer: save yourself by cooperating. The only difference is that Jackie admitted it, and Jonathan hasn't.

"I hope you didn't agree to that," Jonathan says, trying to match her smile, but certain that he's fallen far short.

"I told him that I'd think about it. And then I asked some questions about whether they'd allow us conjugal visits. You know, once you're in jail, after I turn on you."

Jackie laughs. "Jesus, Jonathan, you look like you're afraid that I'd actually do that. But no such luck, I'm with you until the very end."

How much does Jonathan want to believe it's true? That he and Jackie are in this together.

"Jonathan?"

Jonathan is momentarily startled by the sound of his name, which has come from behind him. He turns around to see Natasha.

As always, she looks stunning. She's wearing a low-cut black dress and a diamond necklace that Jonathan knows he didn't give her. But that's not the accessory that's caught his eye. It's the man holding her hand: Harrison Kaye. Apparently, their former Hamptons real estate broker isn't gay after all.

Now it makes sense how Natasha's been able to stay in the co-op without any income with which to pay the mortgage and maintenance.

"Natasha," Jonathan says, her name coming out like a question. He stands and kisses her on the cheek. "Um, this is Jacqueline Williams. We went to high school together."

He watches Natasha's eyes go up and down Jackie's body. Jackie offers her hand, and Natasha appears reluctant to shake it, as if Jackie's about to pass on some contagious disease—being in love with Jonathan Caine—and having rid herself of that malady, Natasha wants nothing to do with it ever again.

Natasha finally takes Jackie's hand, and when she does, she immediately turns back to Jonathan and says, "You remember Harrison Kaye, don't you?"

Harrison has no similar hesitation about shaking hands. "Nice to see you again, Jonathan," he says.

Harrison's grip tightens around Jonathan's hand, but Jonathan has no interest in a dick-measuring contest. He couldn't care less who shares Natasha's bed these days.

"How have you been, Jonathan?" Natasha asks, her eyes still on Jackie.

He considers how to reply. Certainly not with the truth. *Remember when I was most worried about being homeless and convicted for securities fraud? Well, things have gotten a lot hairier since then.*

"Up and down, I guess is the honest answer," he says. "My father died a week or so ago."

He had thought about calling Natasha after the funeral, but decided against it. With each passing day, his life with Natasha seemed like it had happened to someone else, and he had no desire to revisit it.

"I'm sorry," she says.

It sounds as perfunctory as the condolences made by the people at Lakeview, who barely knew his father. Natasha was his daughter-in-law for three years, for chrissakes. Natasha, too, has seemingly left her old life behind without regret.

"Thank you. And how have you been?" he asks, solely to be polite.

"Very well," Natasha says in a businesslike tone. "Harrison's now working the New York City market as well as the Hamptons, so I'm splitting my time between both."

There's an awkward silence, the small talk having run its course. "Well, you two enjoy your dinner," Jonathan says.

"So that was the famous Natasha," Jackie says after Natasha and Harrison have left them.

"The one and only."

"She seems to have landed on her feet. Nothing like finding a partner to pick up the slack, right?"

Jonathan feels as if the comment is directed at him as much as it is about Natasha. He wishes he knew Jackie's tells better. If he did, he might be able to discern whether she's made the point to remind him that he has a lot to lose if she goes to jail.

35

Jonathan has an uneasy sleep. Alone in his childhood bed, he can't stop the endless loop playing in his head. Jackie giving him up to the police, Natasha laughing at what a sap he turned out to be in the end, the clank of a jail cell locking as he yells out protestations of innocence.

The flashing colors wake him. Jonathan knows almost immediately that they're police lights, even if he can't hear any sirens. At first he thinks it's part of a dream, but as his head clears he knows the truth. It's all too real.

When the police came the last time, it was in a single, unmarked car. The unmarked car has returned, but the addition of a police cruiser must mean that they're not here just to talk.

They've come to arrest him.

Jonathan's phone is on his night table. He thinks first about calling Jackie, but decides better of it. For all he knows, she's the reason the cops are here.

It's too early to call Alex Miller, so he texts his lawyer.

Being arrested in EC. Help!

By now the knocking on the door is growing louder. "Police. Open up."

Jonathan quickly realizes that if he doesn't answer the door, the police are going to kick it in. So he throws on his father's robe and heads downstairs to face the music.

* * *

Jackie hadn't been able to sleep. All night her mind raced with the parade of horribles she saw as her future: being strapped down about to receive a lethal injection, or alone in a jail cell.

After her kids leave for school, she decides to try to burn off her anxious energy by going for a run. She jogs what she considers her shorter route, a four-mile loop through her neighborhood, which is referred to as the Revolution section due to the fact that the streets are so named thematically. Her run takes her down Constitution, up Bunker Hill, through a long stretch of Washington, and concludes at the dead-end part of Yorktown. From there she walks back the half mile during her cooldown phase.

She first sees the lights flashing in her driveway as she makes the turn back on Redcoat. She thinks about turning around but knows that would be pointless. They've already spotted her. When she reaches her driveway, she sees Detective Martin standing beside his car. Without saying good morning, he tells Jackie that she's under arrest for the murder of Richard Williams.

* * *

The police cruiser pulls up to the back entrance of the station. On the door is a green sign with white lettering: POLICE PERSONNEL ONLY. When the doors open, Jonathan is pulled past three cells. None of them is occupied, but Jonathan assumes he's going to see the inside soon enough.

The police allowed Jonathan to change out of his pajamas, so for his perp walk into the East Carlisle Police Department, he's attired in the same ensemble he donned for the reunion: Brioni suit, white shirt, Gucci loafers. As a result, he looks far more like a lawyer than a defendant.

Jonathan searches about for some glimpse of Jackie, but she's nowhere to be found. He again wonders whether she's already given him up. Could it be that it was her statement that he killed Rick that prompted his arrest? That she's snuggled softly in her bed while he faces punishment for a murder she committed?

The cops put him in an interrogation room that's much smaller than the ones he's seen on television. A small metal table is pushed against one wall and three metal chairs surround it. There isn't a one-way mirror, but Jonathan sees a video camera hanging from the corner of the room.

The uniformed cop who read him his rights in the squad car removes Jonathan's handcuffs. He can't be any older than twenty-five. The kind of kid Jonathan terrorized on the trading floor in his former life.

"You're going to be here for a little while," the cop says. "So you should make yourself comfortable. The door's locked from the outside, FYI."

Jonathan was relieved of his phone upon entry, so he has no idea of the amount of time that's elapsed, but it seems like he's already been incarcerated for at least an hour. He's tried to stay focused on the fact that this part will be over soon, even though he knows that what awaits him is even more distressing.

When the door finally opens, two men enter the room. Jonathan recognizes them from the visit they paid him two days earlier. He can't recall the younger cop's name, but he remembers the mustache is McGeorge.

"Mr. Caine, as you may remember, my name is Detective McGeorge, and my partner is Detective Swensen."

"Yes, of course," Jonathan says.

Detective McGeorge takes a seat beside Jonathan. He taps the metal table twice with the wedding band on his finger, as if it's a gavel and he's calling the meeting to order.

"Well, we have ourselves a bit of a situation here," Detective McGeorge says with a heavy voice. "We've spoken to the Acting DA, and based on the evidence we've already collected, she'd like to try you and Mrs. Williams together, as co-conspirators in her husband's murder. I can't say that I blame her for going that way. What went down here, it's pretty cold-blooded, if you ask me. And I'll tell you another thing. We've arrested this guy Ariel Kishon." Detective

McGeorge mispronounces the name—making it sound like the Disney mermaid—but Jonathan assumes that the proper pronunciation is R-E-L, like the former Israeli Defense Minister, Ariel Sharon. "He's a smart guy, for a hit man, I mean. Smart enough to be cooperating with us as much as he can to save his own ass. He's already signed a confession admitting that he ran down Rick Williams. Also admitted he was paid ten grand to do it. Whatever we want, he's giving us. But some guys have all the luck, and you, my friend, must have been born under a lucky star, because Kishon can't tell us who hired him, you or your girlfriend. Not yet, anyway. And that means you got a chance to help yourself, although that window will close real fast. So my advice to you is that you tell us what happened here and do it right now."

Detective McGeorge stops short, undoubtedly hoping that Jonathan will blurt out a confession. Jonathan stays mute.

"Look, you seem like a really smart guy, Mr. Caine," Detective McGeorge says. "So I assume that you're very familiar with the concept of supply and demand. The way it works here is that the first one who tells us what happened gets a deal. The other one gets to die in prison. Question for you is: Which one do you want to be?"

Jonathan anticipated something along the lines of Detective McGeorge's little monologue, although truth be told, not quite so over-the-top. Jonathan's one and only takeaway from it is that Jackie hasn't turned. At least, not yet. She must have been arrested, too, and is being held somewhere else.

Detective McGeorge stares hard at Jonathan, as if his gaze alone can force Jonathan to confess. Jonathan has been stared down before, so he finds it's rather easy to stare right back.

"You like movies, Mr. Caine?" Detective McGeorge finally says, breaking into a smile.

Jonathan decides there can't be any harm in admitting that. "Sure. Who doesn't?"

"You remember a movie . . . God, I'm old, because it came out a long time ago. It was called *Body Heat*? Young Kathleen Turner. Back when she was hot? Man. And the guy . . . John Hurt."

"William," Jonathan says.

"What?"

"The guy in *Body Heat*. It was William Hurt. John Hurt was the Elephant Man."

Detective McGeorge chuckles. Looking at his partner, he says, "What do you know? This guy really does like movies." Then, turning back to Jonathan: "Okay, so *William* Hurt plays this lawyer, and Kathleen Turner, she gets him to kill her husband. The poor schmuck thinks that they're going to live happily ever after, but she double-crosses him. He ends up rotting in jail, and if I remember correctly, the movie ends with her on a beach somewhere sipping a drink with one of those little umbrellas in it."

"That could very well be the play here," Detective Swensen chimes in. "In fact, it wouldn't surprise me one bit if your girl-friend is spinning it that way. We already know her husband beat her, and so no one could blame her for wanting him dead. And honestly, no one would blame you one bit if she got you to do it. If that's what happened . . . well, the weight of it falls on her and not you. And it really wouldn't even be so bad for her. I mean, spousal abuse is a great defense. All that post-traumatic-stress stuff. Juries eat that shit up. The important thing is that you not let her play you for a chump. If she killed her sack-of-shit of a husband, there's no reason for you to rot in jail for it like that guy in the movie. Am I right?"

After his partner's speech, Detective McGeorge looks at Jonathan hopefully, as if they might go out for a beer as soon as Jonathan explains that yes, he did indeed murder Rick Williams because Jackie asked him to. If this is police interrogation at its finest, Jonathan can't believe that anybody ever confesses to anything.

"I'd like to call my lawyer," Jonathan says.

And poof, Detective McGeorge's smile is now a million miles away.

He looks as if he'd like nothing more than to beat the crap out of Jonathan.

"I'm so happy you said that. I really am," he says.

His expression belies the words. The last thing Detective Mc-George looks to be is happy.

Detective McGeorge slowly rises. Once he's upright, he leans over until his face is right against Jonathan's, as if they're an umpire and a manager arguing over a called third strike. Jonathan can smell the reek of coffee breath.

"I saw your girlfriend when she came in," Detective McGeorge continues, "and I was thinking to myself, I hope he's stupid enough to ask for a lawyer because that'll mean he's going to go down for this. Your girlfriend, she didn't strike me as the murdering type. But you? Oh, I'm betting *you* pushed *her* into it. You see, I was a little worried that you'd be the one to cut the deal with us, but it looks like it's going to end up just like it should. She's gonna turn on you, and be out soon, and you'll be bending over daily while some fucking animal in Rahway makes you his bitch."

In the last few seconds Jonathan has developed a deep-seated hatred for Detective McGeorge. Jonathan knows better than to say anything, though. He lets his stare indicate what he thinks.

The silence is broken by a sharp knock on the door.

"Ah. You know what that means?" Detective McGeorge says, the smile back again and stretching his mustache out across his face.

Jonathan doesn't reply. Detective McGeorge, however, is all too happy to answer his own question.

"It means your girlfriend just gave you up, asshole."

* * *

Jackie can't deny she's scared to death. It takes all her focus not to shake.

"I really wish it didn't happen like this, Mrs. Williams," Detective Martin says, like he's seen this mistake a hundred times, and it pains him at every turn.

They're in a dingy interrogation room with a small metal table and three chairs the only furniture. The female FBI agent, Murray, sits in the center seat, Jackie to her left, Detective Martin to her right.

"I was really hoping that you were going to tell us the truth when we talked the other day," Detective Martin continues. "We were prepared to give you a complete pass if you'd told us that Mr. Caine set it all up, and that would have been that. And believe me . . . I get it. You want to protect him, and you think that he's going to protect you, but that kind of thinking is only going to land you in jail for the rest of your life."

Jackie can't believe that there's any silver lining to her predicament, but then it dawns on her that she's been arrested by the East Carlisle police, which means it's not a death penalty case. Detective Martin just said as much. If she's convicted of the crime, she's not going to be put to death. The worst that will happen is that she'll spend the rest of her life in jail. Hardly a cause for jubilation, but still.

Agent Murray pours a cup of water from the small plastic pitcher sitting on the corner of the table and delivers it to Jackie. Jackie's hand shakes as she receives it.

"Jackie, we have all been there," Agent Murray says in a soft voice. "Trusting a man who then turns around and betrays that trust. But you've got to keep your eye on what really matters here. Your kids. As mothers, we always say that we'll do anything for our kids. Well, this is one of those times when that's put to the test. You have to choose between your kids and your boyfriend, and . . . I'm sorry, but that's actually not really such a tough choice at all. Not for a mom."

"Where are my kids now?" Jackie asks. She's trying her best to sound composed, but even she can hear the fear in her voice.

"At the moment, of course, they're still both in school," Detective Martin says. "Your son is eighteen, so he's free to stay at your house. But your younger one, we can't leave her with your son because he isn't over twenty-one, and so unless other arrangements are made, an officer is going to pick her up at school and bring her here."

"She's sixteen," Jackie says. "She can stay in the house alone. And she won't even be alone. Robert will be there with her."

"I'm sorry. That's protocol. Now, depending on what you tell us, you'll either be sent back home to be with your children—maybe even before school lets out—or you'll be put through processing—mug shot, fingerprints, the whole nine yards—and then you'll go to lockup while you await arraignment. This is a murder case, and so I'm certain the DA is going to ask that you be held without bail, and if the judge agrees, then you're going to be our guest for the foreseeable future. Which means that unless someone over twenty-one takes responsibility for your daughter, she's going to be put in the system, too. Child Protection and Permanency."

Jackie's panic is now ten times worse than before. This is cruel. Using her children as pawns.

"My mother can stay with Emma," Jackie says. Her voice now sounds shakier than ever. She can't deny that the police are getting to her. Weakening her resolve. "But I need to call her and it's going to take her a few hours to drive up here."

"Then right now would be a good time for you to start telling us what really happened," Detective Martin says.

Jackie looks to Agent Murray. She knows better than to think that just because she pretended to bond with Jackie over the motherhood solidarity speech, she actually cares about Jackie's well-being, or that of her children. Still, any port in a storm.

"He's right, Jackie," Agent Murray says. "This goes away real fast if you just tell us the truth." She looks to Detective Martin. "Hey, Quincy . . . I don't know if this will fly, but maybe we can talk with Jackie . . . off the record? Just to hear her story. See, if Mr. Caine was really calling the shots, and Jackie . . . you know, was more an aider and abettor type. Maybe she only found out after it was done, even. Then we can give Jackie a sense of how the DA will react to what happened. After that, Jackie can either give us a formal statement, or not. Her choice."

Detective Martin considers the plan. "If we're going to do that, we need to do it right now and we need to get the full truth," he says, looking intently at Jackie. "Any BS, we shut it down and you go straight to lockup."

"What do you say, Jackie?" Agent Murray says. "Tell us what happened here and we can help you assess it. Totally off the record. If you don't like what we think the outcome would be, it'd be like it never was said. Sound fair?"

Fair. The word rings in Jackie's ears. It has no meaning in this context. It's fair that Rick is dead. That she knows for sure. Beyond that, she's far less certain.

36

There's a second knock on the interrogation room door. Detective McGeorge crosses the room to open the door, and when he does, Alex Miller is on the other side. A Hispanic man wearing a coat and tie is beside him. Jonathan realizes instantly that he's the cop in charge.

"You got two minutes, Counselor," the boss says. "After that, we're going to book your client, and you can see him at his arraignment."

Alex addresses the detectives. "Gentlemen, if I only have two minutes, I'd like to use every second of them. Please shut the door behind you on your way out."

The cops leave the room with unhappy faces. For the first time since his arrest, Jonathan smiles.

Jonathan speaks the moment he and Alex are alone. "Do they record in here? Can they hear us?"

"No. We're privileged. Even in here. That being said, there's no reason for you to say anything. In fact, we're in complete Cone-of-Silence mode. You don't say anything to anyone."

"Was Jackie arrested?" Jonathan asks. "The cops said she was, but I never know when they're lying to me."

"I honestly don't know. After I got your text, I called Mark Gershien. He's on his way, but as of about ten minutes ago, he hadn't heard from Jackie."

"Can you find her, make sure she's okay?"

"Yeah. As soon as I leave you, I'll check to see if she's here. Does she also know that this is a say-nothing-and-invoke-your-right-to-counsel situation?"

That's the question Jonathan has been asking himself since the arrest. "I honestly don't know. They were pushing me hard to turn on her, and I'm sure they're doing the same thing to her. I mean, if she hasn't given me up already. You need to do whatever it takes to keep her calm. Tell her that we're going to get out today, that we won't have to spend the night in jail."

"I don't know if that's right, Jonathan. The judge might deny you bail. And I know you know this, but even if he imposes bail, how will you post it?"

Jonathan's far less worried about having to stay in jail than he is about failing to secure Jackie's release. He'll be able to tough it out, but fears that being denied bail will push Jackie over the edge—and into the waiting arms of the prosecution. If that happens, he'll never get out.

"Alex, listen to me. You said it yourself. Jackie's best play here is to turn on me. The more pressure she's under, the more likely that's going to happen. So if you want to defend me, what you need to do is tell Jackie whatever you have to tell her so that she remains calm, and that means convincing her that she's going to be home, with her kids, tonight."

"Okay," Alex replies, but he sounds unsure whether he can pull it off.

* * *

Before Jackie can respond to Agent Murray's off-the-record proposal, there's a knock on the door. It's loud enough to indicate urgency.

Jackie's relieved to have the distraction. From the look on Detective Martin's face, she can see that he doesn't share that sentiment. He obviously thinks Jackie is this close to cracking, and this unwanted intrusion is going to set back all his good work.

An older Hispanic man, wearing a sports jacket and tie, pokes his head into the room. "I need to see you guys," he says.

"We'll just be a minute," Detective Martin tells Jackie. "I suggest you use this time to consider what you want the rest of your life to look like."

As soon as they've left, Jackie allows herself a deep exhale. She's completely scared out of her mind. This is not the life she imagined. Sitting in a police station, wondering whether Jonathan is going to give her up. Contemplating the rest of her life behind bars.

She flashes on an image of the cops outside this room talking, and what she imagines they're saying is that Jonathan has already taken the deal. Whatever they want him to say, he's willing to go along with it, as long as they understand he had nothing to do with Rick's murder, and it was all her.

She shakes her head. No. Jonathan won't do that, she tells herself. But now it feels like she's whistling past the graveyard. Maybe he already has.

The door opens again, and it's the same Hispanic guy with the sports jacket. Behind him is a familiar face: Mark Gershien.

Mark pushes past his escort, taking the seat next to Jackie, where Agent Murray sat during her speech about the responsibilities of motherhood. "Are you okay?" he asks.

Jackie looks to the door. Detective Martin and Agent Murray have crammed into the entrance behind the other cop. She thinks Detective Martin looks hopeful, as if Jackie might decline her lawyer's help.

"A little privacy, please?" Mark says.

"Jackie, is this man your lawyer?" Detective Martin asks.

"I just said that I was, Detective."

"Let's hear it from her, Counselor," the cop in the sports jacket and tie says. "Mrs. Williams, my name is Lieutenant Alvez. I'm in charge here. Is Mr. Gershien your lawyer?"

They all wait for Jackie to cast the only vote that matters. Even Mark looks at her like the result is in some doubt.

"Yes," she says softly, barely above a whisper.

"Okay. Now that that's settled," Mark says, "you all need to give me a few minutes with my client, please."

Detective Martin doesn't budge. "You're making a big mistake, Jackie. Very big," he says.

"I'm not going to ask you again, Detective," Mark snaps. "You get out right now, or I swear I'm going to get a court order and haul your ass out of here."

Detective Martin first glares at her lawyer, and then slowly moves toward the door, slamming it hard behind him.

* * *

As soon as the door closes behind Detective Martin, Jackie asks her lawyer, "Did they arrest Jonathan, too?"

"Yes. That's how I knew to come down here. Jonathan texted Alex, and Alex called me."

Of course, that's right, Jackie thinks. She's so out of it that she didn't even remember that she hadn't called Mark. She hadn't even told the police she'd retained a lawyer.

"How are you doing?" he asks.

"I'm scared. Really scared."

Mark nods. "I'd be worried if you weren't."

"You need to call my mother. They said that Robert, my son, can stay alone because he's eighteen, but they're going to put my daughter, Emma, in . . . I don't know what they called it, but some type of children's welfare agency. They said that because Emma's only sixteen she can't stay alone with Robert. A neighbor can watch her after school—or one of her friends' parents even—until my mother comes, but I don't want her . . . under arrest, too."

Jackie begins to break down. She can't help but compare how freely the tears flow now with how difficult it was for her even to feign crying after Rick died.

Mark puts his hand on top of Jackie's. "I'll call your mom and I'll make whatever arrangements are needed for your daughter. Try your best not to worry about them, so you can focus on what's going to happen with you today."

"Thank you. Really, Mark, thank you so much."

"Let me explain how this is going to play out, so there are no surprises. I'm going to tell the police that you're invoking your right to silence. That means the questioning is going to stop, and they're going to process you. Don't be scared. It's just fingerprinting and a mug shot. Don't smile in it. Just look straight ahead. Then you'll be arraigned. It might take a few hours, but I'm certain we'll see a judge today. The arraignment is by video. You'll be in a courtroom in this building, but the judge, he's going to be in New Carlisle. All you do at the arraignment is say 'not guilty' when the judge asks you to enter a plea. That's it."

"Am I going to get to go home after that?"

"I hope so. I'll ask for bail. Now, it's possible that the prosecution is going to argue that you be held without bail. The judge might agree because this is a murder case. But you have no prior arrests, and strong ties to the community—you grew up here, right?"

"Yes. And my children go to school here."

"Good. That also will work in our favor. What can you afford in terms of bail?"

"I don't know . . . Not very much, and what little we do have I was saving for the kids' college."

"You're not spending it, Jackie. You're only *posting* it. You get it all back as long as you show up at trial. How much is your house worth? Ballpark?"

"Five hundred thousand. Less, I think."

"Any mortgage?"

"Yes. I don't know how much."

"How about your parents? Do they have any assets?"

"My mom. She owns a house in Baltimore without a mortgage. I don't know how much it's worth, but it's a nice house. It was my grandmother's."

"Okay. We'll see what the judge imposes. Normally all you have to do is post collateral equal to some percentage of the bail amount. Between your house and your mother's, we'll likely be able to do that—if he permits bail, that is."

Even with her lawyer's caveat, it's the first bit of positive news Jackie's heard today. Maybe she's going to get out of here.

37

Having no idea where Jackie is frightens Jonathan much more than his cell mates in lockup. Jonathan assuages his concerns by telling himself that female prisoners are held in a separate area, but like before, he can't rule out the more sinister explanation that Jackie's already cut a deal to cooperate and is comfortably back in her home.

He's in captivity for more than three hours. The other prisoners chat among themselves, but Jonathan doesn't engage them.

When a name is finally called by one of the guards, it's not Jonathan's. The man who answers to it is escorted out of the cell and through a double door that has no signage. After no more than five minutes, a second name that is not Jonathan's is called, and that man repeats the drill.

The first man never returns to the cell, which Jonathan takes to mean that he made bail. Of course, it might not mean that. For all Jonathan knows, there's a postarraignment cell waiting for those unfortunate souls who are denied bail or unable to post it.

When it's finally Jonathan's turn to go through the double doors, he sees that they lead to a courtroom. It's less grand than Jonathan had imagined. This place reminds him of a third-grade classroom.

As he has every prior instance he's been thrust into a new space, Jonathan searches for any sign of Jackie, and like all the times before, she's nowhere to be seen.

Alex Miller is already positioned behind the podium. The guards deposit Jonathan beside his lawyer, at which time Alex breaks from whatever he's reading to address his client.

"You know the drill, right? You say nothing other than 'not guilty' when the judge asks you to enter a plea."

"Okay," Jonathan says. "What do you know about Jackie?"

"She was arrested, too, but she hasn't been called yet. Mark Gershien is here." Alex points to Jackie's counsel, who's sitting in the third row. Jonathan hadn't noticed him before when he scanned the gallery looking for Jackie. "Mark told me that Jackie was holding up all right," Alex continues. "She's concerned about her kids, and Mark made arrangements for Jackie's mother to come up. So, it's all good."

Good? Jonathan thinks. It's most certainly not all good.

In the place where the judge would otherwise sit, behind the bench, is a large monitor. Video cameras are positioned at the counsel table, focused on the two of them. Jonathan turns to see that a similar camera is atop the prosecution table.

"Oh, yeah," Alex says, apparently realizing Jonathan's confusion. "They do this all now by videoconference. The judge is in a courtroom in New Carlisle, and that's where the trial in this case would be held. To avoid the time and expense of transporting people for a short arraignment hearing, they do it this way."

As Alex is explaining this, the television screen comes alive. The picture is of an empty, high-back leather chair. Everyone in the courtroom stares at this unchanging image until a voice comes through the speakers in the courtroom.

"All rise. The Honorable John E. Turner of the Superior Court of Middlesex County, New Jersey, Criminal Court, presiding. Come forward and ye shall be heard."

Alex and Jonathan are already standing, as there's no place to sit behind the podium, but the fifteen or so people in the gallery rise. Then Judge Turner comes into focus on the screen as he takes his seat in the leather chair.

He's an older man, probably closer to eighty than seventy, with the whittled-away look that some men get at that age, as if he was once an imposing figure, and he's the last to know that he no longer cuts that swath. Jonathan isn't sure whether it's a distortion caused by the monitor, but the judge appears to have an enormous head, which lacks a single hair on top, but thick white eyebrows dissect his forehead. There's an unmistakable intelligence to his gaze, as if he's already figured everything out and is waiting for the others to catch up.

"People versus Jonathan Caine," an off-camera voice says. "Counsel, please state your appearances."

"Assistant County Prosecutor Lydia Rodriguez, for the State of New Jersey," says the woman standing behind the other podium. She's young, probably no more than thirty, with a mass of long, curly hair that screams that she's from New Jersey.

"Alex Miller, Peikes Selva & Schwarz, New York City, Your Honor."

Judge Turner smiles. "You know, even through the monitor I can tell whenever you gentlemen from New York City enter my courtroom. Counselor, do you recall when you traveled here from the Big Apple that you went . . . I don't know, over a bridge or maybe through a tunnel?" The judge doesn't pause to allow an answer. "You might have even seen a sign that said Welcome to New Jersey, the Garden State? Does any of that ring a bell with you, Mr. Miller?"

"I'm well aware, Your Honor, that I'm not admitted to practice in this state. I was hoping that the court would hear me on bail, and then I would arrange to file for admission *pro hac vice*. I would have done so prior to today, but my client was only arrested this morning."

"Oh, I see, Counselor. So you're one of those New York lawyers who come to our great state and decide our rules are voluntary, to be applied only when they're convenient. Unfortunately for you, my oath didn't include any carve-outs for when clients are arrested in the morning. Which means I can't accept your appearance."

Jonathan doesn't like what he's hearing. Not one bit. Did the judge just say that Alex can't be his lawyer?

"Your Honor—" Alex says, but he's immediately stopped by the judge's voice.

"Let's not get on the wrong foot here, Mr. Miller," the judge says. "I'm going to take a short recess. During that time, I strongly suggest that you go find yourself local counsel. With any luck, there are some fine lawyers who are admitted to practice law in this state sitting right there in the courtroom. And, to show you that we're an accommodating bunch on this side of the Hudson River, I'm willing to take an oral *pro hac* application, under the proviso that you file the necessary paperwork within twenty-four hours."

He strikes the gavel. Then the television screen goes black.

"What the hell was that all about?" Jonathan asks.

"New Jersey helping its own," Alex mutters. "Mark . . ."

"Welcome to New Jersey," Mark says with a smile as he approaches. Before leaving the gallery, he stops at the second row, in front of a young woman of Asian descent in a dark business suit, a leather briefcase beside her.

"We worked together before, right?" Mark asks her.

"Yeah. I second-chaired Jonah Gorski in that A&B thing two years ago," she says. "The one with the executive over at J&J."

"Right. So, you up for being co-counsel? At least for today?"

"Sure."

Mark accompanies the woman over to the podium. "Alex Miller, from the wrong side of the Hudson, this is . . ."

"Mina Liu," the woman says. "What's the charge?"

"Murder-for-hire," Alex says, shaking Mina's hand. "This is our client, Jonathan Caine."

"Nice to meet you, Mr. Caine. Sorry about the circumstances."

Jonathan simply nods. He understands that he needs to let the lawyers handle things, especially because he has no idea what the hell is going on.

"All you need to do is move for my admission *pro hac*, and I'll take it from there," Alex says.

"Sure," Mina says. "But Mr. Clean might not let that happen, so you need to give me some facts."

"I'm sorry, Mr. Clean?"

"Yeah, that's what everyone calls Judge Turner. Part of it is that he kind of resembles the guy on the bottle, right? Without the earring. But the other part is that he's a real stickler for the rules, like what you just witnessed. That being said, he's the best judge we got here, even at his age. Although you need to look him in the eye when you're talking to him, on account that I think he's lost his hearing."

"Shit. That's just great," Alex says.

"It'll be fine," Mina counters. "Like I said, he's fair and very smart. But I need to know everything, just in case he makes me make the bail pitch."

Alex grimaces, clearly not pleased with the idea that this woman he just met is going to make the bail argument. This, in turn, makes Jonathan equally uneasy.

"The fifty-thousand-feet version is that the victim is named Rick Williams," Alex begins. "He's the husband of Jacqueline Williams. It's the prosecution's theory that Mr. Caine and Mrs. Williams were having an affair and they conspired to hire a hit man to kill Mr. Williams. I suspect that this hit man is in their custody. As far as we know, there's no evidence directly connecting the hit man either to Mr. Caine or Mrs. Williams. So the entire case is built on this hit man, and I imagine he's getting a very nice deal for his cooperation."

"Got it. Not the strongest case," Mina says.

"Right. Now the bad news. Mr. Caine doesn't really have any ties to East Carlisle. He grew up here, and has been living here for the past month to care for his ailing father, but his father recently passed. Mr. Caine is separated from his wife and has no children. His estranged wife now lives in the marital home, which is located in New York City."

Jonathan can tell that Mina Liu is concerned. "So where's home now?" she asks.

"My father's place in East Carlisle," Jonathan says.

"That's good," Mina says, looking hopeful.

"One more thing," Alex says, which Jonathan knows is the preface to the disclosure that will eliminate whatever hope Mina was clinging to, "just so you're not blindsided by this—you should know that up until about last September or October, Mr. Caine was employed with the investment bank Harper Sawyer. He was let go and the firm is claiming that he engaged in unlawful trading, and now there's a criminal investigation out of the US Attorney's Office in the Southern District. I don't know whether the prosecution here knows any of that, but they might."

"Okay . . ." Mina says, her tone indicating that she realizes that bail has just become a much longer shot. "Any prior convictions?"

"No," Alex says quickly. "I guess you also need to know about me if you're going to make the application. I'm admitted to practice in New York, and I've been admitted *pro hac vice* in New Jersey and elsewhere, although I don't remember any of the case names offhand."

Jonathan has surmised that *pro hac vice* must be the Latin term lawyers use for reciprocity permitting out-of-state lawyers to appear in court. Alex has just mentioned his Harvard Law School connection to Mark Gershien when the television monitor comes back on.

"All rise," a voice says through the speakers.

The camera captures Judge Turner walking back into his courtroom a town away. He takes his seat on the bench, and once again his large head fills the monitor.

"So, I trust you all worked out your little difficulties," Judge Turner says, "and I'm ready to take your appearances."

"Mina Liu of Firestone and Associates, New Carlisle, New Jersey, Your Honor. If it pleases the court, I'd like to move for admission of my colleague from New York City, Alex Miller."

"Ms. Liu. I trust that you have a long-standing relationship with Mr. Miller, such that you are able to vouch for his bona fides before me?"

The judge says this with a knowing smile, but Jonathan is very uneasy about how everyone is having fun while his freedom hangs in the balance. Alex must sense his unease, because he grasps Jonathan behind the elbow, his way of saying that everything's going to be okay.

"I just met Mr. Miller, Your Honor, but I was introduced to him by his co-counsel in this matter, Mr. Mark Gershien, who is in court today representing the defendant in the companion case to this one. I am acquainted with Mr. Gershien through previous matters, and he attended Harvard Law School with Mr. Miller. Mr. Miller has represented to me that he is a member in good standing of the bar of New York, and has been admitted *pro hac vice* in this state on numerous matters over the years."

"Harvard Law School, eh," Judge Turner says, not sounding very impressed. "I'm class of '57 myself. I want it on the record that I'm accepting Mr. Miller's application to appear *pro hac vice* on the basis of Ms. Liu's proffer, but that his law school affiliation is actually a strike against him."

Alex smiles at the judge's attempt at humor, the kind of look you give your boss no matter how lame the joke. The gallery chuckles, too, as most of them are lawyers who will soon make an appearance, so the same suck-up principle applies.

"Thank you, Your Honor," Alex says.

The judge slightly nods, and then says, "So now that *that* business is settled, Mr. Miller, does your client care to enter a plea?"

Alex turns to Jonathan. It's his one and only turn to speak.

"Not guilty," Jonathan says with a strong voice.

Judge Turner doesn't seem to care. "What's the state's position on bail?" he asks, focusing his attention on the prosecution table.

The prosecutor has been a bystander to this back-and-forth until now, but the assistant district attorney—Rodriguez—stands and says, "Your Honor, the State seeks to have Mr. Caine held without bail. This is a murder-for-hire. Mr. Caine was having an affair with the victim's wife. Together they paid a hit man ten thousand dollars to run down Richard Williams in cold blood. The State's evidence is very strong, as the hit man is cooperating fully with law enforcement. The defendant has absolutely no ties with this community. He is a resident of New York City."

"Ah," Judge Turner says, "and that's where you come in, right, Mr. Miller?"

"It is, Your Honor. I should also add that I've known Mr. Caine since high school, as I'm a graduate of East Carlisle High, class of 1991."

Judge Turner smiles. "Much more impressive than the Harvard Law School."

Like a tennis player watching a rally, the judge then turns back to the prosecutor and says, "Ms. Rodriguez, New York City is not exactly a place without an extradition treaty with New Jersey."

"Your Honor, it's not that we're worried he's going to flee to New York City. We're worried he's going to flee the country. We have been informed by the FBI that Mr. Caine is currently a person of interest in a multibillion-dollar financial crime that is being investigated in New York City. He has no job, no family, outside of a sister in Florida, and every reason to flee."

"Your Honor," Alex says loudly, trying to get back in the conversation. "I don't know what the FBI told the prosecution, but the only charges against Mr. Caine are the ones here, and those have been brought on virtually no evidence. The indictment suggests that they have one and only one witness—a self-proclaimed hit man, no less—and it doesn't take a vivid imagination to know that someone in that line of work will say anything to reduce his sentence. Also, given that the alleged hit man is, under the prosecution's theory of the case, a co-conspirator, that means his testimony alone is not sufficient for a conviction. And that's a big problem for them because we do not believe there is any evidence linking Mr. Caine to the crime."

"How about that, Ms. Rodriguez. I appreciate the guy who did the crime is saying he was hired. Is he saying that Mr. Caine hired him?"

Rodriguez has lost the sharp look in her eyes; she now appears to be on the defensive. "He was paid ten thousand dollars to carry out Mr. Williams's murder. While he does not name Mr. Caine specifically, we have additional evidence pointing to the defendant as a co-conspirator."

"Such as?" Judge Turner asks.

"The affair, to begin with. Phone records indicate that Mr. Caine and Mrs. Williams were having an affair prior to Mr. Williams's murder. They both lied to the police about that affair, which we think speaks volumes. And if that weren't enough, we have reason to believe that there was spousal abuse in the Williamses' marriage. Only two days before the murder, Mr. Caine called the police to alert them to a disturbance at the Williams home."

"Your Honor," Alex says, "I'm not going to get into a discussion regarding the evidence or lack thereof, particularly because, as the court knows, at this early point, none of it has been shared with the defense. But taking the prosecution at its word, the so-called evidence they've cited actually supports the view that Mr. Caine is *not* involved in any plot. If there was spousal abuse, that would seem to indicate that the prosecution's theory is that Mrs. Williams—not Mr. Caine—hired this hit man."

Jonathan wishes that Alex hadn't said this last part. He doesn't want Jackie to know that any effort was made to put the blame on her. He thinks about what Mark Gershien will say when he argues for Jackie to get bail. *The evidence points to Mr. Caine—a man who defrauded his former employer and investors out of billions. By contrast, there is absolutely no evidence that Mrs. Williams—a loving wife for twenty years, who has two children with Mr. Williams—would even want her husband dead, much less hire a hit man to do the deed. If she didn't want to be married to Mr. Williams, she would have just gotten a divorce. No, only Mr. Caine benefits from Rick Williams's murder.*

The prosecutor attempts to rebut Alex's argument, but Judge Turner tells her to stop with a wave of his hand. "Ms. Rodriguez, let me ask you this: What's your position going to be when the wife—I should say, widow—comes up before me on bail?"

"The same, Your Honor. We'll be seeking that she also be held without bail."

"And is it the case that, at this point at least, you view both defendants as equally culpable? In other words, you don't think one of them orchestrated this and the other is an accessory after the fact, or something of that nature?"

"That is correct. Our evidence points to both Mr. Caine and Mrs. Williams as equally responsible," Rodriguez says.

Silence takes over the courtroom. Judge Turner's chin rests on his fist, the very picture of contemplative justice.

"I'm going to hold Mr. Caine without bail," Judge Turner finally says. "I'm frankly concerned about Mr. Caine's lack of ties. He's the poster boy for defendants who could flee without consequence."

"Your Honor—" Alex says, but he's stopped by the same judicial wave that stymied the prosecutor.

"No need, Mr. Miller," Judge Turner says. "You've said all there is that can be said. You're not going to persuade me. Can the bailiff spin the wheel? Let's pick a judge."

The wheel is actually a cage with Ping-Pong balls inside, each with writing. The clerk spins the wheel and then reaches inside to pull out one of the balls.

"Judge Paul Gottlieb," the bailiff calls out, reading the name off the ball.

Judge Turner then says, "I'm going to set this down for a preliminary conference before Judge Gottlieb on Friday of this week. Mr. Miller, you can remake your bail argument to him at that time."

With that, Judge Turner bangs his gavel and the screen goes black.

"I'm sorry, Jonathan," Alex says. "I'll come see you right after Jackie's hearing, and I'll tell you how that turns out."

The guard quickly comes into view, roughly grabbing Jonathan by the elbow. "Hands behind your back," he commands.

Jonathan does as directed. As he's being cuffed, his mind flashes on the movie referenced by Detective McGeorge. A young Kathleen Turner sipping a cocktail on the beach while William Hurt rots in jail.

38

The light is much brighter in the courtroom than in the holding cell. So much so that it takes Jackie a few blinks to adjust. Then she scans the room for Jonathan, but to no avail.

She does see Mark Gershien, however. He's standing behind the podium.

Her police escort deposits her beside him, and then unlocks her handcuffs. Even before the cop leaves, Mark asks, "How are you holding up, Jackie?"

"I've been better. Did you see Jonathan?"

"I did. He was arraigned about an hour ago."

"Is he out now?"

"No, I'm sorry. The judge didn't allow any bail."

"Damn."

"Don't worry, I don't think that's going to be our result," Mark says. "Jonathan had no ties to East Carlisle. You have two children who need their mother. I can pull a lot of heartstrings with that."

He's missed the point entirely. Jackie isn't worried about what Jonathan's incarceration portends for her bail application. She doesn't want him in jail. She not only fears for his safety, but can't deny that she has selfish motives, too. She's most worried that life behind bars will make Jonathan desperate to say what he can to get out.

"So what happens to him?"

"He'll be held at the New Carlisle jail until Alex can make a bail application before the trial judge. Unfortunately, that won't be until Friday."

"What if I don't make bail? What happens to my kids?"

"I think you will, but just in case, I called your mother. She's on her way. I also spoke with your son and daughter and told them what's going on. They were worried, of course, but I promised them that you'd be home tonight. That put them at ease. They wanted to be here, but I told them that wasn't a good idea and the best thing that they could do for you was to go home right after school and you'd see them later tonight."

Jackie feels like she's drowning. The sensation of not being able to breathe and being pulled under.

"Can I have some water?" she asks.

Mark leans over to fill a paper cup out of a small plastic pitcher sitting on the counsel table behind the podium. As he's handing the cup to Jackie, the monitor comes alive.

"Appearances," the bald-headed man in the screen barks.

"Assistant County Prosecutor Lydia Rodriguez, for the State of New Jersey," replies the woman standing at the other podium.

"Mark Gershien, Your Honor, of Gershien and Kennedy in Princeton."

"Good to see you in my courtroom again, Mr. Gershien," the judge says with a smile. "Does your client care to enter a plea?"

Mark nods at Jackie. "Go ahead," he whispers.

"Not guilty," Jackie says, her voice only slightly louder than a whisper.

"Very well. Ms. Rodriguez, this is the companion case, correct?"

"Yes, Your Honor."

"What is the people's position on bail?"

The prosecutor smooths over her jacket. "As I stated in connection with Mr. Caine's application, we request that Mrs. Williams also be held without bail. This crime is very serious—murder-for-hire. As I stated in the application involving Mr. Caine, the state's evidence is very strong. Accordingly, we request that the court reach the same determination regarding Mrs. Williams that it did in connection with her co-conspirator, Mr. Caine, and deny bail."

"What say you, Mr. Gershien?" the judge asks.

"I say that Mrs. Williams is a lifelong resident of this community, Your Honor. She also has two children who presently attend East Carlisle High School. Now, I don't know how much you know about teenagers these days, Judge, but I've got one and I can tell you from hard-earned knowledge that it's difficult enough to convince them to go with you to the movies, and there's no way they're going to give up their lives in East Carlisle and live on the lam in . . . I don't know where Ms. Rodriguez thinks Mrs. Williams is going to flee to. And there's also no way Mrs. Williams is going anywhere without her children. As any parent knows, being separated from your kids, that's far worse than jail. So, we ask that the court impose a reasonable bail for someone of Mrs. Williams's modest means—a woman who has just lost her husband, who was the only wage earner in the family."

"Mr. Gershien, that sounds a little like that old joke of the defense lawyer who asks for leniency for a child convicted of murdering his parents because the boy is now an orphan."

"Your Honor, it's not a joke, it's the reality of this situation. Mrs. Williams has not been convicted of anything, and she finds herself a single mother with two children who need their mother more than ever, now that their father has been taken from them. Imposition of a high bail is tantamount to denying bail. Bail should be set at an amount that is sufficient to ensure the defendant appears at trial. That can be accomplished here with a reasonable bail. In fact, that can be accomplished without any bail at all."

The prosecutor begins to speak, but Judge Turner talks over her. "I'm afraid it's your turn to lose one, Ms. Rodriguez," he says. "But don't worry, I haven't gone completely senile yet. I'm not letting a murder suspect go without bail." He smiles for a moment and then rules. "Bail is set for Mrs. Williams at one million dollars. Bond or cash equivalent."

Judge Turner strikes his gavel, and the television screen goes dark again.

"Is that it?" Jackie says.

"That's it," Mark answers. "Between your house and your mother's, we'll be able to post the million dollars. I'll get the paperwork together and you'll be out in a few hours."

* * *

Jackie is released three hours later. Alex and Mark are standing side by side, waiting for her to exit the prison.

Mark gives her the good news first. "Your mother's already arrived, and she picked up Robert and Emma from school."

"Thank you," Jackie says. "So much."

She turns to Alex, silently asking him to tell her about Jonathan. He apparently understands the prompt.

"Jonathan's good," Alex says. "He's very concerned about you, so he'll be very happy that you made bail. I'm going to tell him as soon as I leave you. I just wanted to be able to report that I saw you get out with my own eyes."

Jackie wonders whether Alex is playing her. Her ears ring with Mark's warning that Jonathan is the greatest threat to her freedom. Maybe Alex was only telling her what she wanted to hear so she'd be lulled into a false sense of security that Jonathan was standing with her, when in reality he'd already decided to give her up to save himself.

"Can I come with you to see him?" Jackie asks.

Alex shakes his head. "Not this time, Jackie. I need to talk to him about defense stuff, and if you're there I can't do that because the conversation won't be protected by the attorney-client privilege."

Jackie is not willing to take that as the final word. "I can wait and see him after you're done, Alex."

Alex looks to Mark to support his position. "You can see him very soon," Mark says, "but Alex is right that now is not the time for that. Until we know more about the state's case, we don't want to concede anything about your relationship with Jonathan. I know the prosecutor said they have evidence of the affair, but she may have been bluffing, or the evidence is open to interpretation. If you run over to visit him, we're creating evidence that will later be used against both of you, and that's the last thing we want to do. On top of that, your conversations with Jonathan from inside the prison will definitely be recorded, and we need to all strategize about what can and cannot be said before that happens."

Jackie is afraid of what Jonathan will think if she doesn't see him. Will he imagine she's abandoning him? What will he do if he thinks that?

"Please," she says.

"I'll tell Jonathan how important it was to you to see him," Alex says. "And I'll emphasize to him that it was my advice that you couldn't. So he'll know you wanted to come."

"Jackie," Mark says, "let me drive you home. Your kids are waiting."

Jackie doesn't want to leave Jonathan in jail, but she knows the lawyers are right. Of course, that doesn't mean that she's not worried. For Jonathan, and for what he might do to her.

*　*　*

There's a gauntlet of press waiting outside the courthouse, but Mark escorts Jackie past them and shouts "no comment" in response to their pleas that she tell them whether she murdered her husband. Even standing beside her protector, Jackie finds the scene terrifying. Like she's defenseless against the mob.

"Will they be at my house, too?" she asks.

"Probably," Mark says.

Mark drives a red Porsche convertible that seems out of character for him. Midlife crisis, Jackie assumes. At least he's keeping the top up.

"Where do you live?" he asks once they're behind the closed doors of his car.

"What?" she says, still listening to the reporters scream.

"Where am I taking you?"

"Oh. Redcoat Drive, off Bunker Hill, in the Revolution section of East Carlisle."

"I think I know where that is," he says as he puts the car in gear.

Not another word is said between them during the ten-minute drive from the police station until they pass the sign telling them that they've entered Revolution Oaks, at which time Mark breaks the silence.

"Jackie, have you ever heard of a game called the prisoner's dilemma?"

It sounds vaguely familiar, but because she doesn't know for sure what it is, she says, "No."

"It's a logic game, part of game theory. It's used by social scientists and mathematicians to assess how people will react in a given situation. It goes something like this: Assume there are these two prisoners. Let's call them Blue and Red. The police offer each one the same deal—if they turn against the other one, the turncoat goes free, but the other one gets five years in jail. If they both take the deal—each turning against the other—then they each get two years. Oh, and this is important, both Red and Blue believe that if they both stay quiet, they'll both go free, because there's not enough evidence to convict either of them without one of them betraying the other. With me so far?"

"All except that they're called Blue and Red and not Jonathan and Jackie," she says.

"Yeah, that's where I'm going here, obviously. Now, from a purely rational perspective, both prisoners know that if they both keep quiet, that's going to be the best outcome—neither goes to jail. But if Red believes that Blue won't turn, then Red gets the same outcome, whether or not she turns. That means that if Red acts purely in her own best interest, Red should turn on Blue. That way, Red gets no jail if Blue is quiet and only two years, not five, if Blue betrays her."

"Can you get to the point, Mark, without the colors of the rainbow?"

"Certainly. What I'm saying is that you and Jonathan are in a prisoner's dilemma. If you are confident that he won't turn on you, I might say that it makes sense for you not to turn on him because that's the best outcome for both of you as a group. Understand, though, unlike in the prisoner's dilemma, there is no guarantee in your case that, if you both stay quiet, you both go free. Our reality is quite the opposite. You both could end up doing life in prison. That really ratchets up the stakes here. Let's put all that aside, though. My point is that even if the best result for you and Jonathan together is to keep quiet, he's still going to go through the calculation for himself, and he's going to conclude just what I told you—that it's in his individual best interest to turn on you."

Jackie hopes she's hiding that her faith in Jonathan is slipping. She wishes she was firmer in her belief that Jonathan will stand with her to the end, but the truth is that she's not. She has no idea what's going through his mind.

"I'm going to mix metaphors for a moment," Mark says. "You know that joke about the bear and the hikers?"

"No," Jackie says.

"Well, these two hikers are awakened by a grizzly bear outside their tent. And one of them starts to lace up his sneakers. The other one says, "Are you crazy, you can't outrun a grizzly bear," and then the sneakered hiker says, "I don't have to outrun the bear, I only have to outrun you.""

Mark takes his eyes off the road to see Jackie's reaction to the joke. She smiles, weakly conveying that she understands the punch line was not meant to be humorous as much as cautionary.

"It's up here," Jackie says. "You need to make a right at the next street, and then I'm the third house on the left."

Mark nods, and as the Porsche approaches the turn, he says, "So both stories really are about the same thing. Do you trust Jonathan that he's not going to sell you out? Because if you don't, then you have to think about beating him to the punch. And when you consider how firm Jonathan is going to be, you need to factor in that he's in jail now, and he's wondering how much he can trust you not to turn on him."

The Porsche turns onto Redcoat, and Jackie sees what she's feared. A row of news vans camped out on the street in front of the gate to her home. A few parked cars surround them. Rubberneckers. Her neighbors coming to see her disgrace up close and personal.

"Same as before," Mark says. "You walk right by them. You don't even need to say 'no comment.' Just look straight ahead. Keep your front door in your sights and walk straight toward it. Don't run. They may be filming and you don't want to look scared. You want to look calm."

Calm is the last thing Jackie is at the moment. Nonetheless she nods, psyching herself up to make the short walk to her front door as if it's an Olympic event.

39

After the arraignment, Jonathan is transported by a small van with metal grating on the window to the detention center in New Carlisle. One of the other prisoners, a guy who has done this drill before, explains that when they think you're going to stay for a while, they move you to New Carlisle.

At the New Carlisle jail, Jonathan is relieved of his designer clothing and given a gray canvas prison jumper. He's also introduced to his cell mate—a large man who calls himself Rino—who is still bloodied from the drunken brawl that landed him in prison.

Four hours into his incarceration, Jonathan hears one of the guards shout out "Caine," followed a moment later by "Visitor."

Jonathan exhales deeply, careful not to smile. No one he's encountered so far has smiled.

"Who is it?" Jonathan asks.

"Don't know. Don't care," the guard says. "Hands behind your back."

* * *

Alex Miller is sitting at a small wooden table in the middle of an otherwise empty room. There are six other tables there, but apparently no one else has a visitor right now.

The guard unlocks the handcuffs and allows Jonathan to enter the room unescorted. Before shaking hands with Alex, Jonathan looks behind him to the door to determine whether such contact is permitted. The guard has stepped outside the room, however. With no one to object, Jonathan extends his hand.

"How you doing?" Alex says.

"I feel like I should offer some type of sarcastic quip about the lack of concierge service, but I don't have the strength."

"Understood. So let me tell you what's happening. Jackie got bail, and she's out. Different circumstances. She's got kids, she's a lifetime resident, and she's not the target of a second criminal investigation. She said she wanted to visit you, but Mark and I thought that was inadvisable. There's no privilege between you, which means that the prison can record your conversations, and Mark also made the good point that we might want to deny you two have the kind of relationship that would cause her even to want to visit you in prison."

Jonathan shakes his head in disagreement. He wishes that Jackie had visited, so he could gauge her level of anxiety, calm her down, and hopefully stop her from turning on him. But he's got no say in the matter now. He's locked up, and others are making these decisions.

"I do have some good news, though," Alex says. "Right before I came to see you, I got a call from the prosecutor who was in court today. She's pretty junior, so I don't think she has any authority, but she told me that she'd spoken to her boss, and they're willing to be very generous with you because they figure that it's got to be Jackie who set everything in motion. Now, for all I know, Rodriguez had the exact same discussion with Mark Gershien in which she put the blame on you. But the truth of the matter is that I think now is your best—maybe also your last—chance to get out from under this. With any luck, I might even be able to roll the securities-fraud thing into any deal we make on the murder."

None of this surprises Jonathan. The Jersey folks just want someone to pin the murder on—they don't care who, and even Jonathan's rudimentary knowledge of the workings of the criminal justice system includes the understanding that murder trumps a white-collar charge.

"And what if I went to trial? What are my chances of an acquittal?"

Alex pauses, reflecting on this most important question. Then he shrugs.

"Like I said before, my guess—but it's only a guess—is that they don't have much beyond what this Kishon guy has to say. Now, they more than likely have the affair—the prosecutor said in court that they did—so that gives you motive, but Kishon must not be able to identify either of you as his patron. So, at trial, you and Jackie could point at each other, hoping that the jury has reasonable doubt as to which one of you hired the hit man. That's a risky strategy because a jury could conclude you were in it together and convict you both, but I've seen it work. Another way to go is to put Rick Williams on trial. An asshole like him must have pissed off tons of people. That creates a lot of reasonable doubt.

"But," Alex says with emphasis, "and this is the wild card, the only chance you have of beating this is if Jackie keeps her mouth shut. And that you can assess better than I can. But I'll tell you this: I sure as hell wouldn't trust the Jacqueline Lawson I knew in high school to do the right thing."

"She's probably thinking the same thing about Wall Streeter Jonathan Caine," Jonathan says. "Can't trust that guy."

"That only proves my point, Jonathan. These deals are first come, first served. I saw Jackie when she got out. She looked scared to death. And people scared to death . . . You don't have children, Jonathan, but I do, and so I'm going to tell you, people with kids will do anything to stay with their kids."

"I'm pretty fucking scared, too, Alex. And I didn't kill Rick—she did. She told me so."

There, he'd said it. Alex Miller now needed to know. Jonathan was innocent and Jackie was guilty.

Alex doesn't look the least bit fazed by Jonathan's charge. Jonathan wonders whether that's because he'd already figured it out, or because he didn't necessarily believe it was true.

"In that case . . . you should definitely think very hard about cooperating against her. At least you'd be telling the truth."

Jonathan considers what life would be like for him if he throws

Jackie under the bus. She'd go to jail, and he'd be alone. Not exactly the happy ending he was hoping for.

"I can't do that, Alex. I just can't. I know you think it's too soon, that I've only known Jackie a short time, but I'm in love with her. The only future I can see for myself is one in which I'm with her."

Alex doesn't say anything in response. Jonathan has the feeling that Alex's silence is driven by the fact that he thinks his client has lost his mind. What grown-up falls hopelessly in love in a month? And with a murderer, to boot?

"Jonathan . . . I'm a believer that like a therapist, a defense lawyer shouldn't share anything of his own life with his client," Alex says slowly, as if he's still unsure whether he should be disclosing anything of his own life, "but since we know each other from way back, I'm going to break that rule with you. A few years ago, I thought I had it all. I was a partner at Cromwell Altman, pulling down a million a year. Fancy apartment, designer suits, the whole nine yards. And I won't bore you with the psychobabble that's been thrown at me since then, but I became involved with an associate at the firm. I didn't know her very long, but I imagine it was something like what's going on between you and Jackie. I felt alive for the first time in years. I was blind, and now I could see. Rebirth. Whatever crazy metaphor you want, that's how bad I had it. Being with her was all that mattered. Sound familiar?"

It does. All too well.

"Yes," Jonathan says.

"Well, the folks at Cromwell Altman weren't such romantics, and they fired me. I felt like . . . well, like I had nothing. Like I wished that instead of firing me, they'd shot me in the head. Again, sound like anyone you know?"

This time, Jonathan offers only a nod.

"But I had a daughter, and so dying wasn't really an option. Which meant I had to go about rebuilding my life. It wasn't easy. There was more than a little bit of drama that followed, but eventually I focused on what truly mattered, and that was my family. And then I got this job at Peikes Selva, and now this is my life. I won't lie to you—there are times when I'm in my little dinky office and wonder, my God, how the hell did I end up here? But a few years ago my wife and I had our little boy, and . . . I have to say, I'm happier now than I've ever been. So it's a long way of saying that, even though I know things are bleak for you right now, a lot of good things can still be yours. Don't waste your life by going to jail for a crime you didn't commit."

Jonathan flashes on his father's dying words, imploring him to be a better man. What would that better man do?

And then he thinks about the motto that has guided him for as long as he can remember: *I want what I want.*

What is it that he truly wants?

It's the moment of truth. As Alex said, time is not on his side. For all Jonathan knows, Jackie is close to making a decision herself. He has to act before she does.

"Okay," Jonathan says. "You're right. I'm willing to make a deal."

40

A night in prison has hardened Jonathan's resolve that the path he is about to travel is the only course. So the next morning, when he once again hears his name called out by the guard, Jonathan girds himself for the battle to come.

Like before, Jonathan's hands are cuffed behind his back, and a guard leads him through the prison. But this time, they walk past the visitors' room where Jonathan met Alex Miller the day before, and enter a room at the end of the hallway.

Once inside, Jonathan sees that it's a full house, seven people crowded into the space. The only face among the attendees that Jonathan recognizes, aside from Alex Miller's, belongs to the New Jersey lawyer Alex needed to vouch for him at the bail hearing.

While the guards unlock Jonathan's handcuffs, Alex says, "Let me do the introductions. You all know Mr. Caine, of course. Jonathan, this is Juliana Scillieri. She's the acting county prosecutor for Middlesex County." Scillieri looks to be Jonathan's age, and smiles the way you would if you were introduced to someone at a dinner party, which couldn't be more incongruous in this setting. "Lydia Rodriguez, you may remember, was the prosecuting attorney at the arraignment. Standing beside her is Detective Quincy Martin. He's the lead detective on the matter." Detective Martin nods, but even with that limited gesture, Jonathan can tell that Detective Martin is a formidable guy. "Next to him is David Geller. David is the head of the criminal division in the US Attorney's Office in Manhattan, and next to him is Elliot Felig, who is also an assistant US Attorney in that office." Jonathan recalls that Felig's name was on the bottom of the grand jury subpoena he received on New Year's Day. "The folks representing the federal government were invited to attend because what we decide here will have implications for the securities investigation in New York."

Alex had previously told Jonathan that the first hint of how receptive they'd be to the proposal could be discerned by attendees. *If Felig comes alone, it means that they're just going to hear us out,* Alex had said. *But if his boss joins, then they're ready to deal.*

Felig's superior was present. That meant Jonathan had reason to hope.

The introductions complete, Geller says, "We understand that you have a proposal to make, Mr. Miller. So . . . we're all ears."

"First some ground rules," Alex says. "I assume no one has any objections that this is an off-the-record meeting, for settlement purposes only. Meaning that if we end up going to trial, nothing anyone says here will be repeated there. Agreed?"

"Yes, of course," Geller says.

Scillieri nods her assent. "Agreed."

"Good. So let me get down to it, then. Our proposal is that Mr. Caine will cooperate against Mrs. Williams in connection with the murder charge, in exchange for full immunity on that charge and also the securities fraud charges still being investigated in New York."

"What is the nature of that cooperation?" Scillieri asks.

This is another good sign. The lead prosecutor isn't negotiating, but inquiring.

Alex turns to Jonathan. "Tell them what you know, Jonathan." Then, as if he can sense Jonathan's apprehension, Alex adds, "Don't worry. It's all privileged as settlement discussions."

It's now Jonathan's turn to tell them what they want to hear. The words he had never thought he'd ever utter.

In as unemotional a tone as he can muster, Jonathan says, "Jackie admitted to me that she hired a hit man to kill her husband."

The statement hangs in the air. There's no going back now.

"That's just your word against hers," Scillieri says. "She'll say you're lying to save yourself."

"She got the $10,000 she used to pay the hit man by pawning some jewelry," Jonathan says. "I can tell you where she pawned it. I can also corroborate the hit man's story about where the money was left for him."

This disclosure is met with stone-cold silence. Jonathan knows that's yet another good sign. They believed him.

Scillieri finally says, "We can live with giving Mr. Caine immunity as long as the deal is contingent on Mrs. Williams's conviction."

Alex laughs. "No. It doesn't work that way. The deal is based on my client providing you with certain agreed-upon information and then testifying truthfully to the best of his ability at trial. End of story. He's not going to jail if you guys screw up the case against Jackie."

"That's too risky for us," Scillieri says.

"Not really," Alex says. "You have nothing on Mr. Caine on the murder, so giving him a pass isn't really much of a price to pay. And, as I said, this is a two-part deal. We need immunity on the securities fraud charges, too."

"Nope. Not going to happen," Geller says quickly. "I really appreciate you guys inviting me to your plea negotiations, but I'm not sure why I'm even here. I understand what Ms. Scillieri gets out of it. If all goes well, she's going to walk out of here with a murder conviction. But what do I get? Nothing. And that's exactly what I'm prepared to give in return."

"I can say the same thing to you that I said to Ms. Scillieri," Alex says. "If you had a case to make against Jonathan, you would have already made it. You don't have anything, and so closing up the investigation isn't really much of a concession."

Geller shakes his head. "No, I could say the same thing to you. If you really don't think we have enough, then don't link our investigation to the murder case. And if you're right, *you* haven't lost anything because we won't indict Mr. Caine, or we'll lose at trial."

Jonathan hates people talking about him as if he weren't present. It's something that never happened when he was ruling the roost at Harper Sawyer. Unfortunately, it seemed to be business as usual with lawyers.

"If I'm turning on Jackie, I'm going to have to start my life over," Jonathan interrupts. "I can't do that if I'm worried about getting indicted tomorrow for securities fraud. I want to leave the Northeast, maybe go somewhere warm. My sister lives in Florida. None of those things are possible with this thing hanging over me. I need to know that it's all over for me, or I'm not going to do it at all."

"As much as I'm touched by your change of circumstances, Mr. Caine," Geller says with sarcasm, "I only came to this little soiree because I thought I'd end up leaving with a guilty plea and some jail time out of you. I'm willing to be reasonable with regards to a sentencing recommendation in consideration of your acceptance of responsibility for your crimes . . . but if you think you're getting a deal in which you never see prison, you are sadly mistaken. Worse than that, you've wasted my time."

Jonathan knows that Geller isn't bluffing. If he wants a deal, he's going to jail. Shit. The question in his mind is for how long.

Alex then asks it. "What kind of jail time would you be looking for?"

No one says anything. Jonathan can feel his heart race.

"Give us a moment," Geller finally says. "We need to talk among ourselves."

* * *

"What do you think?" Jonathan asks Alex once they're alone.

They've been returned to the prison's visitors' room. Visitors aren't permitted at this hour, and so they're alone.

Alex considers the question for a moment. "Scillieri obviously wants the deal. She needs this conviction to get the 'acting' part off her job title. It seems that it's just like we thought. The arrest was a Hail Mary pass to try to get either you or Jackie to turn. So it's a safe bet Scillieri is going to be putting maximum pressure on Geller to make an offer we can live with so he doesn't screw this up for her."

"And what will he want?" Jonathan asks.

"Hard to say. But you heard him say that it's definitely going to be jail time."

"Damn."

"Let's not get ahead of ourselves. First things first. We need to hear what the offer actually is."

* * *

The wait isn't long. The federal prosecutors enter less than a half hour later.

Neither Geller nor Felig sits down. Felig has apparently been tasked with doing the honors, because he says, "The best we can do is five years on the securities fraud. Immunity on the murder."

"No way," Alex says. "Five years? We could lose at trial and still do better than that with the right judge."

"Or you get the wrong judge and it's twice as long a sentence," Geller says.

Alex audibly sighs. "Now we're going to need a minute," he says.

After Geller and Felig leave, Alex turns to Jonathan. "So you got that, right? For giving them Jackie, the murder charge goes away, and on the securities fraud, it's five years. And like I told you, you serve all of it. Last six months in a halfway house, but other than that, you're inside the whole time. No time off for good behavior and no parole."

"Where would I serve the time?"

"We'll insist that part of the deal is that they agree to a joint recommendation, and we'll ask for a minimum-security facility. That decision is ultimately made by the Bureau of Prisons. The Bureau is free to disregard our deal, and even the judge's recommendation. But the securities fraud is a nonviolent offense, and the agreed-upon sentence is relatively short, plus you're a first-time offender, so I'm reasonably confident that you'll get minimum security. As to which minimum-security facility, we'll put together something of a wish list where we rank them. Otisville is the place of choice for most New Yorkers. Fort Dix is on an army base in New Jersey, and it's about an hour from here. There's a good one in Pensacola, Florida, that's popular. Pleasanton, which is near San Francisco, is supposedly okay."

"You make it sound like I'm applying to college."

"It is, a little bit. But I want to be straight with you. Even if you're in minimum security, the days of Club Fed—you know, the places with tennis courts and lobster for dinner—those are long gone. This deal gets you out from under the murder charge. So right there, that's worth it all by itself—although I know, it's a murder you didn't commit. But looking at it solely through the prism of the securities fraud, five years is steep. In my own head, I was hoping we'd end up closer to three. Besides, we have no idea if they're even close to getting an indictment. This entire thing could be a bluff by the New York guys to get you to plead guilty and serve time when they know they can't make a case. So, if it was just the securities fraud we were talking about, I'd advise you to turn down the deal, and wait to see what an indictment looks like—or even if they can get a grand jury to indict."

"Okay. I get it. On the one hand, and on the other hand. What I need to know is what you're telling me to do."

"There's an old joke in the legal world that says that no matter what I tell you, you're the one who has to serve the time. So, it's really your call here, Jonathan. My job is to present the options and the risks associated with them."

"That's not much of a joke," Jonathan says with a smile.

"Nothing funny about this, I'm afraid. And, at the risk of showing you yet another hand, you need to consider one more thing. There's no way I can represent you for free in two big-time trials. My partners are already upset about the time I'm putting in now pro bono."

Jonathan nods. "I know you can't devote two years of your professional life to me without seeing a penny."

"So you'll have a public defender representing you in both cases. Some of those guys are great, maybe better than me, especially on the murder charge because . . . full disclosure, I've never tried a murder case. But they're also overworked, and the securities case requires extensive analysis of the trading records, and all that stuff takes time and bodies."

Jonathan understands. If he doesn't take this deal, he'll be facing a two-front war with an overworked, underpaid public defender being the only thing between him and a lifetime in jail.

But five years. Jonathan will be pushing fifty when he gets out. If he isn't killed inside. And he'll be a convicted felon, which means he'll never be able to assume anything approaching his old life. As an ex-con, he couldn't even work in the mailroom at a bank.

"Okay," Jonathan says with a sigh. "I'll take it."

41

lex arrives back at the prison the following morning. In his hand is the paperwork setting forth the plea deals. The documents have already been executed by the prosecutors in New York and New Jersey. Now all that awaits is Jonathan Caine's John Hancock.

Jonathan reads the terms several times, making sure each deal says exactly what they agreed: In exchange for truthful cooperation, which included, but was not limited to, his identifying the pawnshop that provided the ten thousand dollars that was used to pay Ariel Kishon, and his truthful trial testimony that Jackie admitted to murdering her husband, the State of New Jersey and the Department of Justice agreed that all charges against him relating to the homicide of Richard Williams would be dismissed with prejudice, and he would receive full transactional immunity from prosecution for any criminal conduct relating to the death of Richard Williams.

The federal securities fraud deal with the New York prosecutors was even more straightforward. There all Jonathan had to do was to tell the truth about what he'd done, and the US Attorney's Office would request a jail sentence of five years. Alex had gotten the deal to include the joint recommendation that Jonathan serve his sentence in Fort Dix, and that Jonathan had the right to withdraw his guilty plea if the judge imposed any greater sentence. As icing on the cake, the deal also included that no one else would be prosecuted for the securities fraud, which was the least Jonathan could do to repay his debt to Haresh Venagopul.

"Does Jackie know about any of this?" Jonathan asks, staring at the signature pages.

"No," Alex says. "I didn't want to say anything that would potentially derail it. But I suspect our friends in the county prosecutor's office are going to share it with Mark Gershien as soon as I deliver the signed documents."

Jonathan tries to imagine what Jackie will think when she hears that he's turned against her. His only frame of reference is how he would have reacted if she had betrayed him. It's a thought too horrible for him even to fathom.

Then without further hesitation, he signs both plea deals and pushes the papers toward Alex.

"It's the right thing to do," Alex says, taking the paperwork in hand.

Jonathan smiles at him but doesn't otherwise answer. He thinks he's done the right thing too, but for vastly different reasons than Alex.

* * *

Later that day, Jonathan is brought to the same room where he turned on Jackie, once again to meet with the acting county prosecutor, Juliana Scillieri, and Detective Martin. Alex Miller is also there, but Jonathan knows he's largely going to be a spectator. This is Jonathan's show now.

"You got what you want," Detective Martin says, "and so now it's our turn."

Jonathan takes a deep breath. Then he tells them what they want to hear.

"Jackie raised the ten grand by pawning some jewelry and her father's Rolex. She took them to some place called We Buy Gold 4 Less. It's located in Asbury Park. She told me the guy she dealt with was fat with a bad comb-over."

"How'd she find the hit man?" Detective Martin asks.

Jonathan smiles. "Believe it or not, the Internet. She created a Gmail account and just e-mailed the guy. She never met him. Never spoke to him."

"So how'd she pay him?" Scillieri asks.

"Jackie told me she saw that part in a movie. She e-mailed him where the first payment would be, and she just left it there. She left it under a garbage can in a park in Monroe Township. The second one was at the pavilion on the boardwalk at Bradley Beach. She made the drop in Monroe on her way down to Baltimore and then did the one at Bradley on her way back."

Scillieri wears a smile as big as Texas. Detective Martin looks equally pleased. He even says thank you as they leave.

* * *

Four hours later, Jonathan is hauled back into the visitors' room. Alex Miller is waiting, and he's alone.

"We have a problem," Alex says. "The pawnshop guy says *you* sold him a Lange & Söhne chronograph watch. He described you like he was looking right at your face. Like he'd seen you in the last week."

"Did he, now?" Jonathan says, not even attempting to hide a smile. "Well, if he did, he's a goddamn liar."

Silence from Alex. Jonathan knows his lawyer is more than smart enough to have figured it all out by now.

"Scillieri is threatening to blow up the deal," Alex says. "She says that if the pawnshop guy is going to say you sold the watch, she can never get a conviction against Jackie, even with you testifying against her. Mark Gershien will say the evidence points to you, not her. And your testimony at trial against Jackie is now less than worthless because you got a sweetheart deal and there's no corroborating evidence to support that she did it."

"That does sound bad," Jonathan says. "I'll bet a smart guy like Jackie's lawyer will also put the busboy from the Hilton on the stand. He'll testify that a day before the murder, Rick was beating the shit out of me. That also can't be good for the prosecution's case against Jackie. Not to mention that I did once own a Lange & Söhne chronograph and now I don't."

Alex gives Jonathan a knowing look. "I bet Mark will also say that the pawnshop guy has no motive to lie. It's not like somebody paid him off, right?"

Jonathan knows the attorney-client privilege would protect him if he chose to tell Alex that he gave the pawnshop guy his Bentley in exchange for Mr. Comb-over going to his grave swearing that it was Jonathan who pawned that watch. Still, the less Alex knows, the better.

"I honored my part of the deal," Jonathan says. "I'm ready, willing, and able to put my hand on the Bible and say Jackie set up the hit, pawned her jewelry, and used the proceeds to pay a hit man. If the pawnshop guy says it was me, maybe they should prosecute him for perjury. But I'm telling the truth."

Alex shakes his head in disagreement. "Look . . . fun and games aside, Jonathan, if you pawned the watch, then the evidence is pretty good that you hired Ariel Kishon, not Jackie. Scillieri will claim that you lied to her when you said Jackie did it. And if you lied to them about Jackie's guilt, that blows up the deal."

"But I'm not lying about Jackie," Jonathan says. "I didn't set up the hit. Jackie did. I'll take a lie detector test. My guess is that Jackie would, too. That's not admissible against her anyway, right?"

Jonathan had tied this up tightly. Even if it was too early to spike the ball, Jonathan knew he had won. From the look on Alex's face, Jonathan could see that his lawyer knew that, too.

"Okay," Alex says. "I'm going to go straight to Scillieri's office from here. I'll tell her that you held up your end of the bargain, and that there's no room for her to renege. Hopefully she'll understand that trying to undo a plea deal is not a very wise career move. I'll also put in her head the idea that if she cuts Ariel Kishon a little slack, maybe he'll recant the whole murder-for-hire thing. That will allow her to claim she got the guy, and then she can announce that she's dismissing the indictments against you and Jackie because she's now convinced that Kishon acted alone and it was just a hit-and-run. With any luck, Scillieri might be able to salvage her career from this little debacle."

"Everybody wins, then," Jonathan says.

"Something like that. Although not everyone is getting away with murder."

"I'm still going to jail for five years," Jonathan says.

"Jackie's got to be grateful for what you did for her."

"I love her, Alex. She's my happy ending."

42

The Federal Correctional Institution at Fort Dix is housed on the Joint Base McGuire-Dix-Lakehurst. It's forty miles outside of Philadelphia, a little more than a half-hour car ride from East Carlisle.

More than four thousand inmates serve their time within its walls, which makes it the largest federal prison by population in the United States. A lucky four hundred are in the minimum-security section, which is more of an army barracks than a prison, and the rest serve their time in the low-security portion of the facility.

Alex had lobbied the Bureau of Prisons for Jonathan to be admitted to the minimum-security section, but after the epic bait-and-switch that landed Jonathan at Fort Dix, there was no way that anyone was willing to make Jonathan's incarceration more comfortable. And while minimum security was a second-best option, as Alex had warned, it was no vacation. Many of the inmates were hardened criminals, doing their second or third stint.

Jonathan's main understanding of prison comes from *The Shawshank Redemption*, and what he recalled most is the line that prison time is slow time. If his actual experience didn't much resemble Andy Dufresne's stint at Shawshank, the quote rang true. Sometimes Jonathan felt as if time had literally stopped.

It gave Jonathan ample opportunity to reflect on how everything had unfolded exactly how Alex had predicted. Ariel Kishon recanted his claim that he was a hit man and pleaded guilty to vehicular manslaughter. He was sentenced to eight years, which was less than what he likely would have pulled on a murder-for-hire charge, even with his cooperation. At a press conference to tout Kishon's guilty plea, Juliana Scillieri announced that the county prosecutor's office was dismissing all charges against Jackie and Jonathan, telling assembled reporters that the arrests were part of an interjurisdictional effort that successfully resulted in securing Jonathan Caine's guilty plea and significant prison time for securities fraud.

Like Alex Miller had said, everybody won. Only the spoils of Jonathan's victory would have to wait five years.

* * *

Inmate visits at Fort Dix were strictly limited to an hour, and one visit per week.

Alex Miller visits shortly after Jonathan's incarceration begins. They meet in a private room, one reserved for counsel visits. Alex tells Jonathan at the outset, however, that it is purely a social call.

"When did you know?" Jonathan asks, without any preface to indicate the topic of Alex's knowledge.

"When you took the deal," Alex says without hesitation.

Jonathan laughs. "How'd that tip you off?"

"Because you so quickly accepted the five years. That told me that you were primarily worried about something besides going to prison. I knew you were worried about Jackie."

"Do you think I'm an idiot?" Jonathan asks.

"Far from it. I think you're probably the smartest guy I know."

"Why, because I tricked some prosecutors?"

"No, because you realized what was really important and made it happen for you. In the scheme of things, giving up five years of your life for that type of happiness is well worth it. Think about all the people who live their entire lives without finding any meaning, any purpose."

Jonathan nods. "You know, for a lawyer, you're quite philosophical."

"Thank you," Alex says. "And for a master of the universe, you're quite the romantic."

* * *

Amy comes up from Florida as often as she can. Usually, her visits correspond with her needing to do something to ready their parents' house for sale. She always makes it clear to Jonathan that she could hold off on the sale if he wanted to live there when he came out of prison. He's consistently told her to sell it. He knows he'll have a place to call home after he's released from prison.

It isn't lost on Jonathan that he and his sister speak, e-mail, and see each other more now than they had in the last twenty years. He promises her that will continue even after he ceases to be a captive audience, and she tells him that she looks forward to getting to know Jackie.

* * *

Jackie comes every Sunday without fail. Kissing and embracing briefly upon arrival and departure is permitted, to a point, which Jonathan and Jackie referred to as the three-second rule. After that, hand holding is the only physical contact allowed.

In addition to the litany of regulations imposed by the institution, Jonathan has one rule about these visits. He communicated it to Jackie through a game of telephone—in which he tells Alex, Alex tells Mark Gershien, and then Mark tells Jackie—to keep it all within the attorney-client privilege.

It is that she can never admit to killing Rick. Ever.

Jackie's first order of business upon arrival is always to ascertain whether Jonathan has any bruising. She tries to be discreet about it, but Jonathan knows that she always makes it a point of studying his face and his hands even before a word is exchanged.

Jackie has a job working in the mall. It doesn't pay much, but it's enough to keep them afloat in the short term. She's also gone back to school, using some of Rick's life insurance to pursue a master's degree in child psychology, with the long-term plan that she'll practice in East Carlisle when she finishes her degree. Robert is heading off to college; the life insurance was also enough to cover in-state tuition at Rutgers. Emma is doing well too. Living her life as a normal high school student, going to football games and hanging out with her friends.

Jonathan's favorite topic of conversation is when they imagine their lives upon his release. The plan is for him to move into her house in East Carlisle, but at other times they talk about starting somewhere new. Florida. California. London, even.

What either of them actually says about their future together is almost beside the point, however. What mattered is that they both wanted that future and were willing to wait for it. For Jonathan, that sentiment is brought home by the way Jackie smiles every time she visits. The same smile that had captivated him in high school.

It has taken him a lifetime, and brought him to the depths that a person can go, but Jonathan knows that true happiness lies ahead. He would be with the woman he loves, and who loves him. After spending his life in pursuit of false idols, he had finally found something real in his love for Jackie.

He finally has what he wants.

ACKNOWLEDGMENTS

Thank you so much for taking the time to read *The Girl from Home*, and for going above and beyond by venturing into the acknowledgments. My favorite part of the writing process is hearing from readers, so please, if you've made it this far, go a little further and send me an e-mail at adam@adammitzner.com and tell me what you thought of *The Girl from Home*, or any of my other books. Also, although it would truly be above and beyond, please post a review on your favorite website.

Now to thank the people who made *The Girl from Home* what it is: Scott Miller, my agent at Trident Media, and his colleague, Allysin Shindle, who are my first stop for advice on all things about books (and some other stuff, too); Ed Schlesinger, my editor at Gallery Books, who breaks my heart with his every critique but makes the book something I'm proud to deliver to the world in the end; Stephanie DeLuca, who handles the publicity at Gallery Books and has been a great promoter of my work; and Fauzia Burke and Leyane Jerejian at FSB Associates, who spread the word on social media and the blogosphere.

My friends and those who visit my Facebook page know that I'm a huge Batman fan. The closest I get to actually being the Caped Crusader, however, is that I have a secret identity as a mild-mannered lawyer, and it is only at night and on weekends that I become a writer. Those who have been entrusted with my secret identity have been incredibly supportive of my dual existence, and special thanks goes to my partners and colleagues at Pavia & Harcourt, the New York City law firm where I spend my days.

My thanks also go to those who read and commented on drafts of *The Girl from Home* (and voted on the title), who include many of the same people who have been reading my work since the beginning: Clint Broden, Jane Goldman, Gregg Goldman, Margaret Martin, Benjamin Plevin, Bonnie Rudnitsky Rubin, Ellice Schwab, Jessica Shacter, Lisa Sheffield, Jodi (Shmodie) Siskind, and Susan Steinthal.

As has been my practice in all of my books, some real-life people have contributed their names to the characters, but rest assured, Cathy Bachman, Elliot Felig, Mark Gershien, Yorlene Goff, Jonah Gorski, Paul Gottlieb, Harrison Kay, Erica Murray, Aaron Pratt, Peter Stemblack, Haresh Venagopul, and our dog, Nixie, in *The Girl from Home* are fictional in every way.

The Girl from Home is dedicated to my parents, Linda and Milton Mitzner, who unfortunately passed away before my first book was published. Given the subject matter of this book, I spent a lot of time thinking about my parents while writing it, and though the usual disclaimer applies that the father in the book is not my father, the one thing that I did take from real life is that both of my parents always urged me to be the best person I could be. (That and the story about the father pushing the car, which *is* truly something my father did.)

Lastly and mostly, I owe a tremendous debt of gratitude to my family. My writing as often occurs around the dining table as it does at my computer, listening to ideas and critiques offered by my wife and children. And so my thanks to Rebecca, Michael, Benjamin, and Emily for being everything they are, and to my wife, Susan, for allowing me to at least try to be everything I want to be.